CLEAR AS
THE MOON

Also by Chris Stewart

Shattered Bone
The Kill Box
The Third Consequence
The Fourth War
The God of War
A Christmas Bell for Anya

Others in *The Great and Terrible* series:
The Brothers
Where Angels Fall
The Second Sun
Fury and Light
From the End of Heaven

THE GREAT AND TERRIBLE

VOLUME 6

CLEAR AS THE MOON

CHRIS STEWART

DESERET
BOOK

SALT LAKE CITY, UTAH

Library of Congress Cataloging-in-Publication Data

Stewart, Chris, 1960–
   Clear as the moon / Chris Stewart.
      p. cm. — (The great and terrible ; v. 6)
   ISBN 978-1-59038-994-2 (alk. paper)
   1. Terrorism—Fiction.   2. Religious fiction.   I. Title.
   PS3569.T4593C55 2008
   813'.54—dc22   2008031145

Printed in the United States of America
Worzalla Publishing Co., Stevens Point, WI

10 9   8   7   6   5   4   3   2   1

" . . . in this the beginning of the rising up and
the coming forth of my church out of the wilderness—
clear as the moon, and fair as the sun, and terrible
as an army with banners."
—D&C 5:14

"And now, my sons, remember, remember that it
is upon the rock of our Redeemer, who is Christ, the Son of
God, that ye must build your foundation; that when the
devil shall send forth his mighty winds, yea, his shafts in
the whirlwind, yea, when all his hail and his mighty storm
shall beat upon you, it shall have no power over you to
drag you down to the gulf of misery and endless wo,
because of the rock upon which ye are built, which
is a sure foundation, a foundation whereon
if men build they cannot fall."
—HELAMAN 5:12

prologue

ARLINGTON NATIONAL CEMETERY
WASHINGTON, D.C.

The two angels stood on the highest point within the sacred cemetery and looked east, taking in the destruction of the once-mighty city. Behind them, on the west side, below the crest of the hill and thus protected from the nuclear blast, were rows and rows of untouched marble markers surrounded by grass and trees. Farther on, beyond the borders of the cemetery, the capital struggled still to live, but before them, on the blast side of the hill, the center of the city was nothing more than ash, the cinders so light and feathery they were caught up in the slightest breeze. The center of destruction was utterly bare, smooth as black glass—no trees, no grass, no living thing, certainly no people. Farther from the center of the destruction, the shattered buildings became somewhat recognizable. Here and there, a few marble pillars protruded from the landscape, and the roads were still identifiable by the lines of tumbled cars. Two of the main bridges across the Potomac River lay in a ruin of twisted steel and black cement, but the north bridge was still open although the downtown portion of the city had been abandoned and might never be reclaimed.

Behind them, crowds of people filled the cemetery, for the grassy knolls and open grass had become a makeshift sanctuary. Farther west, the city looked fairly normal, though it was not nearly as busy as it used to be. One in ten people who once lived here had remained. Others were leaving now, but some were returning, too, having discovered there was little reason to go elsewhere. There were no safe havens in other places. Wherever they went, things were pretty much the same.

Overwhelmed with emotion, the two men didn't speak as they took in the devastating scene. Overhead the sky was dark and lonesome, a flat-gray plate of clouds that capped the sky. Finally, after nearly half an hour of earthly silence, the father turned to Teancum. "Too many cities have been destroyed now." His voice was strained.

Teancum nodded sadly. "Parts of Israel. Most of Gaza. Cities in Iran. Other places throughout the Middle East."

The father closed his eyes as he remembered. He and Teancum had walked those parts of the earth together. He knew what things were like there, having seen the devastation for himself. Entire regions of the mortal world smoldered in radioactive ash. Millions were surrounded by hunger and death and despair. Sin and depravity were so overwhelming there was hardly hope at all. "How could they do it?" he asked. "I simply don't understand."

Teancum thought before he answered. "Let's not blame them all," he said. "There are many good still left among them. And that is true everywhere. Whatever country or region you chose to take me to, I could find you good and righteous people living there."

The father brought his hands up to his face, then slowly shook his head. It was just too painful to see the suffering and too frustrating to know it could have been avoided if the people had only seen, if they had only cared.

4

Teancum watched him thoughtfully for a moment, then touched him on the shoulder. "You've forgotten, my good friend, what it was like to live here. You've forgotten how powerful the voice of Lucifer can be. You've forgotten the pull of temptations, the anger, the lust and greed and weakness of the natural man. Your memory has been washed—although just a bit, perhaps—of the intensity of the experience, which is fine. Mortal life can be so acute, so severe and powerful, sometimes it's hard for us to remember how difficult it really was. And the Dark One is even more dangerous now than he was before."

The father shook his head. "No, Teancum, I haven't forgotten. Not a moment. Not an hour. Every day, every emotion, every joy and every fear, every lesson learned is branded upon me. You know we don't forget."

Teancum didn't answer for a moment. "I don't suppose we do," he said at last.

The father shook his head again. "No, we don't forget." Then he nodded to the mortals huddled in the tents below. "They think that we forget them, though."

Teancum smiled, his eyes shining. "A bit of irony, I suppose. I mean, how could we forget them? How could we forget our own children? We love them now more than we ever did, for our love is more perfect, which makes it more powerful."

"If only they knew. If only they believed. If they would just try to listen for us, then they might hear our tender words."

Teancum folded his arms, his face relaxed. It was as if he knew a secret that he wasn't telling. "They are so busy," he answered carefully. "There are so many battles for their time. It's hard for them, just like it was hard for you and me."

The father thought a long moment as he studied the grassy

cemetery that fell below him to the west. "So you think that I can help him."

"Yes, I know you can."

The father hesitated. He was a younger spirit than Teancum and not as sure.

Teancum watched the uncertainty in his eyes. "He's your kin," he reminded him. "The earthly bonds between you are deep, the heavenly bonds even more powerful." He moved his head to the side and pointed to the west, almost laughing. "And remember this, my friend: his mother is out there praying. You've heard her many prayers. They are so strong and faithful, they almost drive me to my knees. Could you deny such faith?" He shook his head. "I don't think either of us can."

chapter one

The room was silent. They were alone. The two men stared at each other before one of them whistled quietly, a nervous habit he'd picked up as a kid, then swallowed and forced a smile. The air in the command center was cool but arid as the desert, the underground cooling systems breathing out purified, bone-dry atmosphere. The digital clocks on the wall behind them showed the local time in a dozen locations around the world: Moscow, Berlin, Jerusalem, New York, Hawaii, and a handful of others.

Local time: 0314. A little less than four hours until sunrise. Above the underground complex, the night was dark. To conserve energy, but mostly to avoid highlighting their capabilities to the local population, the base commander had ordered all lights extinguished after sunset. There were already hundreds of civilians at the gates. No reason to make it thousands. The time for riots and gunfights along the base security perimeter would come soon enough without publicizing the fact that the military had electricity. And water. And communications. And pretty much everything else.

Not the kind of things they needed to advertise right now.

But in the end, it wouldn't matter. If things didn't change soon, the base would run out of energy and supplies just like the local population.

Brucius Marino, the Secretary of Defense, was exhausted. He hadn't slept at all in almost thirty hours, and he'd had little more than a couple of hours of sleep during the two days previous to that. He knew he had to find some time to rest; his mind was slow as molasses and he found himself sometimes stumbling on both his feet and his words. Worse, he slipped into microsleep for fifteen or thirty seconds at the most awkward times—while talking to a subordinate, shaving, eating, listening to a security brief. He couldn't read a paragraph without slipping away.

What he needed was a shower. And a hot meal. And twenty hours of sleep.

But not right now. Not until he said good-bye.

This was important. Maybe the most important thing they would do up to this point.

He stared across the table. There wasn't a man in the world he trusted more than the man sitting opposite him. And this was the last time he would see him. Somehow they both knew.

James Davies, the FBI Director, kept his eyes low. He too was exhausted, his black eyes melting into the dark skin above his cheekbones, his curly hair cut to a stubble of black and gray. The portable table, mounted on rubber wheels, moved under the weight of the Secretary of Defense's heavy arms. The military infirmary was all chrome and tile and white cement walls, causing their voices to echo, which created a stiff environment that magnified the awkwardness of it all.

"How does it feel?" Brucius asked.

James turned his head and swallowed, his Adam's apple bobbing at the strain. "Feels like I swallowed a tennis ball."

Brucius flinched.

"If it hurt like that going down, I can't imagine what it's going to feel like coming back up again."

Brucius winced again and subconsciously swallowed. "It's going to be okay, though?"

James clenched his teeth, then rubbed his tongue across the new cap on his molar and nodded.

They were silent another moment.

"You don't have to do this," Brucius said.

"I know that, sir."

Brucius shook his head. "I'm not *sir*, to you, James. I never will be."

"You're the president, sir."

"Not right now. Not yet. We've been through this."

"You are the president, sir. That isn't in dispute. That's why I'm doing this, you know. As much affection as I might have for you, this isn't about you or me or friendship. This is something different. More important." He nodded toward the hallway. "That's why all of us are doing this. It's about the presidency. The country. It's about the Constitution versus chaos. It's the only thing we can do."

Brucius didn't answer.

James broke into a smile. "I love you, Brucius, you know that, but this is much more important than a single man."

There were footsteps in the hallway, the sound of clicking heels moving past, and they fell silent as they listened, both of them lost in their own thoughts.

"We made a mistake." Brucius had a far-off look on his face as he spoke, his mind reflecting back. He had a sense of pain about him—a father reflecting on the passing of his child. He appeared to be racked with torment. What had happened to his country? What might he have done!

James sucked his teeth and waited.

"We should have seen it coming," Brucius continued.

Again, James didn't answer.

"We should have known."

"What are you talking about, Mr. Secretary?"

"The president we elected. He was good and smooth and said all the right things. But he didn't love his country, at least not like you and I do. Not like our fathers. Not like our grandfathers. He saw our country as not that much different from all the others, not much better, in some ways maybe worse. He saw our sins and determined they precluded us from any further greatness. It wasn't that he had an evil heart, he just couldn't see or didn't choose to see the good that was our country."

"Hmmm," was all James offered.

Brucius Marino leaned over and ran his hand over his head, then rested his elbows on his knees and looked up. "It allowed him to surround himself with men like he was, only worse. Men who didn't trust their own people. Men with lust for power. And power, like cocaine, left them unsatisfied, always aching for more. But it was us as much as anyone. We're the ones who elected him. We're the ones who put him there."

"He paid a price for his folly."

Brucius thought of the nuclear attack over Washington that had killed the president and answered, "Yes, he did."

They fell silent another moment. Outside, a powerful storm was raging: enormous black clouds, billowing and boiling, dark and full. Thunderous rain. Constant spiderwebs of blue-white lightning. Something in the atmosphere had been thrown completely out of whack—whether from the EMP attack or the nuclear fallout, no one quite knew. Maybe it was from both. Maybe Mother Nature was just ticked off, but she was birthing storms now that billowed with more fury than

they'd ever seen before. A particularly close bolt of lightning
CRAAACKED and the thunder followed instantly, causing
the air to sizzle with the smell of burning sulfur. Both men
stopped and stared at the window. It was almost as dark as
midnight outside.

"You get in and get out," Brucius Marino said after the
echoes from the frightening thunder had rolled past. "You
understand me, James. Don't you go and be a hero. I need
you here. I'm not being protective or patronizing; it's the
simple truth. You talk about doing this for our country—well,
this is what your country needs for you to do: Complete this
mission but stay alive! You're no good to any of us dead." The
Secretary leaned forward, his weary eyes boring into the other
man. "I mean it, James. If you consider me the president, then
consider this an order. The country will need your loyalty and
expertise. She will need your truthfulness and intelligence. You
do this and get out. *Do not* get yourself killed!"

James Davies stared at his hands, large, rough, and thick-
fingered. His father's hands. His grandfather's hands. The
inherited hands of a former slave. A sudden chill ran through
him. A premonition? A warning? He didn't know. He looked
across the table at his best friend, his mind drifting back. "Do
you remember the first time we ever met?" he asked.

Brucius stared at him. "Are you kidding? I can't remember anything that happened even a month ago. That was back
in college. It seems like another world."

James rubbed his hands across his eyes. "I remember it like
it was yesterday. We were sitting in a physics lab. There were, I
don't know, forty or fifty kids, all of them as arrogant and self-
absorbed as we were, all of them certain they were going to be
the next billionaire or president or power-crazy CEO. You
don't fill a classroom at Yale with the weak in intellect or ego.
An hour into the lab I looked down the row and caught your

eye. You stared at me, then motioned to the back door. We picked up our books and headed out . . ."

"There was a gym across the hallway." Brucius remembered now. "We ended up shooting hoops."

"Yeah. You were taller by four inches, but I could still dunk on you."

"I was jealous of your money," Brucius said.

"I was jealous of your determination," James countered. "The fact you were making it on your own."

"Your dad was paying your way through college. He bought you that cool car," Brucius pointed out.

"Cool! Are you kidding! That British Triumph was nothing but a piece of junk."

"It was a chick magnet."

"The sucker never ran," James complained. "I spent more time on the bus than any poor black kid in Memphis."

They both fell silent, smiling, the memory deep and full.

"I'll always remember," James repeated, his voice low and monotone. He was talking to himself now. "I looked down the row of kids and saw you. You looked at me. And from that moment, before we had ever even spoken, I knew that you were going to be my best friend."

"It was a long time ago," Brucius answered. "But that has proven true."

"You know what else? Out of that whole group of kids, out of that entire bunch of snot-nosed, brilliant, ambitious, arrogant, give-it-to-me-because-I-deserve-it Yale freshman, I don't think anyone would have predicted we would end up where we are. *We* never would have guessed it. Yet . . ." he motioned to their surroundings, "here we are."

"*Audaces fortuna iuvat,*" Brucius smiled. *Fortune favors the bold.*

"Ab incunabulis," the FBI Director answered. *From the cradle.*

This made Brucius laugh. "I've got a better one: *Age. Fac ut gaudeam.*"

James had to think, translating in his head. "*Go ahead. Make my day.*" He wet his lips and laughed. "Gotta love that one."

"I think it's more appropriate than what you said. I'm pretty sure the only useful thing I did in my cradle was bawl. I don't think that I was predestined to—"

James cut him off. "Not predestined. Ordained. And yes, I think you were. I think we both were. We find ourselves here, at this critical juncture in time, not out of happenstance or luck or some perfect storm of time and circumstance. It certainly wasn't inevitable, but I do think there is a purpose and plan to it all."

Brucius didn't answer for a moment. "Maybe," was all he said.

"Not *maybe,* Brucius. What I said was true."

"Maybe. It doesn't matter. It doesn't matter how we got here; all that matters is what we do with this moment we've been given. All that really matters is what we do with right now."

James looked around as if caught in some internal debate, then turned back to his friend. "I had an interesting experience about a year ago. It'll sound crazy, and I'm not sure you'll understand, but I want you to hear it. I know you're not a Christian—despite my best efforts to save you," James gave him a wary smile, "but I know your heart. So I want you to listen to what I'm going to tell you and really try to understand."

Brucius waited, his face unchanging.

"Last Christmas, Emily and I went to a Christmas concert

at the National Cathedral. The Mormon Choir was there. They're pretty good, you know. During the concert, they sang a song that harmonized with 'Silent Night.' In the background they sang these words: 'This is a time of peace. This is a time of joy.'

"As I heard those words, a feeling came over me, a certain assurance, as if a voice were speaking to me from God. It *was* a time for joy. It *was* a time for peace. It was the great breath of air before the deep plunge, the great calm of peace before the dark and deadly storm. It was the final moment of quiet, the deep sigh of hope before the last cage was opened to the darkness of a stark and evil world. The Lord's angels were waiting to sound their trumps, but evil angels were also waiting to unleash their hate upon the world.

"And as they sang, I started wondering, how long will this last peace last? Now we know. It is over. How deep will be the darkness? Only time will tell. But on that night, in that cathedral, the impression was so clear. *Strengthen yourself,* the voice whispered to me. *Prepare for what is true. The time of darkness is coming. Find joy in this day. Live, love, and be happy! But also know He is preparing His kingdom, and soon He will appear. Are you willing to help Him? Are you worthy of His cause? The battle lines are drawing. Which side are you on? No one can stand on the sidelines, hoping the storms will pass them by. This battle will sweep every generation and every people on earth—the young and the old, the cowards and the true. So prepare now while He gives you this final moment of peace. Prepare now for the darkness that is building before the final storm . . ."*

James trailed off. He didn't know any better how to explain it. And he didn't know why it was so important to him that Brucius understand.

Brucius looked at him awkwardly. "I don't . . . you know, James, I'm just not that kind of guy. I left the church when I was just an altar boy. It killed my family and the local priest, but it just was not my thing. I wanted to believe. I *still* want to believe. But there were too many holes, too many things that didn't make sense. Still, I don't begrudge you your faith or beliefs. In fact, I'm envious. And, in my own way, I'm still searching. But I have to be honest with you when I say I just don't see too much in all of that. This thing that happened to you in the cathedral, this premonition or whatever, I don't doubt it for a minute; I just don't think the same thing will ever happen to me. And I don't know that it means too much anyway.

"To me, this thing is pretty simple. Some guys have stolen the presidency. I'm going to round them up and kill them. You're going to help me. Everything else is purely smoke."

James looked deeply at his friend, thought a long moment, then nodded.

"You okay with that?" Brucius asked.

James stood up from the table.

Brucius pushed to his feet and leaned into him. "I mean what I told you," he repeated. "Don't take any chances. Get in, get out, and get back here. Simple as that. You got me?"

James watched him another moment. Did Brucius understand at all? Maybe not. Probably not. But, one day, James knew he would.

Brucius watched his friend's cheeks protruding as he moved his tongue around his teeth. "Don't break it," he told him protectively. "No good for you to starting throwing up right here."

"I'm not a fool," James smiled weakly.

Brucius nodded to the door behind them. "It's time to go," he said.

James moved around the table. He too was tired, that was obvious from the stiff and gingerly way he moved his legs.

Brucius put his arm around his shoulders. "You don't have to do this," he said a final time.

James scowled. "Don't insult me, friend."

"Trust no one. Don't expect any of them to trust you. Always expect they will be watching. Everything you do, every word you say, every glance of your eyes and inflection of your voice will be noted. If they could read your mind, they would do it. Plan on the worst case and go from there."

James raised an impatient eyebrow. "I got it."

Brucius took his hand and shook it. "I just want you to come back to us."

James grunted and took his coat. "I want to come back too."

chapter two

T he army officer stood on the back porch of the white-paneled house, his dark hair blown back across his neck. His name was Joseph, but even here at home he still thought of himself as Bono, the nickname so deeply ingrained that everyone considered it his name. His skin looked especially tan in the dying light, his eyes alert, his demeanor calm, his shoulders slacking. The same cold wind that just a few nights before had passed over the frigid waters of Lake Michigan to gust at Sara Brighton and her family atop the old railroad building in East Chicago had rushed down from the north and mixed with the moist air sucked up from the Gulf of Mexico to form a cold and constant drizzle over most of the Tennessee River Valley. The soldier looked up at the clouds passing over the trees and open fields, estimating the ceiling at just a couple of hundred feet. The dark clouds rushed past him, billowing layers that were driven eastward by a powerful force.

He watched a moment, then stepped down from the porch and walked across the grass, his head up, his eyes on the rushing skies. The gentle rain wet his face, but he didn't seem

17

to notice, and he never wiped the falling drops away. As he stared toward the heavens, he sensed an unseen power. Something up there. Something moving. Something alive and full of evil energy—watching, listening, looking, waiting. Yes, that was it. Something waiting. Just like he was. Just like they all were. *He* was up there waiting, watching and hoping, the dark spirits that surrounded him filling his ears with their constant cries, their boiling agitation driving them to froth.

The young soldier kept looking up, his heart beating rapidly. As he sensed the presence of the evil, a sudden realization rested upon him: *Lucifer hated the thought of passing time.* Far more than the mortals, the Dark One felt old and used and tired. He felt wrinkled and bent and hopeless, *for he knew his time would pass!* There was no hope for his future, nothing to look forward to at all. So he didn't want the final battle to ever end. He feared it. He dreaded it. He knew that he would lose, and when he did, the outcome would lead to his destruction. He would be cast out, expelled from the empire he had worked so hard to lead, thrust out from the kingdom he had built upon this earth.

The Last Days were just the beginning for the righteous, but they were the final days for him.

As Bono thought, the rain and mist gathered deeper all around. He took one last look at the skies, then slowly bowed his head.

He didn't hear her slip out of the house or walk across the wooden porch, the padding of her bare feet lost in the sound of the blowing wind. She stood quietly watching him, the rain dribbling from the roof before her face.

And though he didn't see her leaning against the white pillar on the porch behind him, he sensed her spirit and knew that she was near.

*　　*　　*

Caelyn watched him a long moment. He was so beautiful. So strong. So sure. So gentle and concerned. He wasn't perfect, not by any means—his smile was a bit crooked, he was far too arrogant, and she hated the way he wore his hair, more like a Bedouin warrior than a U.S. Army Special Forces officer—but she saw none of these imperfections as she looked upon him now. She had never loved him more. No man had ever made her feel the way he did. From the first time she had seen him—and she remembered that sunny afternoon back on the campus at UCLA very well—she had never even considered another. That night, for some reason she didn't understand, she had closed her eyes to pray. And the voice that had come to her was as real as the yellow square of moonlight that had spread across her bed. *"You will marry him,"* the voice had said.

She had opened her eyes and looked up at the darkness. "I will *what!*" she had demanded.

"The life you will share together will be difficult, but I will also make it sweet."

Looking back, she realized that time had proven the premonition true.

Caelyn shivered and drew her arms around her chest. Bono turned and looked at her, then extended his hand. She left the porch, her feet getting soaked as she walked across the wet grass. She lifted his arm, twirled underneath it, turned her back to him, and leaned against his chest. Together they studied the weeping sky, their faces growing wet.

Bono pressed his nose against her neck, the fragrance of her hair lifting in the wind. "I love you, Caelyn," he whispered to her.

She leaned against his shoulder and closed her eyes.

"I love you more than anything." His voice was hardly more than a breath.

She smiled, but there was a sadness in her posture that her husband couldn't see. She tilted her head against his chin. "You love me, babe. I know that. But there are other things that you love, too?" Her voice was half teasing, half true.

He nuzzled against her neck but didn't answer.

"You love your country. You love our freedom."

She felt him move against her arms.

"I love you more than *anything*," he told her.

She stared out blankly at the growing darkness, holding herself motionless as he grew tense.

She wanted to believe it. *Most* of her believed it. But there was another part of her, a part deep inside the feminine emotions of her soul, that couldn't quite fit the pieces into place. He would do anything for her, she knew that. He'd make any sacrifice. But he wouldn't leave the military. *That* he would not do. And it wasn't so much that he wouldn't, but he *couldn't*. She might as well ask him to sell his soul to the devil as to ask him to quit serving his country right now.

Funny thing was, if the country had been at peace, if the battle wasn't raging now around them, he would have resigned his commission without her even asking him to. It wasn't just the service to his country that attracted him, it was serving during a time of war. At first, that hadn't made any sense to Caelyn. It was as strange as if he had said he wanted to start eating grass and living outside with the cows. However, over time, after being around him and his friends, she had begun to understand at least a little of why the soldiers felt so compelled to serve. It was something deep inside them, something she couldn't ever really feel in exactly the same way as they did.

Why would a man throw himself into battle, cast his life

into the wind while rushing forward against a hail of metal and fire and smoke and death, feeling the splatter of the dying all around him? Why would men choose to leave their homes, their wives, their families, clean showers, flushing toilets, microwave ovens, and soft beds, to live on the razor's edge? Enduring 120 degrees of summer heat while dressed in full combat gear. Surviving bitter winters in the mountains. Through it all, they would grumble and complain, yet when it came time for another tour of duty, all of them went back. None of them were forced to. There certainly was no draft.

"We knew what we were getting into," she remembered her husband saying. "We go outside the wire, we see cut-off heads and tortured children, and we do our best to fight it. And when it's over, we'll know we did something that really matters. How many people can ever say that about their lives?"

Now Caelyn finally understood. *"Who more than self their country loved, and mercy more than life."* It really was that simple. At the end of all her pondering, it pretty much all came down to that.

And when she really thought about it, she realized that she was just like them.

She too loved her country. She too felt the sacred obligation of doing something meaningful in this world. Deep in her heart, she knew, just like her husband, that the Spirit of God was the spirit of freedom, and that it was worth the heavy price. Yes, family members sacrificed in different ways from their husbands, but their willingness to lay it out there was the same.

Her mind drifted back to a conversation she and Bono had had a couple of years before. Early in the morning. A spring day. He had called her on his unit's satellite telephone from Afghanistan.

"Peter Zembeic went AWOL from the field hospital down

in Kandahar," he told her, his voice scratching through the military phone.

Caelyn had to hold her finger in her other ear to understand him. "Say it again," she said.

"Peter Zembeic went AWOL from the field hospital down in Kandahar."

"You're kidding. He went AWOL? I don't believe it! No way Peter takes off on you guys!"

Bono started laughing. "Listen to me, this is funny. He went AWOL from the field hospital, okay? Not from our unit. He got shot in the leg a couple weeks ago. Took out a pretty good hunk of flesh. He tried to dress it himself and keep it quiet, but it started to get infected, and the boss sent him down to Kandy to the field hospital. They told him they were going to keep him there a couple weeks and then send him home. He'd have none of that. He tried to check himself out of the hospital. They wouldn't let him. So he packed up his gear and took off. Got a ride with a couple Navy Seal pukes heading north and showed up back here at our unit. The guys down at the hospital thought he'd flipped out and headed home. Put out a huge search party. The boss finally had to call them and tell them we had their guy up here. We all thought it was so funny . . ." Her husband started laughing. "He's the only guy I know who went AWOL to get *back* to his unit!"

Caelyn laughed too, but inside her mind was racing. "Why did he do that, babe?" she finally asked when he quit laughing. "He had a ticket out. No shame in being wounded. He could have come home."

Bono hesitated, uncomfortable with the sudden change in the tone of her voice. "He said Lieutenant Horace owed him from the poker game the night before. Said he had to come back to get his money."

Bono tried to laugh again, but Caelyn's voice was serious. "I don't get it," she repeated. "He could have come home."

After a long moment of silence, Bono said, "I don't know, babe. Guess someone's got to do it." He hesitated again. Both of them knew they weren't talking about Peter Zembeic any more. "Someone's got to do it," he repeated. "And they probably won't do it as good as me. I've got my brothers back here, Caelyn. None of us went looking for this fight . . ."

"Every one of you is a volunteer."

"Yeah, but what I said is true. None of us asked for this. All of us would just as soon be home. But the situation is what it is, and since it is, we might as well try to do a little good. And as long as my guys are here, I've got to be here too. If something goes wrong—and it will—no one else can take care of them like I can. I want to be beside them. There's not much more I can say. If I don't stick with them, what will they think of me? What would *you* think of me?" He paused to swallow. "What would I think of myself?"

Caelyn had thought about that conversation many times through the years. Somehow, it made it easier.

✳ ✳ ✳

The rain slowed to a heavy mist. Both of them were wet now, their clothes, their skin, their hair. Caelyn felt the warm heat of his body and pressed against his arms. "I'm so glad you're here with me," she whispered. "I needed you right now." He only held her tighter, and she turned around to face him. "If you die, I'm going to kill you." She punched him on the arm. "I mean that, Lieutenant! If you die, I'm going to kill you. Don't you leave me here alone! I don't care what you have to do, you stay here in this world. You stay here with me and Ellie. Even if you're never home, as long as I know that you're out there somewhere, I can handle it. As long as I have the hope that you'll come back to me, I know I'll be okay.

"And remember, we deserve you as much as anyone does. Ellie needs her daddy. I need my husband. My life would remain forever bleak and empty if I couldn't know that you were somewhere in this world. I have to know that when I look up at the night sky, you are out there too. So I want you to promise me again. I want to hear you say the words."

Bono looked down at her. She felt him breathe in deeply; then he leaned over and whispered in her ear, "I swear to you with everything inside me, with every fiber of my soul, with every authority I have been given, I will find a way to come back home."

He reached down and took her hands, holding them tight. She looked up at him, staring into his eyes, their faces only shadows in the darkness. Then she felt a single teardrop fall from his cheek and rest upon her eyelid. She brushed away its warm, wet sting.

It was the thousandth time that she believed him.

* * *

Later that night they lay beside each other in their bed. Ellie was sleeping with a bunch of blankets on the floor, unwilling to be separated from her father. Neither of them was sleeping, and Caelyn turned to him. "What are you thinking about?" she whispered so that Ellie wouldn't wake.

He looked up at the darkness, the outline of his face barely visible in the moonlight.

"What are you thinking about?" she whispered once again.

"Seventy-three," he answered.

"What's that? The number of medals you're going to win?" she teased.

His expression didn't change, and she laid her head upon his chest.

"What is it, babe?" she pressed him.

He cleared his throat and touched her hair. "How many hours before I have to leave."

chapter three

Caelyn awoke and rolled over, felt the empty bed, opened her eyes and looked at the rumpled sheets and covers, then extended her hand. The side of the bed had grown cold, and she turned to look at the floor. Ellie's blankets had been rolled up and pushed aside. She heard quiet footsteps in the hall, whispers, then a giggle, then two sets of bare feet moving down the stairs. She rolled over to the window. The sun was up and shining brightly through the eastern pane, two full fists above the horizon. Later than she thought—it had been a long time since she had slept in. She rolled to her side, fluffed the pillow, watched the sun stream through the window, then fell back into a warm and peaceful sleep.

*　　*　　*

Ellie followed her dad out the back door and onto the porch. Bono stood for a moment looking across the empty fields. The rain had cleared and the morning was calm and peaceful—a little cold, with light mist along the lower fields,

26

but the air was still and smelled of wet grass and hay and rich, dark earth. He took a breath and held it, sucking the smell into his lungs. Beautiful. Full and fragrant. He smiled and let the air out with a satisfied sigh. There was something about the earth, the ground, the rain on the harvested fields that surrounded him; he longed for them in a manner that he couldn't quite explain. It wasn't like he was an old farm boy—quite the opposite, he'd grown up in a stucco-and-brick house set among the San Fernando mountains—but there was something about the land, the open sky around him, the trees, and the rolling, green terrain that beckoned him in a way that was . . . ? He didn't know. He couldn't explain it. Was it old? Permanent? Something from the premortal world?

He remembered talking about his feelings with a fellow soldier in Afghanistan. The colonel had been raised on a cattle ranch in Oklahoma and it seemed all he ever talked about was the BarZ ranch back home. Most guys carried pictures of their kids. He carried pictures of his prize bull and his dog. They had just finished a short sacrament meeting in a camouflage tent with dark bread and bottled water when they had a few minutes to talk. Bono explained some of his feelings, saying he was jealous of the colonel and how much he loved the land.

"I think if we understood how well we knew this earth before we came here, we might be surprised," the colonel had said.

Bono had thought a lot about that and decided it was true.

Either way, it didn't matter. He loved the farm. He loved the earth. "Caelyn, one day, you and I are going to live on a place like this," he remembered having promised his wife. "We're going to raise our family in the country. That will be our reward for what we're giving up right now, a gentle place where we can be together and get a little rest. We'll build a little house, a little . . ."

He caught himself in the memory. Did the things he used to dream about even matter anymore? Was such an ambition even possible, given what had happened in the world?

He didn't know. He liked to hope. It wasn't as if all life was over. Who knew what lay in store?

Ellie came up behind him and slipped her hand into his. He looked down at her and smiled. "Ready for our walk?" he asked.

"Roger that, Daddy!" she answered. Bono laughed. Something about *Roger* and *Daddy* in the same sentence just didn't seem to work.

"You gonna be a soldier?" he asked her.

"Hurrah, Daddy!" she laughed back.

Hurrah and *Daddy*. Same thing. It didn't work.

They started walking, Bono glancing guiltily back toward the house. "Shhh, don't let your mother hear you say that," he whispered conspiratorially.

Ellie watched his eyes. "It's okay, Daddy. Mommy knows I want to be a soldier," she said with confidence.

"She thinks you'll change your mind."

"She knows I want to be like you."

Bono almost froze, his mind racing back to scenes of bloodshed, scenes of violence, the memories quick and jarring. He frowned. "No, honey, you don't want to be like me." His voice was sad but not unpleasant.

It wasn't uncommon for little girls who craved their missing fathers to fantasize about being like them. Some army staff psychiatrist had explained it to his regiment at their last predeployment briefing. "Don't worry about it if your daughters talk about wanting to follow you," she had told the group of departing soldiers. "It's a way for them to share something with you, even if only in their minds. They imagine themselves going off with you to war, a handsome knight and his little princess. Sometimes it's the only way they can figure out a reason for you to be together. Don't try to convince them it is silly. They'll grow out of it with time." The briefing from the psychiatrist was supposed to have made them feel better about some of the fallout from their family separations. Bono remembered it as one of the most depressing briefings in his life.

He looked down at Ellie, her blonde hair, so light and bouncy, her beautiful eyes and flushing cheeks. She wore glasses now, thin wire frames that sat on her nose, lending a bit of seriousness to her face. Looking at her, it was impossible for him to think about her growing up at all, let alone growing up to be a soldier, this perfect and innocent little soul.

He shook his head.

A soldier? Not his little Ellie. She'd always be a little girl, playing with her china dolls and squealing over a new set of clothes.

She looked up at him and squeezed his hand. "I want to be like you, Dad," she said as if she'd read his mind.

It tore his heart to hear her say it. "That's not such a good idea, honey. You'd be much better to be like Mom."

He tugged her hand and they cut across the straw-covered field toward the path that led to the windbreak trees. The morning sunshine was bright but slanted and didn't give much warmth. The air was clean, visibility above the mist a hundred miles. Walking with his daughter, Bono was as happy as he had ever felt. He had only a few days with them, the reminder always tugging at the back of his mind, but the time together was so sweet and happy, it overshadowed the fact that soon he'd have to leave.

They walked for a while in silence until Ellie said, "Something bad happened, Daddy."

Bono turned to look down at her.

She pointed toward the fields on the other side of the trees. "Miller is dead," she told him.

Bono stopped and knelt beside her. "I know that, baby."

"I saw him. It was kind of yucky." She kept her eyes straight ahead, not looking at him. "Mom knows something about Miller that she won't tell me, something about how he died."

Bono thought a moment, measuring his words carefully. He knew everything that had happened, of course. He was the one who had buried the old dog. He knew that Miller had been shot. "Those were some bad men," was all he answered.

"Yeah. You should have seen Grandma. She was *really* mad. I thought she was going to hit one of them."

Bono put a hand down and touched the wet earth to balance himself but didn't say anything.

"Grandma can get really mad sometimes," Ellie said.

"Yes, she can. But you can understand that. Those men weren't very nice."

Ellie's eyes turned down as she remembered. "Not nice at all." She glanced back toward the house. "They said bad words, Daddy." She hesitated, looking at him with a worried face. "Lots of s-words."

"Whoa, the s-word. That's not good."

"You're not supposed to say *shut-up*, right, Daddy?"

"No, you're not. It sounds mean."

"Well, one man said it to another man *at least* five times. I knew when he kept saying that, Grandma was going to get really mad."

Bono couldn't help it. He started laughing out loud. "Well, you can understand that," he repeated.

Ellie nodded, unsure of what her father was laughing about.

Bono stood and they walked again in silence. "I'm sad about Miller," Ellie said.

"He was a good dog, Ellie. But good dogs go to heaven. And he was getting old. I think he was ready to move on. In fact, I think he's glad to be in heaven. He's happy there right now, barking and playing in the sun."

"Do you think he misses me, Dad?"

"I'm sure he does, baby doll."

"But there are other people up there, right? I mean, he's not in heaven all alone? There are other kids to play with, other kids to scratch his ears? What good is heaven if he's alone? He needs someone to feed him and give him baths."

"Yeah, baby, there'll be someone there to play with him and scratch his ears."

Ellie thought for a moment. "Do you think God likes Miller, Daddy?"

"I think He does, baby. I think God loves all of His creations."

"So He'll take care of him. He won't yell at him if he barks or make him eat that one yucky kind of dog food, you know, the kind that makes him sick?"

"No, baby, He won't. Miller will be happy. Heavenly Father will see to that."

Ellie smiled, apparently satisfied.

They walked on, reaching the trees. Bono waited for his daughter to choose the way and she turned left, away from the field where the gang had been a couple of days before. He walked beside her and for a while she sang quietly to herself, a tune that Bono didn't know. Finally he realized that she was making it up. The path was covered with wet gravel, and the small rocks crunched with every step. The trees were full of blackbirds, hundreds of them calling from the branches, their shadows falling across the path. Bono slowed his pace and looked up at them. "Ellie, you know that I can't stay with you and Mommy for too long," he said.

Ellie looked away. "How long, Daddy?"

"I only have a couple more days."

"When Mom says I can have a couple of jelly beans, sometimes I take eight."

Her father shook his head. "I don't have that many, baby."

Ellie pursed her lips. "Sometimes I take five."

It broke his heart to listen to her. "Honey, you know that I would stay here forever if I could."

She didn't answer.

"You know that it's the hardest thing I ever had to do, leaving you and Mommy here alone."

"Mommy's worried about something, Daddy. I don't think you should go."

"I know she is, baby, but she's going to be okay. Heavenly Father is going to watch over both of you."

She looked down. She was trying to be brave. Bono recognized the determined crunch across her forehead, but though she tried to hold back the tears, her clear blue eyes brimmed over. She wiped them, embarrassed and unsure. "Don't go, Daddy," she started pleading. "Please, don't go away right now. If Mommy wasn't so worried . . ."

Bono suddenly felt like crying himself. He felt like weeping for his daughter, for Caelyn, for himself. He felt like weeping for the world, all the lonely children, all those who'd lost so much happiness, so much innocence, so much joy in this dark time. He felt like weeping for the days that lay before them, the things this little girl would have to endure. The knot inside his stomach seemed to crawl into his throat, so tight and restrictive he thought he would choke. He tried to talk but couldn't—it was just too painful, and he had to catch his breath and look away. He couldn't let her see the tears. He couldn't let her watch his shoulders heave. He quickly wiped his face, looking across the open field, then took a deep breath and steeled himself before bending down to her again.

Ellie kept her face low, frightened and frustrated.

"I'm so sorry, baby. Do you know that? I'm *so* sorry I have to go."

"You could tell them you have a stomachache."

"I could do that, baby, and they might let me stay awhile. But Ellie, there are other little kids out there, little boys and girls just like you, who don't even have any grandmas or mommies to take care of them. They live in places around the world where they don't have anything at all. I need to help them. I need to help their moms and dads. If I can help them, then maybe I can make things a little better. I know it's hard for you to understand, but I think that's what I should do."

"I don't care about those other kids." Her voice was angry now. "I want you to stay here with me and Mom."

He reached out and touched her cheek, and she leaned against his palm. "I know you do, Ellie. I understand that, I really do. But there are things I have to do out there, things that I can do to help. And I'm not the only one. There are others too. Other soldiers. Firemen. Policemen. Doctors and nurses. People like that. They have to leave their families, at least for a while. Do you understand that, honey? Do you see why it's important?"

Ellie didn't answer.

Bono cupped her face against his palm. "Look at me, baby."

She shook her head defiantly.

"Ellie, can you look at your ol' dad?"

She kept her head down, brushing her hands against her face, first one side and then the other. Then she took a deep breath, firmed her shoulders, and looked up.

"Do you believe in Jesus Christ?" he asked her.

Ellie thought, then slowly nodded.

"Do you *really* believe He loves you?"

"I know He does, Daddy."

"How do you know that, baby?"

"You and Mommy taught me. And I believe you. And I can feel it sometimes," she moved her hand, "here, inside my heart."

"That's true, baby. That's the way it is. Everything you've been taught and believed is true. Jesus loves you. He knows your problems. He is our Savior. And that's the *only* thing that matters. This is going to be okay."

"But Daddy, when you go away, I get so lonely. And I feel so bad for Mommy. I think she misses you lots more than you know. She needs you, Daddy, like I do. I think sometimes she gets scared."

Bono quickly straightened up and held his hand to hide the tremble in his chin, the tears wetting the creases around his eyes. "Heavenly Father is going to bless you and Mommy," he finally told her. "Sometimes I have to leave you, but He will never go. He is always with you, Ellie, He never leaves your side. He knows you. He loves you. He wants you to be happy, and He will provide a way."

"But I can't be happy when you are gone. I worry about you, Daddy. Mommy does too."

Bono shook his head and closed his eyes. *Help me, Father, to know what I should tell her. Help me, Heavenly Father, to comfort this little girl.*

The answer came to him in a rush of warmth and peace. It didn't make any sense, and it wasn't something he would have ever thought of himself, but he knew it was the answer.

"She wants to help!" the Spirit told him.

He thought, then knelt down and looked into his daughter's

face. "I need you to do something for me, baby. Something really important, okay? But it will be fun."

Ellie looked up, her eyes expectant.

"Mom's birthday is in a couple of weeks. I want you to make her a special cake, okay? I'll talk to Grandma and make certain she gets the things you'll need, but I need *you* to make the cake. And when you do, I need you to tell her that it's from both of us. Can you do that for me, baby? Can you make a special cake for Mom?"

Her face brightened. "Can I decorate it the way I want?"

"Any way you want. I know you'll make it beautiful."

Ellie looked off, her face crunching as she thought. "I could decorate it to make it look like Miller, a cute dog with floppy ears. I saw a picture of a cake decorated like that in a magazine. The doggy was *so* cute. He was brown and had chocolate kisses for his eyes and licorice strings for whiskers. It was *so* neat, Daddy . . ."

"Beautiful, Ellie. You make it look like Miller. Grandma will help you, but I'm going to tell her that it needs to be your cake."

Ellie broke into a smile.

"There's something else I need you to do for me."

Ellie nodded urgently.

"I won't be here to take care of Mommy. And I think you're right—she is a little worried. So I need you to help take care of her, okay? Keep her smiling. Keep her spirits up. Make sure she says her prayers at night. Make sure she thanks Heavenly Father for all the blessings we've been given. I know we've got some problems, Ellie, but Heavenly Father loves us. He loves you more than you could ever know. You remind Mommy of that, okay? You tell her every day. Every day, you go up to Mom, pull her down to you, put your arms around her neck, and look into her eyes. When she is looking at you,

Ellie, then I want you to say these words: 'Heavenly Father loves us. Daddy loves us. We're going to be okay.'"

He looked at Ellie and waited until she nodded.

"If you do that for me, it will help both me and Mommy. If you do that, then every day I'll know that, no matter where I am, someone gave Mommy a hug and reminded her that we love her and that everything will be okay."

"I'll do it, Daddy. I'll never forget."

He put his hand out. "Pinky swear."

She interlocked their little fingers. "Pinky swear."

They pressed their thumbs together, making a snapping sound. "I've got your promise now," Bono said, standing up.

"You can count on me, Daddy."

"I know I can."

She grabbed his legs and held onto him. "You can count on me because I love you."

Bono reached down and picked her up and held her tight against his neck. "I love you, too," he whispered.

He felt her crying in his arms.

chapter four

The Secretary of Defense sat before the electronic console. The command post was almost quiet. Designed to allow a group of thirty or forty technicians and military officers to monitor the strategic situation in a time of national crisis, primarily during a time of nuclear war, most of the tactical screens around him were blank, the work desks empty. A huge computer/television monitor was mounted on the front wall, half a dozen smaller screens beside it. The largest screen showed a picture of the aircraft in the sky along the eastern half of the United States. The number of aircraft was amazingly low—frighteningly low—fewer than forty or fifty in all, and all of them military. On a normal day before the EMP attack, there would have been five or six thousand aircraft in the sky. There was no better indication of the death of the nation than the utter lack of civilian airliners in flight. The SecDef watch a trail of European Airbuses heading across the pond from England, guessing, but not certain, that they were laden with relief supplies. Where they were coming from, where they were heading, what they were carrying, he didn't know. Raven Rock was calling the shots entirely and had been for several days now, choosing not to advise or even pretend to take the counsel of the war planners and military officers at Offutt. Which was fine with Brucius Marino. Let the men in Raven Rock ignore them. Maybe they'd forget about him, too.

Practically the entire world thought he was dead. Fewer than a dozen military officers knew that he was here. It was a very tight secret, kept completely on a highly compartmentalized, need-to-know basis, for it was critical that they protect him until they were ready to act.

Ignoring the large monitor on the wall, Brucius concentrated on the computer screen at the desk where he was sitting. He was waiting for a message and he shot a quick look toward the digital time on the lower corner of the computer screen. 0712 local. A little more than a day since James Davies had left.

They should have heard something from him. They should have gotten the signal before now. James had been in Raven Rock for six or seven hours by this time.

Brucius waited. At his side, a young officer waited with him. A couple of senior NCOs worked the communications console four rows back. Behind the NCOs, at the back of the room, behind a thick pane of one-way glass, the others waited. Some of them paced. Some of them slept in their chairs. A couple of them ate, picking at the salads and sandwiches the cafeteria had sent down.

All of them were nervous.

But none of them were nearly as fearful as he.

*　　*　　*

RAVEN ROCK (SITE R), UNDERGROUND MILITARY COMPLEX
SOUTHERN PENNSYLVANIA

The first thing they did was take his clothes and burn them. Then they stripped him down, searched every inch of his body, sent him through an X-ray machine to check for implants, and left him in the room to wait, naked, cold, and scared.

It was pretty clear that he was not among friends, and just as clear that they didn't trust him. They didn't trust anyone any longer. Anyone outside the coven was the enemy, and there was no way for James Davies to invite himself in without raising deep suspicion.

So they left him in the interrogation room off the entry into Raven Rock while they decided what to do.

Time passed. Hours? A day? He didn't know.

Waiting, James got angry. It was one thing to be careful. This had nothing to do with that. To leave him there for hours, naked, without the dignity of something to even cover himself with, had nothing at all to do with security. It was part of the mental handicapping to bring him under their control, part of the psychological intimidation. *"You're in our world now."*

More time passed. He grew more cold and angry. A small metal chair was the only furnishing in the room. Sitting on it, he glanced in the upper corner, staring at the security camera. "A little clothing here would be nice!" he called angrily toward it, knowing they were watching. He turned to the wall where a couple of nondescript dime-store pictures had been mounted, knowing there were cameras and microphones concealed there as well.

Realizing he was in for a long haul, he did the only thing he could think of. Having been subjected to the most humiliating search, naked, shivering, hungry, and exhausted, he stood up, walked to the corner, lay down, curled up, and fell asleep.

*　　*　　*

The doctor watched the intruder on the television monitor. Though he was middle-aged, the civilian psychiatrist was easily intimidated because he was new, having been recruited to work at Raven Rock just a few weeks before the EMP attack. The military officer standing beside him had three silver stars on his shoulders, but there was something about him that the doctor didn't like. For one thing, he was far too young. How old could this snot-nose be? Middle thirties? And yet here he was, a general? The doctor shook his head. Yeah, things were in upheaval, and tens of thousands of senior officers had been killed in the nuclear attack on D.C., but come on, who was this kid? And who in the world had made him a three-star general? And his age wasn't the worst of it. It was the pride and arrogance that bothered the doctor the most.

He had been in Raven Rock only a couple of weeks, and he didn't understand military protocol at all.

The general watched the closed-circuit monitors for half a minute. It appeared the subject was asleep. "You're certain he's not contaminated?" he demanded of the doctor.

"Nothing, general. He's clean as the day he was born."

"The X-ray?"

The doctor held up a couple of dark gray sheets. "Nothing, sir. Nothing implanted under his skin. I assure you, he's not carrying anything. If he had any covert reconnaissance or tracking devices, we would know."

The general didn't answer as he watched the screen. The doctor had better be right. They couldn't take the chance with this man. They knew far too much about him to ever trust him, and there was no way they were going to let James Davies into Raven Rock without being certain—absolutely certain—he wasn't there to plant a tracking device or reconnaissance bug. And the stuff the FBI had now, the tiny, secret, and amazingly effective bugs—and yes, *bug* was the perfect word to describe them—forced them to take extraordinary measures to be sure.

Extraordinary precautions, yes. But to leave the intruder in the interrogation room for hours without any clothes, that had been *his* decision. A surge of emotion ran through him, the power of the moment tingling in his veins. This was, after all, the freaking Director of the Federal Bureau of Investigation, the most powerful law-enforcement agency in the world. Yet there he was, sleeping naked in his cell.

The problem for James Davies, a problem he apparently didn't know about, was that he'd been replaced. He wasn't the FBI Director any longer. He was nothing but a has-been civilian in a world that didn't appreciate men like him anymore. President Fuentes had put his own man in as Director. This short, fat man was soon going to find out that he'd lost his job, as well as all of the privileges and protections that had come with his former position.

The general snorted to himself. In an hour or two, James Davies was going to find himself on the road that led away from Raven Rock without so much as a ride to the nearest town.

If he was lucky.

And the general didn't believe that much in luck anymore. Far more likely Davies would be killed here. Which was fine with him as well.

But first, the Council wanted to see him. They were a little curious about what the former Director had to say.

Brucius Marino had sent him to them, which meant he was a messenger who might be worth listening to.

"All right," the general said, turning away from the security monitor. "Get him up and dressed. I'll send a couple of marines down to escort him to the executive compound. It might take me a couple of hours. Keep him locked in there until then."

chapter five

James Davies was led down a crowded hall. Military officers and enlisted men along with an equal number of civilians—middle-aged men and women who had the air and arrogance of career bureaucrats—hurried up and down the halls. A recessed light in the center of each hallway was illuminated red. DEFCON at the highest level. A sense of urgency filled the air.

James wore a black, one-piece jumpsuit and white socks with no shoes. The jumpsuit was too small for him, and though he had loosened the waistband, the cover over the zipper still pulled tight. He walked slowly, his legs stiff, and he didn't appear to look around.

He was waiting to find the bathroom, but he had to select the right one. It had to be private, not under surveillance. The entire mission depended on his choice.

They descended a set of cement stairs, working their way lower into the underground government command post, then came to a secure elevator. The two marines stood on his left and right, each of them keeping a firm grip on one of his elbows. He tried to pull away, but they wouldn't let him.

"Look at me, boys. I'm an old man. Do you really think I'm going to run?"

It was ridiculous and they all knew it, but still the guards continued holding tightly, hurting the tendons in his arms.

They stepped into the elevator and one of the guards flashed his security pass in front of the electronic reader, then punched an unmarked button, sending them to the highly secure presidential and executive level. James felt his stomach flutter as the high-speed elevator descended farther into the bowels of the underground command post. The doors opened and he looked out. No more cement floors and bare walls. Deep blue carpet. Expensive artworks. Mahogany and leather everywhere.

They started walking, James almost limping as they moved.

There it was—three doors down, just like they had told him it would be. The door was narrow and outlined in dark wood. A combined man/woman symbol was at the side. A multiuse bathroom, which meant that it would lock. On the presidential level, which meant it was far less likely to be monitored. Passing the deeply stained wooden door, he looked pained, then glanced back.

"I've got to go," he whispered to one of the guards.

The guard firmed his grip around his elbow.

James looked back desperately as they moved away. "I've really got to go!" he said again.

The guard kept moving him along.

James pulled away and stopped. "Look, you fool, I've been locked up for hours. I've had every inch of my body prodded, examined, poked, and explored. Only one of my many deprivations has been a bathroom. Now, unless you want me to go in the middle of the president's office, something I promise you I *will* do, you'd better give me a little time to stop in there."

The guard hesitated.

James moved toward him. "Do you even know who I am?" he hissed.

The guard looked vacant.

"I'm Doctor James Davies, the FBI Director . . ."

"Not any longer, sir. The FBI Director is waiting with the president in the executive suite."

James almost sneered, *He is not the president and I have not been replaced!* but he bit his tongue, barely keeping his angry words from spouting out. The military guard, a spit-and-polish marine, stared at him, his face sympathetic but firm. He wasn't part of any grand conspiracy. He had no idea what was going on; he was just doing his job. As far as he knew—and how could he know any better?—the legally appointed president was commanding Raven Rock.

James glared at him and squirmed. "Look, soldier, I'm not some Cold War spy or Islamic terrorist, for heaven's sake. I'm your fellow American. I used to serve the president. I *was* the FBI Director, even if you say I am no longer."

"We have specific instructions, Mr. Davies."

"Was part of your instructions to make me wet my pants?"

One guard glanced toward the other.

"Please. A simple bathroom break. This isn't a big deal."

The marine looked quickly back and then said, "They told us to escort you without any delay. We need to do that. The president can be very . . ." The marine caught himself and stopped. He was completely and utterly and perfectly loyal. Marines assigned to guard the president were one soldier in ten thousand and, regardless of his personal feelings or observations, he wouldn't hesitate for half a second to place himself in front of a bullet to protect his leader. But his oath extended beyond just that; it included utter confidentiality regarding his personal observations of the president, his secrets, the things he saw and heard. He was allowed to guard the president for one overriding reason: He was as loyal to the office as a dog was to his master. So, like Mr. Davies, he found himself biting his tongue.

He thought, then nodded hastily toward the bathroom. "Please hurry, sir," he urged.

James nodded gratefully and turned.

The second marine followed him as James opened the door and stepped inside. It was a tiny bathroom, barely large enough for one man. The marine was standing next to him. James looked at him, disgusted. The marine hesitated, then backed outside and shut the door.

The room was small and simple. A toilet. A small sink. A cloth towel hanging on the wall. A square mirror. Nothing else. He looked around carefully, searching the corners, the walls, underneath the sink, behind the toilet. No cameras or hidden microphones anywhere, at least as far as he could tell. Satisfied, he stood up and checked that the door was locked. Then, his hands shaking, he bent over the small sink.

He didn't know what to expect. They had told him it would be—how had they described it?—terribly unpleasant, but not painful. But they had also warned him to brace himself, to have something he could hold onto and to prepare himself not to groan or cry out loud.

That made him wonder exactly how unpleasant it might really be.

His pulse was pounding in his ears as he leaned over the faux marble sink, made certain the drain was plugged, opened his mouth, reached back onto the artificial molar, felt the thin veneer give way at his touch, took a deep breath, leaned a little lower toward the sink, and squeezed.

He felt a sudden burning and he forced himself to swallow. The intensely concentrated mix of sodium stibogluconate and ipecac worked just as quickly and as violently as they had told him that it would. In seconds, he was racked with waves of nausea. They came at him with a power he had never felt before, gulping heaves of gut-crushing spasms that made him feel like he was going to explode.

He heaved up his last breakfast. He heaved up the lunch before. He felt like he was heaving up every candy bar he had eaten in high school. Wave after wave, he wrenched in silence, the two tiny plastic capsules, unmercifully, the last things to come up.

Forty seconds later, the heaving was complete. He leaned across the bowl, turned on the water, extracted the two one-inch capsules he had regurgitated, and rinsed them off. Using handfuls of disinfectant soap, he washed his hands, his arms, his face, the sink, dried his hands and face, then caught his breath again. Holding the red capsule to the light, he split it open, examined the tiny contents carefully, then knelt beside the sink. Tucked below the basin was a single electrical outlet. He pushed the receiver/transmitter into the socket and left it there, effectively turning Raven's entire wiring system into a huge antenna. Lifting the blue capsule, he split it open, pulled out the tiny drone, deployed the folded wingtips, and activated the minuscule battery to turn it on. Then, carefully, as if he were holding a live dragonfly, he tucked the tiny drone into his right pocket, constantly aware of the paper-thin wings pressing against his leg.

Dropping the broken capsules into the toilet, he flushed, checked his look in the mirror, opened the door, and walked into the hall.

OFFUTT AIR FORCE BASE
HEADQUARTERS, U.S. STRATEGIC COMMAND
EIGHT MILES SOUTH OF OMAHA, NEBRASKA

The Secretary was startled as he stared wide-eyed at the screen. The team of satellite technicians behind him suddenly came to life, typing at their consoles while talking to each other in hushed tones. His heart rate doubled, his fingers subconsciously clenching the edge of the console in a white-knuckled grip. A single drop of perspiration rolled down his left rib. The image on the main screen flickered, then went blank. He waited, his breath heavy. He strained to follow the technicians' conversation, but they spoke with so many technical terms and acronyms he couldn't understand much of anything they said. Glancing over his shoulder, he wanted to scream for information but held his tongue, knowing it wouldn't do any good aside from releasing his pent-up pressure.

Turning, he looked forward again.

The main screen was still blank.

He waited.

The audio was the first thing to come through. One of the technicians whistled, then slapped the other on the shoulder. Brucius continued waiting, not daring to even hope. Another crackle from the audio.

Behind him, the lead technician left his seat, walked the descending aisle to his right, then approached the SecDef from behind. "Baby Dragon has been activated," he whispered at his shoulder. "We're not getting any visual, and the audio is intermittent, but it's definitely on."

"So he made it into Raven Rock?"

"Yes, sir, he did."

Brucius took a breath and held it. "And he's activated the drone's transmitter?"

"Yes, sir. At the very least, he's turned it on. Again, we're getting only intermittent audio signals right now, but if he's following the plan, that would make sense. The drone hasn't been deployed."

Brucius Marino stared at the top of his desk. "How long

until they realize the security violation? How long until they find the mobile . . . what do you call it . . . the nest?"

"Mr. Davies has been able to plug the receiver/transmitter into their electrical system but we don't know enough yet to estimate how long we have. We're guessing they'll pick up the intrusion fairly quickly. But even if they know they're being violated, it may take them a while to find the bug."

Another man slipped into the room, young and thin, with wire glasses, the SecDef's chief of staff. He moved quickly toward the Secretary. The technician moved away.

"I hear the drone's been activated," the young man said. Brucius nodded.

The chief of staff glanced anxiously behind him. "The security teams in Raven are going to locate the nest, we know that. When they find it, they'll know it's him. I don't think they'll be forgiving. He's got to get out before that point."

Brucius grunted. No. Not forgiving. Not these men.

"It's going to work out," the other man assured him, reading the worried look on his boss's face. "They'll tear Raven Rock to pieces, but the presidential suite is the last place they'll look. He'll have time to get out. Everything will be okay."

Brucius nodded slowly. "That's right," he said.

The two men sat in silence for a couple of minutes. "Sir, if you want to go back and get a little sleep, we could call you when we start to get a good visual or other useful signal," the chief of staff offered.

"No," Brucius shot back quickly. "He's only got a few minutes, a few hours at the most. I want to know what's happening. I want to be here when we start getting signals. I want to be here until we know for certain that he got out."

chapter six

OFFUTT AIR FORCE BASE
HEADQUARTERS, U.S. STRATEGIC COMMAND
EIGHT MILES SOUTH OF OMAHA, NEBRASKA

S he stood outside the metal door, waiting for her meeting with the Secretary of Defense.

The cinder-block corridor stretched for a hundred feet behind her, suspended fluorescent lights illuminating the white walls and off-color cement floor. Over her head, a bundle of electrical cables and air vents hummed silently. The nearest security camera—there were at least a dozen stretching the length of the underground hallway—watched her every move. A red CLASSIFIED BRIEFING IN PROGRESS light was illuminated above the metal door outside the conference room and a small speaker in the ceiling spouted white noise, making it impossible to hear through the heavy door and thick walls—something that seemed remarkably unlikely even without the electronic background noise. Sara Brighton didn't move, her head down, her eyes on the floor, her mind racing, her heart pounding in her ears.

Sometimes she shook her head as if trying to clear it. But she wasn't trying to think more clearly. She wasn't trying to think at all. Too much to think about already. Too much crammed inside her head. Her eyes ached and her neck was stiff. Sometimes it seemed even her brain hurt.

She thought back on everything they had told her: the pictures of the men they said were traitors, where they came from, how they got there, what they intended now to do. The truth was, she didn't believe it. Not yet. At least, not everything. And maybe she never would. It wasn't that she thought they were crazy; she just thought they were wrong. There was no way it could be that bad, no way the government could have slipped so far. A few traitors, yeah, maybe that—she remembered what her husband had told her—but this was very different. This wasn't a tremor, this was an earthquake, and she almost felt the earth moving beneath her trembling knees.

Time passed. She was tired. They had left her waiting so long she was tempted to lie down on the floor.

She glanced up and down the corridor, wide enough for two forklifts to pass each other (which they often did), metal doors that led to offices, small signs with acronyms she didn't know. COMM. INTERN SEC. SATCONTRL. IOFIL. LANDGRASS. SATCOM/LANCOM/SPCECOM. HOSTILE ANGEL. She stared at the metal signs over the doors, then looked to the far end of the hallway. A single elevator was waiting, its door held back, the interior empty. She turned and looked the other way to see nothing but forty feet of cinder block that ended in a cement wall.

Minutes passed. She kept on waiting. Finally the metal door pushed back and a man she'd never seen before was standing there. "Mrs. Brighton," he said.

Sara started walking toward him.

He moved through the heavy door and let it close behind him. "There's been a delay, ma'am. I'm afraid you'll have to come with me." He motioned toward the elevator at the end of the hall and started walking.

Sara didn't move. "I was waiting for Secretary Marino."

"I know you were, ma'am."

"He said . . ."

"The Secretary's been delayed."

Sara watched the stranger. Thin. Wire glasses. Much too young. She wanted to ask what was happening, but she knew he wouldn't tell her. She hesitated a moment, then started following him down the hall.

"The Secretary thought he'd have some time to see you," the man explained in a sincere tone. "He sends his apologies. But frankly, right now there isn't much that he can tell you anyway. The endeavor into Raven Rock has been stalled, leaving us without access to critical information that we need before we can finalize our plan."

"Do you think—"

He cut her off abruptly. "There really isn't any more that I can say. We're still in the information-gathering process. As soon as the Secretary has anything at all to go on, I know he'll bring you into the loop. He has far too much respect for both you and your husband to leave you hanging. More, he realizes what an important role he has asked you to play. In no way, Mrs. Brighton, does he mean any disrespect by leaving you waiting. It's just that he's a little busy. And regarding our efforts into Raven Rock, there's unfortunately nothing I can say. All of us are waiting." They were at the elevator now. He stepped inside, scanned his security card, then punched a button to send it to the main floor. "Someone will meet you when the elevator opens. He'll take you back to your quarters. Your family is all there."

He stepped out of the elevator but held the door as he concluded. "The Secretary wishes for me to thank you. He understands this has been difficult. Again, ma'am, the instant we are in a position to move forward, we'll be back with you."

Sara stepped into the elevator and turned to face him. The door started closing. "Thank you" was all she said.

chapter seven

The former FBI Director let himself out of the tiny bathroom. His hands were shaking and he knew his face was pale but there wasn't anything he could do. If they were suspicious, they would search him. If they searched him, they would find the electrical device taken from his stomach and stuffed inside his right pocket. If they found it, he was dead. There wasn't much more to it. In the next few minutes, he would know.

The two marines were waiting, obviously impatient. They walked toward him as soon as he appeared. One of them glanced inside the bathroom, pushing the door back to check it out. The room reeked. He instantly recognized the smell. He hesitated just a minute but didn't say anything.

If he were being dragged to see the president, he would feel sick as well.

Holding James by the elbows, the marines started walking down the hall.

Inside his pocket, James kept the tiny drone tucked in a loose fist, protecting it as if it were as fragile as a butterfly, which, of course, it was. Ahead of him, he saw the set of double glass doors etched with the presidential seal. According to the briefing, he'd have to pass through a final electronic sensor on the other side of the glass doors.

He had to get rid of the drone before he got there, or they would find it.

Twenty feet or less now.

He had to let it go.

He glanced behind him. No one was there. The hallway up ahead was crowded. More guards waited—two army officers, one of them holding the door. Pulling his hand out of his pocket, the bug tucked gently in the open space between his fingers, he pretended to cough, brought his other hand to his mouth as a distraction, then dropped the bug behind him on the carpet floor.

He held his breath, waiting. The men kept walking. No one said anything. One step. Two. Then three. The set of double glass doors was only ten feet before him now. Turning quickly, he dared look back. The tiny electronic bug was in the air, its paper-thin wings buzzing. It seemed to lurch, then climbed and landed on the ceiling, where it started crawling forward, moving toward the open door.

OFFUTT AIR FORCE BASE
HEADQUARTERS, U.S. STRATEGIC COMMAND
EIGHT MILES SOUTH OF OMAHA, NEBRASKA

The video screen suddenly burst from darkness into light. The image was grainy and halting, but reasonably clear.

"I got it!" one of the technicians screamed from his cluttered console. "I got it! I got it! Okay, he dropped the bug. It's been deployed! I've got good imagery. Partial feedback . . . okay . . . okay . . . we're good to go. I've got control of the Dragonfly. I say again, I've got control. It's responding to my commands now. We've got hover. I'm moving upward. Going to get some space between the drone and the people there so they don't see it. Okay, okay, up on the ceiling . . . hooks deployed . . . we're on the ceiling now . . ."

The tiny lens, no larger than a fly's eye, transmitted from the hallway outside the presidential suite. It showed a picture from about shoulder height, then seemed to hover upward toward the ceiling, where it stopped and hung, suspended. The camera angle suddenly inverted as the tiny reconnaissance drone approached the ceiling, then flipped over as the bug dug its Velcro hooks into the tile. Looking down, the lens continued broadcasting to the receiver/transmitter left in the bathroom forty feet down the hall. Then, slowly, as if on tiny legs, the image started moving toward the double glass doors. Seeing through the bug's tiny lens, the men inside Offutt's command center were able to make out a small group of people in the hallway. Closer, almost directly below them, they saw three men, two of them in uniform, a black man in the middle, the guards' hands on his arms. The audio started cutting through, transmitting the mix of voices from deep inside of Raven Rock.

The technicians shouted congratulations to each other.

Dragonfly was a go.

Brucius jerked forward in his seat, his chief of staff beside him, their eyes intent, their faces drawn with equal fascination and concern. Brucius couldn't believe the image they were receiving from what was essentially a reconnaissance aircraft not much larger than a fly. The grainy image was not perfect—it paused and halted and was gritty as a first-generation security camera—but he could clearly see his best friend walking toward two army officers waiting near a set of etched glass doors.

The Dragonfly was inching forward. James and the two

guards in the hallway moved much faster. It quickly fell behind.

Brucius leaned toward the main screen on the wall. "Can you make it fly to get into the presidential office suite?" he demanded of the technicians.

"We can't risk it, Mr. Secretary. If we fly now, they're going to see it."

The SecDef turned around. "It's got to get through the doorway!" he cried.

The men were now ten paces farther up the hallway. They were walking quickly. The drone was moving forward just a bare inch at a time.

"It's not going to make it," the chief of staff warned. "It's going to get locked outside the door."

The SecDef turned back to the pilot technician. "You've got to take a chance and fly it. If the drone doesn't get inside the presidential suite, all of this will be for nothing."

The technician jerked a finger toward the screen. "If I fly it, sir, they'll see it!"

"If you don't fly it, the door will close!"

The other technician started shouting, "Come on, baby, GO!"

Brucius turned around. James and the two guards were at the set of glass doors now, the drone at least ten feet behind.

One of the officers stepped forward, taking possession of the detainee.

James started walking toward the doorway.

The drone was still too far behind.

The glass door was going to close.

Brucius sat back in his seat and swore.

chapter eight

FOUR MILES WEST OF CHATFIELD
TWENTY-ONE MILES SOUTHWEST OF MEMPHIS, TENNESSEE

The sun was higher in the morning sky and the air was almost comfortable. Winter would come, humid and cutting with northern wind, but now it was early fall and there was still enough warmth to let the sun heat up the earth once it was higher in the sky. Bono and Ellie walked again together, giving them time to talk. Ellie kept up a constant chatter about the secret cake she was going to decorate, the weather, Miller, her mom, pretty much anything that seemed to flutter through her mind. She ran ahead of him, skipped back, grabbed his hand, always moving, her mood happy, the brightness back in her eyes.

Coming across the open field toward the house, Bono was happy to see Caelyn standing on the porch, waiting for them. She looked radiant in the morning sun, her blonde hair illuminated from the back. She wore blue jeans, a light sweater, and leather boots. He stopped. He couldn't help it. It made his heart thump to see her standing there. "Hey, baby," he said in a rather poor imitation of a Humphrey Bogart voice. "Looks like you might be looking for a man." He turned and flexed his biceps, nodding toward his muscled arms with an exaggerated smile.

"As a matter of fact, I am," Caelyn answered while seeming to pay him no attention.

Bono flexed again. She pretended not to notice. He stretched his arms above his head in an exaggerated motion, his T-shirt pulled tight against his chest. Caelyn continued looking past him. "Still looking for a man," she said.

Bono had had enough; he ran to her and lifted her up high, holding her weight easily above the ground. She screamed and started laughing. "Let me down," she cried.

"Go, Daddy!" Ellie joined in, running to him. "Look at this! Look at this. Mom, he could make you *fly!*"

Caelyn punched Bono on the shoulders. "Put me down, you *lunk!*"

"Not until you say it!"

"Say what?"

He kept her in the air, her feet kicking at the emptiness, completely at his mercy.

"Say it!" he laughed.

"Okay, okay, let me down and I will."

He lifted her a couple of inches higher. "Come on, Caelyn, you gotta say it or I'll keep you there all day." He pressed his fingers into her ribs.

She punched at his shoulders again, still laughing. "Let me down first."

"Not until—"

"All right! I love you! There, I said it. Now will you please let me down!"

He lowered his arms, letting her feet touch the ground. "There you go again," he laughed, "getting all smoochy on me."

"I *hate* it when you do that. You make me feel like a little kid."

He smiled. She tried to look angry. Ellie skipped around them, laughing. "Mommy's smoochy, Mommy's smoochy."

Caelyn looked down, feigning anger. "See what you did? How do you expect her to respect me when you do that?"

Bono crossed his heart. "Never again. I swear."

Neither of them believed it.

"You still feel like walking?" Caelyn asked, nodding to the open fields behind her shoulder.

"Are you kidding? Like I would pass up the opportunity to walk in the country with such a beautiful girl?"

Ellie looked up excitedly. "Can I come too?"

"Sure, Ellie," Caelyn answered.

They started walking, Ellie between them. Grabbing their hands, she tried to swing, but she was too big now, and even though she bent her knees, they dragged across the wet ground. The threesome approached the end of the grass. "Which direction?" Caelyn asked.

Bono nodded toward the narrow country road that ran north. "Let's go that way," he said, nodding down at Ellie. "It's much less muddy."

They crossed the gravel driveway and started walking down the road. It was strange to see the country road so vacant and quiet. Half a mile ahead, a stalled car had been pushed off into the barrow pit; behind them, far in the distance, another couple of cars lay motionless where they had died when the EMP swept across the country not long before. Bono cocked his head and listened, noting the empty silence; a hint of wind in his ear, the sound of their shoes against the pavement, their breathing, and the movement of Ellie's polyester jacket were the only sounds he could hear. He glanced skyward. Completely empty. Looked across the fields, left and right. Not a soul or a hint of movement anywhere.

"Kind of strange, isn't it, honey?" Caelyn said, watching his eyes and gesturing to the empty landscape all around them.

Bono slowed and then stopped walking.

"It took a while for me to get used to it," Caelyn continued. "The first couple of days I would sit on the front porch waiting, certain that someone would show up. There I'd sit, staring at the empty road and wondering where everyone had gone. It was kind of like the Twilight Zone. No one was around. For a time I wondered if we were the only ones alive. Then I saw a couple of the neighbors walking with some people who'd come down from Memphis. They stopped to talk. That was the first time I really understood what had happened. Since then, I haven't talked to many other people." She thought about the violent gang and the confrontation in the field. "At least, not many who I *wanted* to talk to."

She fell silent in her memories. The sky overhead was vast, blue and empty, and the wind was pure and cold. She went on. "I really thought it would be different. I don't know, I guess somehow I thought we'd be out with other people, you know, banding together, trying to work something out. It seems like just the opposite has happened. Seems like everyone wants to stay home and see what happens before they take any action. Everyone's too scared to make a move. Guess it's every man for himself."

Bono looked down the empty road. "I think people are kind of catching their breath, you know, hiding out, hoarding their resources, protecting home court before they venture out. Some people are afraid." He nodded over his shoulder toward the house. "Your mom is terrified, it's pretty obvious. She tries to act brave, but that's not how she feels. She's becoming more and more suspicious and withdrawn. It's understandable how she would feel that way." He bent down, picked up a small rock, felt its round edges, tossed it up and down a couple of times, then stood and threw it across the open field. "You should have seen what it was like up in D.C. It was amazing. And scary. Even now, I don't know if I can quite figure it out. It was like everyone was instantly ready to give up. Can you imagine that? I saw people literally sit down on the side of the road and surrender, waiting to die rather than take some responsibility for themselves. It was jarring. No, it was more than that, it was shocking. I mean, they gave it up so easily. Like a bunch of helpless babies. I mean, come on, people, are you kidding me! You gonna quit, just like that? Bunch of spoiled brats. Is that the only thing you got?

"But you know, Caelyn, I thought a lot about it—and it's funny, but I think I realized something I'd never thought about before. They didn't give up so easily because of all the difficulties that lay ahead. They didn't lie down and surrender because the future looked so bleak. That wasn't it at all. It wasn't the difficulty of the future that made them so despairing, it was the emptiness of the present, the meaningless of their lives, the barrenness of how they had chosen to live, detached from their families, their religion, any sense of purpose or worthy cause. *Hey, dude, my iPod isn't working. Guess I'll lie down here and die.* I mean, it was almost like that. *You're telling me my 401k isn't worth anything? My Mercedes won't start? My 80-inch flat screen got quick-fried into smoke? Well, I guess that's pretty much it for me, dudes. Mix up the Kool-Aid and let's get this over with.*"

Caelyn looked at him. He half smiled, his sarcastic humor biting.

"You really think that's the way it is?" she asked. "People lose their easy lives, their possessions, and that's it, they give up? They roll over and just give in? I don't know, honey, I think you might be underestimating your fellow Americans."

Bono ran his hands through his hair, thinking of the hellish highway he and Sam had walked around Washington, D.C. "Maybe, Caelyn, maybe." They started walking again. He didn't know how much to tell her. What good would it do? He didn't even want to think about it himself.

Ellie let go of their hands and ran before them. Bono thrust his fists into his pockets as they watched her go. "I don't know if I can explain it very well, Caelyn, but it was pretty much unbelievable. I saw hundreds, no thousands of people on this highway who had absolutely *no idea* what to do. I understand that they were shell-shocked—I mean, the people in D.C. took a double hit: first the nuclear explosion, then the EMP. I understand that's a lot to live through, but there we were, twenty-four hours after the EMP attack, and some of them were still sitting by their cars. *Sixty miles to make it home. Way too far to walk. Someone's got to help me.* I wanted to shake them. I wanted to scream: 'This is your life. Take responsibility. It isn't over. There is hope. You can make it through this.' It wasn't until later that I realized how many of their lives had become meaningless and sterile, an empty candy wrapper in their hands. *Might as well check out now as later* seemed to be a common attitude. All they wanted was for the end to be painless. Geez, Caelyn, if you had seen it, it would have driven you insane."

She pressed her lips together and glanced down the road to Ellie, who was balancing on the white stripe in the middle of the road, her hands extended at her sides. "I did have a visitor a few nights ago," she said, recalling a different side to the bleak picture. "You probably won't remember him. Brother Simpson. He used to be the bishop of the ward here. We've met him a time or two."

61

"A big guy? Kind of a down-to-earth farmer, as I remember?"

"Yeah, that's him."

Bono leaned toward her, instantly interested. "That's good. That's really good. What did he want?"

"He didn't want anything, really, though he did bring a couple of boxes of dry goods. More than anything he was checking up on some of the members of the ward from these parts."

Bono noted the "from these parts." His wife tended to revert to the country vernacular when she'd been home awhile. "Why did he stop at your parents' house? How did he know that you were here?"

Caelyn thought back on the night the old farmer had shown up. She could remember his words almost perfectly. *"The Spirit brought me to you,"* the man in the baseball cap had said. *"I was going to turn around. I wanted to get home before it got dark. But I couldn't. I knew that someone else was out here.*

"I think you prayed me to you, Caelyn. Your faith is strong enough that God was able to use even an old fool such as me."

She considered her husband's question. "I don't know, babe, it's kind of a funny story, but the long and short of it is that he found me out here. Anyway, they're having a meeting at the church house. They're going to work out a system to check up on each other, help each other, you know, share things if we need to, see who has what, who needs what, that sort of thing."

Bono listened with even greater interest. "That's beautiful, Caelyn. Exactly what I had hoped. That's got to be the plan . . . it will work that way, don't you think? I mean, if we can stick together on this thing, if we can work with our friends and neighbors, then things will be okay."

She smiled at him. "I think when you say 'if we can work

with our friends and neighbors,' what you really mean is 'if Caelyn can work with strangers,' isn't it, babe? I mean, you won't be here. And these really aren't our friends. I don't know any of the people in this ward. Remember, I joined the Church when we were at UCLA, not here."

He stepped toward her. "I understand. And yes, I'm sorry, I was probably making it sound too easy. I'm just so relieved to know there are others here to help you and they've stepped forward. I was planning on going to the church to talk to the bishop before I left. I felt like I had to find someone who could watch over you while I was gone. Even better, Bishop Simpson has reached out to us. I *knew* the members here would be willing to help us . . ."

"But are they *really* willing? Think about it, honey. They don't know me. They've got their own families, their own problems, their own worries and concerns."

He sensed the hesitation in her voice and put his arms around her, pulling her close. "I do, Caelyn. I really do. It's the way that God intended it. Think about it. Did the early Saints cross the plains by themselves? No. They worked together. Did they build Independence or Nauvoo or the Salt Lake Temple by themselves? No, they worked together. I can't believe that God intends for us to go through this by ourselves. He understands, they understand, that I can't be here to help you. They recognize the challenge you will have here, by yourself, with Ellie. They recognize that I'm not off on some overseas vacation. There are patriots and they'll have to help us." He lifted his eyes toward the heavens as if saying a quick prayer. "It's going to be okay."

She watched him, then started walking again. Ellie was forty or fifty feet ahead of them now, looking at something along the side of the road, and it made Caelyn nervous not to have her immediately by her side. It was silly, she knew—there wasn't anything up there that was going to hurt her daughter, but she was skittish now, afraid of so many unseen things. What if Ellie got hurt, bitten by a snake or a spider? What if she fell and twisted her ankle? What if she got sick? Before, a doctor or a hospital was just a short drive away, and they would take care of things: medicines, surgeries, painkillers, antibiotics, the world's best medical care, all at her disposal if she ever needed help. But all of that was gone now. And it scared her. There were so many things to deal with that she'd never had to think about before. So she wanted to be close to Ellie. She wanted to wrap her in a tight cocoon and keep her safe until this thing had passed.

If it ever did pass . . .

If things ever got any better . . .

Would they? Would things get better?

She really didn't know.

The emotion of the moment caught up to her and she turned suddenly toward her husband. "What's going to happen to us?" she whispered, her voice unsure.

Bono squinted while looking straight ahead. "Things are going to work out, Caelyn, I really believe they will. As bad as things appear, I still have hope.

"Some people think this is the end, that God is going to show up from the heavens with a host of angels, that the Millennium is finally here, Satan bound, heaven established here on earth. And who knows, maybe all those things are going to happen really soon. But I don't think so. Not yet. Not right now. There are still some things that have to happen. Cool things. Great things. Maybe some more hard things, too. But I don't think all the prophecies have been fulfilled yet." He stopped and motioned to the empty landscape around him. "Do I think it's going to get better? Yeah, I really do. I don't think that we are finished, not as a people, not as a government. This has knocked us to our knees, maybe even come close to killing us, but I don't believe our heart is gone. It's going to be tough, no doubt. In fact, it's going to be way more than tough—it's going to be horrible. Lots of people are going to die. Maybe millions, maybe a hundred million, I don't know. It will be unlike anything we've ever tried to imagine before. We might not be *okay,* not in the normal sense of how we think of things, but I think we can get through this. I think eventually we'll rebuild."

"But who, baby, *who?* Who's going to rebuild? We don't even have a government!"

Bono nodded slowly. "I don't know."

"All of our leaders in D.C. have been killed. Something isn't right. It just feels . . . I don't know, *bad* somehow. We've got no government, no infrastructure, no medicines, no food. How are we going to do it? Who is going to do it? These are the things that I don't know."

Caelyn waited, hoping he would answer. But he didn't, and she turned back to the road.

Ellie was running toward them now, excited. "Look at this!" she cried. She was holding out a purple thistle, fuzzy at the bottom with tiny filaments of color bristling at the top. Deep purple. A hint of yellow. Beautiful but thorny. Bono took it cautiously. "You've got to be careful, Ellie, this thing has pricklies that can hurt."

Ellie held up her index finger with childish pride. A tiny blot of crimson blood was dripping down the front. "I already found that out, Daddy."

Caelyn took her hand and held it, examining the tiny prick. "That looks like it hurts, baby."

Ellie pulled her hand away. "It's okay," she said before sticking her finger in her mouth. "It's only a little cut." She looked up at her dad. "I took it like a man," she told him proudly.

Caelyn shot a look to Bono. "Like a man?" she questioned.

Bono hunched his shoulders in a don't-blame-me expression.

Caelyn compressed her lips, then examined Ellie's finger again. The blood was gone now, the bleeding stopped. Bono bent down and held the thistle between them, the brilliant colors flashing almost luminescent in the morning light. "You shouldn't have tried to pick it, Ellie. I could have told you that you'd get hurt."

Ellie didn't hesitate. "It was so pretty, Daddy."

"But it already pricked your finger."

"It was worth it, Dad."

chapter nine

James Davies, FBI Director of the legitimate government of the United States, walked toward the presidential office suite. He took a quick breath, his heart lurching. Too many people were up ahead of him. Someone was bound to see the drone! It couldn't get into the compound unobserved with so many people standing there. And the batteries were only good for a couple of hours. Once they were gone, the drone was useless. He had to find a way to get it inside the compound now!

For a moment he wished that he had waited to drop the drone, but, looking ahead of him, he knew that wouldn't have worked. The instructions they had agreed on had been correct. *Deploy the drone before you get into the presidential office suite. There will be far too many people, once you're inside. You'll be surrounded, and they will see it when you drop it. Either that, or the metal detectors will detect it. Wait until you're as close as you can get, then deploy it just outside the door.*

His mind raced. Only four steps to the door. The army officers watched him carefully, two men he didn't recognize. Behind them, there was a security wall and reception desk, then a wide and beautifully furnished hallway that led to the president's den, all protected behind a metal scanner. A red sign had been posted near the doorway.

STOP
PRESIDENTIAL SECURITY AREA
USE OF DEADLY FORCE AUTHORIZED
DO NOT PROCEED UNTIL INSTRUCTED

It was easy to pick out the two Secret Service agents behind the glass walls. Others were there as well, not seen, but watching. Even here in Raven Rock, the barrier between the open corridor and the president was as impenetrable as steel.

One of the army officers, a thin-haired colonel, pushed the door back a little further and stepped across the threshold to meet the unwanted intruder. He didn't extend his hand to James to shake it, but reached out for his arm the way an irritated father would reach for a wayward son. "Mr. Davies," he greeted simply, "come with me."

Without waiting for an answer, the colonel nodded at the two marines who had escorted Davies down. "We got him," he said.

The marines stopped at the door, releasing Davies's arms.

James shot another look back. The fly had disappeared. Somewhere along the ceiling? He didn't know.

He had to give them time to fly the drone through the open door and inside the presidential compound without being noticed. But he didn't know how!

Only one idea came to mind. He turned toward the colonel. The balding man reached out again for his arm. James pulled his arm back defensively and stepped angrily to the side. The colonel gestured impatiently for him to come and he hesitated, then moved gingerly forward, then suddenly tripped. Falling, he slammed his head into the side of the glass door. Bulletproof, the heavy glass didn't break but left a painful gash against his forehead, which immediately started to bleed.

The colonel stared down at him lying in the open door-way. The men on the other side of the glass turned instantly at the sound of the crash. For a moment no one moved; then one of the marine guards stepped back and reached down to the fallen man. James took his hand and pulled himself up, his other hand at his head, a smear of blood seeping through his pressed fingers. "I'm sorry . . . I guess . . . I guess I tripped on something . . . I've been feeling dizzy . . ."

The colonel didn't seem to care. *You'd feel a whole lot worse if you knew what we had in store for you,* he thought as he stared passively at the fallen man.

One of the marine guards reached into his uniform pocket, pulled out a handkerchief, and flipped it toward him. James thanked him and pressed the handkerchief against his head. The marine steadied him while he wiped the blood away. The colonel released the two marines with a determined nod. The marines stepped back and turned around, then started walking down the hall.

Handkerchief still pressed painfully against his forehead, James followed the colonel into the presidential suite.

Behind him, the glass door closed on its smooth, pneumatic hinges.

James glanced back.

Had the drone made it into the presidential office suite? He didn't know. But whether it had or not, there wasn't anything more that he could do.

Offutt Air Force Base
Headquarters, U.S. Strategic Command
Eight Miles South of Omaha, Nebraska

"Go, GO, *GO!*" the second technician screamed. "The door is closing!"

The drone pilot looked intent, his eyes squinting in

concentration, glistening drops of sweat collecting on his forehead. His hands were shaking, his lips so tight they were almost white, every ounce of mental energy focused on controlling the tiny drone. Enormously unstable, slow to respond, inherently unbalanced, with a high center of gravity and an unfathomable weight-to-lift ratio, not to mention the fact that the thing was at the mercy of every draft from every air vent or passing breeze, it took incredible energy and concentration to keep the miniscule drone from rolling over and flopping on the floor.

The technician pilot ignored his comrade's shouted warnings. There could have been an earthquake at his feet, an explosion in the command center, a herd of wild horses stampeding across his desk, and he wouldn't have known, he was so entirely and utterly focused on keeping the unstable drone in the air.

"You got it, you got it!" the geekish major cried. "Keep it up. Get it higher . . . watch it . . . watch it . . . look out, the door is closing!"

"I got it, SIR!" the pilot shouted back.

Hundreds of miles away, the drone dropped down and started flying, a soft buzz in the air.

"Back off! Back off!" the major cried. "You're getting too close . . . they're going to see it! Get back up near the ceiling!"

The flier struggled with the remote controls, one hand on a miniature joystick, the other on a throttle control.

"Through the door!" the major cried. "NOW! You've got to GO!"

chapter ten

T he glass door closed behind them.

Leading James past the reception center and
security desks, they waited while he walked through
the metal detectors, then moved him down the hall. Two
doors down from the Secret Service station, President Fuentes
was waiting in a large conference room. Other men were waiting with him, sitting around a massive wooden table.

Fuentes watched with deep and somber eyes. He seemed
to enjoy the growing tension as James was led into the room.
All the men were silent. There were no women among the
group.

The colonel pushed James to the front of the table, nodded toward Fuentes, then walked out, shutting the door
behind him. The room was dark, a bank of television screens
glowing on the front wall. A bright spotlight in the ceiling
glared in James's eyes, making it difficult for him to see. He
squinted, taking in what he could, but most of the dark faces
were lost in the glare and shadows. He felt powerless in his
black jumpsuit and shoeless feet—which was, of course, how

they wanted him to feel. A heavy silence permeated the air, awkward and unpleasant.

James couldn't see it, but he felt it, and he instinctively reached for the gold cross he wore around his neck. But the cross had been taken from him and he reached at nothing there.

The room was full of evil. He could almost smell the darkness in the air. Whoever these men were and whatever they intended now to do, it was as obvious as the darkness in the nighttime that none of them were friends. He stared at Fuentes. *Where did you get these men?* he almost sneered. *How could you have located so many men willing to betray their own country!*

Fuentes seemed to smile at him, his eyes fixed in a vacant stare.

James watched him, his fury building, then glanced around the crowded table, his eyes coming to rest on a hunched man dressed in a black suit and black tie. His worn jacket was draped across his slumping shoulders, and the hair on his neck was as long as the patches of white across his scalp. And he was old. Very old. James could almost smell his ancient breath. The old man stared back at him, his eyes pale and opaque, red-rimmed and teary. It seemed to James as if there was nothing in the man's eyes, no soul or life, only angry emptiness behind two lifeless balls of glass.

James studied him and realized that there was no seeing in those eyes, no vision or light or revelation. The eyes of a blind man. The eyes of a man who didn't *have* to see.

James shivered, his gut crunching into knots. Suddenly it seemed hard to breathe, the air stale and calm and foul. Something about the smell—what was it? Rank and wet. He didn't know, but it was old and full of rot and terror. The hair on his neck stood on end, the spirit inside him sensing what his brain couldn't know.

Looking at the group of evil men, he realized the ugly truth.

The battle wasn't starting. It was almost over. There was nothing he could do now, no way to stop the coming wave from crashing down. He had walked into a throng of murderers and thieves, a den of predators so full of jealousy and fury that they couldn't reason anymore. These were no comrades here, no friends or patriots who loved their country or a just cause. This was a group of men who'd been hating for many years, each of them having long before made the decision to betray their country. And, in a sad way, James realized they were not really traitors, for none of them had ever pledged allegiance to their country, not in any real sense of the word. They were outsiders on the inside, the cancer next to bone, the disease that would kill the nation after having lain dormant all these years.

The realization crushed him like a boulder, turning his warm blood into ice.

He stared at them, his eyes finally adjusting to the light, his heart racing with fear and anger as he recognized the faces that had been hidden in the dark. All the men were dressed in suits, but some of them were not Americans. He recognized their ethnic features: men from the Arab peninsula, Syria and Oman, the prime minister from Malaysia, the foreign minister of Russia next to him. The young Arab beside the old man was King Abdullah. Other leaders from around the world were in the crowd.

None of the men were friends or allies. He slowly drew another breath.

That was when he knew it. That was when he finally understood.

It had been a terrible mistake to come here.

And he knew that he was dead.

A sudden calmness came over him, sweet and full of warmth, a sense of peace so real it caused his mind to race. Time suspended and he drifted back, reliving the happiest moments of his life: the warm sun on the front porch of his ranch house, the ocean and the beach, the sound of his daughter's laughter, the touch of his wife's hand, the feel of the Good Book as he read it, the assurance of the Spirit that he had felt so many times before. There were no memories of the pain or heartaches or the challenges he had overcome, just the joy and happiness, and he couldn't help but smile.

"The battle will go forward," the Spirit told him. *"You've done your part, and I am grateful. There is nothing more for you to do."*

The old man sensed the presence of the Spirit and he snarled as he rose with surprising strength and quickness, his fang teeth showing, his eyes wild and full of hate. He moved up to James, leaned into his neck, and whispered in his ear, "Your work is finished here. Yes, my friend, you're done. Soon, I will dismiss you. But before I do, I want you to understand." He pulled away and looked into James's eyes. "Perhaps you wonder about where these men came from and the cause that binds us here today? I want to tell you, brother.

"You see, *Mr. Davies,* all of us together," the old man motioned around the room, "are bound in one purpose, one privilege, one plan. It didn't start out that way, of course. Foolish to think of a dark, smoke-filled room with a group of conspirators conceiving a step-by-step plan to destroy the entire world. It was nothing like that. We are—how would you say it?—more laissez-faire in our approach. Market-based and opportunistic. We let the free will of the people work. They

make a choice. We let them wonder. It's not much more complicated than that."

His voice was tart and dripping with so much sarcasm that
James felt like recoiling at his breath.

The old man huffed in pride. "You think it was some
great, grand conspiracy from the beginning? Such a stupid
fairy tale. A few years ago, none of us even knew each other.
We were independent in our thinking, operating on our own
while moving toward the same unspoken goal. Yes, the paths
we took to get here have wandered through many lands, but
all the while our master taught us so that when the opportunity finally presented itself we would be ready. Then we
emerged from the cracks of life together. Like spiders, these
brave men scurried from the shadows when they heard their
master call."

He paused and looked around the room, his teeth showing in a wicked smile. "Rats draw to the smell of a carcass. The
U.S. is our carcass. Good men, it's time to eat!"

The group of dark men smiled weakly at his humor, but
their pleasantness was forced and unnatural, their lips tight
beneath their smiles.

The old man turned to Davies and waited, then decided to
tell him the entire truth. It wouldn't matter. They were going
to kill him anyway. No harm if one man knew. "The ropes that
bind us are thin and gentle as a woman's hand," he explained.
"But together they are more powerful than anything known
to man. The oaths come by degrees, of course, line upon line,
a single step and then another, each coming in its time. For
some men, it can take a lifetime." He stopped and glanced at
Fuentes, flashing a knowing smile at him. "For others a few
short days. The first step is fairly innocent: *We need for this to
happen. Let us agree upon this plan.*

"Then, when the first obstacle comes up—which it will,

because our master will place it for us—we justify the next principle of our oaths. It is beautiful and simple and something you've heard before: *Better for one man to die than for our plans to fail.*

"The next oath is based primarily on an argument of practicality. But humans are so very practical in their nature, and that can be a useful thing. *We've come this far. Much too difficult to turn back now. Come on, brother, let's see this through.*

"The next step is where we finally acknowledge the motivations that really drive us: *I'll kill them if you provide a good enough reward.* Everything that happens after that comes down to greed, lust, jealousy, pride, and power.

"Then comes the final oath that binds us: *I'll never lift a hand toward a brother. I'll die to protect our cause. I'll never desert the brotherhood. If I do, then you must kill me, my family, and my children. You must take everything I have ever loved or worked for. If I betray you, you take it all. The oath is the only thing that matters, and I seal my pledge in blood.*"

The old man smiled, his crooked teeth yellow with time and age. "Do you understand what you're up against? The oaths we have taken are more powerful than the earth. More eternal than the stars. Do you see that you can't defeat us? We're totally committed to this cause. You have no hope. You have no power. There is nothing you can do. Yes, Brucius Marino may be alive now, but believe me, he won't be for very long. It will hardly matter how we do it; we will kill him in the end. Then we'll move on, forgetting both of you, never speaking your names again."

The old man stopped and cleared a wad of dry phlegm from his throat, spitting into a frayed handkerchief before he sneered, "Now, tell us, *Mr. Director:* Why exactly are you here?"

James glared at Fuentes. "You are *not* the president," he

said, his voice low but powerful. "Brucius Marino is the president. And he *will not* let this stand!"

He narrowed his eyes. "It doesn't matter what you do here; in the end you cannot win. There are more of us than there used to be. And He is on our side. You win a skirmish, we win the battle. You kill a few of us, but we win the war."

The old man shook his head. "I don't have to kill you to win this battle. But there's always pleasure in the kill."

James straightened his back in proud defiance. "I'm not afraid of dying. Unlike you, I have nothing left to fear."

The old man snarled with frustration, his eyes black and red and full of hate. "You *will* fear me!" he cried in fury.

James looked at him and smiled. Against all reason, his eyes were bright and full of life.

chapter eleven

It was a simple device: small, easy to use, accurate, and lethally intrusive. Developed for critical and time-sensitive interrogations on the battlefield, the device was no more complicated to operate than a cell phone. Slip the sensors on. Ask some questions. Wait for the light. Red light, the subject was lying; yellow, the computer didn't know; green, the subject was telling the truth.

Accurate to something more than 92 percent, the computer was no larger than a deck of cards with a couple of wires attached, two electrodes that measured the subject's stress through changes in electrical conductivity under the skin, a third that evaluated cardiovascular activity through a pulse oximeter on the fingertip, and a clip on a fold of the skin under the elbow that measured blood pressure. The military called it a PCASS, or *Preliminary Credibility Assessment Screening System,* and although the early versions had been troublesome, the algorithms coming under constant stress and tweaking, the latest models were as accurate as any polygraph ever made. Initially envisioned as a combat triage device to identify who or what situation needed attention first, the PCASS had proven to be an extremely accurate, easy to administer, highly portable polygraph device. It was this simple: Pull the subject aside. Slip on the sensors. Give the subject instructions: *Look at me. Answer all my questions. Is it raining right now? Do you have shoes on your feet? What color is my name tag? Look at your watch and tell me what time it is. Okay. Good. Now, what is your name? Where do you live? Do you admire Osama bin Laden? Who are your friends? Are you associated with any militia? Do you support your government leaders? Do you have any weapons? Are you a member of the Taliban? Do you know how to work with explosives or any other dangerous material? Have you ever contemplated or plotted to harm Americans?*

It was like talking to a prophet. The controller of the PCASS could discover anything.

Because the PCASS had proven extremely effective, over time its uses had been expanded into other areas of interrogation, most of which were legal, but some of which were not.

*　　*　　*

Even though deception measures had proven completely ineffective against the PCASS, the group had still ordered sodium pentothal to be administered to the patient to bring him completely under their control. The professional interrogators had argued against the drug, knowing it was unnecessary, but the Brothers had a proven zealousness that amounted to overkill. It simply wasn't in their nature to take chances, their operating philosophy falling more in line with "why drop a single bomb when a dozen bombs will do?"

James Davies was propped up in a chair, the drugs flowing heavily through his veins, dilating his eyes and lowering his pulse and blood pressure until his head bobbed atop his neck as if suspended on a string. His eyes were unfocused, his lips pulled back in a grimace of a smile. The PCASS electrodes were slipped around his fingers and under his arm, and the questions began. They started out very simple, then became more probing, more dangerous, more telling and instructive as the interrogation wore on. Inside the functioning part of his mind, deep inside his ventromedial prefrontal cortex where his moral compass and ethical judgment lay, James struggled with all his might to keep from answering, but the mental resistance he tried to exercise never quite made it to the surface of his brain. As hard as he tried, the answers were impossible to avoid. He tried to lie. The interrogator caught him. He tried remaining silent. The sodium pentothal made him talk. And some of the questions didn't need a truthful answer; knowing when he was lying was enough.

"Is Brucius Marino alive now?"

A long hesitation.

"Is Brucius Marino alive?"

Finally a struggled answer. *"I don't know."*

Red light. With one option eliminated from a yes-or-no question, they didn't need to ask again.

"Does Brucius Marino realize he's next in line of succession to be the president of the United States?"

A long, long pause. A very pained face. Eyes rolling. Dry lips smacking.

"Answer the question for us. Does Brucius Marino believe he has a claim upon the presidency of the United States?"

"I don't know."

Another lie. Again, no reason to follow this line of questioning any further.

"Is he planning at this time to make a claim upon the presidency?"

Another long moment of hesitation. *"No, I don't think so."*

A couple of seconds for the computer and monitors to evaluate, then another red light.

Even as he answered their questions, stabs of fear cut through James's mind. He knew what he was saying but he couldn't stop himself. Deep in his brain, he focused his determination, willing himself to say the right thing, willing himself not to tell them everything, willing himself to shut his mouth and not say anything at all. "SHUT UP! SHUT UP, YOU FOOL!" he screamed from deep inside himself. But the heavy drugs had made him talkative, giving him a false sense of contentment that led to a willingness to share his secrets with his new friends.

In the end, his resistance didn't matter. Despite his best efforts to deny them, it took only a few hours until they knew.

* * *

Minutes after the interrogation was over, a small group of men gathered in the private office of the president.

"Brucius Marino is alive," the first man said.

The other men demurred. They had suspected he was out there somewhere, but this was not welcome news.

"He's holed up in the Strategic Command Operations Center out at Offutt."

More murmurs. It was the last place they wanted him to be.

"We could kill him," one man offered. He was the new FBI Director and had always favored the most direct approach. "Better to eliminate him before he can do us damage."

Five minutes of conversation followed. Most of the men agreed.

Then the old man stepped forward, the air pungent with his smell. "Yes, we could kill him," he offered simply. On the surface it appeared that he was seeking their support, but none of them bought it. They all knew the final decision would be his. "As a matter of principle, I think we've pretty much established that we'll do what we have to do in order to make this work. But there are important considerations before we take such a course. And the truth is, my good Brothers, there's a better way. There is something we could do that would utterly eliminate Secretary Marino as a threat, perhaps more effectively than if we put a bullet in his head. More importantly, my suggestion has the added and powerful benefit of establishing our authority while legitimizing our new government and making everything that we do after this perfectly justifiable and legal."

The men fell silent. Whatever he came up with, they knew it would be brilliant. And they knew that it would work.

"How many members of the Unites States Congress are still alive?" the old man asked.

"One hundred and twelve," the FBI Director answered. "Thirty-eight senators, seventy-four congressmen."

"How many of them are here in Raven Rock?"

"All but twelve. The others are in various stages of arrival, but it may take a few days. A couple of them . . ."

The old man raised his hand. "It doesn't matter. We have enough," he said.

*   *   *

It took almost a day to complete the second interrogation. All they were trying to do was gather enough video footage of James Davies talking to be useful. To do that, they had to moderate the drugs to make him coherent yet sedated enough to keep him under their control. In the end, it proved to be impossible. He was simply too bullheaded, his will too strong to get anything useful without showing the obvious effect of the drugs.

"It doesn't do us any good to put him in front of the cameras if he looks like he's stoned out of his mind!" the old man screamed. "Go back! Try again! Poke him! Prod him! Deprive him and drive him. Do whatever it takes to wear him down!"

Back to the conference room. More interrogations. More drugs. James did very little talking, leaving them with pretty much the same result.

Three hours later, the old man watched the newest video footage of the Davies testimony, then cursed in a constant string of rage. "Screw it!" he commanded when he'd seen what they had. "It'll have to be enough. We'll take the little bit that's useful and digitally manipulate the rest. They can take care of it down in the communications center. I've already talked to them.

"Okay then, let's get ready. Send out a notification through the Emergency Broadcasting System that the president will address the nation tonight."

* * *

Although individual operating radios and televisions were incredibly difficult to find, there were enough scattered around the country, most of them recently provided by the Department of Homeland Security, that a fair portion of the populace watched the emergency broadcast that night.

chapter twelve

T he shepherd stood atop a granite cliff, looking down on the narrow valley some two thousand feet below. Half a dozen shacks—not quite huts, with their clay walls and leaf roofs and mud floors—lined the deep river that cut through the valley floor. Ancient rock fences, some of them older than the Prophet, crisscrossed the valley, separating the land into separate pastures. The fences hadn't been built to acknowledge private property—earth was the great gift from Allah and land was held in common among the village folks— but they did make for more efficient management of the sheep and goat herds that provided the milk, meat, leather, and woolen blankets the village people needed to survive. To the villagers, their animals were almost sacred, for they lived or died according to the health of their herds. Every part of the animals was used: the internal organs cooked into stew, the blood boiled and packed into intestines to make sausages, the horns worn for adornments or hollowed out to pack tobacco, the skins tanned, the wool stretched and dyed and sewn, the hooves pounded into magic potions they called medicines, the teeth ground into various concoctions, most of them unhealthy.

The old man tugged on his hairy chin as he looked out. The rock cliffs around the valley were smooth and gray and sheer, with buttress outcroppings that looked like enormous castle walls. The grass in the valley was brown now, the harvest having come and gone, and the river was running slow. Looking up, he watched the clouds sink toward him. Winter was coming early. The nights were already bitter cold, the days covered with the slate clouds that hung around the mountaintops, creating an artificial ceiling to a valley that sat very near the top of the world.

As he watched, a cold wind blew down from the mountain peaks, wet with drizzle. In a few minutes, it would rain. By nightfall there would be snow. Fall was even shorter than summer in the mountains, and the coming winter would be long. The old man's face was beaten and deeply creased, reflecting a long, hard life. It was a harsh land that he looked out upon— unbelievably cold in winter, fire-hot and dry in summer, unforgiving, remote, brutal to outsiders, utterly unmanageable except for the few herdsmen and mountain sheep who had the courage to traverse the steep and rocky trails.

The old man watched the single road that ran into the valley from the treacherous mountain pass to the east. His eyes were not as good as they once had been, and he cocked his head to listen as the military jeep reached the highest point on the dirt road and began descending into his valley. Other military vehicles followed. In all, he counted five. They stopped outside the rock wall that surrounded the tiny village, only four feet high now, a thousand years of neglect and erosion having worn it down. Two men got out of the first vehicle and looked around, their weapons hanging under their arms, always ready.

The shepherd turned to his dear friend. Omar watched without speaking, his face tan and tense as he stared down.

"You know them?" the shepherd questioned.

Omar thought a long time before he finally nodded.

"They came for you?"

He shook his head.

The old man glanced back at the shepherd hut set among the scraggly mountain pines near the entrance to a narrow canyon. The boy was waiting there, standing by the goatskin door that covered the small opening to the hut. Omar followed the old man's eyes to watch the boy. They called him *Larka ka aik Heera*. Boy of the Diamond. Omar hated the name—it was demeaning and too descriptive—but he'd never said anything. For what his old friend had risked to protect the child, he could have called him *Son of a Christian Warrior* and Omar wouldn't have complained.

The two men watched him. The boy waited, afraid to move. But Omar could read his body language. He was pent-up, coiled metal, ready to spring if the men gave him but a word. "He's a good boy," Omar observed quietly to the shepherd.

"He's got the spirit of a stallion, but the manners of a colt," the old man complained.

"You gave him that, my friend."

The old man shook his head.

Omar continued, "No, *Rehnuma*, that is the gift you gave to him. His breeding is deep inside him, rich as blood and deep as bone. It will drive him with ambition when he gets older, that is assured, but it will destroy him if not bridled. That is one of the reasons I brought him to you. He needed the seasoning only you and the mountain could ever give him. He needed the humility of being hungry, the gratefulness of being cold, the discipline of herding stupid sheep, the faith of hanging on the mountain with only your word to guide him home."

The old man thought, then nodded. "The manners of a colt, perhaps I nurtured that. But the stallion that runs inside him, he got that from somewhere else."

"His father gave that to him."

The old man's eyes narrowed to suspicious slits and he turned back to the valley and the military vehicles down below. "They are looking for him," he said.

Omar didn't answer.

"You have not told me. I have not asked you. But it isn't hard to figure out. The diamond he carries is worth more than every man, woman, and child in every village within a five days' walk of here. His shoulders are too proud, his neck too long. He doesn't come from Peshawar. He doesn't come from Persia or Pakistan or anywhere even close. He's too royal. You can see it. Young as he is, I could not hide it. If they see him, they will know."

Omar cleared his throat and spat, then pulled out a square of brown paper, tapped in a short line of tobacco, rolled, and licked the edge with a dry tongue, taking less than thirty seconds to roll the smoke. He shoved the narrow roll into his mouth and lit it with a paper match.

The shepherd nodded to the military vehicles again. "They're looking for him?"

Omar pulled a drag and held it.

"They will find him," the old man said.

"Not if we're careful."

"No, *dost* (friend), that isn't true. They'll find him. They'll take or kill him, depending on who he really is. I can't keep him here forever. They know too much. They've come back here too often now. They must know that they are close.

Someone in the village—I have my own enemies, you surely know—they must be talking, and I can't stop them.

"Listen to me, *dost*. I am old now. I'm not afraid to die. I would welcome a chance to sleep, but if Allah were to grant me a few more years, I would take them with great pleasure. I'd like to see my grandchildren safe before I die. I'd like to touch the sea. I'm tired of these mountain walls and winter."

He fell silent. Omar smoked. The wind was picking up and getting wetter, blowing the first raindrops from the mountain-tops over their heads.

"No," the old man said, "I'm ready to face my Master. But the boy, he's far too young." He shot a look to Omar. "He's too important."

Omar almost snorted. *If his old friend only knew!*

The shepherd watched and then concluded, "He is not safe here, not any longer. You've got to decide where you want him to die—here or somewhere else. Leave him and they'll find him, and when they do, he's dead. Take him away and they might get him—or maybe not. But stay here and it's decided. So what are you going to do?"

Omar smoked again. "I'm going to get us help," he answered.

The shepherd grunted. "And where will this assistance come from?"

Omar crushed the half-smoked cigarette against his hand.

"Where will this assistance come from?" the old man prodded, his voice full of doubt.

"The Great Satan," Omar told him.

The old man shook his head.

"They need him as much as we do. And I can't fight this battle by myself."

"We have been placed on earth in troubled times. We live in a complex world with currents of conflict everywhere to be found. Political machinations ruin the stability of nations, despots grasp for power, and segments of society seem forever downtrodden, deprived of opportunity, and left with a feeling of failure.
We who have been ordained to the priesthood of God can make a difference."
—President Thomas S. Monson

"We are strengthened by the truth that the greatest force in the world today is the power of God as it works through man."
—President Thomas S. Monson

chapter thirteen

OFFUTT AIR FORCE BASE
HEADQUARTERS, U.S. STRATEGIC COMMAND
EIGHT MILES SOUTH OF OMAHA, NEBRASKA

Sam Brighton was tired of waiting. He was tired of the uncertainty. He was tired of being held in the small office and not being told what was going on. He was a warrior, and the frustration of inactivity burned like a hot coal inside him. He could feel the sense of urgency in the pace of operations all around him. There was a real war going on and it was going on without him, which was driving him insane. Here he was, stuffed away inside a waiting room, no weapons, no information, no plan. He felt agitated, almost angry, wanting to get in the fight. He missed the vital sense of purpose that came with battle: the chaos, the noise, the uncertainty, the rush of adrenaline, the action, the ecstasy, the sure feeling that no matter what happened to him he was doing something good. All of that was missing now. He was ready to move.

The office door opened and his mother walked into the room. He moved anxiously toward her. "So?" he asked before she could even shut the door.

She shrugged her shoulders. "They cancelled the meeting," she said.

Sam gritted his teeth. "Are you kidding me? What have you been doing? You've been gone for almost two hours."

"They left me waiting. I was close, I think, but something came up."

"They didn't give you any explanation? They didn't tell you anything about what's going on out there?"

"No, Sam, they didn't. And let's not flatter ourselves, we're not that important right now, not in the big scheme of things. We're lucky even to be here. I'm certainly not going to complain."

Sam turned away and ground his teeth again. "Sure, Mom," he said.

Behind him, his brothers were sitting on the floor of the small office under the only window, which looked out on the military base three floors below. They'd pushed the metal desk aside and laid out their sleeping bags for padding. Azadeh was sitting apart, against the back wall. Mary and her daughter were not with them; they'd been taken to the base hospital for a checkup the day before. Kelly Beth's obvious poor health and low weight had raised enough concerns that the medic who had been assigned to them had wanted to check her out.

Sara smiled as she remembered Mary trying to explain to the young medic what had happened to her daughter. "Two weeks ago, she was dying of cancer," she had started. "She was right on death's door. But the good Lord sent an angel to bless and save her. The good Lord sent that young man and his family over there." She pointed toward Sam. "He blessed her with righteous oil and now she's healed as well as you can see . . ."

The medic had responded with a patronizing grin. Mary had gone on, but the attendant wasn't listening anymore.

Before Mary had left with Kelly Beth for the hospital, Sara

had pulled her aside. "I don't know if I'd be telling everyone about what happened to Kelly Beth," she whispered quietly.

Mary looked at her with intense surprise. "Oh, I'll be telling everyone," she said. "Everyone who will listen and even those who won't. The Lord reached down and saved my daughter, clutched her right from the very hands of death. He saved her sure as He raised Lazarus. It's a miracle, and I don't think anyone could stop me from shouting it from the housetops just like the Bible says. It's like a burning in my chest that I have to quench by getting out. I'm going to tell everybody. I'm going to tell the whole world."

Sara had thought for a long moment, her eyes down. It was a very fine line, and who was she to say, but still she had to wonder. "I just . . . I don't know, Mary, I just think there may be some things that are particularly sacred."

"Sacred, yes it is, Sara, but we can't be quiet on this thing. Miracles like this are the only thing that's going to save us now. You know that better than anyone. Miracles are all we've got now. We've got to get everyone to know." Mary had lowered her voice and shot a quick look toward Sara's youngest son, Luke. "You've got your own miracle over there, baby. You know it. I know it. I think the Lord *wants* us to go and tell."

Sara had thought for another moment, then smiled apologetically as she reached out to touch Mary's arm. "You're right, Mary. Of course you are. Most people will think we're crazy, but some of them will listen, and it will help those few who do. All around us now there are people who are searching desperately for any sign of hope, any little thing that they can cling to. We have hope because of miracles. God has blessed us so. Who are we to remain silent? You are absolutely right. You tell whoever you think you ought to. Heavenly Father would want us to shout it from the housetops. Thanks for helping me to see."

✳   ✳   ✳

Sara smiled as she thought back on the conversation that had taken place the day before. Where Mary and Kelly Beth were now, she didn't know. She hadn't heard from them since they had left for the base hospital. When would she see them again? she had to wonder. Maybe soon. Maybe never? There was no way to know. But there was no doubt in her mind that right now, sweet Mary Dupree was hovering over her little girl, explaining to everyone within earshot how Kelly Beth had been cured. The image in her mind made Sara want to both laugh and cry. It made her sweet and peaceful and reminded her again: *Yes, I saved this girl. This is my world. You are my children. As the Evil One grows stronger, so also will my Light. I will send more power from the heavens to counter the growing darkness of the world.*

Sara smiled sadly, wishing Mary was with her now. She missed her dearly, her optimism and simple faith. *I will send a child to lead them.* There was a bond between them now that was good and strong, and it hurt Sara to think she might not see Mary and little Kelly Beth again. But something told her that she wouldn't. Their role in her life was over. Mary and Kelly were on their own.

Azadeh had stood up against the back wall, listening to Sam and Sara talk. Now she moved forward carefully, her eyes on Sara. Her face showed great relief at the woman's return. Being the only female in the room was extremely uncomfortable for her, her culture and its teachings deep and strong, leaving her off balance and unsure around the three young men.

Sam watched her move forward to stand at Sara's side, seeing the look of relief on her face. He and his brothers had tried to be careful around her, no man jokes or "dudes" or talk of things she wouldn't understand, but it was difficult—

impossible, really—to put her at ease. There was a world between them, a world that would have been difficult to bridge under the best of circumstances. As things were, with the U.S. having been turned upside down and smashed on its head by an enemy that was certainly from the Middle East, it was that much more difficult for either party to really be at ease.

Sara looked at Azadeh standing at her side and beckoned her to the window. Having spent twenty-five years as the only woman in the house, being married to a man who was nothing if not a warrior and raising three sons who were as much like their father as any sons could be, Sara immediately understood. She was first and foremost a woman, and she could see more in Azadeh's anxious eyes than her sons would ever understand. When Azadeh didn't move, she took her by the hand. Leading her to the window, she pulled her down beside her and they sat side by side on the floor.

"Didn't you learn anything?" Ammon pressed after his mother had sat down.

Sara ignored him for a moment as she studied Azadeh's face. She was so beautiful, with her enormous eyes and soft, brown skin. She looked . . . Sara didn't know; she had to think about it. And then it came: She looked royal. Noble and imperial. "You're lovely, Azadeh, do you know that?"

Azadeh kept her face down as tears pooled in her eyes.

Sara pulled her close. "It's going to be okay," she said.

Azadeh tried to pull back, but Sara wouldn't let her. "It's going to be okay, Azadeh. It's going to be all right. You've got us now. We are your family. You're not alone."

Azadeh's shoulders started shaking. A single teardrop slid from her cheek and fell silently to the floor. No one saw the falling tear but Sara, and she pulled the young woman close once more. Azadeh fell against her shoulder, hiding her face

95

against Sara's neck. "It's okay . . . it's okay," Sara repeated again and again.

Her sons sat silently by, dumbfounded. Where had these tears come from? They had no idea Azadeh had been feeling . . . what? They didn't know. One moment she was smiling at them, trying to follow their conversation with her halting English; the next minute she was crying in their mother's arms. Sam shot a look to Ammon and Luke, who only shrugged their shoulders. They remained silent for a moment until Sam knelt down and touched Azadeh on the arm. She turned to look at him, embarrassed as she pulled away from his mother's shoulder.

"I'm sorry," she whispered while drying her eyes. "I'm not bad. I feel not bad. I just . . ."

Sara put her finger across her lips. "It's okay, Azadeh. Frankly, we all feel like crying sometimes."

"No kidding," Ammon muttered from behind her. "Every time I smell Sam, I want to cry."

They were silent for a second; then they started to laugh. What began as mere giggles soon burst into long, deep, tension-releasing roars. Luke was rolling on the floor. Ammon bent over, holding his side. No one said anything for a moment. Sam sniffed his armpits. "Holy cow," he said.

Azadeh laughed the hardest, though she wasn't even certain what they were laughing about.

Sam looked at her, embarrassed, then sniffed himself again.

Glancing at Azadeh, he couldn't help but feel better. It was so good to see her smile.

"What can you tell us, Mom?" Sam asked after they had finally settled down. "Did you learn anything at all?"

Sara wiped her eyes a final time. "No. I really didn't. I didn't see or talk to anyone. Honestly, I don't know anything more than you do."

"Is Secretary Marino really going to be the next president of the United States?" Ammon asked.

Sara thought carefully. "As I understand the situation, yes, he should be."

"Are you certain?" Sam pressed her.

Sara nodded in a barely perceptible movement of her head. "Near as I can tell, it's true. But I don't know who else is out there. None of us do. Is there someone who should be ahead of him? He tells me they're all dead."

Sam took a breath and looked away. "I believe him," he said.

"So do I," Sara answered. "I've known Brucius Marino for many years. I trust him. More importantly, *way* more importantly, your father trusted him. He told me many times . . ." She suddenly stopped. The room was quiet for a moment. "Your father and Secretary Marino met frequently over the past year or so," she continued carefully. "Neil considered him a trusted friend."

Ammon slid a little closer. "Do you think we're being listened to in here?" he asked in a hushed voice.

Sam glanced toward the door. Sara looked surprised. "Us! Here? Of course not, Ammon," she said. "There's no need for them to do that. What could they possibly learn from us?"

Sam didn't argue as his eyes swept the room. He wasn't nearly so sure.

"It's just too weird," Ammon offered in a frustrated tone. "A month ago, yeah, sure we had our problems, but we didn't have anything like this! Nuclear detonations over the Gaza Strip and then Israel. What's happening over there? We don't even know. Haven't heard a thing. Anti-ICBM interceptor missiles pop up everywhere: Iran. Iraq. India. Russia. Most of Europe on hair-trigger nuclear alert. A nuclear explosion over D.C." He paused, all of them thinking of their husband and father, their hearts as heavy as melted lead. "Then the EMP attack across our country. From coast to coast, it hit us all. Now there's a struggle to save the government, a death match to see who has power, who's in charge. Think about that. We don't really have a government, so many of our leaders have been killed. We don't even know who's in charge! For the first time in our history, two men have claimed the presidency. The entire federal government has collapsed into shambles. I never would have dreamed it. I never *could* have dreamed it. Not here. Not in *this* country." He fell silent, exhausted at his own words.

Luke had been mostly quiet but now he spoke up. "Remember what happened in the Book of Mormon," he said. "Now, I don't claim to be a big scripture genius or Bible scholar or anything—"

"I don't think any of us were thinking that," Ammon cut in.

Luke ignored him. "Okay, we won't talk about my seminary grades," he eyed Ammon again, "but at least I didn't go just so I could sit by Heather Babe-a-licious or whatever that girl's name was . . ."

"That's because she didn't like you . . ."

"I *do* have a point here."

Ammon shrugged his shoulders to apologize. "Sorry. My bad."

Luke took a deep breath and waited. "Okay, like I was saying—and I'm trying to be serious here—I think this is a point worth making. Think about what you just said, Ammon. We never thought it could be like this, not in *this* country. But that's how the people in the Book of Mormon must have felt. Think about Amalickiah and the guys who tried to make him their king. They were Nephite dissenters, their own people, not Lamanite enemies. And they almost destroyed their own nation. Amalickiah wanted to be king. His crew, those pukes who supported him, were mostly lesser judges. The main reason they pushed to make him king was that they wanted to share his power. They started a civil war, an inside battle for their country, that lasted for years and almost destroyed the entire Nephite nation. Kind of like what we're going through right now."

Ammon eyed his brother, caught up in the mental vision. "Gotta love Captain Moroni. What a stud. Tears his shirt off, hangs it from a pole, and goes marching through the streets to rally the troops. Not many guys could pull that off. I'll bet he was ripped, know what I mean. Bet he'd bench-press at least 360. Wanted to show a little muscle."

Sara wanted to interrupt them and get them to be serious, but Luke went on before she had to, realizing they'd wandered from his point. "Yeah, yeah, maybe all that. But think about what I was saying about how the Nephite people must have felt. Just a year before, they had fought the Lamanites and won the greatest battle they had had up to that time. Now here it was, just a few months later, and ol' Amalickiah goes off trying to steal their country. Nothing like that had ever happened to them before. You got to believe there were a bunch of ticked-off Nephites sitting around saying the same thing Ammon just said: 'I never thought this could happen to *our* country!' They had their constitution. They had their laws. Now someone was trying to destroy all that and make himself king. But they didn't let him. They fought back. And they got through it. Just like I think we can get through this. It isn't over yet."

The room was quiet. None of them had ever thought about it quite like that before. "In memory of our God, our religion, and freedom, and our peace, our wives, and our children," Sam finally said.

His brothers looked at him. "Got that right, brother," Ammon said.

Sara listened, thinking. "There's no doubt who should be the president," she said.

"Are you certain, Mom?"

"Absolutely, Ammon. Secretary Marino should be the next president, assuming there's no one else higher in the line of succession that we don't know about, and I don't think that there is. Brucius would have no reason to deceive me." She paused. "I just don't think he would lie." She was speaking to herself now, making her evaluation. "If there's no one ahead of him, the Speaker of the House, the president pro tempore of the Senate, etcetera, then he's the president. He's certainly ahead of Fuentes—*that* we know for sure."

"Who is this Fuentes guy, anyway?" Sam sneered. "Where did *he* come from? Who's ever even heard of him?"

No one answered.

"Is Secretary Marino . . ." Sam hesitated. "Is he going to go and claim the office, then? Does he have the guts to do it?"

Sara bit her lip. "He does. And yes, he will."

"You're going to help him, aren't you, Mom?"

Sara looked away.

They were silent for a moment. Outside, they heard birds calling in the nearby trees, but it wasn't a pleasant sound. They were large birds, dark and greasy looking, with black feathers and a constant, hungry cawing that grated on the people's nerves. They listened, all of them thinking.

Sam looked down at his dirty uniform, still covered with coal dust from the railroad yard back in East Chicago, mud from the ditch he'd waded through after jumping from the air force tanker and running through the night, a splatter of blood from when he'd tied up the shooter on the beltway that ran around Washington, D.C. A tinge of smoky scent still lingered from the fires that had been burning through the western quadrant of the city. Sniffing at his clothes, he thought back. All if it, from the first bomb over Gaza to the chaos they found themselves surrounded by now, had taken place in not much longer than a month. But all of it was blurred now, the old life—the good life—a faded memory. They didn't used to drink from dirty water. They didn't used to worry about where their next meal was coming from. They used to sleep in beds in heated homes, drive cars, talk on cell phones. They didn't used to panic about infection from every scratch or every upset stomach, knowing there were doctors and medicines around.

They didn't used to look at every passing stranger and wonder, "Will he try to kill me for my food?"

They didn't used to look at senior government officials and wonder, "Is this guy on our side?"

They didn't used to wonder if their government would survive.

But everything was different now.

Another day. Another world. The old one was so far gone it was hard to even remember what it had really been like. So much was different now. None of them would ever be the same.

Sam fingered the nylon laces on his filthy leather boots. "You know what today is?" he asked.

Sara shrugged. Luke kept his head down. Ammon looked confused. "I have no idea," he said. "I couldn't tell you what day, what month, I'm not even sure what year it is anymore. It's like there *is* no time here; it's all just one long, never-ending circle of bad things and really weird stuff like . . ." he nodded to the windows, "strange birds with red eyes that look like mini-vultures waiting to swoop down and claw our eyes out." He took a breath and laughed. "Nope, don't know what day it is."

Luke looked up. "It's Sunday," he said.

"Sunday," Sara breathed. "Oh, that sounds good. I *love* Sundays." She turned to Azadeh. "Sunday is our holy day," she explained.

Azadeh nodded, understanding. "I like Sundays too," she offered, hoping to please them.

"Sunday comics," Ammon said. "*Dildog* or whatever that thing was called. Man, that used to make me laugh."

"Sunday afternoon meant ice cream. It was the only day your dad would let you eat it, remember?" Sara said.

"Which is why we always hid a couple of spoons in our bedrooms," Ammon laughed, glancing at his brothers. "We'd slip down to the freezer in the basement, spoons in hand. Go through half a gallon in one night."

Sara smiled at them. "You know what's really funny about that?"

They looked at her and waited.

"Your dad used to do the same thing."

Ammon stood up and pointed to his brothers. "I *knew* it!" he cried. "I *told* you guys I caught him with a spoon once. He looked so guilty standing there with a wet spoon sticking out of his shirt pocket."

Sara started laughing. "You want to know something else that's funny? You guys didn't think we knew, but we could hear you every time you snuck down there. Your voices would carry up through the heat vents. Yeah, we always knew."

"Did not!" Sam shot back.

"Every time!" his mother laughed.

"But you never said anything?"

"Didn't you guys ever notice there was always another fresh container of ice cream in the freezer? You could finish off a gallon and go back two nights later and there'd be another gallon waiting. Didn't you think I'd notice the empty ice cream containers? How could we not have known?"

The guys were silent. Ammon shook his head. "Wow, all these years we thought we were really getting away with something. And all the time you knew. It kind of . . ." he looked away wistfully. "I don't know, it takes away some of the sense of accomplishment somehow."

Listening to them, Azadeh smiled.

"It's still a good memory," Luke offered.

Sam pulled his pant legs tight around his boots, then stood up and started walking to the door.

"Where you going, dude?" Luke asked.

Sam looked back. "To get some bread and water. It's Sunday. We're going to have the sacrament." Turning, he walked out the door.

chapter fourteen

T hey gathered around the small plate of broken bread. Sara held Azadeh's hand. She had spent a few minutes explaining what the sacrament meant, and though Azadeh watched the others, she didn't participate, sitting slightly behind them on the floor.

Sam pulled out his set of small military scriptures to read the sacrament prayer, held them in his hands a moment, then looked up at his family and cleared his throat. "I used to laugh at these," he said. "I'm sorry to tell you that, but it's true—I used to think it was ridiculous. I mean, come on: angels and gold plates and John the Baptist appearing out of thin air and all that. I used to read things about the people down in Central America just to try to prove it wrong. But then a good friend—you've heard me talk about Bono—asked me a very simple question. 'Someone had to write the book,' he said. 'I mean, you hold it in your hands. It's there. Someone wrote it. Now the only thing you have to figure out is this: Did the man who wrote it know Jesus Christ?'

"So I thought about it—a lot. Did ancient prophets really write those words, and did they know Jesus Christ, not just *know of* Him, but *know* Him?" Sam dropped his head, his voice cracking. "By the power of the Spirit, I know they did. And that testimony gives us more power than anything else we could hope for in this world."

He fell silent, his eyes staring at the floor, then looked up at them again. "You don't know how many nights I have thanked God that He gave me such a family. I mean, you guys know about my mom and dad. I would have . . . I would have been like them, I know that. But from the first day I came to your house—and I'll remember this forever—from that first day I was thrust into your home, you always made me feel loved. I don't know how or why you'd do that, but I am grateful. You're my family, and I would do anything for you."

His voice trailed off. No one said anything. Azadeh watched him carefully. She understood only a little of what he was talking about but there was something in his words, something in his eyes, a lost look, an orphaned look, that she immediately understood.

Sam looked at them, then bowed his head and said the sacrament prayer.

They took the bread and ate it. Luke said the blessing on the water and they drank.

Finished, they looked at each other. All of them wanted more.

"Do you remember how, when we were kids and traveling, we used to say our favorite scriptures in the car before we'd fall asleep?" Luke said. "Let's do that now. That can be our Sunday talk."

They went around the circle, Sara going first. Sam was last. He thought a minute then told them, "I don't have a single favorite scripture. Mine is a series of scriptures, but they tell the story of my life, I think. So this is how I see the Lord. This is how I see myself."

Sara watched him carefully, sensing this was one of those rare moments when she would get to see what was inside one of her children's hearts.

Sam cleared his throat again. "Okay. Three things. A leper went to Jesus and begged Him, 'Lord, if thou will, thou can make me clean.' A weeping father brought his suffering son and placed him before the Savior. 'Heal him, Lord,' he begged. 'I will if you believe,' the Savior told him. 'I believe, Lord,' the father said, then he caught himself, realizing the true weakness of his faith. 'Lord, help my unbelief,' he begged again. Last one, okay? Two men went up to the temple to pray, one a publican, the other one a Pharisee. The Pharisee stood before the others and said, 'God, I thank thee that I am not like these other men, unjust, adulterers, sinners even as this publican.' But the publican stood afar off and would not lift even so much as his eyes up to heaven, but beat upon his chest and cried, 'Forgive me, God, for I am a sinner.'"

Sam paused for a moment. The room was silent. No crying birds. No footsteps in the busy hallway.

"That is who I am," he concluded, his voice low as he looked at them one by one. "You know me. You know how I've lived. It was hard for me. I've always had to struggle to do the right thing. From the very beginning, I knew I wasn't like the rest of you; I was a sinner, rebellious. I had too much of my old man inside of me, I guess.

"Can you see what I'm saying? These scriptures I have talked about are *me:* Lord, you can make me clean. Yes, I believe. I *want* to believe. Please, can you help my unbelief? Forgive me, Lord, forgive me, please, for I'm a sinner.

"But that's not the end of my favorite scriptures. The best one, the one that gives me hope, the one that means more to me than any of the others is so clear. Doctrine and Covenants

106

60:7, 'For I am able to make you holy, and your sins are for-given you.'"

He stopped and stared at the floor now.

"At the end of the day, I know that's true. I'm a sinner. We all are sinners. But Christ has the power to make us holy. He can make you holy. Even make me holy. And that's the only thing that gives me hope."

*　　*　　*

Luke stared at his brother, the Spirit settling like a peaceful blanket over his troubled soul. As he listened, the Spirit told him: *Everything you have been taught and believed is true. Jesus is the Christ. He is the Savior. That is the only thing that matters. Everything else will be all right.*

And from that moment, Luke never doubted. His faith was more sure than even the growing devastation and evil all around him. He could feel the Prince of Darkness's expanding power, but he realized the light of the Savior was still more powerful. He felt a reassurance that God knew them and cared for them and wouldn't stay His hand.

The words of a prophet suddenly came to his ears. He didn't know which prophet it was, he didn't know when he'd heard the phrase or even that it was buried somewhere in his mind, but the Spirit brought the message in words he couldn't miss. *"You are a royal generation. You were preserved to come to earth in this time for a special purpose. Not just a few of you, but all of you. There are things for each of you to do that no one else can do as well as you."*

It was a turning point for Luke. And though the course of his life would turn out to be very different from how he ever thought it would, from that moment on he never doubted what his destiny would be.

* * *

Sitting back a little farther from the circle of the others, Azadeh listened to Sam's words. And as she listened, she felt something that she'd rarely felt before, something inside her, warm and beautiful. It was both emotional and spiritual and it came with overwhelming power. A fire glowed inside her and her mind felt peaceful—alive and pure.

The feeling brought overwhelming memories as her mind went racing back. She was a little girl going through her morning prayers. Her sixteenth birthday, the beautiful morning her father had given her the silver brushes, knowing he'd given everything he owned to buy them for her. The night she was lost on the snowy mountain, the stranger appearing out of the storm and dark to keep her warm.

Yes, she'd felt this burning glow a few times before.

And she would pay whatever price she had to in order to make this feeling a permanent part of her life.

* * *

Lucifer watched them, listened to their words, and then started screaming. "NO! NO! NO!" he cried in unbridled rage and fury. "There is no hope! There is no future. You have nothing! Are you so blind you cannot see? I have taken everything you need to be happy! I've taken everything you need to live. You're going to die, you stupid, brainless mortals, you're going to suffer here and die! Are you so stupid that you can't see that you've lost everything? How can you be happy? How can you have any hope at all! There is nothing left here for you but pain and loneliness. How dare you feel this way! How dare you look upon my Enemy and believe that He will help you! How dare you look to His Great Work and ignore the great work of my own hands.

"I am the Second Son. You are my brothers. I am a fallen

angel, but you have fallen here with me! There's only fury, there is no light. There is no hope. There is no answer. Now I command you to worship me! I should have been the savior. Worship the mighty works I've done. Worship the pain and dread and hopelessness. Worship the darkness I have created and settled upon this wretched world."

He stopped raging and stared at Sam, then clenched his fists and cried again, "DON'T IGNORE ME! DON'T IGNORE MY GLORY. DON'T IGNORE THE MIGHTY WORK I'VE DONE!"

✴   ✴   ✴

Behind him, Balaam watched his wretched master, then slowly turned away.

It was no good. It didn't matter. His heart sank into the most hopeless of all despairs.

It didn't matter what they did to them, they could not steal their light. They couldn't steal their hope or testimony. No matter what they did to them, some of them still knew. No matter what obstacle they placed before them, some of them fought on.

They could fill the world with darkness, but they could not stop the light, as long as some of them were faithful.

He turned and glared at Sara's family.

These were the ones they had to fear. These were the ones who would destroy them. These were the great light in the darkness. Clear as the moon. Fair as the sun. Oh, it hurt to even look at them, they were so beautiful.

Sinking to his knees, he felt the empty hopelessness. But, unlike the lies they'd whispered to the mortals, his bitterness was real.

Trembling like a child, he fought in vain to hold his tears.

chapter fifteen

Sam had barely finished talking when the door opened suddenly and a mustached air force sergeant burst into the room. "You're going to want to see this," he commanded.

They all stood. "What's going on?" Sam asked.

The tech sergeant nodded toward the hallway. "Come with me, sir."

The army lieutenant and his family followed the sergeant down a dimly lit hallway to a common room where a television was playing.

Seeing the TV screen, Sara drew a sudden breath.

James Davies's exhausted face filled the screen. He was speaking slowly, his voice measured as he read from a teleprompter, the text carefully prepared. Though his hands were animated, his face remained unusually passive and grim. And there was something about him, something . . . Sara didn't know, something artificial about the dryness of his voice, his words powerful but not convincing, at least not to those who knew him best. An off-camera voice swore him in, then asked him to begin.

"My name is James Davies. I am the Director of the United States Federal Bureau of Investigation. For the past two weeks, since just before the EMP attack against the United States, I have been working closely with Brucius Marino, the Secretary of Defense. Because of this, I have first-hand and intimate knowledge of what Secretary Marino intends to do, should he attain the presidency of the United States, a goal he is intent on accomplishing.

"First, and most dangerously, should Brucius Marino be sworn in as the president of the United States, he would order an immediate and massive retaliatory nuclear strike against the twenty largest Muslim cities in the world. Even now, he is working with military strategic forces, through the Strategic Command Center at Offutt Air Force Base, so as to implement this strike within a day of his being sworn in.

"Second, if Secretary Brucius Marino is sworn in as the president of the United States, he intends to sever all alliances, treaties, military agreements, and diplomatic accords with any allies who may have had knowledge of or a hand in the nuclear attack upon D.C., the EMP attack upon the United States, or the nuclear strike against Israel, this last despite the fact that Israel was the first to strike using nuclear weapons. The severing of these relationships and agreements will include but not be limited to expelling the United Nations from U.S. soil, severing all military agreements presently in place through NATO, as well as other agreements with our allies across Eastern Europe and the Pacific Rim.

"Further, Secretary Marino and his staff are drawing up plans to target those nations that may have assisted any of our enemies in the development of their nuclear programs, including Russia, North Korea, Saudi Arabia, and France. These retaliatory plans include severe sanctions, sea and aerial blockades, support of opposition parties within these governments, pro-insurgency operations, destabilizing propaganda, and, in some cases, covert military operations, including assassination of key leadership positions.

"Should Secretary Marino be sworn in as president of the United States, he will order our military forces to take the oil fields of the Middle East, including those in the allied nations of Saudi Arabia and Iraq. This will be the largest military operation since the invasion of Europe during World War II. But he will not stop there. He intends to occupy, using massive ground forces, the entire region, from Iran across the Persian Gulf to the Red Sea, including Bahrain, Qatar, and the UAE. If it is a Muslim country with significant oil reserves, he will invade it, claiming it for his own.

"Finally, you should know that even as I speak here, the Secretary is putting his plans in place to assume his rightful place as the president of the United States. And yes, it *is* his rightful place, for as outlined in the Constitution, he *is* next in line to become the president of the United States. Yet knowing what he and his supporters intend to do—and I speak now as one of his dearest friends and most intimate professional advisers—I beg the Congress not to let this happen. They must take action. If Brucius Marino is allowed to ascend to the presidency at this severe time of crisis, he will take a most desperate situation and make it infinitely worse. He will cause war to fall upon one point five billion innocent Muslim people, raining nuclear death upon their cities, all for no other reason than revenge. He will destroy every conceivable friendship or alliance that our country desperately needs in order to survive. Winter is coming on and we can't clothe, house, or provide heat and living accommodations for our own people. Our hospitals, police, and other emergency services are completely overwhelmed. Right now, we have no choice but to rely upon our friends and allies. Secretary Marino is going to make it impossible for them to help us. Worse, with the plans he and his military advisers have devised to launch a massive and incredibly deadly ground war throughout the entire Middle East, we won't have the resources we need to feed ourselves. We need these troops at home now, helping us to rebuild this great nation. Without them, we don't have the manpower, we don't have the resources, we don't have the international goodwill to rebuild. Without our military resources, we can't provide for the welfare, safety, or well-being of our own people. To launch a massive ground war now would be national suicide."

Here James Davies stopped, still staring directly into the television cameras. His dark eyes were filled with powerful emotions, his face now strained as if he were in great pain, the treachery of betraying his friend only slightly less powerful than the real fear he felt for his country. He wet his lips and concluded in a raspy voice: "I have known Secretary Marino for many, many years. He is a good man. I love him like a brother. But he is the last man on earth who should lead our nation right now. He is the last man who should be the president during the most critical crisis we have ever faced. Valley Forge, Gettysburg, the D-Day invasion of France, none of those turning points in history were as critical or dangerous as the crisis we face right now. Brucius Marino, in his single-minded lust for revenge upon our enemies and in his unwavering resolve for the continued domination of U.S. power, will end up destroying our nation, or what little nation we have left.

"I ask the remaining members of the Congress that are gathered here in Raven Rock not to let him do this. You have to save our country. You simply have to act.

"Do your duty. Save our country. God bless the USA."

*   *   *

James Davies finished speaking and the television cut to a government public service announcer.

Sara and her children stood in silence. No one spoke. The air was heavy. They weren't listening to the announcer any longer.

Sara stumbled backward, feeling for the seat behind her, and fell into the leather couch.

chapter sixteen

James Davies was hauled away, his feet dragging across the floor, leaving a thin trail of red blood across the dark blue carpet from the powerful dart that had pierced his neck.

The first order of business out of the way, the real meeting was finally able to begin. It lasted for almost five hours before food was brought in; then the lunch was quickly eaten and the men went back to work.

At three in the morning, they had their final agreement. They signed it, some of them smiling, some frowning, though in truth most of them were relieved.

It had gone better than any of them could have dreamed.

The world's spheres of influence divided and allocated, the meeting was adjourned.

*   *   *

The old man met the king at the back of the room and pulled him aside. "This is the last time you will come here," the old man said. He glanced behind him after speaking,

115

shooting a nasty look toward the president of the United States. "It makes it difficult for the others. You are far too recognizable."

The king of the House of Saud stared at the old man, his eyes cold. Their relationship was strained now, tight and accusing and barely even civil. There was no balance any longer. The old man had delivered everything that he had promised the king: his brothers, the weapons he had used to destroy America, the kingdom with its uncounted wealth and pride and unfathomable power. Everything they'd ever talked about, the old man had delivered, leaving King Abdullah to stand beside Nebuchadnezzar in the historic halls of power. But what the old man could build, he could destroy; what he had given, he could take back. Worse, the king had little purpose now, and the old man was through with him. He didn't want to kill him—he wouldn't need to, the king would kill himself soon enough—but he certainly wanted him dead.

Like an infected wound, the king's heart was fully putrid now. Everything that he was, he owed to the old man, which made him hateful and resentful and ripe with pride, a deadly combination for any king, but especially for a king of Saudi Arabia descended from a long line of proud and powerful men.

The king didn't answer for a moment.

"You have everything you've asked for. I gave it all to you. Now I need for you to listen. You must stay away. Stay away from Fuentes. Stay out of the country. There is nothing for you to do here. No good can come from it. If you're invited, decline politely, but do not come. It will make our work much more difficult if you are identified at this critical juncture. I know you'll understand."

The king cocked his head, tempted to rebut him, but the red smolder in the old man's eyes seemed to tame him, turning his wrath aside. "Agreed," he answered simply, a dog before his master, his tail between his knees.

The old man watched and smiled, laughing inside himself. None of them were equal to him. None of them. They all wore down, some of them more quickly, some of them more stubbornly, but all of them would fall. Once he started talking to them, once they looked him in the eye, they would fall. Their defense against him would have been so simple: All they had to do was walk away. But as long as they listened to him, then *all* of them would fall. He could wear them down eventually if they listened to his words.

The old man leaned toward Abdullah and lowered his voice to plant the seed. "The child-king is still alive, you know."

Abdullah stared at him.

"I've told you before, it is a problem. You've got to take care of him. He will grow, and when he does, he'll come to kill you. Do you think he won't come for his kingdom? Do you think the men who have him now won't prepare him for that day? He is the only son of the oldest son. He should be king. He has been taken and hidden for a purpose. Every day you let him linger, they grow bolder, thinking you have forgotten the bloodline that survives."

Abdullah turned his eyes away, looking past the old man. "I have time . . ."

"You will lose your kingdom then, you fool. Everything that we have worked for, everything that we have killed and died for, all of it will be gone. You risk your own good, but you risk mine as well. Mine and that of all your Brothers. We will not endure your foolishness. You must act—or we will."

Abdullah moved his shoulders slightly. His breath smelled like Arab chai and cigarettes, his armpits like sweat.

The old man knew that the king was hesitant and he

pressed the seed a little deeper, pushing into more fertile mental soil. "Think back over time," he whispered now. "How many empires, how many kings have been brought down by a child who had claim upon a throne? I can name you at least a dozen, including the greatest kings. And whether you like it or not, King Abdullah, this young prince has claim on you. You killed his father. You killed his brothers and their children. You killed his grandfather, the *real* king," the old man emphasized the word, digging into Abdullah's soul. "You stole it from him, Abdullah. He knows it. Those around him know what happened, which is why they risk their lives to save him. But I've told you all this before." The old man let his voice drift away now. He had him; he could tell that from the agitation in his eyes.

"I'll do it," King Abdullah said.

The old man frowned and leaned toward him. "Do it now," he sneered.

"I'll do it . . ."

"You know where he is. I've already shown you. The Persian mountains are his hiding place, but they build strength and power there. Don't give them time to build an army around this young prince. Do it now and you will fight a dozen others; wait ten years and fight an army. The choice is up to you. No! That isn't right. We will not let you choose if you choose wrongly. You will do what we tell you now."

Abdullah pressed his lips. "I agree with you," he said.

"I knew you would." The old man smiled.

※　　※　　※

Twelve feet to their right and ten feet up on the wall, nearly completely hidden in the corner where the wall and ceiling met, the Dragonfly caught the last of the conversation and broadcasted the grainy images and barely understandable audio signal back to the relay still hidden in the bathroom down the hall.

Twelve minutes after the conversation between the old man and King Abdullah ended, the batteries on the tiny drone reached the end of their useful power. The minuscule drone sent out its final signal. Then, using the last of its battery power, it dug its tiny, hooked appendages deeper into the corner of the wall, ensuring that it would cling there even after all of its power was depleted, the design engineers knowing it would be much more difficult to locate and identify the drone up in the corner than if it had fallen onto the floor.

chapter seventeen

Seven stories below Sara and her family, Brucius Marino sat in the underground command center watching the last of the proceedings that were being broadcast from the assembly room in Raven Rock. Sometimes he paced. Frequently he swore. Once or twice he slammed a fist on the conference table. Through it all, his eyes never left the television screen.

When it was over, his staff sat in stunned and unbelieving silence until Brucius glanced down at his watch. "Got to be a record," he said, his voice so sarcastic he was almost laughing. "I was the president for what . . . less than ten minutes? Going to make some history there."

His staff stared at him, too dumbfounded to reply.

Brucius snorted again. "You've got to admit, it was brilliant. Brilliant and effective. As a means of making it impossible for me to make any claim upon the presidency, this was it. Think of what we just witnessed here: In just under four hours, the only remaining member of the Supreme Court swears me in in absentia, making me the president of the United States. The House of Representatives immediately begins impeachment

120

proceedings against me, presents testimony—with my good friend James Davies as the star witness—then votes for impeachment. The House sends its impeachment to the Senate, which convicts me, and bam, that's it, I'm out of office the same day. No appeal. No legal grounds to take it to the American people. Swear me in. Impeach me out. Put their guy back in place." He shook his head in disbelief. "It's beyond amazing. It really is. I tell you what, none of us saw this coming. It was brilliant—inspired, really—you've got to give them that. I was afraid they were going to try to kill me, but hey," he laughed sarcastically again, "this was a much, much better plan than that. The entire country knows now. There is nothing we can do. Yeah, it was a much better way of getting rid of me than putting a gun to my head." He sat back, suddenly exhausted. "James, oh, James . . ." he muttered to himself.

His chief of staff leaned forward. "Sir, you know that he was drugged. You must know he didn't have a choice."

Brucius only shook his head. Maybe that was true, maybe it wasn't. Either way, James should have done something to stop it, even if it meant taking his own life. There was just too much at stake, millions of lives, the entire future of their country, everything that mattered. And it all turned on just one man. He shook his head again.

His COS watched him, recognizing the signs of building rage. Like most powerful men, Brucius had a temper to match his ego, ambition, and intellect. The COS added quietly, "He was drugged, sir. We all know that. He can't be held accountable. We don't know what they did to him."

Brucius bit his lower lip so hard the COS thought he might draw blood and stared down at his hands.

It was like a dream, bizarre and surreal. He reviewed the proceedings in his mind, unable to force the images from his mind: being sworn in as president via proxy; James Davies

121

testifying against him, his voice as heavy as leaded weight; additional testimonies from a couple of other witnesses; the short debate; the findings from the assembled members of the United States House of Representatives; a single article of impeachment approved; the trial in the Senate, presided over by the only surviving member of the Supreme Court. The final vote: thirty for conviction, four against.

A Senate vote of conviction was final. Once a president was convicted and impeached, there was no appeal.

"It's over, then?" he asked his staff, his eyes smoldering with building rage. His voice was heavy but determined, his hands moving constantly on the table. "You're telling me I can't fight it? There's nothing I can do?"

No one wanted to say the words. Military and civilian advisers flanked him on both sides of the enormous conference table, but Brucius Marino kept his eyes on the group of three attorneys who sat packed together opposite him. There were two United States Attorneys from the Justice Department in Washington, D.C. (two of the few who had survived from their entire office) and a third man who was the general counsel of the navy, a politically appointed civilian who'd been serving in the Pentagon for almost four years. He was the one who finally spoke. "Sir, it was extremely clever—"

"Clever!" Brucius almost screamed. "I don't want to hear that it was clever! I don't want to hear that, you understand me!" The Secretary swore, his rage and frustration rolling up like a volcano that couldn't hold back the pressure anymore. He'd been simmering for weeks, building smoke and ash for days, splashing hot licks of lava and fire now for hours as he forced himself to remain calm. The forced calmness was over. He was about to blow. "I don't want to hear how we've been politically outmaneuvered or legally outfoxed. This isn't a game or competition! This isn't a battle of legal wills! We don't congratulate the winners, shake their hands, and go home." He swore again, his voice still rising. "You call them *clever*. Yeah, they're clever *traitors!* They don't deserve our respect or admiration. You understand me? I don't give a flying load of crap how *legally clever* they are! I want to know how to defeat them. I want to bring them down!" The Secretary slammed his fist on the table, spit and fury flying from him. "I want to crush them! We're going to crush them. We will not let this stand!"

The room was heavy with silence, awkward and full of pain. Some of the men, the brave ones, stared at Brucius Marino. Most looked down, unable to meet his eyes or his rage. Everyone could hear his heavy breathing as he stared back at the men. "Okay," he said again, only a little more in control. "Tell me. Is what they've done legal? Can they swear me in by proxy? Can they impeach and convict me the same way, leaving me no ability to defend myself, no opportunity to face my accusers? And I don't want to hear you say you've got to study it. I don't have time. None of us have time. We've got to act. I've got to know!" He jammed an angry finger to his right. "Think about what we know now, gentlemen. Think about what the Dragonfly has shown us! Think of the video footage we have from the drone. Think of the foreign leaders we know are in Raven Rock right now, King Abdullah not least among them, and tell me there's nothing we can do.

"We know what they're planning to do! We know how they're going to do it! We know where Abdullah's heading. We have to take them now. We *can't* sit here while they do this! Legal or illegal, we've got to act!"

The lawyers glanced painfully at each other. The lead Pentagon attorney spoke, his voice slow and measured, an even-tempered balance to the Secretary's rage. "It's difficult, Mr. Secretary. I'm sorry, but, legally, this matter leaves us on very unstable ground. You've asked for our opinion, but we're talking about a situation that is unprecedented in every conceivable way. There is nothing here for us to go on. We're treading virgin ground. If you want us to voice a preliminary opinion, this is what we would say: There are obvious problems with the conviction, but this is a political process as much as a legal one, and the Constitution is very clear. There is no appeal process from conviction. Our only hope lies in the Supreme Court. And as we all clearly saw, the only surviving member of the Court presided over the Senate proceedings. His entire purpose was to assure the constitutionality of the process. What are we going to do, ask him to overturn himself?"

Brucius Marino sat back, his face taking on color once again. "Is that possible?" he demanded.

The attorney shrugged. "I think, sir, in this situation, almost anything is possible. But does it even matter? With only one member of the Supreme Court still alive, we have very few realistic options, not with him sitting with the others down in Raven Rock. And we all know one of the first things President Fuentes is going to do is name new members to the Court. He'll choose people who will support him." The legal counselor hesitated, looking down, then raised his eyes to meet Brucius's vicious stare. "I'm sorry, sir, but it seems to me this might be over."

The SecDef raised his hand. "But if we had other members of the Court?"

"I just don't know, sir. I suppose . . ." he glanced quickly to the other lawyers. "I think we would agree that if you were to locate and assemble other members of the Supreme Court, they might be willing to issue a finding. But they're dead, sir. We all know that. None of them survived."

For the first time in weeks, Brucius Marino leaned back

and almost smiled. "If we had some other members of the Supreme Court, we might be able to overrule them?"

The lawyers hesitated. "It is possible," the lead attorney said. "But in this situation, it doesn't matter, sir."

Brucius turned to his right, looking at his chief of staff. The COS barely moved, but it was enough for Brucius to know.

"Good enough," Brucius said. "We're going to do it! We're going to do it now."

The COS started protesting. "Sir, it is too dangerous. Your plan has enormous risks—"

"Everything is risky now!" Brucius shot back. "Everything we do now is by definition a risk. But the truth of the matter is, in a couple of hours, a couple of days, all of us could be dead.

"So yes, I understand it's risky. But we don't have any choice. We've got to do it to save our nation, and if that means that all of us are going to die here, that's a small price to pay."

He shifted his eyes, looking at the other men. "All of you get ready. I'm not waiting any longer. We're going to do it now."

chapter eighteen

Caelyn and Bono sat talking on the porch under the light of the stars, her head resting on his shoulder. The moon was just a sliver of white against the dark sky and the countryside was completely void of any light, a long, broken line that seemed to stretch forever beneath the starry horizon. Above them, a single yellow candle flickered in Caelyn's parents' bedroom. The sun had been down for almost two hours and their eyes had had time to adjust to the dark. Caelyn had rarely experienced such darkness, and it amazed her how well she could see, given only the flicker of natural light from the stars. Bono was not surprised, having spent many nights out on patrol in desolate areas.

They sat on the porch swing, a cold breeze pushing dry leaves across the grass and along the lane to pile up against the picket fence. As they talked, there was a rustle of movement to their right and Bono immediately turned and listened. Caelyn seemed not to have noticed. Bono cocked his head. The sound of footsteps? Could it be? He listened again, certain he had heard it. Who? Why were they out there? Caelyn started to speak but he lifted a hand to hush her. She turned to him, sensing his growing tension.

He peered into the darkness. His pistol was hanging on his web belt upstairs in their bedroom closet, hidden away from Ellie; now he wished that it was at his side.

Caelyn didn't move. Bono listened. Silence. The wind blew, moving leaves again. More movement with the rustle. Empty blackness as far as he could see. More motion beyond the tree line. An animal? Maybe nothing?

No, he was certain of what he'd heard.

Slowly, his footsteps light, every motion tight and under perfect control, he stood up from the porch swing, motioned to Caelyn to stay still, moved toward the steps, grabbed onto the pillar that held the slanted roof, then swung onto the grass in one movement. He crouched there, getting low enough to change the angle of his view so he could use the starlight to look up against the horizon. The existing light was weak but enough to illuminate the ground, the barns behind the fence, the trees in the backyard. Another sound. The sense of movement. Bono took a step forward, glanced back to Caelyn one more time, held his finger to his mouth, turned and started moving forward, still crouched. One step. Two. Stop to listen. Stop to look. Low, still using the starlight to look for shadows against the horizon. Another step. Another look . . .

The sound of running footsteps erupted across the grass, light and furious. Bono started running after them. A squeal of fear before him. Cries. A couple of voices, very young. The sounds of *children*?

"Hey there!" he called out.

"GO!" someone screamed out from the darkness. Bono ran again, but lost the sound of their footsteps when his own feet started crunching through the dry leaves under the huge oak. Without enough light to follow them, he stopped and listened, having to rely upon his ears. Darkness. Silence now. He listened, frowned in frustration, then rushed across the lawn, coming to the picket fence. Turning his head, he strained to hear again. The footsteps faded in the distance, the voices hissing and whispering as they ran.

Children! Had he heard children in the darkness?!

The voices were high and childlike, the footsteps short and quick, but the cries were also different from children's voices somehow—more conspiring, more agitated, more conniving and devious. He peered across the open fields behind the fence, but the retreating footsteps were gone now, faded into the distance. He stared into the darkness until Caelyn came up behind him, moving quickly to his side.

"There was someone out there," she said. "I could hear them running." She was fighting to keep her voice under control.

Bono stared without answering.

"Did you see them?" she asked.

"No, not really."

"Did you see *anything?*"

He couldn't see the expression on her face but he sensed her fear and agitation from the aggressive shaking of her head. "No," he answered simply.

"Who could it be?"

"I don't know, babe."

He glanced back toward the house. "Come on." They moved across the dry lawn together, running toward the porch.

"They were children," Caelyn whispered as they ran. She was speaking to herself but Bono heard her anyway. "I saw their shadows. I heard their voices." She stopped and gripped Bono's arm, her fingers digging into his bare skin. "Children!

Do you understand that? There were children out there in the darkness."

"I don't think so. Not really children. They were something else."

"Something else?"

"Kids. Teenagers, maybe."

She shook her head but didn't answer.

Bono watched her carefully, glanced back toward the darkness, then pulled her across the lawn, onto the porch, and into the house. He shut the door behind them, locked it, and peered through the window. Feeling the kitchen table behind him, he turned and walked down the hall and up the stairs, his footsteps almost perfectly silent against the wooden floor. Thirty seconds later, he reappeared. Caelyn couldn't see anything but his shadow, so she reached out, touching the canvas holster against his chest. "Baby, what are you thinking? You put that thing away!" Bono stood by the window, looking out intently. "You hear me, Joseph? Put that thing away. There are children out there, honey. You can't even think about—"

He reached out and put his finger to her lips, nodded for her silence, then moved down the hallway toward the front door. He checked the deadbolt, making certain it was locked, then waited, his head close to the thin pane of glass in the middle of the door, listening, his eyes looking down so he could concentrate on what he heard. Caelyn waited in the kitchen. From where she stood, all she could see was a hint of his shadow. Taking a breath, the darkness and silence all around her, she felt a sudden sense of fear, bone-deep and gut-wrenching.

There was *something* there!

Outside the door! Out on the front porch!

She couldn't see it. She couldn't even hear it. But she knew. She sensed it. Something was there. Her heartbeat skipped and then doubled, pounding suddenly in her throat. She moved half a step to get a better look down the hall. Bono was crouching at the doorway, his body outlined by the faintest hint of starlight that bled through the living-room windows. He crawled to his right and she sensed the motion. She waited, watching, hardly breathing, then glanced above her, thinking of the bedroom on the second floor where Ellie slept.

Bono crawled over to the front window but didn't look out, keeping his head below the glass. He listened, hearing movement against the wooden porch. Heavy. Deliberate. More than one set of footsteps. A couple of men, opposite him now, on the other side of the wall.

He inched back toward the door, his weapon ready, put both hands across the deadbolt and slowly slid it back, moving the metal a fraction of an inch at a time to keep it silent. Listening again, he realized that the footsteps had faded away and he motioned toward Caelyn to wave her back. Instead she inched forward, her bare feet silent against the wooden floor. Bono gestured with more urgency, waving her into the safety of the kitchen. Defying him, she ran forward, turning at the bottom of the stairs and racing up. Stopping at the top of the stairs, she positioned herself at the end of the hall. There she waited, looking back. What her plan was, she had absolutely no idea. All she knew was that she had to get herself between whatever was out there in the darkness and her child.

Bono watched her go up the stairs, then turned back to the door. Reaching up, he grabbed the handle, holding his weapon at the ready. With a jerk, he threw the door open violently. It swung back on its hinges, crashed against the doorstop, and swung halfway closed again. He didn't move, waiting and listening against the wall. Silence. The sound of his own breathing pounding in his ears. Then, with a flash of movement, he stood and ran across the threshold, falling into the night.

Caelyn almost screamed when she saw the white-hot double flash of fire. At the same instant she heard the crashing impact of two bullets against the wall beside the door. Two more flashes of light and two ear-crushing sounds, these two much closer, having come from Bono's gun. Screams sounded from behind her—Greta crying from her bedroom at the unexpected noise. Footsteps and voices hurtled across the porch and Caelyn's heart slammed into her chest. Her husband was gone now, having disappeared into the darkness. She cried and started running, descending the stairs two or three at a time to follow him, almost falling as she ran. Halfway down she stopped and looked back. Up? Down? Her husband? Her child?

"*Don't leave Ellie!*" an unseen voice seemed to cry in her ears.

Turning, she ran back up the stairs and down the narrow, picture-lined hallway. She reached the first bedroom, the white outline of the door frame barely visible in the tiny hint of light. "Mom, come with me!" she shouted as she burst into the room.

Her mother was standing in confusion beside her bed. The bedroom was dimly lit, the moonlight in the east filtering through the upper windows. Her mother ran toward her. "What is it? Who is it?"

"Go get Ellie. Stay with her!"

"Who is it? Who was shooting?"

"I don't know, I don't know. Now GO, GO, GO!"

Caelyn ran back into the hallway. Her mother ran behind her, then turned and sprinted down the hall toward Ellie's bedroom. Caelyn rushed toward the empty stairs.

Halfway down she heard the scream.

She stopped, her blood frozen in her veins. The contents of her stomach rose inside her and she almost threw up on the floor. Cold shots of fear ran through her, spiderwebs of terror that spread across her back and down her arms.

Ellie cried out from her bedroom once again, then was muffled into silence.

"JOSEPH CALTON, GET UP HERE!" Caelyn screamed toward the porch.

Bono was already on his way, rushing through the door and bounding up the stairs. She recognized the raging glare in his eyes as he ran by. *Not my daughter! Not my child!* the furious look on his face screamed.

He ran up the stairs in wild anger, calling as he ran, "ELLIE! WHERE ARE YOU, ELLIE!"

He hurtled into his daughter's bedroom, his eyes flashing left and right. Greta lay across the bed, holding onto Ellie, who was crying in her arms. The bedroom window was open, a cold breeze blowing the curtain back. Caelyn rushed into the room behind him. Ellie's tears were glistening in the moonlight, her fingers clinging at Greta's clothes. Bono's eyes darted around the room again, taking in the open window, the blowing curtains, a deserted burlap sack and string of rope left in a heap on the floor. He heard the sound of heavy footsteps across the wooden shingles on the roof. He ran toward his daughter, dropping to his knees beside the bed. "Are you okay, baby?" he whispered to her as he reached out to stroke her head. She buried her face into her grandma's shoulder and didn't answer. Caelyn rushed forward and pulled Ellie into her arms.

Bono looked at Greta. "Is she hurt?" he demanded.

"I don't think so," Greta answered. "I got here just in time. Someone had her. They let her go when I came into the room. They ran out . . ." she nodded toward the window.

Bono stood and leaped toward it, staring out.

The roofline sloped gently toward the south. A huge oak tree at the corner of the house spread its branches over the roof. There was movement across the yard now, but it was too dark to see. He turned back to Ellie, put his hand atop her shoulder, and whispered to Caelyn, "*Is she okay?*" He needed to be assured.

Caelyn didn't answer. Greta looked across the bed toward him. "She's okay. I got here in time to stop them."

Satisfied, Bono turned and crawled through the open window. The women listened as the sound of his footsteps across the wooden shingles quickly faded into the night.

Outside, Bono jumped, swung on a low branch to catch himself, then dropped onto the ground. Reaching for his holstered weapon, he raced into the dark.

Three minutes later, he returned. The women had moved to the other bedroom and were huddled together on the corner of the bed. Caelyn's father was standing guard, a baseball bat—autographed by his favorite Yankees—in hand.

Bono moved up the stairs, found them in the bedroom, and knelt in front of Caelyn and Ellie. Reaching out, he pulled his daughter close. "You're okay, Ellie, you're okay," he whispered to her. "It's going to be all right."

"Daddy, Daddy," she started crying.

Handing her to Caelyn, he stood up once again. "You'll be okay," he assured his daughter in a hurried voice. His eyes were always moving. His mind was somewhere else.

"Where are you going?" Caelyn asked him, sensing his thoughts.

"I'll be back. I'll be okay."

"Don't you leave us, honey."

He tried to smile to reassure her, squeezing her hand. The

moment lasted less than half a second. Then he turned and disappeared into the hall and down the stairs.

*　　*　　*

The sun was just coming up when Bono returned to find Caelyn in the kitchen huddled over a propane burner, cooking a batch of pan bread. He stepped into the room. She turned and took a step toward him, then stood still. Her face was almost sick with fear and worry. "Where did you go!" she demanded in a panicked voice.

He slowly shook his head.

Unable to hold back, she ran toward him and grabbed him so tightly he could hardly breathe. Moments passed. He felt her shaking; then she pushed back to look into his face.

"Are you okay?" she asked, looking him over from head to toe.

He was covered with dirt and mud: his clothes, his face, his hands, his arms. Even his eyelids and ears were caked in mud. It took her a moment to realize he had camouflaged himself. "What did you find out? Who was out there?"

He slowly shook his head. "Gangs. Roving bands of thieves and . . ." his voice trailed off as his eyes darted to the stairs, "worse," he finally offered.

Caelyn's hand shot up to her mouth. "But why, baby, why? Why us? Why here?"

He didn't want to answer as he eased onto the nearest chair. His eyes were red-rimmed with exhaustion, his shoulders drooping, his hands resting on his lap. "It's getting crazy out there, Caelyn. Groups of thugs have come down from the cities. Other gangs have moved up from the south, most of them from across the border. They're rampaging and stealing, taking everything they can find."

"No, no!" Caelyn shot back. "That isn't why they were

here last night. This wasn't about food or money. They knew what they were doing. *They had to be watching the house!* They knew where Ellie slept! They knew they could get into her bedroom from the roof. This had to be planned out. The voices in the dark, designed to lure us out. Someone had to be on the roof even when we ran across the backyard. Don't try to sugarcoat this for me, honey; I'm strong enough to take it, but I want to know what we're up against!"

Bono closed his eyes and leaned his head back. She studied him carefully, noting the creased lines around his eyes, the heavy hands and heavy voice. He was frightened, she could see that, and she realized that she'd never seen him scared before.

She knelt beside the chair and grabbed his hand. "Tell me what we're up against," she asked again as she held desperately onto his dirty fingers.

"All the demons and evil of the world," he finally whispered as he stared blankly down at her.

chapter nineteen

Y ou're not going to leave me here, baby. No way you're going to leave me and Ellie here all by ourselves."

They were sitting opposite each other at the kitchen table. Greta was down the hall, in the living room with Ellie. The old man was on the porch, staring at a blank television screen and cursing the fact he couldn't watch his Yankees or Padres, as if anyone was playing baseball anymore. The house was quiet and Bono knew that Greta was listening, so he kept his voice low. There was tension in the air, palpable and edgy. Bono felt as if he were suffocating. He actually had to work to breathe. His expression was crestfallen, confusion clouding his eyes. Caelyn was just as emotional, her face tight, her lips pressed, her hands moving constantly. "You *can't* leave us here," she whispered, her eyes unflinching. No more pleading. No more asking. She was demanding, and in this matter she would get what she needed, no matter what the cost. "We can't take care of ourselves, you can see that. Look at what happened last night. Can you even imagine if it had been just me and Mom? They would have taken Ellie! Someone would have been hurt,

136

maybe one of them, maybe one of us, it doesn't matter—someone would have been hurt or killed."

Bono shook his head but didn't answer, thinking for a long moment. "What do you want me to do, Caelyn? What *can* I do?"

"I want you to stay here. I want you to act like every other father, like every other husband, like every other man!"

The words cut him and he sucked another breath, his heart racing with uncertainty and frustration. Caught in the middle of two impossible choices, two mutually exclusive paths, he felt like he was being split in two, cut through the middle with a jagged knife. He couldn't desert the army. For one thing, they would come and find him and arrest him. A run-of-the-mill officer who worked in admin or supply or logistics or something deep within the bowels of the machine might get away with it . . . maybe, with all the chaos that was going on. But not a Special Forces soldier, especially a member of the Cherokees. He was a national asset. They would come looking for him. Far more important, he couldn't shame his honor or his brothers. To even think about it cut his heart out, making him feel dirty and ashamed.

Yet he couldn't desert his family, either. He couldn't leave them here, not in the situation they were in.

The knife cut. He felt the tendons stretching. He was being ripped in two.

And though his emotions welled inside him, he wasn't angry at Caelyn. Quite the opposite. He knew that she was right—or at least that she had the right to be demanding. All she was concerned about was the safety of their child. And a mother's instinct for protection was not to be ignored. No, he didn't want to argue with her. He *couldn't* argue with her. There was just nothing for him to say.

Caelyn leaned toward him, resting her arms on the table.

Her eyes were softer now, but her face was just as determined. "This isn't going to work, babe, not the way things are. You understand me; it isn't going to work to leave us here all by ourselves. A month ago, a year ago, hey, a *week* ago, you could have left us and we'd have been okay." Her eyes glanced toward the back door and the darkness. "But not now, not with the way things are going. Mom and Dad will be okay, I think people are going to leave them be, but not us, not me and Ellie."

She sat back and fell silent, her heart sinking as she considered what her husband had told her about the things he'd seen the night before. And he hadn't told her everything; that too was very clear. He didn't want to tell her—and frankly, she didn't want to hear. All she knew was that he had come back more frightened and discouraged than she'd ever seen him. In her innocent mind, she couldn't imagine what he might have learned, but the fact that someone had come after Ellie told her everything she needed to know.

She watched her husband, thought a moment, then looked away. Sitting there, she realized something about herself she hadn't considered before.

Ever since the afternoon out in the straw field, she hadn't been quite the same. She thought differently. She felt different. She was different in almost every way.

She didn't trust the world. Skittish and withdrawn now, she never felt relaxed. Worst of all, she lived in mortal fear for Ellie, crushed by the burden of trying to protect her from all the evil and blackness in the world. She was a mother and her defensive instincts had kicked into hyper gear. But in order to protect her daughter, she had to take care of herself, which was nearly impossible right now.

She shook her head in frustration.

She needed her husband's help.

A cup of warm water sat on the table, and she pressed it to her lips to hide the grim tightness of her mouth.

It was demoralizing and insulting to think about, but the truth was that they had slipped back to her great-great-grandmother's world, back to a time when it was virtually impossible for a woman alone to take care of herself.

From the beginning of recorded time, from the very first caveman (if there even was such a thing) through the ancient peoples who built the first cities along the Euphrates, from the Egyptians to the Hebrews, from the Assyrians to the ancient Greeks, from these very beginnings all the way down to medieval Europe and the frontiers of the American West, a woman wasn't anything without a man. She wasn't listened to, she wasn't considered, she wasn't a person, not in any real sense. In a world where food and shelter and safety and protection were the only concerns, where the luxury of a full stomach and a safe place to sleep were never taken for granted, where there was always some army or king or thick-necked thief threatening to take it all away, a woman always found herself in need of the protective custody of a man. The more beautiful the woman, the more that this was true. And as much as she hated the feeling of dependence, she knew that it was as true now as it had ever been. She needed her husband's muscles and defensive skills. She needed his ability to navigate through a brutal world.

She sat there, angry and confused, her emotions boiling over in a way she couldn't understand.

But why was she so angry?

She really didn't know.

Why was all her fury directed at the only man she'd ever loved?

Again, she didn't know.

*   *   *

Though she couldn't understand what she was feeling, the dark angel who stood beside her understood it very well. His powerful whisperings were the source of her anger, and he was concentrating on her spirit with all of his dark and forceful might.

This was the last chance he had to get her, his best chance to take her down.

What he was doing wasn't original—he was a faithful servant but not creative or innovative—and the things he whispered to her now had been taught him long before.

Incite her rage and anger. Confuse her. Convince her she is alone. Get her to blame the one who loves her, the one who would sacrifice his very life to save her. Get her to turn her anger on him and her soul will rebel, pushing her further from her loved ones. Then she'll feel forgotten and abandoned and the cycle will start again.

These were the emotions that could kill the love between them. And if the adversary could destroy the trust between them, it would leave them with nothing else.

So far, with these young mortals, it had proven difficult. But the dark angel was persistent, for he truly loved the evil plan.

*   *   *

Caelyn looked at her husband intently, fighting the inexplicable emotions that were boiling now inside her. "I understand your position, honey, but you've got to think about your family now," she said. "Me and Ellie . . ." her eyes wandered to the hall. "It's impossible for us now and it's only going to get worse. And think about this, baby. I'm the last person in the world to complain. I've been independent all my life, you know that—you know me. I've never, from day one, complained about the time you've had to be away, about the way you've had to leave us for months at a time, not knowing where you were, what you were doing, when you'd be back home. I've never said a word. But this is different. Surely you can see that. I can't take care of Ellie. We won't survive a week here by ourselves."

Bono lifted his face to look at her but there was nothing he could say.

"We've got to do something," she continued. "We've got to come up with another plan. There's got to be someplace you can take us, someplace where the army can protect us. I mean, is that asking too much? If the army demands that you leave us, don't they have a responsibility to take care of the family members you leave behind?"

Bono breathed again, grasping for her hand, but she pulled back. "We've got to think of something. If we stay here, I don't know, I have the worst feeling. Things *will not* be all right. I don't know what's going to happen, but it will not be good."

Bono sat back against the chair. "We'll figure something out," was all he offered.

Caelyn watched him, forcing herself to calm down. Finally she reached across the table and grabbed his hand. "I love you, babe. I always have. I always will. I love you more than anything and I'm so proud of the man you are. I understand your position. I know you can't stay here, but we've got to think of something. And we've only got a couple of days."

chapter twenty

OFFUTT AIR FORCE BASE
HEADQUARTERS, U.S. STRATEGIC COMMAND
EIGHT MILES SOUTH OF OMAHA, NEBRASKA

The day and night passed slowly. The family was told to remain in the small office, able to leave only for showers in the gym and to eat. After some begging and ordering and finally some fairly believable threats, Sam convinced the old tech sergeant who had been assigned to look after them to let him use the gym. He spent the next three hours running, boxing on the shadow bag, and lifting weights. Sweating and completely exhausted, he showered and fell asleep.

The next morning he was as agitated as he'd ever been. This time, he wasn't alone. Sara paced as well. Luke and Ammon watched them, leaning against the far wall. Azadeh sat on the rolled-out sleeping bags, reading to work on her English skills.

"Unbelievable," Ammon muttered as he watched his brother pace.

Sam shook his head, thinking on the broadcast they'd watched the previous day. "How do you describe it?" Sam asked in an incredulous voice. "Swearing him in and then impeaching him, all in the same day!"

Sara kept on pacing. "It looks that way," she said.

"How stupid," Luke muttered. "It seems like—"

Sara cut him off. "No, it wasn't stupid. It was brilliant. I mean, think of this. They found out Secretary Marino was out here. With him holed up here at Offutt, there was no way to get him short of a military attack upon the base. Were they willing to risk that? Clearly not. Would they be able to assassinate him like the others? Highly unlikely. Brucius isn't stupid. His security forces can take care of him. And this was better anyway, much better. By swearing him in and then impeaching him, they utterly removed him as a threat. Fuentes is the president. Legally, Brucius is completely powerless. There is nothing he can do."

"But why? Why would the Congress do that?" Luke asked. He kept his face down, a little bit embarrassed that he didn't understand. He'd spent too many weekends climbing rocks, too many nights texting all his buddies, too much time chasing the babes whose pictures used to fill his cell phone, too much of all of that to pay attention to the things that mattered. His father had tried to warn him, tried to get him to take life a little bit more seriously, but he had always figured he would have time to grow up later on. "I don't see what we can do now," he finished. "I don't think there's anything . . . I mean, I don't see how we're going to win."

Sara stared at him. "I still don't think it's hopeless," she said. "We're not fighting the whole world, Luke. I don't think there are a lot of them. It's a tiny group, maybe no more than a handful of people. And I don't believe they've been plotting this for very long. They have been waiting, men of like mind, but I don't think they've been plotting, not actively, anyway. I think they've been watching for the opportunity, and when the attack took place, they took action, knowing the time to strike was now." She kept pacing as she talked, turning toward him now. "No, I don't think we're facing more than a handful of men. But they're powerful. Very powerful. And growing more and more so.

"It's going to take a miracle to stop them."

She smiled, trying to look hopeful. But her eyes showed how she really felt.

Sam watched his mother, then clenched his jaw. "You want to know what I think?" he asked.

They turned to him and waited.

"I think God showed us a couple of miracles. For that, I think we're all grateful. But I think it's time to create some of our own miracles now."

Sara looked closely at him.

By the end of the day, she would know that it was true.

chapter twenty-one

OFFUTT AIR FORCE BASE
HEADQUARTERS, U.S. STRATEGIC COMMAND
EIGHT MILES SOUTH OF OMAHA, NEBRASKA

The soldier came for Sara and Sam. It was late at night, but none of the family was asleep. Instead, they lay awake inside the tiny office they'd been mostly confined to since they'd been rescued from the rooftop in East Chicago, talking quietly in the total darkness about the future that looked so bleak. The army colonel opened the door, the thin beam of his penlight intruding in the night. "Lieutenant Brighton," he said.

Sam sat up on his sleeping bag and looked at him.

The colonel shifted his eyes, looking for the women. "Mrs. Brighton?" he asked gently.

Sara was sitting with her back against the wall, her knees pulled up, her arms around her legs. "Yes," she answered simply.

The colonel moved into the room, his light flashing a narrow beam of white that illuminated his outline as a shadow behind it. "Will you please come with me?"

Sara stood up. Sam stood up beside her. "Where are we going?" he asked.

"Secretary Marino needs to see you."

Sara looked down at her other sons. "What about them?"

The colonel moved the thin beam of light. "Guys, if you'll just stay here?" He said it like it was a question, but it was clearly a statement. Luke and Ammon nodded at him. "Okay, sir," they said.

The beam of light moved again. Azadeh had been sitting next to Sara. She remained on the floor, her eyes down. The colonel stared at her a long moment, started to say something then seemed to change his mind. Turning, he motioned to Sam and Sara while glancing at his watch impatiently. "Please hurry," he urged them, his voice on edge. "The Secretary is waiting. Believe me, guys, the dirt or whatever is flying out there has hit the fan."

Sam took his mother by the arm. "Come on," he said.

Sara glanced down at Ammon and Luke again, patted Azadeh on the shoulder, and followed the officer to the door.

They walked down the hall. Sara caught a look at Sam as he moved. He looked both relieved and excited.

This was what he'd been waiting for.

*　　*　　*

Sam and Sara followed the colonel into the Operations Center (OC). It was a large room stuffed with computers, video screens, telephones, encryption equipment, and open workstations. The lighting was dim and a red DEFCON ALPHA sign was illuminated in the front corner. The floor sloped gently downward and rows of theater chairs lined both sides of the central aisle. A large projection screen and elevated stage took up most of the front wall, with multiple smaller monitors on both sides of the main screen. The SecDef, Brucius Theodore Marino, was talking with some military aides at the front of the room. Half a dozen officers waited in the chairs, a few civilians scattered among them.

The colonel led Sam and Sara through the metal doors at the back of the room, gestured to the SecDef, then disappeared. The two of them waited, looking around anxiously. Time passed and no one spoke to them. Brucius continued huddling with his aides, his face tense. Ten minutes passed. Finally a young lieutenant colonel broke away from Brucius, came to the back of the room, asked them to follow, escorted them to the front row, and invited them to sit down. Brucius caught Sara's eye as she moved forward and nodded at her.

A three-star general moved to Marino's side. "We're ready, sir," he whispered at his ear.

Brucius immediately stopped talking to the officers and turned around. "Okay," he said. He turned and walked toward Sara, leaned over, and kissed her cheek. "Sara, are you okay?"

She nodded quickly.

Brucius gave Sam a quick look then turned back to Sara. "Your other sons, that Iranian girl, they're doing all right?"

"They're fine, Brucius. A little cabin fever, maybe. A little . . . I don't know, nervous, but doing fine."

"Okay. Good."

Sam kept his eyes on the Secretary as the man interacted with his mom. Brucius was trying to show concern, but Sam could tell his heart wasn't in it. His mind was far away, the creases on his forehead deep and furrowed. "Let me show you what we have here," he finally said.

The Secretary nodded to the control console at the back of the OC. The room grew darker and the large screen on the front wall flickered with a grainy light.

Every eye turned toward it. A broken image filled the screen. It jumped and halted, then came back in a grainy black-and-white video. As they watched, the army general started to explain. "This is from a micro-drone we were able to get into Raven Rock a few days ago."

Sam nodded in amazement. He'd never worked with the micro-drones, never even seen any of their intelligence products, but he'd heard the Black Box guys were close to pushing some of the early models out of testing and into the field.

The general saw Sara's puzzled look and gave a brief explanation. "A micro-drone is a tiny, robotic, remotely controlled, fly-like reconnaissance machine. Some of them, like the one we were able to slip inside Raven Rock, are no larger than an insect. Amazingly effective, very difficult to identify or locate, their only drawback is a very short life span. Issues with expanding their battery capabilities are still being worked—"

"How did you get one into Raven Rock?" Sara interrupted. The look on her face indicated she already knew.

The general hesitated.

"James snuck it in for us," he told her.

Sara nodded. "All that stuff we heard, then, the statement he made on the television broadcast?"

"Clearly he was drugged or operating under duress."

"Have you heard from him since he got into Raven? Do you know—"

"Please, Mrs. Brighton," the general interrupted. "We are really tight on time right now."

Sara glared at him, then turned to Brucius. "Is he okay?" she demanded.

The Secretary looked strained. "We don't know."

She sat back, her face determined.

Brucius watched her, then offered the only thing he had. "We're trying to get in touch with him." He wished he had a better answer. It was important. It would matter a great deal when she found out what he needed her to do.

"Do you have allies in Raven Rock who can help you?"

"No, Sara, we don't."

She nodded grimly. "Okay, go on."

Brucius waited a second, then continued. "Not only was James able to get the drone into the presidential working area, we actually got it in position to monitor their critical meeting. Because of this, we learned much more than we ever could have hoped for." He stopped and eyed her carefully. "If you believe in God or heaven, and I know you do, then He must be on our side here. Getting the drone inside the presidential conference room was, to say the least, fortuitous. Getting it there when we did was nothing short of a miracle. If you're praying or counting sacred beads or whatever you Mormons do, keep doing it, please, for it has been enormously helpful, as you're about to see."

The general stepped forward, motioning toward the image on the screen, which was frozen on pause. "We're going to show you selected video from inside of Raven Rock; then we'll answer your questions," he explained. He nodded and the video started playing. The grainy image showed the inside of a conference room, a dozen men around a large table, more standing at the wall. Fuentes was standing in front of the conference table, an old man at his side. At first there was no sound; then the audio started coming through. Sara watched carefully as the other men around the table came into view. Some of them she recognized. Most she didn't know.

When she saw King Abdullah standing by the old man, she sucked a breath and frowned.

* * *

Two hours later, Marino summed it up for them. "Okay, so this is what we know.

"First, they're going after Israel. We don't know when or how, but they're going to destroy it, that much is very clear. That by itself would be reason enough to stop them—but, as you've seen, there is much more.

149

"They've also set up agreements to carve the world into spheres of influence, allocating who and what among themselves. Abdullah will control the Muslim world. Europe will be split among the others. Fuentes and his buddies will keep the Americas, a couple of goons we've never heard of having their way in Mexico and South America; Xian Cheng is left with China. I could go on, but I think you know. Bottom line—we're going to end up with half a dozen men controlling the entire world. They have military agreements between them that say, in essence, *'Hands off! What I do in my sphere is none of anybody's business. Stay out of my affairs.'* Through these military noncompete agreements, they're essentially promising never to intervene militarily outside of their own spheres. Suffice it to say, I don't think anyone's going to be filing any human rights violations against any of the others. They'll reign with blood and money. What else is there in their world?

"China has promised to provide nuclear expertise, technology, and hardware to Middle Eastern countries, making them impervious to attack. Once that is done, who would dare to go after them when they can destroy the world in retaliation? Give him a year and King Abdullah will have consolidated the entire Muslim world into a caliphate that controls 83 percent of the world's oil fields."

Brucius stopped. They'd seen the video. They'd heard the leaders talking. Everything he had just told them, they already knew.

He started pacing before the stage, his face intent. Stopping in front of Sara, he looked into her eyes. "I need your help to stop them." He shifted his eyes to Sam. "I need you both."

Sara started to answer but Brucius cut her off. "Before you say anything, I want to be very clear. I have to know you *really* understand. I've been sworn in and impeached. I am *not* the president. I'm not even Secretary of Defense any longer." He gestured to the men in the room around him. "Everyone you see here, everyone who is helping me right now, is guilty of treason. All of us could be tried and hung. Do you understand that! Is that clear? As of twenty hours ago, everything I've done here is illegal. I can't call upon military units to support me, not any longer." He knelt down before Sara and lowered his voice. "All of the power lies within the walls of Raven Rock. A few men, those you have been watching on the video here, control everything right now. To them, we are nothing but a group of power-hungry rebels who have to be crushed. I need to know that you appreciate what is happening, what you are getting yourselves into."

Sara shot a look to Sam. He nodded back at her. "We understand," she said.

Brucius's shoulders seemed to relax. "Let me say it a final time. Neither of you is bound to help me. I don't have authority to ask anything of you. And you'll be taking an enormous risk. The painful truth is, in private moments, I realize we're almost certainly doomed to fail. If that happens, it could mean death or at least prison."

He waited, giving them time to think.

Sara leaned forward. "How long have you known me?" she asked, her voice so determined it sounded almost hard. "How long did you know my husband? Is there anything about us, anything from all those years of experience, that would lead you to believe I wouldn't do anything you asked me? If not for you, then for my country, which is what you represent right now. Our entire future, the presidency, our government, the Constitution, all of it is hanging by a thread. I'm not so naïve or foolish that I can't see that. I'll do whatever it takes to help you."

Brucius watched her carefully.

151

"Now quit apologizing and tell me what you need," Sara concluded.

Brucius took a deep breath and shook his head in a gesture of appreciation that bordered on disbelief. Shifting his weight, he turned to Sam. "You understand I have no authority to give you any orders. I'm no longer the SecDef. I have no right—"

"I understand," Sam shot back. "Come on, sir. Let's get the party rolling."

"But how, Brucius?" Sara demanded. "How can we possibly help you? What can either of us do?"

He glanced at the floor a moment, steeling himself, then lifted his eyes to look at Sara. "I'm going to send you into Raven Rock."

She stared at him dumbfounded and shook her head. "No, Brucius, no. Look what happened to Davies. The same thing . . . the same thing is going to happen to me."

He leaned into her intently, his hand upon the arm of her chair, his jaw square. "Daniel Jefferson is down there. If you can get to him and bring him out, we can turn this thing around."

Sara almost shuddered, the fear growing deeper in her eyes. Daniel Jefferson. The last surviving member of the Supreme Court.

Brucius looked up at the nearest aide, who gave him a quiet nod. "There may be other options, but we can't count on them," he told her. "Until we know for certain, we have to assume that what they told the nation was true. Jefferson is the only living member of the Supreme Court. But he knows you, Sara. He knew your husband. If you can get to him, he'll listen to you. He had no idea what was going on out here. You're going to go in and tell him and you're going to bring him out."

Sara didn't answer, her shoulders sagging as she closed her eyes.

Brucius turned to Sam. "And you, soldier. We have to stop King Abdullah. He'll never rest until Israel is a heap of rubble. And his attacks upon our country cannot go unanswered. The future demands that we do something. But we have only two options: retaliation or justice. Those are the only two paths we have. Retaliation doesn't help us. Justice is what we seek.

"Even as we speak, the king of Saudi Arabia is on his way to Iran, into the Zagros mountains, to find and kill the only person in the world who has a claim upon his crown. You're going to meet him there. You're going to find him. You're going to bring him back here, where he'll stand trial for what he's done."

He paused and stood back, his eyes intent. Much of the power was gone out of his posture now and he looked weaker, less confident, more needing and unsure. "This is the only chance we have," he almost pleaded.

Sam stood up and squared his shoulders. "Cool. This is going to be a good one. But I'm going to need some help."

"You name it and you've got it."

"I want to choose my team." Sam stopped, thinking quickly as he looked off. "And we're going to need a decoy. Someone who can get us to the king."

The Secretary was ahead of him. "We've thought of that," he said.

Sam almost shuddered, reading the look in the Secretary's eyes.

Brucius saw that Sam understood what he was thinking. "She's here. She's trustworthy, at least as far as we can tell. And the truth is, we couldn't find a better candidate if we looked through the entire Department of Defense. We've known that since she got here, the answer obvious the first time she followed you through the door. She has knowledge of the area, she knows the language, she is familiar with the local customs. She's a tactical asset we would be stupid to ignore."

Sam shook his head. "It's just not fair to ask her."

"Is anything fair right now?"

Sara looked up, her eyes now angry. She guessed what they were thinking and it made her furious that they would even consider it. "You can't do that!" she cried in protective desperation. "Azadeh is innocent. She didn't ask for this."

Sam studied his mother, then turned away.

No, she hadn't asked for this. And no, it wasn't fair. But fairness didn't seem to be the priority anymore.

chapter twenty-two

M iss Pahlavi?" The deep voice emerged from the dark.
Azadeh stood and nodded slowly, dazed with
sleep.

The colonel had worked his way silently into the room, using a small flashlight with a lens attached to dim the light. He looked her up and down, then nodded to the open door. "Will you please come with me?"

Azadeh glanced fearfully toward Ammon and Luke, who had stood up beside her.

"It's okay, Miss Pahlavi," the colonel attempted to assure her. But his voice was so brisk, it did little good.

Azadeh didn't move, her eyes wide, her hands shaking. She was acting out of instinct now, a lifetime of fear and paranoia kicking in. For eighteen years she'd been trained to be terrified of strangers, to say nothing of men, government officers, the West, Christians, Americans, but most especially soldiers. All of those fears had been rolled into one package that was staring at her right now while commanding her to come with him. Her instincts for survival rose, and she backed against the wall.

The colonel turned and illuminated the way, shining the

155

light back toward the door. He started walking. "Come quickly," he commanded.

Azadeh looked from Luke to Ammon, not knowing what to do. "Why do they want me?" Her voice was pleading.

Ammon turned toward her. "I don't know. I think you should go with him, though."

"They're going to send me back. I didn't do anything wrong. I didn't have anything to do with—"

"No, no," Ammon assured her. "Don't worry about that, Azadeh. It has nothing to do with any of that. They're not going to send you back. They're not going to hurt you. I promise you, they're not going to do you any harm."

"They are. I know it. I have seen it so many times before."

"No, Azadeh . . ."

"Why else would they want me!" Her voice was rising. She sounded weak and terrified. She stared desperately at the brothers. *Please! Can't you help me!* her eyes said.

Ammon moved quickly to her, holding her shoulders in his hands. He looked directly into her eyes, gripping her tightly. "No one's going to hurt you. I swear to you, it'll be all right."

Her eyes shot wildly around the room, as if looking for a way to escape.

"Go with him, Azadeh. He's an American officer. He's not going to hurt you. I promise, it will be okay."

Azadeh looked at him, then nodded slowly, her eyes still racing.

Then, because she didn't have any choice, she trusted him enough to take a breath and follow the colonel out the door.

chapter twenty-three

The H-60 Blackhawk army helicopter was large, black, lean, and low. Everything about it screamed serious combat aircraft. The two GE T700 turboshaft engines, each putting out more than 1600 horses, and four composite titanium rotors could lift a fully equipped infantry squad and transport it at almost 200 mph. Its protective armor was able to withstand hits from 23mm shells, and with its two door-mounted M60D 7.62mm machine guns and M144 armament subsystem designed to disperse chaff and infrared jamming, it could give as well as it could take.

Standing on the tarmac near the helicopter's rear cabin, Sam could see that both the door guns were mounted and manned, their metal ammo containers full and ready. He looked forward, nodded to the crew, then slid the combat gear off his back and dropped it on the metal floor. "Ready when you are, sir," the pilot called from the left seat. The chopper's engines weren't running yet, but it was cocked and ready, only waiting for his word. Sam nodded to the chief warrant officer and pulled his leather gloves on. Someone behind him called his name and he turned. Secretary Brucius Marino was walking toward him. He hadn't heard the staff cars pull up. His face and body grew tense and he stood ramrod straight. "Sir." He saluted briskly.

"A word with you, Lieutenant."

"Sir."

Brucius took Sam's arm, leading him away from the chopper. As they walked, Sam looked around. The army chopper was sitting on the hammerhead at the end of the runway at Offutt Air Force Base. The main runway stretched northwest for almost two miles. Lines of military aircraft, parked in rows of four, and a string of enormous hangars lined the runway, the largest of the hangars sitting midfield. Two black SUVs had pulled up beside the chopper. Half a dozen civilian guards stood their posts. Behind them, another dozen military security police moved around. Halfway down the taxiway, two camouflaged HUMVEEs with .50 caliber machine guns and automatic grenade launchers waited. Glancing up and down the runway, Sam knew there had to be snipers watching. One of them, he guessed, had a bead on him right now, keeping his high-powered military sight on Sam's heart while others kept watch over the long expanse of runway as well as the cavernous hangars and long, brown grass on the other side of the runway. It frightened him, seeing the impenetrable wall of security that surrounded the Secretary now. These were more than just precautions. These were guys who expected a fight. Turning from the runway, he looked at the Secretary. He wore a dark suit and, looking closely, Sam could see the narrow outline of a holstered weapon tucked at his left side.

The soldier in him smiled. If it came to an open battle, the men in Raven Rock were going to get a fight. Good for Brucius. He liked a man who wasn't afraid to go down shooting.

The Secretary kept his arm across Sam's shoulder as they walked. When he started to talk, he spoke with urgency. He didn't have much time. "Do you understand your mission?" he asked.

"Yes, sir."

Brucius stopped and turned to him. "I'm not sure you do."

Sam waited.

"No offense, Lieutenant Brighton, but I'm just not sure you do. Not yet. Not completely. And I've thought about this, wondering how much I should tell you, wondering if it helps or hurts to put the pressure on, but I think it's only fair for you to know. Hard to feel any more pressure than you already feel, I suppose, and I just think it's important for a man to know what he's up against before he walks into a fight." A military aircraft suddenly flew overhead and they both glanced up as the F-22 fighter circled to land after providing CAP (Combat Air Patrol). They didn't speak for a moment as the gray fighter flew parallel to the runway, opposite the direction from which the pilot intended to land, then broke hard to the left, dropped its gear, descended while turning sharply, and lined up for the runway, its nose high now, its speed brake extending for half a second to slow it down, its dark canopy muting any light flashes from the sun. One of the HUMVEES turned to face it, its gunner keeping the fighter in sight.

The sound faded quickly as the pilot pulled his engines back to idle and the Secretary turned to Lieutenant Brighton again. "I don't think it's excessively dramatic or even an overstatement to say that, in many ways, the future of our world depends on what you and your team do now," he said.

Sam kept his mouth shut, the creases on his forehead furrowing deeper with concentration.

"Sometime soon, if your mother is successful—and we both pray she will be—I hope to be sworn in as president of the United States. Once that happens—if that happens—do you have any idea the pressure I will come under to retaliate against King Abdullah for the EMP attack? I've got a dozen generals and a couple of dozen civilian advisers who are begging me to do it now, take whatever resources I can muster and launch a counterattack. Of course I can't do that for several reasons, the most important of them being that I am not the president. But if that time comes, the pressure to retaliate will increase manyfold. And how can I blame them? It's exactly what I want to do as well. More, it's been the strategic doctrine of our country for more than eighty years that we would retaliate if we ever suffered from a nuclear hit. Same thing for the EMP attack, which, you can see, has proven much more deadly and difficult to survive than a simple nuclear strike. They got us. They *almost* have us. We know that King Abdullah funded, coordinated, and ordered both attacks. It's going to be enormously difficult for me not to order retaliation once I become the president."

A cool wind blew across the open runway and Brucius sucked in a breath of air.

"The only problem with the doctrine of retaliation is if you happen to be one of the fifty million innocent Arabs who are going to die. They didn't choose their king. They certainly don't control him. They have no more say in their national leadership or foreign policy than the poor old goatherds did over the most powerful caliphs a thousand years ago. It just seems, I don't know, a little bit ineffective to order the death of fifty million innocent civilians. And a conventional attack is not an option, not right now, not with virtually all of our military forces required here at home—not to mention the lack of blood and treasure to fund such a massive land attack. But we have to do *something*. We can't walk away from this fight, our tail between our legs.

"And let's say I did order retaliation. Let's consider the

implications for future relationships between the Middle East and the West. It would take a dozen generations to get beyond this. In fact, I don't think we ever would. I think that hundreds of years from now, such an action would still define our two worlds. I believe such a retaliatory strike would create the death match between our cultures, leading to both of our downfalls.

"But we know something about King Abdullah and his intentions that is proving incredibly valuable. We know where he's going. We know when he'll be there. Fool of fools, outside his own nation he's going to be vulnerable. So desperate is he to kill the only son left living from his brother, he takes an enormous risk.

"We have this one chance. If you can get him, if you can locate and extricate King Abdullah, then we can punish him. Justice will be served. We could stop the final world war. I know that sounds like something out of a poorly written movie, but it really is the case: Find him. We will try him and hang him. Don't, and we'll have to retaliate."

Sam felt his stomach muscles tighten, and he was already feeling sick. His mouth was so dry he didn't know if he could talk. "I understand, sir," he answered simply. "We'll do the best we can."

"Remember this, it is important: As long as the boy is alive, Abdullah has no legitimate claim upon the kingdom. Protect the boy and he will be king. But let Abdullah kill him, and it's over. We have no chance for a legitimate or friendly government in Saudi. Worse, let Abdullah slip away, and we lose the only chance we have of averting a potentially world-ending war."

Sam stared ahead and swallowed.

Marino eyed him carefully. "You have a good team?" he asked.

"The best, sir."

He watched the young soldier. "I hope so. We need the best right now."

Sam waited, expecting to be dismissed.

"A couple of other things you might want to consider," Marino told him as the cold air blew his suit jacket, pressing it tight against his waist, exposing the outline of his gun. "We have to demonstrate to the rest of the world that, despite some of their great hopes and deep-seated desires, the United States hasn't been rendered completely helpless. We have to demonstrate that we're not neutered, that we have the will to fight. We're not going to turn in on ourselves and abrogate our responsibilities to the world. We have to show that we are capable of and, much more importantly, still willing to mount a military operation in order to protect ourselves, that we are not a broken nation, that we can get up from our knees. Do you understand that, Lieutenant Brighton? I know I'm asking you to think much larger; I'm asking you to think on a much more strategic level than a junior officer is expected to have to think. This is political. This is perception. But many times, *most* times in geopolitical situations, perception is far more important than the reality. And that's what we're dealing with here."

Sam nodded. The band of black-coated personal body-guards drew nearer, hating the fact their charge was exposing himself like this, out in the open, unmoving, not under any cover. Might as well stand in the middle of the runway with a target on his coat. They moved closer, gathering in a loose circle, all of them facing out. Marino looked at them, then turned back. "One more thing," he said, biting his lower lip. "And this is perhaps the most important thing that I can tell you. If I'm sworn in as president, once we start to rebuild and resecure our nation, do you think King Abdullah is going to stand by? Do you think he came this far to watch us build again? He knows that once we set our minds to it, once we dedicate the people and the resources, we'll be back in the fight. It won't even take us very long, once his allies in the government have been destroyed. That being the case, do you really think he'll let us? Or will he attack again?"

Sam's eyes opened wider. He had thought that it was over, that the worst of it had passed. It had never really occurred to him that the battle would continue or that King Abdullah might attack again.

Marino watched his face and read his mind. "He's prepared. He has other weapons. Biological agents. The most dreaded diseases. If he uses them, it'll make the plagues of Egypt look like a weekend cold. He's got at least another twenty nuclear warheads, we know that. He's got . . ." The Secretary stopped. No sense going on.

The two men stood in silence for a long moment. The cold wind cut through Sam's military jacket, sending a shiver up his spine.

"We have to stop him," Marino muttered almost to himself.

Sam waited. The Secretary didn't speak again. "Yes, sir," he finally said.

Marino took a final breath, then placed his hand on the young man's shoulder. The beefy flesh was strong and heavy. "No pressure, okay?" He cracked a smile.

Sam smiled back. "Not feeling any, sir."

"It's only the entire freaking future of the entire freaking world, that's all that's on your shoulders. Ain't no big thing." He smiled again, but his eyes were serious.

Sam brushed a piece of blowing sand out of the corner of his mouth.

"Just wanted you to know what you were fighting for."

"I appreciate that, sir."

The Secretary slapped him on the shoulder. "I know how good you guys are." His eyes were smiling now, his face brightening with sudden confidence. "I know how incredibly difficult the process of being selected for the Cherokee program is. You guys have been culled and strapped and trained to an infinite degree. You're the best warfighters in the world. I think you're probably the best warfighters the world has *ever* seen. There is no one like you, and frankly, Lieutenant Brighton, this is exactly the kind of thing the Cherokees were created for. Now go. Do this mission. I'll see you in a couple of days."

The Secretary turned and nodded to his people. One of the black SUVs roared to life and sped across the tarmac to pick him up, saving the short walk.

Sam watched the Secretary climb inside, then turned to the waiting helicopter and started running as the low whine of the electric motors began to spin the jet turbine engines up.

Three minutes later, he was in the air.

chapter twenty-four

He lay with his eyes open, listening to Caelyn breathing, wanting to reach out and touch her but not wanting to wake her up. Through the bedroom window, the stars formed a huge, bright saucer that stretched from one end of the horizon to the other, a hundred million points of light. The moon had waned to hardly more than a sliver on the southwestern horizon, but there was just enough light to allow him to see as he slipped out of bed and moved quietly toward the bedroom door.

The first thing he wanted was to get clean. After years in the ickiest of the Ickistans, it had become an obsession, and he was always aware of dangers of bacteria and disease now. The old farm was blessed with several springs that had been used to water the small herd of cattle, and over the past couple of days his father-in-law had rigged a holding tank, curtain, and showerhead in some trees out past the hay field. He grabbed a towel and slipped down the stairs, out the back door, and across the porch, where he stopped and took a deep breath, drawing the cold air into his lungs. Soon it would be morning and it was chilly, maybe only 40 degrees, but dry and clear. As

165

he sniffed, he smelled smoke, its acidic fragrance tinging the air. Campfires. The people from the cities were getting closer. Hordes of them, some of them camped together, some of them trying to make it on their own, some in families, some with others, some forming larger groups with guns, some with money trying to buy their way with paper bills nobody valued anymore. They had abandoned the cities and were moving through the country now, searching for food and water.

What would a good man do to save his children once he realized they were going to starve to death? What would a mother do to help her infant while holding her baby's weakening body in her arms? He sniffed the smoky air and wondered, then headed across the grass.

The water from the spring was ice-cold but invigorating, sending the adrenaline surging through his blood. He lathered up, rubbing the cake of soap against his body, rinsed in the icy water, sputtered from the cold, then lathered and rinsed again. Feeling better, he dressed in his military fatigues and headed back to the house.

The sun was just breaking across the horizon when he got back, the eastern sky having turned from deep purple to pink. He'd already positioned his gear on the back porch; now he pulled his heavy pack over to him and sat down on the steps. Opening the pack, he extracted its contents and laid the equipment out to check and organize it. He started with the clothes: two sets of camouflage fatigues; a heavy jacket; thick socks, reinforced in the toes and heels; three sets of gloves, one insulated, one heavy leather, one a pair of fire-resistant Nomex that an air force pilot had traded him for a set of Iraqi playing cards; a rain poncho; a knit hat that covered his ears; another with a hood that snapped onto his military jacket. The clothes were clean, having been thoroughly hand-washed the day before. He folded them carefully, then rolled them into tight bundles and packed them into the zippered compartments on both sides of the pack. His leather boots were drying on the porch from the waterproofing he'd applied the night before. He checked them, satisfied, then pulled them on. Next he extracted his military gear: knee and elbow pads (considered by many soldiers to be the most important pieces of gear they had), a GPS receiver (with encryption to prevent the user's location from being triangulated by enemy forces), emergency satellite locator, protective eyewear, first aid kit, sunglasses, whistle, firestarter, space blanket, pencil and tiny notebook, two heavy-duty trash bags, chem sticks, wire saw, fifty feet of nylon webbing, Ensolite pad, signal mirror. On top of the pile of gear was a six-inch knife, razor-sharp, along with his own custom-built M1911 .45 pistol as well as a military-issued 9mm Glock. Already strapped to his leg was the tiny pearl-and-plastic .22 that he'd been given by a buddy in New York City the day before his first deployment to Afghanistan. The weapon wouldn't kill anything unless shot at short range, but it had great sentimental value and, like many soldiers, he was superstitious enough to believe the Saturday Night Special had become one of his good-luck charms.

Other gear would follow once he got back to his unit: an HK416 Delta-issued assault rifle, lighter and smaller than the older M-4s and M-16s, more reliable and easier to shoot, especially in close quarters. When he got in-country again, he'd pick up another AK-47, partly to blend in with the locals, but mostly to take advantage of the plentiful supply of ammunition. Before leaving his unit he would also take up his Interceptor Body Armor (IBA); a Laser Target Location System, which would provide both day and night capability to locate targets; miniature binoculars; and an Improved Spotting Scope with a tripod and a monocle lens that would attach to his helmet and fit over his right eye, allowing him to see a digital image of his own men superimposed over a satellite-powered map. The same monocle could also be attached to his weapon, allowing him, in effect, to shoot around corners without exposing himself.

It was a boatload of equipment, all in all. And though it was designed to be as light as possible, allowing the soldier to fight and move more quickly, taken together it weighed more than sixty pounds.

He had just finished checking, cleaning, and packing his combat gear when the back door opened and Caelyn looked out. He glanced over his shoulder at her, the Glock in one hand, a velvet-soft cleaning pad in the other. She looked out at him, saw the backpack and guns, then frowned and stepped onto the porch.

"You're getting ready to go?" she said.

"Not really, honey. I'm just keeping things in shape."

"No, babe, you don't have to try to hide it. You're getting ready."

"Not getting ready. Just making sure that I'll be ready. There's a difference."

If there was a difference, she didn't see it. She looked away. The sun was just above the tree line and the morning was growing warmer.

Bono slipped the gun into the backpack, knowing it made her uncomfortable. "Ellie still asleep?" he asked.

Caelyn nodded, then knelt on the wooden porch and cuddled up behind him, wrapping her arms around his chest. "You smell fine," she whispered.

He leaned back against her. "It was a little nippy, but the shower sure felt good."

She breathed, her nose pressed against his hair. "I'm going to go and take a shower too."

He turned and smiled at her. "If you wait a couple of

hours the water in the holding tank will heat up to thirty-six degrees or so."

Caelyn shivered. "That bad?"

"Wait until you feel it."

"Okay, don't come running if you hear me scream."

"I'll know you just turned the water on."

She laughed, then put her lips to his hair and pulled it gently. It was long and black and smelled like soap. "I don't know about you Special Forces guys. What do they call you now? Last I heard, it was Cherokees. Look at you, baby. Long hair. Never clean-shaven. Dark sunglasses and lots of ugly gear. If I'd wanted to marry a Hell's Angel, I would have stayed in California."

Bono lifted his jaw. "You should see me on my Hog. It makes me sexy, baby."

She laughed and pulled his hair again.

They heard it at the same time, the rotors first, then the whine of the twin jet turbine engines. It came in low, barely over the tree line, the scream of the engines beating on their ears, the massive black rotors sending miniature shockwaves that thumped against their chests. It swooped over the house, then rolled quickly onto its side while slowing, completed the 180-degree turn, and came to a hover over the grass in the backyard. Bono was already standing. Caelyn struggled to his side and grasped his arm, her other hand shielding her eyes against blowing leaves and sand. The army Blackhawk settled to the grass, the thick, black tires bouncing lightly. Then the cabin door shot open.

Caelyn gripped her husband's arm more tightly. "No, baby, no," she called above the roar of the blades and engines. "Not yet! Not now! You're supposed to have more time!"

Bono felt her fingernails digging into his arm. He kept his eyes on the chopper. The pilots didn't roll the engines back, though they'd taken the pitch out of the blades, and the sand and blowing debris weren't biting their eyes anymore. A soldier jumped out of the rear cabin and started running toward him. Bono recognized the face and long strides. Sam Brighton ran up and stopped before him.

Caelyn was panicked. She leaned toward her husband, almost falling into his arms. "No, no, not yet," she cried as she beat her fists lightly against his chest. "Not now." She put her arms around him and held him closer. "You *can't* leave me here. I don't know what I'll do. How am I going to protect Ellie? *What are we going to do!*"

The back door to the house swung open and Greta was standing there, holding her fingers in her ears. Ellie hid behind her grandma's knees, then ran out and jumped off the porch into her father's arms. He barely caught her with Caelyn holding him so tight.

Bono held his daughter while feeling Caelyn's weight as she leaned against his shoulder, her tears wet against his cheek. He stared at Sam, who took off his dark glasses to look at him.

"What are you doing here?" Bono cried.

Sam nodded to the chopper. "Something's come up."

"What something? We had two weeks."

"Not anymore."

Bono nodded to the farmhouse behind him. "I can't go now," he cried.

Sam shook his head. "Sure you can."

"No, I can't go. Not yet."

All of them knew he had to. And all of them knew he would.

Sam turned to Bono's wife. "You must be Caelyn?" he shouted above the roar of the rotors.

Caelyn pulled away from Bono and glared at Sam. She

wiped her tears away angrily and accused, "You've come to take my husband."

Sam shot a look at Bono, then extended his hand. "My name is Samuel Brighton."

"I know who you are."

Caelyn turned to Bono. "Please," was all she cried.

Bono glanced at the house again, looked at the ground, then leaned toward Sam. "I'm not going to leave them here alone," he shouted to him.

"Of course you're not going to leave them, buddy. That's one of the reasons I'm here."

Sam turned back to Caelyn. "How long will it take you to get some things together?" he cried.

She looked at him, her eyes wide with disbelief.

"You and your daughter are coming with us, Caelyn." Sam turned and motioned to the pilots, spinning his fingers slower around his head. The engines decelerated, making it easier for them to talk. Sam turned back to Bono and his family. "Let me help you grab some clothes and things. But please, we've got to hurry. We don't have much time."

chapter twenty-five

T he military helicopter was incredibly noisy and uncomfortable. It vibrated with force and energy and noise and wind, all the combined energy of the turbine engines, the four main rotors, and the smaller tail rotor at the back. The seats were nothing more than thin nylon cushions stretched over aluminum framing, and the floor was dirty steel.

Bono sat in the right corner, looking out the large Plexiglas window. Caelyn sat beside him, resting her head against his shoulder. She stared straight ahead at the cockpit where the two pilots were working, but she didn't really watch them, her mind racing. She was thinking of her parents. The army had promised to send someone to help them, and all she could do now was hope that they would. Ellie was asleep beside her, her head upon her lap, the adventure of the helicopter ride having quickly worn off. Azadeh was sitting on one of the seats facing the rear of the helicopter, her back to the pilots. Sam and a couple of other soldiers, one of them the Blackhawk crew chief, sat on the other side of the cabin. The center of the floor was taken up with the soldiers' packs and weapons, all of the gear strapped down.

The chopper was flying at 145 knots, 300 feet above the ground. The air was clear of clouds but hazy, the ground beneath them having turned brown and dead from the coming winter. Bono watched the passing terrain in wonder. Every road they crossed was lined with dead cars and semis—all of them already looted—and rows of walking people. He looked across the open fields. Miles and miles of makeshift camps. Fires, smoking white, dotted the landscape in every direction. He frowned as he looked. The fires were too big. Completely inefficient. Fools! Why didn't they save their fuel for the winter? A small fire to cook with would have been enough. Soon they were going to need that wood for heat.

The chopper crested a low, tree-covered ridge, the ground orange and yellow from the fallen leaves, then crossed a small lake. His eyes opened wide as they flew over the brackish water. At least a hundred boats of all shapes and sizes were sitting on the water, fishing lines stretched from all sides. He tried to count them all but quickly lost track. He didn't know how many fish were in the lake, but it was pretty clear there were a lot fewer today than yesterday, and there'd be even fewer tomorrow.

The refugees were hungry. But it was going to get much worse.

He leaned forward, looking behind the helicopter as it passed the lake, amazed at the absurd number of boats he had seen. He could have walked across the lake without getting his feet wet by jumping from boat to boat.

They passed over a major highway, Interstate 30 or 40 or something, he didn't know, but the helicopter followed it until it turned slightly south to bend around a low hill. He looked down intently as they flew. There were bodies there. Some had obviously been carefully placed along the side of the highway; others had been left where they had fallen, their legs and arms and heads stretched at awkward angles. He cringed as he watched. Men. More women. A few children. It made him sick to see it. It was depressing and discouraging and it made him miserable. Watching the despair, he wanted to cry.

They had to get help. They had to turn it around. And they had to do it soon or it might actually be too late. There was a tipping point, a point where things would crumble and decay beyond their ability to put them back together. How many Americans were down there starving? Had they come to the point where they were killing each other now? How many had already killed themselves? He swore as he looked down. Where was the government? Where were their allies? Wasn't there any help!

He turned and looked across the helicopter toward Sam. As if he knew, the other soldier turned away from his window and looked at him. They both had on military headsets that plugged into the helicopter's intercom, allowing them to communicate by pressing a button on the microphone cord that extended from the communications panel overhead. Bono pressed the button. "It's as depressing as anything I've ever seen."

Sam nodded grimly. "Did you see that family along the lake?" he asked.

Bono shook his head.

"There were four or five of them. It looked like—"

Bono cut him off. "Does this story have a happy ending?"

Sam closed his eyes and shook his head.

"I don't want to hear it, then."

"I wish I hadn't seen it. It looked like—"

Bono lifted an angry hand. "Really, I don't want to hear about it. I've seen enough myself."

Sam turned, looking forward now. They flew along in silence until Bono asked, "How long till we get to D.C.?"

One of the pilots turned and talked to him over his shoulder, speaking through the intercom. "We'll have to stop for fuel at a little field outside of Charleston. Shouldn't take much time. We'll be there sometime after dark."

"Got it. Have you been able to talk to anyone at the command post at Langley?"

Langley Air Force Base was their destination, the same place from which, ten days before, he and Sam had caught separate flights. At the time, he hadn't expected that they'd both be back so soon.

"The HF is still down," the pilot told him.

Used for long-distance communications, the high frequency radio had a reputation for being spotty. Even on the best of days, a user was as likely to get in touch with an HF command post in Tuli, Greenland, or one of the outskirt radar sites along the Bering Sea as to get a hold of a command post within the States.

"HF radios been almost worthless since the nuclear and EMP attack," the pilot continued. "No one can explain it. Too many crazy ions racing around the atmosphere, I guess."

Bono nodded and sat back and Caelyn rested her head against his shoulder again. The chopper bobbed lightly in the turbulence. The afternoon sun poured through his window. He didn't try to fight the weariness. Closing his eyes, he fell asleep.

chapter twenty-six

OFFUTT AIR FORCE BASE
HEADQUARTERS, U.S. STRATEGIC COMMAND
EIGHT MILES SOUTH OF OMAHA, NEBRASKA

The civilian aide paused at the glass door and knocked but didn't wait for Brucius Marino to answer before he pushed it back and slipped into the room.

The sun was just rising outside, the day coming alive, but deep in the basement compound, no one would have known that unless they were looking at the clock. In the sterile, carpet-and-cement rooms, there was no sense of day or time, no sense of light or darkness, weather, rain, heat, or cold. It had been a week since Marino had been out of the command post for more than a few minutes, and his normally tanned skin was turning pale from lack of sun and air. He was sitting at his desk, slumped back in his leather chair, his fingers interlaced together under his chin, his eyes closed, his breathing heavy and strong. The military lawyer from the Pentagon waited a long time, knowing Brucius was asleep. Listening to the Secretary's breathing, the aide hated to wake him, but he finally cleared his throat.

Marino sat up, instantly awake, his eyes moving as if he were trying to figure out where he was.

"Sir," the lawyer said.

Brucius focused on him. The first thing he noted was the satisfied smile.

"We got them, sir," the lawyer told him.

Brucius shook his head in disbelief. "You didn't!"

The lawyer's smile widened. "Yes, sir, we did."

"Both of them? They're alive!"

"We got them both. It was easier than we thought it would be. Our guys found them holed up like a couple of scared Chihuahuas out at Sanner's country estate."

Brucius sat back. He had to think. "No kidding?" he muttered, his mind racing, almost unwilling to accept their good fate. It was the first bit of good news they'd received since the nuclear warheads had been exploded over the four quadrants of the United States—certainly the first bit of good news he'd received since arriving here at Offutt—and he was almost gunshy, thinking there must be some mistake.

The aide watched him carefully, reading the look on his face. "It's true, sir. They're on their way here."

"How did Raven Rock miss them?"

The bald man shrugged his shoulders. "Like everyone else, they thought that they were dead."

Brucius humphed. "It's not like them to make such a big mistake. It's not like them to make any mistake at all."

"Perhaps not. But I suppose they're mortal, like the rest of us, and they're going to screw it up from time to time."

Brucius was suspicious but didn't say anything. "They're on their way here?" he repeated.

"Yes, sir. It will take a little doing. We've had to walk a fine line, you understand, using their position to get our hands on government transportation but at the same time trying not to draw too much attention to the fact that we have—"

"If you commandeered government assets to transport them, then Raven's going to know."

The lawyer hesitated. "Probably, sir."

"They'll follow them here to Offutt."

"Maybe, sir. But we've been careful."

Brucius shook his head. "Careful or not, they'll find them. They know how important this could be. If they're out there, the word will spread, especially if you used government assets to bring them in."

"It was either that or have them hike across the country," the lawyer answered.

A moment of silence followed as both men thought. Brucius put his hands together and vigorously rubbed his face. "I don't think you did the wrong thing, I just want us all to understand and be prepared. They're going to know. They're going to try to stop us. They can't let this stand. They know those two individuals could turn their entire plan up on its head."

"Even with them, we still need Jefferson . . ."

Brucius immediately thought of Sara Brighton, his heart sinking in his chest. "Is that true? Does the Constitution even say?"

"Are you kidding, sir?" the man scoffed, not so much at his boss as at the absurdity of it all. "No, sir, it doesn't say. I don't think our Founding Fathers were sufficiently premonitory, even in their greatness, to see this day. The Constitution is mute on the number of Supreme Court justices that even constitute a court, let alone any direction in such a situation as we face today. But this much we do know: A majority is the key."

Brucius stepped toward him. Their entire future rested in the answer to the question he was about to ask. Inside, his gut crunched, and though he didn't know it, his breathing stopped. "And how do we stand? What do these two have to say?"

"Sanner will rule for us. Gainsborough is unwilling to say for now."

Brucius slammed his fist into his palm. "In order for what we want to do to be constitutional—which is, after all, the entire freaking point—we need at least two of three. Far better to be unanimous. Think of how powerful that would be. No split decision. No muddled middle ground. A clear decision. A clear direction. It could set this whole thing right again."

The lawyer pressed his lips together thoughtfully. His scalp was greasy and he smelled. They'd been rationing their water, their food, their electricity, pretty much everything, and he'd lost track of the last time he had showered. He thought a moment, then said, "If Sara Brighton can get to Jefferson, we could really turn this thing around. As it stands, we need him, for we can't count on Gainsborough's vote. If we have two, good enough. If we get all three, so much the better, but again, it's not required."

Brucius chewed his lip, his hands shaking with fatigue. He turned to the large map they had pinned up on the wall, reached up, and gently tapped the red pin that depicted Raven Rock in Pennsylvania. "We'll know soon enough. One way or the other, by the end of this day, we ought to know."

The lawyer nodded toward Brucius, then turned for the door. Before he could leave the room, Brucius called him back. "Any word from Stalker?"

Stalker. The code word they had assigned to the mission to Iran. The aide considered for a moment. "General Foot will be in to brief you soon, but from what I understand, the aircraft is crossing the Persian Gulf about now."

Brucius's face was tense again. So much going on. *Too* much going on. And none of it was within his control. He hated the helpless feeling and turned back to the map again. "The world will change today," he whispered slowly.

The aide couldn't hear him. "Sir?" he asked.

Brucius moved his eyes across the map. "It's been a couple of thousand years since we've seen such a pivot point in human history. I can almost feel it, the weight, the pressure cooking down. I feel its heat. I sense its power. The world is going to change today. And I pray for the result."

The aide hesitated, then tried to smile. "I didn't think you were a praying man."

Brucius didn't answer or turn around.

chapter twenty-seven

Brucius Marino waited by the door of the executive office in the back of the command center. The room was built on a small platform that was eighteen inches higher than the downward sloping floor below it, and a wide, tinted window looked out on the operations center, which was a beehive of activity now. Men and women manned almost every workstation, intent, focused, and frankly a little scared, the tension hanging like extra oxygen in the air. They had a plan. They had a mission. No more waiting. No more wondering. They all knew what they had to do. There weren't as many people as they needed to get the job done, and everyone had multiple tasks to perform, but they were focused and intent and relieved to be doing *something*.

The entire future of the country came down to what they did right now. There was no time for indecision or hesitation, and certainly no time for fatigue. In a few hours it would be over.

Sara walked toward him, and he put his arm around her as he led her into the conference room and shut the door behind them. They stood together by the tinted window. He was frazzled, being pulled in every direction. She was in a hurry as well. They would have to make it quick.

"Are you ready?" the Secretary asked her.

Sara nodded hesitantly.

"Do you have any final questions?"

She thought for a while, looking off. "I have a thousand questions, Brucius." He waited. She looked back at him. *No time for all my questions,* her expression said.

"Okay. Okay," he said. "We've been monitoring the access protocols. They only open the personnel tunnel into Raven Rock once each day. You've got the proper code words and authentication. No one's going to question you, Sara. There's not going to be any problem getting you in, of that I'm pretty sure. People are coming and going every day. They're preparing to bring all their operations topside, at least for a while, and a couple of hundred personnel go in and out of Raven Rock every day. Getting you in will be easy. You're going to be okay."

She looked at him, her face expressionless. She knew it wouldn't be that easy but there was no use arguing the point right now.

"Once you're in, you've got to find him. Don't delay for any reason. As you've no doubt been told, there is a designated area within Raven Rock for members of the Supreme Court, but the truth is, he might not be there. If he's not, I'd expect to find him on the executive level, somewhere near Fuentes and his staff."

Sara listened carefully. All of this she knew.

"Get in. Talk to him. Tell him what's going on. Tell him I'm out here. Tell him that most of what James Davies testified isn't true. Convince him to come with you. He knows you. He'll trust you—"

"He'll think it's a trap."

"No. He'll realize there will be danger, but he'll know you wouldn't set him up."

Brucius hesitated. He walked away from her, then turned back and leaned against his desk. He looked at her intently. "Sara, we've found two other surviving members of the Supreme Court. They are the last ones left alive. All the others have been confirmed dead. We're bringing them out here. They're on their way to Offutt even as we speak."

Sara had already heard the rumors. "It seems to me, that being the case, there is little need for me to go to Raven," she said.

"I wish that were true. In fact, it's just the opposite. It's even more important now. I'm almost afraid to tell you because I realize the added pressure doesn't help, but here's the situation. Right now, one of the justices is for us. The other one's against. In fact, Justice Gainsborough was at first uncommitted, but now is demanding we take her directly to Raven Rock. She doesn't even want to come here. It's making it, umm . . . awkward, as you can imagine, forcing her to come out here."

It took Sara less than half a second to understand what Brucius was really saying. "You've got a split decision then. With Justice Jefferson in Raven Rock teamed up with Justice Gainsborough, that would be two against."

"But Jefferson doesn't understand the situation. He has no idea what's going on out here. Remember that, Sara, *he doesn't know.* I'm certain he will side with us once he understands the facts."

"Which means it's even more important."

"Yes. It's even more important that you get to him. Without him, we are through. It's one for us, two against us. This is the only chance we have."

Sara thought again, then nodded. "I'll do what I can,

Brucius. I'll do anything you ask me to. I'd give my life for my country. Millions of us would. But you've got to remember, I'm not a soldier, I'm not a spy. I'm nothing. I don't have any skills or background that would lead any of us to believe I'm going to be successful. I wonder if we're all crazy. Are we storming the castle walls with the only thing we have left, a middle-aged mother like myself?"

Brucius shook his head. Very little about Sara came across as middle-aged. And she was far more capable, far more intelligent and resourceful than she was giving herself credit for.

"I'm the last choice, the least likely person to be successful in this thing," she concluded with a worried look.

"No, Sara, that's completely wrong. Completely wrong. Yes, we're sending you into the lion's den; there's no sense pretending this is anything else. It would be stupid and patronizing to minimize the danger. But if you *can* get in there, if you can just talk to him, then you're not the only choice, you're the best choice. You have no dog in this fight, not a thing to gain. You're just a friend. Someone he can trust. Someone who was willing to risk her life just to talk to him. You won't be asking any favors. You'll want nothing in return. He'll listen to you, Sara. He's a good man. He respects you and Neil. Once you talk to him, I believe he'll do the right thing. I think it's going to work."

Sara drew a long breath. "Is there anything else?" she asked as she stepped toward the door.

Brucius hesitated. "They're giving you a weapon. A small handgun. It's light and simple to use. I know you don't want to take it, but Sara, you can't be foolish or compassionate or whatever you might want to call it, not right now. If you have to use it, then you *do it,* you understand? If you need to use it to protect yourself or to protect others, don't you hesitate. You have an obligation to see this through. There's too much riding on this." He swallowed awkwardly and took a step toward her. "I know how difficult this must be for you, Sara, but *this is war.* You can't hesitate to act. If you do, you'll be dead—and if not you, then maybe Jefferson or someone else. You've got to make a commitment. You've got to make the right decision now. Put aside your normal motherly instincts, close your eyes, and make the decision that you'll do anything necessary to make this work."

"I'm not taking the gun," she said. Her voice was firm with determination. "There's no reason I should take it. I couldn't use it anyway. I couldn't shoot a sparrow; there's no way in this world I could shoot another human being."

"You would if you had to. If the mission depended on it, I think you'd do what you had to do."

"If it's likely to come down to that, you'd better send someone else."

He looked at her and waited, unsure of what to say. "Please take it with you, Sara."

She only shook her head. "Is there anything else?"

"Think about your children."

"I think about them every day. Every moment. They're the only thing I think about."

"Then do what it takes to protect yourself."

"I'm not going to take the gun."

They stared at each other angrily. She was so stubborn. He was so determined. She didn't understand how it might help her in a desperate situation. He didn't understand the sense of kindness in her heart.

"Please," he tried a final time.

She headed for the door. "My flight is waiting."

He reached out and touched her arm, turning her around. She looked at him, her eyes hard. His voice was soft and pleading now. "Please be careful, Sara. Please go and get him out of there."

She glanced down at his hand then took another long breath. "Things will be okay." She patted his arm and turned around.

He watched her go, the glass door closing behind her softly. For a long time he stood there, considering the last thing she had said.

"Things will be okay."

He wondered what that meant.

chapter twenty-eight

C losing their eyes, the three of them slipped away, drifting into agitated and restless sleep.

Half a world apart, two of them dreamed in the darkness while one dreamed in the light. One of the dreams was a dream of warning; while two were dreams of peace.

All were premonitions of the future.

And all would change their lives.

*　　*　　*

She slept inside the moving aircraft as it cruised at nearly supersonic speed across the vast emptiness of the North Atlantic Ocean. They were high, above 43,000 feet. It was early evening and because they were heading east, the day was short, the sun setting behind them in a third of the time it normally took for darkness to come on.

Azadeh sat near the back of the high-performance military executive transport. Sam and the other soldiers huddled near the front. The aircraft was too small for them to stand and the seats were close together, the aisle narrow, so they bunched up behind the cockpit door, which was open, allowing them to see the rows of multicolored panels and other cockpit instrument displays.

Azadeh watched and listened for as long as she could force herself to stay awake, but sheer exhaustion eventually overcame her and she drifted off to sleep.

✳   ✳   ✳

It was a dark world, filled with noise and rubble and filth and smoke. It was hard to breathe, the air tart and acidic with the burning fuel and rubber from the line of destroyed cars that littered the dark and empty streets. Behind her, she could hear the muffled but heartbreaking sobbing of a mother who'd lost her child. Azadeh pressed her scarf to her face, holding her palm against her nose to filter the dirty air. There was something else in the odor, heavier, more powerful, and it made her stomach turn. The smell of decaying flesh. A hot wind blew up from the south, swirling pieces of paper and tattered garbage at her feet.

Without warning, there was a terrible roar behind her; she didn't even have time to turn before the fighter aircraft—dark with heavy bombs hanging from its canted wingtips, its two engines spouting blue flames—screamed over her head. It was so low she could actually feel the heat from its engines, the roar so powerful she could feel it in her chest, the passing air so piercing she had to slap her hands against her ears.

The fighter disappeared as quickly as it had screamed up from behind her, leaving her with the emptiness again. The crying mother was silent now. There was not another soul around.

She stood there a long moment. She felt so desperate and alone. The empty street stretched on before her, straight, without any intersections or cross streets, an unending canyon of buildings on both sides. Everywhere she looked it was the same hopeless devastation, the same fatal sense of despair. Moving to a smoldering car beside her, she stepped up on its crooked bumper and looked down the street for as far as she could see. It grew darker in the distance, the details swallowed up in the dying light.

She took a breath and squared her shoulders.

She had no choice but to walk it.

She shivered, stepped down from the car, and started walking. The street continued stretching out before her. She moved faster now, feeling a sense of urgency she hadn't felt before.

Farther.

Faster.

She almost broke into a run.

Something was up before her. Something important. Something good.

She saw a flash of movement and slowed her pace. A thick darkness had gathered all around her but she didn't feel afraid anymore.

Realizing the peace inside her, she stopped.

For the first time since the day on the mountain when her father had been killed, it was true: She realized she wasn't afraid any longer. She felt sure and peaceful. She felt warm and full of joy.

A little boy emerged from the shadows and walked into the street. She didn't move, her heart beating in her chest, her eyes wide in awe, her hands brought together in surprise. He was so beautiful. Flowing hair. Wide, almond eyes. Dark skin. Beautiful teeth behind a flashing smile. A little girl followed him. Azadeh sucked in her breath again. A brother and his little sister. She was as beautiful as he. The little girl walked toward her older brother and he turned to help her to navigate the cluttered street.

Looking up, the little boy finally caught sight of Azadeh. Seeing her, he stopped.

He was close now, so close she could read every expression in his eyes.

He looked back and pulled his sister to him, then turned to her and smiled.

She felt so beautiful and peaceful. The smoke and death and darkness and fear were gone now. It was just her and the children and she almost wept with joy.

She knelt down and extended her hands, beckoning to them carefully, but the children didn't move. She moved forward slowly, afraid that they might flee. They stood their ground as if waiting, and she beckoned to them again.

Suddenly she stopped.

She couldn't get any closer to them. It was as if she had hit a wall. Some unseen barrier lay between her and the children and it wouldn't let her pass.

She cried in desperation, gesturing for them to come.

"Not yet," the little boy whispered to her.

Turning to his sister, he led her away down the street.

"Please don't go!" Azadeh called out to them.

Their forms started merging with the darkness and they almost disappeared.

"No, no," Azadeh cried. "Please, do not go. Tell me your names. Tell me who you are! Tell me why I'm here alone."

The little boy stopped and turned toward her.

"Who are you?" Azadeh cried.

"We are Tomorrow," he whispered to her, then waved goodbye and turned around.

✳   ✳   ✳

The king of the House of Saud—perhaps the most powerful mortal in the world, for the moment at least—slept restlessly, always turning, sometimes snoring, his eyelids fluttering. Though the thermostat was set at 58 degrees, the line of powerful, industrial-sized air conditioners that cooled the ancient castle churning out a constant stream of cold air, he was sweating from head to toe. Rolling and mumbling constantly, he never woke, leaving his sheets damp and clammy with drying sweat.

As he tossed and moaned, he dreamed.

* * *

He was sitting on a throne of gold. Twice the size of a man, it was tall and noble and adorned with precious metals and all the jewels of the Nile. Jagged eagles' talons were fashioned at the four legs and stone jaguar heads sat below the armrests where he placed his hands. A cavernous hall lay before him, narrow and full of light. Two rows of enormous marble pillars stretched into the distance, but there was no ceiling overhead. A deep, maroon carpet lay between the marble pillars, extending from the foot of the throne as far as he could see.

The king waited.

He fidgeted.

He swore and cursed.

But still he waited. And he didn't even know why.

Hours later, he checked the time again. His golden watch was broken. He didn't know what time it was. He didn't know how long he'd been waiting, but it felt like days. He was hungry and thirsty, exhausted and angry. Whatever he was waiting for, he wanted it over. He was ready to have it done. He tried standing up to leave, but a great weight kept pushing him down and he fell back, exhausted, knowing he couldn't go.

Suddenly, far in the distance, he heard an unseen door open on mighty hinges. Footsteps. The click of metal. He squinted into the distance, his heart racing, sweat pouring down his sides.

The American warrior emerged from the last pillar to his right and started walking down the heavy carpet toward him.

Young and proud, broad-shouldered and strong-armed, the young man walking toward him was wearing modern battle gear. Twenty paces before the king, he stopped, lifted his assault rifle, and aimed at him.

Abdullah tried to scream. No sound came out. He tried to flee but couldn't move.

Uncertain, the young man moved his eye away from the scope atop his weapon, looked at the king, cocked his head as if listening to some unheard voice, hesitated as if resisting, then angrily lowered his weapon and walked a few steps closer. The king felt a growing surge of fear as the young man drew near. It sank into him, deep and penetrating and far more powerful than any emotion he'd ever felt before. Black and consuming, the fear made him sick inside. He felt his stomach rising. He swallowed to keep it down. "Stop! STOP!" he cried in horror.

At the sound of his voice, the young warrior was instantly gone.

The king's dead brother stood before him now, his face rotted with death and maggot-eaten flesh. He smiled harshly as he spoke, his teeth protruding through split lips. "My son will be the cause of your destruction," his brother said.

The king tried to cry out but the breath was frozen inside him.

His dead brother's eyes were vacant as he spoke. "My son will cause your death."

The king felt his heart quake again. He tried to cry out. He tried to run. He tried to turn away. But all he could muster was the smallest movement of his head. "Not if I kill him first," he finally had the strength to answer in defiance.

"Especially if you try to kill him."

The king forced himself to sit up straight upon his throne. Raising his fist, he cried out to the corpse, "This is my world. You are gone now. There's nothing you can do to stop me!"

"Beware, my little brother, or you're going to stop yourself!"
The dead brother glared at him, howled like a banshee, then
lowered his eyes and disappeared.

✻　　✻　　✻

Sara's dream was short and intense and she wakened with a start.

Her eyes shooting open, she looked around anxiously, taking in her surroundings: the bright sun to her right, the dry leaves on the passing trees, a long line of brown grass below a razor-topped fence. They were riding in a military van, heading southeast along the main aircraft parking ramp at Offutt Air Force Base. She turned her head against the back of the seat and glanced toward Ammon and Luke, who were sitting at her side. Ammon looked at her and forced a smile. "You doing okay, Mom?" he asked.

She had dreamed. It was important. But it was fading . . .

It wasn't until then that she remembered where she was going. Her heart leapt inside her chest.

The military vehicle sped along the airport taxiway. The driver kept his eyes ahead, taking in the sentries who were posted at the entrance to the aircraft parking ramp. The major in the passenger's seat turned and spoke over his shoulder. "Just about there, Mrs. Brighton."

She nodded but didn't answer.

"Have you got everything?" he asked her for the second time.

She nodded again.

Ammon shifted in the seat and looked ahead. "The aircraft is waiting for you."

Sara followed his eyes. The military jet was blue and white and had no markings other than a small USAF emblem and U.S. flag on the tail. Her personal ride to Raven Rock. A fresh

193

surge of adrenaline rushed through her and she took a deep breath to keep her heart from racing.

She turned to her sons and whispered so the men in the front seat couldn't hear. "I had a dream," she told them.

They looked at her. Something in her voice told them it was important, and they waited for her to go on.

"A young man came to me. He was white and beautiful."

Ammon cocked his head, his eyes solemn, his face expectant. "Who was it, Mom?"

She looked away and thought for a moment before she turned back. Her two sons waited. A reverent feeling filled the car.

"I don't know, I don't remember. It's right there, so close, sitting on the tip of my tongue, but I can't quite remember. If I just had time to think about it . . ."

The major turned around again. "This is it," he announced. The van was slowing down. "They radioed ahead and the flight crew is waiting for you."

The vehicle came to a stop and a waiting guard slid the rear door open. "Mrs. Brighton," he said as he extended a hand to help her out.

She glanced anxiously toward her sons. The door on the other side of the van was opening as well, and another guard was standing there.

There wasn't time to think about the dream now. It would have to wait.

She shrugged and stepped out of the van and into the light of the bright sun reflecting off twenty acres of white cement.

Her sons came around the car to talk to her. There were a lot of men around so Ammon pulled them all aside.

"You don't have to do this, Mom," he said again.

She patted his arm reassuringly. "I know that, son."

"You could come back to the hangar . . ."

She cut him off. "I know about my options." Stepping toward her sons, she pulled them close. "It's going to be okay," she said.

Ammon's face was hard. He wasn't certain. Luke's cheeks were wet with tears. He bent and held on to his mother—he was six inches taller than she was now—and kept his face buried in her shoulder. Ammon watched his brother's forehead turning red.

They held each other until Luke pushed back. A cold wind blew across the empty tarmac and a spatter of dry leaves danced around their feet. Ammon started to say something, hesitated, then glanced at Luke. Luke acknowledged his darting eyes and nodded back. Ammon took a breath as if steeling himself, looked up and down the runway, then turned back to his mother. "Mom, Luke and I've been talking."

Sara cocked her head. The introduction was familiar. It was common for them to stand together when they had some news to bear.

Ammon glanced again at Luke. "You're going, Mom. Sam's already gone. We feel useless here. Useless and alone. There's nothing for us here. Fact is, we've been pretty much useless since this whole thing started. We've been baggage, someone you had to worry about, that's about all."

"No, Ammon, that's not true." She shot a shocked look at Luke, then turned back to Ammon. "Don't think that. It's not true. Think of all the good you've done."

"We could argue it, Mom, but we don't have time and we don't want to anyway. But what I said is true. We haven't contributed anything; we're just a couple of young guys who've been along for the ride. We feel compelled to do something useful now."

"What . . . what are you saying?"

The two young men didn't dare look at her until Luke finally shrugged his shoulders. "Mom, we just want to help."

"What are you thinking!"

"You're leaving. Sam and Azadeh are already gone." He was repeating himself now. "If we stayed here, we'd just be hanging around and hoping they like us enough to feed us. *Everyone* is doing something. We think that we can do something useful too."

The wind blew again, gusting a strand of blonde hair in front of Sara's eyes. She swiped at it quickly, brushing the tears away at the same time.

Ammon gritted his teeth. "We were talking to one of the sergeants at the security desk. You might have noticed him. Tall, black guy. Young. Anyway, he found out that we were Mormons, so he came to talk to us. It turns out that he is too. Seems they're looking for . . ."

The two jet engines on the military aircraft started turning. A low grumble erupted from their cores as the fire within them started, the sound growing instantly louder and more powerful. They were standing fifty or sixty feet in front of the transport aircraft and they had to almost scream to hear each other now. A sergeant in camouflage fatigues ran toward them. "They're waiting for you, Mrs. Brighton," he said in Sara's ear.

She nodded to him, then lifted a single finger. He acknowledged her request for more time and stepped back, giving the family a final minute to say good-bye.

"What are you thinking?" Sara demanded again.

They huddled close together, Luke and Ammon continuing to shoot anxious looks between themselves. What were they going to tell her? How was she going to take it? They didn't know. "The Church is asking for volunteers to go around and help some of the most devastated regions," Ammon said. "They're sending men to Washington . . ."

"Back to D.C.?"

"Apparently."

"Is it even safe to go back there?"

"I guess so, Mom. But that's not all. They're sending volunteers to Jackson County."

Her mouth flew open. "Jackson County! Why?"

"We don't know, Mom. But we want to go."

She looked at them, terror in her eyes. "Jackson County? Jackson County . . ."

"Mrs. Brighton," the sergeant cried, taking a step toward them. She tried to brush him off again but he was pulling on her arm now. The aircraft was starting to slide forward, closing the space between them. Ammon took a step toward his mother and she pulled out of the sergeant's grasp. "Don't worry about us, okay, Mom?" he said. "Luke and I will stay together. We're going to be all right. But we want to do something—we *need* to do something to help. We know where to find you. We'll let you know that we're okay . . ."

The sergeant was becoming agitated now. "Mrs. Brighton, we *really* have to go!"

"Go, Mom. Be careful. Don't worry about us. This is what we're supposed to do—this is our time, our calling. Think of us like the men who volunteered for the Mormon Battalion." Ammon smiled at her proudly. "We'll be all right. And we'll be back . . ."

The sergeant tugged on Sara's arm again, almost dragging her away. She went with him for a step or two, then pulled away and ran back. Grabbing her sons, she drew them close and held them tight. All of them were crying now, but they were no longer tears of fear. The Spirit settled on them. "I love you both so much," she said. "I love you more than anything. I'm so proud of you. So proud. There's never been a mother more grateful for her sons."

She pulled away and looked at them, her eyes opening wide now in surprise. "My dream . . . my dream . . . it just came to me, I remember it all so clearly now. The messenger who came to me, I remember every word he said."

"What is, Mom? What did he tell you?"

She brought her hand up to her mouth and leaned toward them, her face peaceful and full of light. "He said he was a messenger sent from Elijah." She closed her eyes and smiled. "He said he wanted to remind me that the sealing power was real."

*"And seeing the people in a state of such awful
wickedness, and those Gadianton robbers filling the
judgment-seats—having usurped the power and authority
of the land; laying aside the commandments of God, and
not in the least aright before him; doing no justice unto
the children of men;*

*"Condemning the righteous because of their righteousness;
letting the guilty and the wicked go unpunished because of
their money; and moreover to be held in office at the head
of government, to rule and do according to their wills,
that they might get gain and glory of the world, and,
moreover, that they might the more easily commit adultery,
and steal, and kill, and do according to their own wills."*

—HELAMAN 7:4–5

chapter twenty-nine

RAVEN ROCK (SITE R), UNDERGROUND MILITARY COMPLEX
SOUTHERN PENNSYLVANIA

The tunnel was narrow, with a slippery cement floor and gray, cinder-block walls. It sloped gently downward, leading toward the access door. There were at least six other entries into Raven Rock, most of them hidden inside various administration buildings scattered around the surface complex. There were also two deep tunnels that ran for many miles to the presidential compound at Camp David.

The main access door into Raven Rock was hidden in the trees and protected by more guards, cement barriers, and bunkers than the gold at Fort Knox. Large enough to drive a truck through, the main access was not far from the main road. Its huge metal doors braced on massive hydraulic pistons had not been opened since the senior surviving leaders of the government had fled to Raven after the EMP attack.

In addition to the main entrance, there were other access doors, and the underground complex was not completely sealed. Some of the other entries were used for supplies and service; some of them, like the one Sara waited near now, were secret entries used exclusively for the exchange of personnel.

She stood in line with forty or fifty other people. None of

them were friendly and no one spoke to her. All shared the same concerns: their families left up-top, how they were going to find food and shelter, their government, the future, the whole mess of a thing. Looking at them, Sara could see the same cold desperation in all their eyes. The vast majority were in military uniform, but there were a few civilians in casual attire and business suits. All of them wore coded, picture ID passes on colored lanyards around their necks: blue, red, yellow, green—the color of the lanyards obviously meant something, but what it was, Sara didn't know. She glanced down nervously at her own ID. She had rehearsed her name and story and her reason for entering Raven Rock so many times she could have explained it in her sleep, but still she was nervous, her hands shaking, her mouth so dry she could hardly talk. If anyone stopped or questioned her she would probably just throw up on their shoes. She swallowed, trying to keep the bile down, but her stomach kept on fluttering like the wing tips of a bird.

Turning, she looked back up the sloping tunnel. She had already passed through two security access points, the first on the military bus that drove them through the main gate into the surface compound, and the second at the door of the nondescript warehouse building that housed the entry tunnel into Raven. The final—and most secure of the three security checkpoints—was still ahead.

She checked her watch for the third or fourth time, then glanced down the line of waiting people. The line started moving and her heart lurched into her throat.

One by one they stepped up to the final checkpoint. Three armed and very unfriendly military police checked their IDs, asked a few questions, and scanned their pupils with a portable IR scanner, passing the red beam in front of their eyes. The computer checked the electronic scans of their irises for a positive ID, then compared the scans against the database of personnel approved for entry into the compound.

This was the most critical of the checkpoints. This was where it could all break down. This was where they would know if Brucius Marino's people were any good. Had they been able to plant Sara into the access system? They had assured her yes, but the truth was, they didn't know. No one could know until she got there. She thought of James Davies, her mind racing with worry. Surely that had not gone according to their plan. Would she be another failure?

They were about to find out.

Moving forward, she wiped her sweating palms and took a calming breath. *No big deal, no big deal,* she gently reassured herself.

She was next. She waited like the others behind a red line on the floor, an obedient member of the flock, then stepped forward when the first guard told her to.

He lifted her ID hanging from the red lanyard around her neck. "Sara Brighton," he called to the second guard behind him while scanning the coded information on the back of the ID. Sara waited, trying her best to appear uninterested.

The second guard stared at his computer screen, which Sara couldn't see, then motioned to a black keyboard mounted on the bulletproof glass wall that separated them. "Enter your access code," he told her. Sara stepped forward. The keypad was covered with a curving black plastic cover, making it impossible for anyone to see what she was typing. She typed the access code they had given her, a code that changed every six hours.

"Again," the second guard told her.

"Did I mess it up?" she blurted before she even had time to think.

"Again!" the guard answered tartly.

Her heart lurched again. The bile rose, her stomach fluttering. Time to throw up on the floor? She took a quick breath and put her fingers on the keypad, typing the eight-character code again. This time she moved her fingers more carefully and looked down, making certain of every key.

He waited. The guard stared, then motioned to the other. "She's new in the system. Give her a FOX session," he said.

FOX session. She almost froze. She knew from her husband that *FOX session* was Intel slang for "Ask a few tough questions, maybe rough her up a bit."

The guard stepped toward her, his M-16 hanging loosely at his side. Sara turned toward him and almost fainted. He grabbed her ID again. "Sara Brighton? Is that right?"

"Yes, yes, Sara Brighton."

"And what is your reason for being granted access into the complex?" He looked down at her ID again.

After much argument, they had decided back at Offutt to go with something close to reality rather than invent a story out of whole cloth. "I'm a private consultant with the Department of Defense," Sara started. "My husband was Neil Brighton. He used to work for the president. I've consulted with Family Support Services for a couple of years. We're working on an emergency program to ensure support and pay and benefits to military families during a time of crisis, especially for those whose spouses are away."

The young enlisted man didn't look impressed. "Who invited you here?" he asked.

This was where it all could break down. If they checked it out, their plan was over.

"General Cantera. He heads up Family Support Services." She held her breath. They had timed it so Cantera would be in his afternoon briefing when she tried to get into the compound, making it more difficult to reach him if anyone tried to call to confirm her explanation.

The soldier glanced again back to the others.

They had told her to stay with the story and not say more. They had told her to be silent and not to improvise. "Don't screw it up!" they had warned her. "Silence is much better than handing them the rope to hang yourself. You're not good enough, you haven't been trained enough, to fake your way through." But they hadn't predicted that she'd be FOXed, and she knew she had to say something now. Her instincts kicked into gear. And her instincts were good.

"Look, maybe you don't know how bad it is up there right now," she said quickly. "Maybe to you it's no big deal, all safe and sound down here. But if you're a soldier with a family, a wife and kids, and you're not able to be home to help take care of them, then yeah, it's a big deal. We've got to figure out a way to help those who can't be there for their kids. Military members and their families are one of our highest priorities right now. We have to ensure your families are taken care of. If they're up there starving on the streets, none of our troops are going to stay at their stations. Our desertion rates will sky-rocket. We've got to figure out a way to make sure the supplies of food and water are getting to the right people, and right now military dependents are one of the highest priorities we have." She did her best to glare at the soldier. "I'm sure you agree. You want your family taken care of. That's why I'm here. If we don't do that, our military members will do what they have to do to help their families. If that means leaving their posts to feed their children—well, I think we both know what a mess that could be."

The soldier lifted his face and looked at her, his eyes now sad. "I've got two kids," he said.

Sara didn't answer. Time to shut up now. Anything else

she said would be redundant, and she needed to let him figure out for himself the importance of what she had said.

He glanced behind him, then leaned toward her. "How bad is it out there?" he whispered. "They won't let us leave the compound—"

She cut him off. "It's bad. But we're trying."

He watched her, then stepped back and lifted his portable iris scanner. She felt a slight sting as the IR light scanned her right eye.

They waited. Sara tried to breathe. Had they been able to plant her identity into one of the most sensitive military databases the Pentagon had ever maintained?

Ten seconds passed. The soldier glanced at her. She heard a soft beep.

He stepped aside. "Step through the X-ray and metal detector. Take any electronics out of your briefcase," he said.

She almost cried with relief but caught herself. Exhaling visibly, she stepped toward the X-ray.

Four minutes later, she was in.

chapter thirty

Everything about her said *leave me alone.*

She sat in the corner of the main cafeteria, a sheaf of papers spread out before her, pen in hand, a laptop pushed to the side of the table. She looked busy and she kept her head down, not talking to anyone. The mess hall was always busy: day, night, it didn't matter, the staff at Raven Rock worked around the clock and the cafeteria remained open 24/7. Though she appeared consumed with her work, shuffling her papers, scrawling notes in the margins, tapping on the computer, she kept her eyes moving, always looking for him.

She glanced at her watch. Almost eleven at night. She'd been inside Raven Rock for more than seven hours. Still no sight of him.

It had taken her a while to find the Supreme Court annex to the underground complex, a row of small but finely furnished apartments with tiny offices lining a narrow corridor with the Supreme Court chamber at the end. All of the offices had been empty. She didn't know which office Jefferson had claimed, since he had his choice of nine, but not a justice, secretary, clerk, or lawyer could be found. She had waited near the hallway for a couple of hours, trying not to look conspicuous, but after being approached by a security guard, she'd moved on.

Standing in the main corridor that led into the mountain, she had stopped to think. No way to get down to the executive office level. She'd already tried. The elevator was guarded and she didn't have the access codes. He wasn't coming to the Supreme Court wing; it was pretty obvious he'd set up his office somewhere else. And why wouldn't he? Who would want to sleep and work in an empty chamber, only to be reminded constantly of his dead friends? Where else could she find him? Where else could he be? The gym? Not likely. Jefferson was five-foot-seven and pushing 240 pounds; it had been a few legal briefs since he'd seen the inside of a gym. The central cafeteria? Maybe. But surely they provided food services on the executive level. Would he really come up here? The recreation hall? She'd already been down there. Rows of Ping-Pong tables, computers, arcade games, poker tables, a couple of billiard tables, banks of televisions that were mounted on the wall. It was pretty obvious that Raven Rock designers expected recreation to be the last thing on the minds of its long-term occupants. No, he wasn't going to show up there.

Which left her with . . . nothing.

Finally, after wandering the halls for a while longer, she'd taken up a table near the back of the cafeteria from which she could survey the hall. There she waited. And hoped.

Now it was approaching midnight and she had nothing.

More than four thousand people had been crammed into the underground complex. What were the chances she might see him in the cafeteria in the middle of the night?

Not very good, she knew that.

And even if she found him, how would she ever get him to listen to her, let alone convince him to leave the safety of Raven Rock and venture in their cause?

chapter thirty-one

She didn't know where to sleep. They were hoping she would have found him and gotten out before it mattered. But here it was, the middle of the night, and she had nowhere to go.

There were temporary quarters for guests and newly assigned members of the underground compound, but they required written orders. She had them, but they would have to be verified, and she didn't want to chance it. She simply couldn't stomach the thought of another encounter with a security guard. She had already decided that she would sleep in the women's rest room before she'd take the chance of checking into the visitors' quarters.

Time passed. The cafeteria stayed equally busy, the pace of operations fairly consistent from night to day. Looking around her, she realized there were many others working at tables. Staffing had reached war-footing levels and she wasn't the only one who didn't have a place to work.

She glanced at her watch: 1:20 in the morning.

Resting her head on her arms, she fell asleep.

*   *   *

Twenty minutes later she woke up. Something inside her made her tense, and the soft hair on the back of her neck stood on end. Her heart raced and she felt disoriented as she struggled to come awake. She kept her head down, trying to understand what had jarred her.

Then she heard it. His voice was deep and resonating and distinct enough to jolt her from her sleep—the voice of the old friend, a man she and Neil had known since his first assignment at the Pentagon.

He was the national security adviser to President Fuentes now. She had seen his picture just a couple of days before when Brucius Marino had shown her photographs of the meeting of conspirators that had taken place somewhere overseas.

This was the man who was responsible for the previous president's death.

She kept her head down, her heart slamming in her chest.

If he saw her, he would recognize her.

If he saw her, she was dead.

She kept her head buried in her arms, wishing she could tunnel under a pile of papers, wishing she could climb under the table, wishing she could disappear.

She didn't move. She kept her head down, her shoulders shaking.

Ten minutes later, she finally looked up and he was gone.

chapter thirty-two

She'd waited as long as she could stand it, but it had been almost twenty hours and she simply couldn't wait for him any longer.

She stood up from the cafeteria table she'd been hoarding for almost half a day, then headed down the main hallway. At the elevator, she pushed the button for the executive suites. Two stories above the presidential level, this floor was accessible but dangerous for her to venture down to. She knew she had no other choice—and she might find him there.

The elevator opened to a dark blue office suite. A receptionist was seated behind a small desk and a guard was standing there. She flashed her badge to them while glancing at her watch, pretending to ignore them. It was 12:39 in the afternoon. They let her pass.

As she glanced at the armed guard, her heart skipped another beat.

She didn't know where it was, but she guessed, not wanting to indicate that she hadn't been on the executive level before. Down the main hallway and to her left, she found it: the executive dining hall.

Looking through the etched glass, she took a deep breath. This had to be one of the most dangerous places she could be. It was far more likely that she would be recognized here than in the crowds upstairs, but she didn't care anymore. She was running out of time. And she had already run out of nerves. Better to get it over with than to die a thousand deaths of fear.

She pushed into the small dining room, stopped, and looked around. Tables with white linen and yellow silk flowers spread before her. She searched the sparse crowd and found him sipping coffee while reading at a table in the far corner of the room. She almost cried out in relief. Walking quickly, she moved toward him, coming to a stop beside the table. He looked up, irritated at the intrusion, then realized who was standing there. His expression immediately changed to one of shock and he quickly looked around. "Sara Brighton!" he mouthed. "What are you doing here?" His eyes darted again, sensing danger.

He made no motion toward the chair across from him, but Sara sat down anyway. "Daniel, I need to talk to you."

He looked at her and shook his head. "I can't imagine you have anything to say that I'm going to want to hear."

"Maybe not. But you're going to listen. There's far too much at stake for you not to at least hear why I've risked my life to find you."

chapter thirty-three

Sara leaned across the table and whispered to the justice.
"Brucius Marino is alive. He's going to fight to claim
the presidency. He will not let this stand."

Daniel Jefferson, the last surviving member of the United
States Supreme Court—at least as far as he knew—stared at his
old friend, his eyes wide, then looked around anxiously. He
sensed that there was danger, though it wasn't clear from
what.

"Secretary Marino has found two other members of the
Supreme Court," Sara blurted out, all of her carefully prepared
remarks fleeing from her now. "He's taking them to his headquarters at an air force base in the Midwest. The impeachment
proceedings that convicted him were based on forced and fab-
ricated testimony. He is going to ask the two surviving justices
to overrule the impeachment proceedings or at least to allow
him to defend himself."

She stopped. How much should she tell him? She didn't
know. Jefferson raised an eyebrow. "And how do my col-
leagues feel about this, I wonder?"

Sara nervously fingered the cuff of her dark suit, deciding

to tell him the truth. "The two justices are in disagreement. One is sympathetic, one is not. We need you to come and join us. To put it simply, we need your vote."

There was much more to it, of course, but that was the essence of why she had risked everything to find him, and she wanted to lay it out.

Jefferson stared at her, his eyes narrowed to careful slits. Sara looked around at their surroundings. She was scared, her eyes always moving, her face tight, her hands almost trembling on the table before him. He considered her behind the hood of his heavy eyelids, keeping his emotions in check. Then he started asking questions. Some of them, she answered. Some, she kept the answers to herself.

Twenty minutes later, he ordered another coffee, sat in thought for a long moment, then said, "You're in great danger here. You spread that danger to me when we're together. Go now. I'll think about it and let you know."

Sara watched him. He had clearly already thought about it. This was his way of telling her to get lost. "Please come with me," she begged him. "If you'll just—"

"Go, Sara. It is dangerous for you to be here. I'll consider—"

"No, Daniel," she insisted. "You can't push me away like this. I know what you're thinking, I know that this is difficult, but please, you've got to understand!" She stared at the emptiness above his head, searching for the right thing to say. She could beg him, she could plead and reason and maybe threaten, but none of that would matter. He was a proud and independent man. He'd been an independent and even rebellious thinker all his life, and nothing she could say to him was going to change his mind. None of her persuasion, no thoughtful or reasoned argument was going to convince him now.

The only thing she had to offer was in her heart. "When I was asked to come and talk to you, I accepted the assignment with enormous trepidation," she whispered honestly. Jefferson watched, listening, and she took another breath. "I didn't want to be here. I didn't want to be the one who talked to you. I didn't want the responsibility. What if you wouldn't listen? What would happen if I failed? But I was the only option. You and I were . . . are . . . friends—at least I hope we are. You've known Neil and me for many years. We all thought that maybe you would trust me. And that's all that I can do now, talk to you and hope."

Jefferson wrapped his fingers around his mug of coffee, letting the warmth soothe the arthritis in his hands. He felt a rising brooding. Part of him wanted to stand up and walk away from her. He wasn't a fool—he could see the terror in her eyes. She shouldn't be here. How did she get in? And it was a dangerous message that she brought, which made him angry at her. He wished that she would just go away. And yet, part of him wanted to listen to her. He wasn't afraid of a good fight. He'd been a fighter all his life.

She looked at him, sensing his rising impatience and darkening mood, then went on as quickly as she could. "This day is fraught with peril. The state of our nation is unsure."

"Sara, you don't have to tell me that," he said. "I've been up there." He leaned toward her and lowered his voice. "You just came from up there. I can see it in your eyes and smell it in your clothes. We both know what's going on up on the surface. It's terrible now and it's going to get much worse. There's simply no way around that. Who knows how many people are going to die? But these guys," he nodded toward the hallway behind him, "they've got a plan. It isn't pretty, I'll give you that, but it might be necessary. And right now, it's the only thing we have. Yes, things are going to change, but that's only because things have *already* changed. They didn't do that. *We* didn't do that. These days were thrust upon us. All we can do is try to pull it all together and rebuild from the pieces that have been left us—"

"Into *what*? What are you rebuilding, Daniel? What do you have in mind?"

The Supreme Court justice looked at her squarely and answered, "That's not for me to decide. My role is very simple. Are they complying with the Constitution? That's all that I can do."

"But you know what they're proposing! It will rip our Constitution into shreds!"

Jefferson sat back again, his agitation growing. "I've heard rumors, same as you have. I don't believe them. They can't be true. And if these men attempt to implement any of the things people are saying they *might* have considered, we will stop them in their tracks."

Sara looked at him, her eyes widening in surprise. In that moment, she knew that they were going to kill Justice Daniel Jefferson. They would keep him for as long as he was useful, but they would never let him stop them. No one was safe from their wrath.

In an agony of fear, she leaned forward and took his hand. "You have to fight them," she whispered across the table. "You have to fight them, Daniel. Please, don't let them win."

He sat back and pulled an unlit cigar from his jacket pocket. Stuffing it in his mouth, he sucked the wetted tip. Only half a box of the illegal Cubans were left now. No way of getting any others. He had to treasure every one. "It's not that easy anymore, Sara. It's not like it used to be. It's much more complicated now. And it might be time to make some needed changes anyway. It might be time to move beyond the mistakes of the past. We are the most despised nation on the earth at the moment. No one trusts us. No one likes us. We can't function like that any longer. We have to make some changes; I think that's a given. We've made mistakes—far too many— to pretend it doesn't matter. Maybe it's time we paid the price now. Maybe our dues have finally come."

Sara shook her head. "No, no, no. This isn't about international politics and power. This is about America. Americans. Nothing else. We live or die together. There's no way around that now."

"Sometimes I wonder, Sara. Sometimes in the past few weeks I've wondered if any of it's worth saving anymore."

She narrowed her eyes defiantly and squeezed his fingers so tightly the skin turned white. "I say this with great assurance," she told him. *"The United States of America is a special place.* It will *always* be worth saving! The world needs us. We are the only hope they have.

"Think about it, Daniel. Maybe they don't teach these kinds of things at Ivy League schools anymore, but what would have happened to Europe during either of the World Wars if not for the United States? What would Japan or the Pacific Rim be like under totalitarian regimes? The Philippines, Korea, Afghanistan, to say nothing of Israel? What would those places be like if it were not for the U.S.? It's impossible to overstate the positive impact the U.S. has had on the world over the past hundred years.

"Yes, we have fought many wars, but we are not a warlike people. We don't fight to conquer nations; we fight to set nations free. We don't fight to enslave a people; we fight to set a people free. And the only territories we've ever kept are the tiny pieces of pasture where we bury our soldier-dead.

"This country is a beacon in the darkness, but its future is not assured. We have to fight to save it, but its future is worth fighting for." She gestured angrily toward the hall. "Some of them don't believe that. They think they have a better way. But I know you, Daniel—I know you don't think like that. You've walked through the military cemeteries, you've touched those stone-cold markers, you've recognized the sacred ground.

"Think about that, Daniel. Think about what's going on. We can't betray those dead now. Think of all those who died in Washington! We can't let them die in vain." She lifted her eyes, indicating the topside world. "Think of all those who are dying right now. They look to us for hope!"

Jefferson lifted his coffee and sipped, realized it was only warm, and gulped it, taking down half the cup. He was old now, overweight, balding, red patches aside his cheeks. The truth was—and even he would admit it—he shouldn't have been on the Court any longer. He had trouble hearing and concentrating and was generally more concerned about the length of time between bathroom breaks than about the arguments before him. He was old and cranky to the point of being ostracized by his peers—little love and less respect between them. There was one element of the Constitution that he held most inviolate and dear: Supreme Court justices served for life. Didn't matter their mental, physical, or emotional health, they took their place on the bench until their bodies were cold and dead. Such an attitude guaranteed him power, but it certainly wasn't endearing to either his friends or his enemies.

Worst of all, over the years Jefferson had taken the journey from being a proud defender of civil rights to being a proud defender of extreme liberalism to becoming a hard-core cynic. Few things mattered much to him anymore. He'd lost faith in his government, in his nation's people, in the law.

Which was why, Brucius Marino and his people knew, the conspirators had decided to let him live.

Sara stared at her old friend, searching for the bit of life that used to shine in his eyes, her mind flashing back to dinner parties around Washington where he used to argue, his deep voice booming, for the oppressed and the minorities.

Was that patriot still alive inside him?

From the blank look on his face, she didn't know.

She searched herself a final time, seeking desperately for the right words to say. But nothing came. Her mind was blank.

She stared vacantly at her trembling hands, then cleared her throat and looked at him again. "This is the Promised Land, Daniel. I don't know any other way to say it. It isn't perfect—far from it, I know—but there is nothing else even close. God has guarded His work in this magnificent cause, for He knew it was essential for this country to survive in order that it might guarantee the same freedoms to other people. Think about it, Justice Jefferson. It started as early as Jamestown. For years they struggled against starvation, disease, hunger, danger, a sometimes hostile Indian population there. Eighty percent died in the cause. Yet, despite this overwhelming failure, God saw that it was good and He helped the seed survive. Within just a couple of generations, the United States had the highest per capita income of any nation in the world.

"Think of the original thirteen colonies against the entire British empire. I mean, come on. The Battle of New York during the American Revolution. No way Washington and his army should have survived. But the fog came and gave them shelter and they lived to fight another day. The Battle of Gettysburg. Even in the face of utter failure, Lincoln knew God had taken the whole business into His hand.

"But it's a new day now. And like it has happened during the rise of fascism we've seen so many times before, I have to wonder why free men don't speak out. An amoral society can't exercise moral judgment. If we are no longer able to see the difference between right and wrong because we don't believe they exist, then we have failed as a nation.

"Our Founding Fathers believed our government could survive only if the Constitution ruled over a moral people.

"Are we a moral people, Daniel? Are we worthy of the fight? Is any of it worth fighting for? I'm here to tell you that it is. I love my country. I know you love it too. Now it's time to man-up and find the courage to join us in this cause."

chapter thirty-four

OFFUTT AIR FORCE BASE
HEADQUARTERS, U.S. STRATEGIC COMMAND
EIGHT MILES SOUTH OF OMAHA, NEBRASKA

The Secretary of Defense was in his office. The lights were turned down, the shades drawn, the door open. He had three computers on the credenza behind him, all of them glowing, and a pile of papers across his desk, most in red folders marked "TS—SBI" (top secret, special background investigation). Each red folder, he had to sign for, and he couldn't let them out of his sight.

Although he was sitting at his desk, Brucius Marino was asleep. He hadn't meant for it to happen; he'd only closed his eyes to rub them, but his wire glasses had fallen into his lap, his arms slumped awkwardly across his lap, his chin heavy upon his chest.

Sometime after ten, one of his assistants had poked a head into the room and called his name, but Brucius hadn't moved. The captain had repeated his name, this time more softly, but again had gotten no response. He listened to the SecDef's breathing for several seconds, then silently left the room.

Brucius slept in his chair for almost three hours without moving, the longest period of uninterrupted sleep he had had in almost two weeks. At 0113, another man walked into the office without knocking. "Sir," the four-star general said softly. Brucius didn't move. The general took a couple of steps toward him and raised his voice. "Secretary Marino."

Brucius finally woke. He looked up groggily and shook his head. "What time is it?" he wondered aloud as he glanced down at his watch. "Did I sleep here through the night . . . no, I mean, it's not afternoon, it's still nighttime . . ." He quieted himself to settle his brain and collect his thoughts.

"Sir," the four-star said again, his voice now urgent. "She got him. He's coming out!"

Brucius stared at the general. Neither of them had shaved and all of their eyes were red with fatigue. "Who . . . Sara Brighton . . . she got him?"

"Yes, sir," the general said. "She found him this afternoon, yesterday afternoon now, I guess I should say. He's coming with her."

"Are they . . . ?"

"Yes, sir. They're already out of Raven Rock. The helicopter met them up at the pickup point a few minutes ago. They'll be here by midmorning."

Brucius stared, almost unable to accept the good news. "You're certain?" he demanded.

"Yes, sir. I talked to Mrs. Brighton myself. Got a patch through on the HF. She sounded pretty good."

"And Jefferson is with her?"

"Yes, sir." The general hesitated. "Apparently he's not too happy, though."

Brucius sat up in his chair. His legs had fallen asleep and he had to shift them with his hands. He stood up gingerly and smiled. "What did she do? How'd she do it? She never could have brought him out against his will. The old coot is as stubborn as a mule with broken legs." Brucius started laughing with relief.

The general didn't share the humor. Laughing wasn't his job. "Sir, all I know is that she did it. She really did it. And both of them are okay."

Brucius rubbed his hands across his face to wipe the sleep from his eyes. "All right," he said. "They'll all be here by morning. The other justices are waiting. I want them assembled by one o'clock. We're going to lock them in a room and not let any of them out. We're not going to interfere with their decision or deliberations in any way. We'll provide any assistance they might ask for, give them anything they want, but we're going to keep them locked up until it's over. I want a decision from them. One way or another, I want to know."

The general took a breath. "The good news is, Mr. Secretary, that we've got three justices now. Either way, it'll be at least a 2–1 decision. There'll be no tie vote."

Brucius looked across the desk at him. "Yes, that's the good news. The bad news is that we don't know which way this thing will turn."

The general stood with his eyes on the wall.

Brucius moved toward the low coffee table set between two leather couches on the other side of his desk. "I want to show you something, General Hawly."

The general followed him around the first couch and looked down at the table.

The engineering charts, construction blueprints, and infrastructure layouts were piled two inches thick. Brucius tapped them eagerly.

"What are these?" the general asked.

"All the engineering blueprints of Raven Rock. We've got charts that show every access door, the ventilation systems, communications antennas, power generation stations, air purifiers, the whole bit. See, that's the problem with a place like Raven Rock. It was always assumed that friendly forces would be up-top. But I'm not feeling friendly, General Hawly. And I'll bet that you're not either."

Maybe for the first time since he had known him, Brucius saw the general smile. "What are you planning, Mr. Secretary?"

"Give me the right Supreme Court decision and I'm going to rock their world. We're going to cut them off and kill them. We're going to take their underground encampment and use it to trap them like the rats they are."

*" . . . according to the Spirit of God, which is also
the spirit of freedom which is in them."*

—Alma 61:15

*"The one great revolution in the world is the revolution for
human liberty. This was the paramount issue in the great
council in heaven before this earth life. It has been the
issue throughout the ages. It is the issue today."*

—President Ezra Taft Benson

chapter thirty-five

At 0208, the helicopter landed at a remote fire base in the extreme mountains of Afghanistan to pick up the final members of the military team. The last of the Cherokees climbed aboard, two men who knew the local area as well as any men alive.

The team complete, the chopper lifted again and flew northeast.

The Cherokees, six of them now, were bunched together at the front of the helicopter, an Air Force Special Forces MH-53J Pave Low, the largest, most powerful and technologically advanced helicopter in the world. The Pave Low was crewed by six: two pilots, two flight engineers, and two gunners who manned the powerful 7.62mm miniguns (6,000 rounds per minute, 100 rounds per second, a beautiful line of destruction in the middle of a firefight). The chopper was huge and ugly and all business, with protruding antennas and guns and in-flight refueling probes, darkened glass, flare and chaff dispensers, and protective armor. Unlike a modern fighter, it wasn't sleek or sexy. Hardly. The thing was boxy and black, a barnyard dog begging for the fight. The two GE engines

227

generated almost 9,000 shaft horsepower between them. The Order of Battle communications package allowed for instant updates on target and threat locations while creating a bird's-eye view of the battlefield. The terrain-following/terrain-avoidance radar, forward-looking infrared sensor, inertial navigation system, global positioning system, and computer-generated moving map display enabled the crew to fly at night or in the weather (Special Ops rarely flew without cover of darkness) while following the contours of the earth at just a couple of dozen feet. Officially, the Pave Low's mission was *"low-level, long-range, undetected penetration into denied areas, day or night, in adverse weather, for infiltration, exfiltration, and resupply of Special Operations forces."* More simply put, the chopper was designed to sneak in and sneak out, avoiding the enemy when it was possible and engaging them when not.

Despite almost 40 million dollars in avionics upgrades, the inside of the helicopter was anything but luxurious. One of the most combat-proven assets of the Dark Side (as Special Operators were known), the chopper was bare-bones and well used: canvas seats, ratty paint, every piece of equipment worn but functional.

As the Pave Low flew northeast, the winds suddenly kicked up, gusting down from the mountains to the cooler valleys, swirling and circling between the enormous peaks to create turbulence so severe the men felt they were on some diabolical roller coaster.

Too turbulent to work. The soldiers quit talking and held on.

Two of them had already been sick. Azadeh hadn't thrown up yet, but that was only because over the previous two days she'd been too nervous to eat anything more than a handful of nuts and a couple of bananas.

As they settled into the valley, the ride became suddenly smooth and the men went back to work.

Azadeh sat watching as they pointed to their maps, debated, sometimes argued, all the while scribbling in little notebooks. She was relieved to see that, as far as she could tell, Sam was one of the officers in charge. She watched him closely. He had cut his hair, dyed it darker and trimmed his facial hair into a neat beard. With his dark skin, he could easily have passed for a local. Watching him, she thought back to the battle on the streets of East Chicago, the episode having instilled in her mind a completely unrealistic confidence in Sam.

"Be cool," he had told her.

She had a better understanding now what that meant.

Staring at him, her stomach fluttered and she quickly looked away. Her emotions for him were becoming far too complicated. Far too deep. *He's doesn't care about you, Azadeh,* a nagging voice inside her seemed to say. But something about the way he looked at her made her wonder, even hope, that maybe he did. And even if he didn't, it didn't change the way she felt. Like some mythical Greek god, he seemed invincible. She would do anything he told her to. She would place her life in his hands.

Which was exactly what she was doing now.

And she wasn't the only one taking a risk. The other soldiers were placing their lives in *her* hands, too.

The responsibility was crushing. But it made her even more determined to do whatever it was they needed of her. After all that she had been through, she wouldn't let them down.

She adjusted her headset to relieve the pressure on her ears and listened carefully as the soldiers talked.

The other officer, she thought his name was Bono, leaned

across the large map the men had spread across the helicopter's floor and shone his red-lens flashlight. "Okay, guys," he said, pointing with his finger. "We're here now. We're heading here. Twenty minutes to the LZ."

Sam glanced at his illuminated watch. "Almost three minutes behind schedule."

Bono didn't seem to care. "No worries. The pilots assure me they'll more than make it up on the downside of the hill."

Azadeh glanced through the tiny window cut into the cabin door to her right. The darkness was so deep she couldn't see anything, which was a good thing, for if she'd been able to see how close the helicopter was to the ground, roaring along at more than 150 miles an hour and barely half a rotor's length above the rocks and trees, she would have panicked.

Sam looked at her and it was as if he'd read her mind. "The mountains in this area form a rough triangle that meets at the Pakistan, Afghanistan, Iranian border," he told her. "We're following the contours of the mountains northeast, basically skirting between the border of Pakistan and Afghanistan." He motioned at their feet, signaling the river valley they were flying over. "Not any good guys around us right now. The mountains ahead of us are as steep and treacherous as any in the world. We're operating on the footstool of the Himalayas, the greatest mountain range on the planet. K-2 is not too far from here. Mount Everest is off our right, though still a long way off.

"The only things below us right now are bad guys and rock." He was talking to his team now. "This ain't the place we want to go down. Not the place we want to have any problems. We all understand that. There isn't going to be any cavalry coming to the rescue. We're going in alone."

Listening to him, the soldiers were attentive and serious. No bravado. No excitement. Like the chopper that was carrying them, they were all business. It was a lousy job before them and the only thing they wanted was to get it over with.

Sam looked grim. "There are no rescue assets in this area," he concluded. "There'll be no Close Air Support, no suppressive or protective cover. With the exception of the weapons we've got in our hands, we'll be on our own. Got some marines up north, but they're way too far away to be any help. You understand what I'm saying?" He paused.

"Alone. Outgunned. Afraid," one of the other soldiers snorted. "Pretty much a normal mission."

The air force door gunner patted the Gatling gun positioned at the window. "A hundred rounds per second of burning slugs of joy. I'd hardly say that you're outgunned. Not with this baby in my hands."

A soldier named Slapper pointed to the ammo box beside him. "Yeah. Sure. At that rate of fire, you have, what? five or six seconds' worth of ammunition? Anyway, what does it matter? You're going to drop us off and head back to the carrier, where you'll sip some coffee before getting on the computer to check in with your wife. After you unload us, we're nothing but six pukes in the middle of the bad guys." He snorted again. "Yeah, you drop us off, then take off with our miniguns. *That's* when I get afraid."

The gunner smiled. "Guess that's why they give you all that combat pay."

Sam nudged the sergeant on his knee to get his attention back. Slapper turned, then tilted his head toward Azadeh. "And the girl?" he asked as if she weren't there.

The other soldiers turned suspiciously toward her. The expressions on their faces asked the question, *What are we going to do with her?*

"She's going to get us close enough to the king to get

him," Sam told them. "She's key to the entire operation. Without her, we don't have a chance of pulling this thing off."

Slapper shook his head. "I dunno, boss. Looks like you pulled her from the cover of some fashion magazine, but Abdullah's used to beautiful women. I don't think he'll be all that impressed." He kept his eyes on Azadeh but still spoke as if she weren't there. "And she looks as soft as mud to me. I say she wets her pants the first shot that gets fired."

Sam leaned toward the younger soldier. "She's got a spine as solid as yours, Slapper. Don't underestimate her because she's pretty. She's seen things, been through things, you could only dream about."

"Yeah, like running up against her limit on the old man's credit card?"

Sam's eyes turned hard. "She's part of us. *I trust her.* You're going to have to trust her too. All of us are going to have to trust each other or this thing is going to blow up in our faces." He nodded toward Azadeh but kept his words directed to the man. "You're going to have to trust me that I know what I'm doing with this, okay?"

The soldier was silent.

Sam leaned toward him, his bulky shoulders creating a wide shadow against the aircraft's bulkhead. "Any further questions on this topic?"

"No, sir."

"Didn't think so, Slapper."

The soldier turned and smiled vaguely toward Azadeh. "Welcome to the team. If you screw it up, they're going to kill you, but hey, that ain't no big deal. Don't go and worry your pretty little head about all that. Just be cool, little darlin', and let's get this over with."

Azadeh only stared back at him.

There it was again. *Be cool.*

232

Bono moved toward the center of the group. "Okay, this is what we know," he started. "We've got a resource somewhere here on the mountain. For lack of a better name, we'll call him . . ." he shot a look at Azadeh, his eyes illuminated by the red lights overhead, " . . . tell you what, we'll call him Omar, since that happens to be his name. He's in contact with the Saudi prince. In fact, he's the young boy's protector. Over the past few days, he's been moving him across the mountains, positioning the prince closer to the Afghani border where it will be a little easier for us to get to him."

"Who is this guy?" one of the soldiers asked, his face hidden in the dim light of the bouncing chopper.

"Omar?"

"No, the kid. Who is he and why is it worth my life to save him?"

Sam leaned forward to take the question. "He's the son of the crown prince of the House of Saud."

The soldier shook his head. "The crown prince is dead. His brother got him. From what our Intel pukes told us, Abdullah pretty much took care of everyone in the family who had the guts to stand in his way."

The soldier was a thirty-year-old enlisted man who was one of the best NCOs the Cherokees had ever produced. He had a bachelor's degree in physiology and a master's in international relations. He spoke four languages, including Arabic and Urdu, the predominant language of the region they were flying over right now (predominant in the sense that more people spoke it than most of the other forty different dialects and languages used by the Pushtin rebels, government soldiers, and nomadic herdsmen of the mountains). Yet he was willing to work in the grime and filth of one of the most hostile locations on the earth, all for something like $45k a year. Some things men did for love of country or adventure, not for cash. His name was Dallas Houston (his old man having been drunk when he filled out the birth certificate, and his old lady having been thrilled with the choice of names), and the soldier was like his namesakes: big, powerful, hot, and sweaty—in general, the kind of guy you wanted with you in a dirty fight.

Sam lowered his eyes, his mind flashing back. His father, Neil Brighton, had been close friends with the crown prince of Saudi Arabia. In fact, his father had sent a rescue mission to save the prince's son after the prince had hidden him in the village in the mountains of Iran.

His heart raced at the memory, but he forced himself to focus his eyes on Houston. "You got it right," he answered. "Abdullah popped everyone in his immediate family: all his brothers, their wives, their children. But the crown prince wasn't stupid. He got his youngest son out before Abdullah could kill him. Took him to the remote mountains of Iran. But Abdullah soon found the location of the village where his older brother had hidden his son and sent an assassination squad to kill him." He pointed toward Azadeh. "She was there. She saw it all. Her father was killed by the Iranian soldiers. It was Omar, one of her father's closest friends, who got the boy out of the village before he could be killed. He's been hiding him ever since, although we lost track of him up until a couple of days ago. That's when Omar sent us word that he couldn't protect the boy any longer. He needed the U.S. to come and get him."

"Okay," Houston answered after a moment's thought. "And we care about this because . . ."

"Because the boy is the legal heir to the Saudi kingdom. Because the young prince is the only hope we have of establishing a pro-democratic, pro-West, pro-American government in the kingdom. Because if we don't save him, King Abdullah wins. It's pretty much that simple. We've got to get this kid out and protect him or King Abdullah retains power—a completely hostile leader sitting on the throne of one of the most powerful and important nations on the earth."

The soldiers were silent for a moment.

"Because if you don't help him, King Abdullah is going to kill him," Azadeh said, breaking the silence. Her voice was quiet but her eyes were firm.

All the soldiers turned to look at her.

"Yeah, there's that, too," Bono said. "We've got a chance to do a good thing. Nothing wrong with that."

"But listen to me on this," Sam cut in quickly. "This is important. Saving the prince is *not* our primary mission. It's critical you understand that he's a collateral objective. Frankly, the main reason we care about him is that we're using him as bait. If we can save him, cool, but that's not the reason we're here. We're here to track down King Abdullah."

"Why in the world would he be stupid enough to leave his kingdom?" Houston asked. "Why would he come to this forsaken place? And how do you even know he's here?"

"A little birdie told us."

Houston nodded, knowing Sam was talking about a micro-drone.

"Turns out the little birdie was right." Sam slapped a high-resolution satellite photograph on the floor that showed two military transports, the Arabic script and sword of the Saudi flag upon their tails. "We got these pictures sometime yesterday. King Abdullah is here to kill the prince."

"Why wouldn't Abdullah just send an assassination squad?"

Sam shrugged. "Seems Abdullah's a hands-on kind of guy, you know, a leader who likes to take care of some of the dirty work himself."

"Okay, boss, so what's the plan? How are we going to pop him off?"

Sam shook his head. "We're not going to kill him. Let me say that again: *We're not here to kill him.* We're going to capture him and take him back to the States, where he's going to stand trial for crimes against humanity, genocide, unlawful warfare, fratricide, offending U.N. officers, breaking pollution standards, stealing bubble gum out of gumball machines—there isn't a crime on the books for which this guy won't be charged. And he's not going to spend his life in some cushy federal prison hanging out with convicted senators and Wall Street executives. No, this guy is going to hang, and hang quickly. It's the only way we have of avoiding an overwhelming push toward a war of retaliation." Sam stopped and stared around the circle of his men. Looks of confusion had crept onto several of their faces.

"Here's the deal," he concluded, slipping the final piece of the puzzle into place. "Even as we speak here, there's a constitutional battle being fought for the very soul of our country. If that goes well, and it had better, then Secretary Marino—"

"Brucius Marino!" Slapper exclaimed. "I thought he was dead."

"Quite the contrary. He's the one who authorized this mission."

"They said he killed himself after the impeachment."

"Afraid that's demonstrably untrue. All sorts of rumors going on out there right now. And if he is able to claim the presidency—"

Dallas Houston raised his hand. "Nyet, nyet, nyet. Fuentes is the president . . ."

"Not if Brucius Marino is alive."

"He's been impeached already."

"That remains to be seen. It isn't clear that the proceedings against him were even legal. In many respects, they were very clearly not."

Sam quickly told the soldiers of the move to gather the three remaining members of the Supreme Court. After he finished speaking, they sat in stunned silence for a long moment, the helicopter bouncing all around them.

"Holy cattle," Houston finally said.

"You got it, baby. Very holy cattle. Do you see now what we're doing here? Do you really understand? If Secretary Marino is sworn in as president, there's going to be overwhelming pressure to retaliate for the nuclear and EMP attacks. He doesn't want to have to do that. But justice *must* be served. The only way to do that is to capture King Abdullah and take him back to the States.

"Knowing what you know now, is there any spot of doubt inside your minds how critical this mission is? Can you see that right now the world is hanging by a thread? We do our job, and we've got a bit of hope here. Fail, and I don't know."

The group was silent.

"We can do it," Houston said.

Sam knelt beside the map in front of them. "And this is how."

* * *

His instructions took less than five minutes. When he was finished, the soldiers stared at him.

"That's it?" Dallas Houston wondered.

Sam shot a look at Bono. "It's the best we could come up with, given our limited resources and time."

Houston shook his head.

Bono shrugged with nonchalant confidence. "It'll work," he assured his men.

"And you say that because . . . ?"

"Well, for one thing, it'll catch them off guard."

Houston almost laughed. "That it will, Lieutenant. I mean, it's so absurd, how could you even think of such a plan!"

Bono kept his face serious. "Yeah, okay, it's . . . uhhhh . . . less *direct* than what we usually do. But if everyone does their job, things will be okay."

"Dude, I wouldn't describe this as a work of Einstein," Houston shot back. "I mean, I've seen some pretty screwed-up plans before, but I don't think I've ever seen anything quite like this."

"You don't think it'll work."

Houston didn't answer at first. The look on his face said it all. Finally he responded, "I don't know, boss, I'm not saying it's completely hopeless, I just wonder, you know . . . I just, I mean, what are we going to face, maybe a hundred of the king's special security forces?"

Sam shrugged. "Maybe not a hundred."

"Okay, eighty or ninety, then?"

"Yeah, that sounds about right."

"And these guys are not slouches. All of them are graduates of the finest training the United States could provide them, I'm sorry to say. All of them were hand-selected for their dedication and ruthlessness. I've worked with some of those guys, Lieutenant—all of us have. They're good. And anything they lack in tactics they more than make up for in their lack of fear."

Sam shrugged again. "Yeah, okay, I'm not going to argue."

"All right, then, just to make sure I've got it. We're going up against at least three teams from the Royal Security Forces, with something like twenty-five to thirty men in each team.

They've got the advantage of defensible positions and superior firepower, not to mention the fact that, when it's all over, we don't have any way to evacuate the area, no way of getting out of town. There's six of us." He looked at Azadeh. "Well, six and one girl who, if we were going to assault some modeling agency in Paris, I think she'd be okay. But this ain't Paris, this is Ickistan. And I'm supposed to feel good about this gig?"

Sam's face remained calm, his eyes bright. He didn't feel scared. "Yeah, Houston, you're supposed to feel good about this thing. Come on, man! This is guts and glory, the kind of mission that they write songs about."

"No one writes songs about things like this anymore."

Sam looked dejected. "Well, they used to."

"Not anymore, Lieutenant."

"Still, they should."

Houston stared back at him, then started smiling.

"And there's one *really* important thing you didn't mention that's in our favor," Sam said as he slapped Bono on the shoulder. "The quality of your leadership is unmatched anywhere in the world. If anyone can get us through this, believe me, this man will."

Houston nodded, then glanced at his watch. Outside, the night was turning pale, the last cold glimmers of the falling moon forming shadows among the mountains.

"LZ in two minutes," one of the flight engineers announced over the chopper's intercom.

The men stood and started unstrapping their gear from the helicopter's metal floor. They had a very long hike ahead of them and very little time, for they had to be in position before the sunlight broke over the enormous mountain peaks almost 15,000 feet over their heads.

Three or four hours of running. Uphill. Among sheer

cliffs. With seventy pounds of guns, ammo, and equipment strapped around their chests and atop their backs.

Most men couldn't make the hike in two days.

They had a little more than three hours.

Sam braced himself for the physical battle that lay ahead. By the end of the day, all of them would be utterly exhausted, every muscle, every bone, every tendon, and every ounce of energy pulled and stretched and used and drained.

By the end of the day, they'd be either successful or dead.

He stood up and threw his pack across his shoulders. A surge of adrenaline pushed through him, sending a shiver through his veins.

But this was more than just the adrenaline. There was something else . . . something around him. Something he didn't recognize. A feeling, foreign and powerful, warm but unfamiliar. A premonition, maybe? He swallowed and looked away, his mind tumbling, a wave of vertigo making him reach for the nearest brace.

Turning toward Bono, he felt a sudden sense of sadness sweep across him. It hit him like a black and heavy blanket, covering his entire soul.

For no reason he could explain, he felt like weeping.

For no reason he could explain, he felt like walking toward Bono and holding him in his arms.

chapter thirty-six

The village was too small to even have a name. It sat beside a swiftly flowing river, which was dark and muddy and frothing now from three days of severe rains. A collection of rock huts and wooden shanties had been built around a crumbling central market, the walls of which were covered arches, the blue and green paint faded now, the white script almost entirely unreadable. The entire wall was pockmarked with bullet holes, some from the brutal Russian military, some from the Taliban militia, some from U.S. soldiers, some from the local warlord's henchmen, some from celebratory shots fired after a wedding party. Behind the village, the land sloped gently upward for three or four kilometers before jutting suddenly toward the blue sky at nearly impossible angles. The valley floor was too rocky to be farmed, three hundred thousand years of retreating and advancing glaciers having deposited a couple of million boulders and man-sized rocks across the gravelly ground. Because the valley was unfarmable, the foothills had been heavily terraced, every inch put to use. The lifeblood of the village, the terraces were richly earthed but dry, the villagers having no practical way of pumping the water out of the gushing river up to the higher ground. Electricity hadn't made it to the village yet. Neither had running water. Nor doctors or medical services. There were a few automobiles, certainly nothing made in the present century, and donkeys outnumbered trucks or cars by at least twenty-five to one. In most respects, the village hadn't changed much over the past thousand years. Battles had been fought here. Battles were fought here now. People had lived and died here. People lived and died here now.

So much was the same.

It was remarkable.

For more than two thousand years, the Pashtun village had lived through a series of horrors known as invasions from the Aryan tribes, then the Persians, then the Mauryas, Kushans, Greeks, Arabs, and Turks. Partly because of this, but mostly because they lived in a land the modern world had forgotten and didn't care about, the Pashtuns were the largest segmentary people on the earth, segmentary in that they stood as tribes, with no other form of government to bind them. The best description of their hierarchy was found in the old saying, "brother against brother, brothers against cousins, brothers and cousins against the world."

Conservative in their lifestyle and devout in their beliefs, the Pashtuns made fearsome friends and terrifying enemies.

Which did Omar stand beside right now? He didn't know.

*   *   *

The village leader's hut sat in the corner of the lowest terrace, the only structure allowed to take up such a precious piece of farming ground, perhaps the greatest tribute to his status in the village that he could ever hope to achieve. Omar stood beside the village leader. It was dim now, not quite morning light but not quite dark, the gray light having washed out the stars. The princeling hung close to Omar's side, and the man looked down at him. The boy was larger now, stronger and more confident. Omar thought of the hidden diamond tucked under his woolen shirt. Looking at the boy, he knew two diamonds were hidden there.

"Who is he?" the village leader demanded.

"He is a child."

"*Who is he!*"

"He needs your help."

"Who seeks him? Are you his father?"

"Many forces seek him. And no, I am not."

The leader studied Omar. "I will not let you bring evil into my village."

"I bring no evil. I bring a child."

"Evil comes in many faces."

"Look at him, Aashir."

The leader of the local tribe was young. Life was too hard to leave many old men on the mountain, and all village leaders had to be young enough to fight. He was called *abbu Rehnuma,* or "father leader," and that was exactly what he was: father of his people, leader of their tribe. He studied the boy, pulling on his long beard. He hadn't shaved—praise to Allah—not even once in his life; his face was virgin, having never touched a blade. He thought for several seconds, then turned around. "Take him away," he commanded. "He's not my charge."

"Aashir, please, in the name of all that is sure and holy—"

"He is not my charge!" The young man looked suddenly nervous. "I hear much now, Allah willing, and I listen. There are foreign forces all around us. And not the devil Americans, no, not from what I hear. These are far more evil, far more dangerous . . ." He dropped his voice to a whisper. "These are the forces of a foreign king: keeper of the Holy Stone, protector of the Shrine."

Omar felt a cold chill. "One day of rest is all I'm asking," he begged. "One day is all I need."

The leader scoffed. "I doubt that, my friend Omar, I doubt that a great deal. One day of hiding the boy and then what, you disappear back to the mountains from which you came? You head on down the river, boy tucked neatly under your goat-hair coat?" The man gestured adamantly toward the mountains. "If I let you stay one day, you will not leave."

"No, no, no. One day and we will go."

His words were met with scoffing. "Few will leave the mountain, especially at this time of year."

The two men fell silent.

"How will you do it?" the young man asked. "If I let you stay, how will you leave me?" He looked down at the child. The boy stood beside Omar's legs, but he didn't hide his face. His eyes were dark and penetrating, his shoulders small but square.

Omar remained silent.

The *abbu Rehnuma* watched him, waiting, then raised his hand. "Not my charge. Not my charge. I have to protect my people. Look at me, look at all of us, my brother—how could we possibly protect ourselves? We are nothing. For a thousand years we've been nothing. For the next thousand years, Allah willing, we'll remain nothing. That's all we want now. Nothingness. Peace. No more foreign soldiers. We want our brothers. Sometimes our cousins. That is all."

Omar took a desperate step toward him. "This is not some *swara*, Aashir, some woman-child I have bought or was given because I was owed. This is—" he caught himself, falling suddenly silent. "This child is something else. Something important . . ." He was afraid to tell.

Aashir turned to him. "This is *who,* Omar? Tell me, who is this child?"

Omar cleared his throat. "We seek sanctuary, Aashir."

The younger man's eyes went hard and he took a sharp breath and held it as if he'd been punched in the gut. He stood there, his mouth open, his face pulled into a frown.

"A single day, that is all," Omar told him. "A single day of sanctuary is all we ask. Then, one way or another, we'll be gone."

"I cannot, I cannot . . ."

"Sanctuary is one of the tenets of your society, a pillar of your faith. You *can't* deny us sanctuary. Allah *requires* this of you. If you want Him to protect you, you *have* to pay the price!"

chapter thirty-seven

The enormous chopper made two full passes, its infrared and low-light sensors searching the ground below. But there was simply nothing there. Every inch of open ground jutted up to meet the rocky cliffs. The ancient pines stretched a hundred and twenty feet into the sky. It took them only a few minutes to realize there wasn't a single patch of level dirt on which they could land.

It was starting to get light now and the chopper was getting low on fuel. And the longer they hovered around the edge of the small lake, the more likely they were to be spotted, if they hadn't been already. Sophisticated as the combat chopper was, nothing muted the roar of its engines or whine of its powerful blades; it sent an audio signal that could be heard for miles.

"What happened to our landing zone?" Sam demanded into his intercom.

"Not here, man," the copilot called back from the cockpit. Looking forward, Sam could see only the left side of the man's body behind the armor plate that was wrapped around his seat.

"There's simply nowhere here to land," the pilot confirmed.

"What about the recon photographs?"

"You got me. Might be some distortion in the picture. Don't know. Don't really care. All I can tell you is there's no place to land down there."

Sam checked the digital image of the satellite photograph once again. That was the problem with this area—so much of the terrain was vertical that the photo images were easily distorted, making them impossible to interpret.

"Isn't there anywhere along the beach?" he demanded of the pilots.

"Nothing, boss. You can come up here and check it out yourself. There are no beaches around this lake, not in the traditional sense. The water comes right up to the rocks and trees."

Sam turned to Bono. "Think we could try to fast rope?"

Bono immediately shook his head. "The trees are way too high. The ropes wouldn't even touch the ground."

"We could use the rescue cable to hoist ourselves down."

"Yeah, if we had an extra hour."

Sam turned back to the cockpit. "You following this, guys?"

"Roger that, boss. Looks like we're calling this mission an abort."

Sam snorted. He knew the pilot was only kidding. Although they didn't know any of the details about the mission—Special Operations were always kept on a strict need-to-know basis as a way to protect the aircrews if they happened to get shot down—the pilots clearly understood this was the highest priority mission they had ever flown.

There was silence for an awkward moment.

"Looks like we're going to get wet," Bono said.

*   *   *

Two minutes later, the enormous helicopter thundered toward the northernmost edge of the lake, then started to slow. Fifty feet above the water, the nose pulled suddenly into an aggressive flare, the rotors spinning up as the pilot took pitch out of the blades. The chopper settled quickly toward the water. Ten feet above the lake, with both side doors open, the chopper came to a momentary hover, then descended into the water, kicking up three-foot waves. Aft, a wall of water moved across the metal floor. The pilot kept the helicopter light, maintaining power in the blades, never allowing the full weight of the helicopter to settle onto the lake although it would have floated even if he had.

With the doors open, the six-man team and Azadeh evacuated the helicopter within seconds. The water was deep. And cold. Bitter cold. With their packs and equipment weighing them down, they knew they had only a few seconds to get out of the water before cramps and hypothermia set in. The Cherokees started swimming, packs on their backs, ammo and weapons around their waists, rifles over their heads. Bono and Sam kept hold of Azadeh, pulling her along.

A couple of the soldiers disappeared below the water. The pilots watched, both of them subconsciously holding their breaths. The two men suddenly reappeared, this time much closer to the water's edge. Approaching the shoreline, none of them were able to walk. The water was just too deep. The pilots watched the soldiers struggle to pull themselves atop the rocky walls that descended into the water for hundreds of feet below.

Counting, the pilot waited until the team was safe; then, getting a thumbs-up from Bono, he pulled up on the collective in his left hand, applying greater pitch to the main rotor blades. Taking deeper slices of air with each rotation, the rotors drooped as the heavy chopper lifted, gallons of clear water rushing out the aft and side doors.

*　　*　　*

Sam watched the chopper lift, turn its tail to the right, and climb higher before dropping toward the water once again. Seconds later, its dark image disappeared, lost in the dim light.

Turning toward the rocks around him, he started climbing. He was shivering already, his body contracting to keep in what little heat it could. But he didn't even think about it. In a few minutes he would be sweating. It would be hours before they stopped to rest.

The last thing he had to worry about was being cold.

chapter thirty-eight

The Saudi soldier was dressed in combat gear, his face hidden in the low brush a third of a kilometer above the village. He kept his eyes on the two men and young boy who were talking down below him. He hardly moved as he watched them, not wanting to give any indication of his position. But the truth was, even if he'd been lying right beside the targets, he would have been impossible to see. Everything about him was camouflaged: his face, eyelids, teeth, clothes, hands, even the boots on his feet. Still, he hardly moved, lying prone across the wet ground, his shoulders and torso stuffed underneath a gnarled *Cydonia* shrub, its low branches meeting the wire grass that clung to the side of the hill, the only thing that kept the topsoil from washing away with every storm. It was barely light, but light enough for him to see, and he watched the men through a long-range lens, the magnification bringing them close enough that he could have read their lips if he spoke the language they were communicating in right now.

But he didn't. He was a foreigner in this land.

A foreigner and a killer.

The sniper rifle was heavy in his hand. It too was carefully camouflaged, tattered pieces of colored burlap wrapped around the stock and 24-inch barrel. Above his fingers, the bolt was seated in the chamber. He was ready to fire.

He held the rifle close to his chest, wanting to keep her warm. It was suspicious, and kind of crazy, but legend was that it was bad fortune to kill a man with a cold rifle, and he didn't want to tempt the shooting gods.

The U.S. Marine Corps M40A3 long-range rifle was an outstanding weapon, one of the world's best. When coupled with the new M118LR ammo, the sniper rifle was capable of extreme accuracy out to 1,000 feet, about the distance he was sitting at right now. He sniffed. No wind. The air was clean and cool and, up here in these mountains, very thin. At this range, give him three seconds and he could put a group of five bullets within a two-inch circle. Give him a couple of seconds longer, and he would group the same shells within three-quarters of an inch.

Three-quarters of an inch. About the same size as a human eye.

Three-quarters of an inch. Accurate enough to do this job.

He eyed the two men and small boy through his lens, then laid it carefully to the side and touched a small button on the clip attached to his lapel. "I have the boy," he stated clearly.

"You are certain it is him?"

The soldier wouldn't have made such a mistake. He knew the danger to himself if he were wrong. His punishment for making an inaccurate call and diverting the other forces from their own searches would have been painful, even deadly.

No, the boy's face was intricately and clearly etched into his mind. So was the face and outline of the fat one. It was part of the art of long-range sniping: accurately identifying the target. "I have him," he repeated curtly.

The radio in his ear was silent for a full half minute. "We are ten minutes away," his commander finally said. "Keep the target in sight. Kill the old man if you have to, but *don't* lose sight of the boy. If you have to, expose your position, but *do not* lose the boy!"

The soldier listened but didn't answer.

"Pile Driver wants the boy alive!" the voice reiterated.

Pile Driver: the daily code word for the king. The soldier listened, then dropped his hand to pick up his rifle once again.

"Confirm!" he was directed.

He quickly lifted his hand to his lapel and pushed the transmit button. "Confirmed," he replied.

Adjusting his weapon, he watched the fat man through the scope. At this range it was as easy to watch him through the shooting scope as with his binoculars, and quicker if he had to shoot him, which a significant part of him hoped he would have the chance to do.

chapter thirty-nine

OFFUTT AIR FORCE BASE
HEADQUARTERS, U.S. STRATEGIC COMMAND
EIGHT MILES SOUTH OF OMAHA, NEBRASKA

Brucius Marino leaned against the desk. Sara Brighton
stood at one of the windows of the large and finely furnished executive office located on the second floor.
Behind her there was a sitting area with two opposing leather
couches and four wing chairs. To her right sat a huge wooden
desk, a bright American flag behind it. A row of dark windows
looked out on the military base. At one time the office had
belonged to the base commander, but no one had seen him in
more than a week, so it had been commandeered. Still, she felt
like an intruder in the stranger's office.

Leaning against the office window, she looked out. The
shades were open, one of the windows, even, and a late-night
breeze was blowing gently against the wooden blinds.

They weren't hiding anymore, not literally and not figura-
tively. There was just no reason any longer. The men in Raven
Rock knew they were here now, knew what they were up to,
knew what they intended. The end game was close now—
upon them, really—and there was no purpose or advantage in
pretending any longer. The path split in a clear fork before
them, and the nation had to choose. No longer were they able

253

to stand and consider or try to stretch between the two alternatives.

She glanced nervously at the wall. The clock stood still. She checked her watch, given to her by one of Marino's aides, then sighed. Time was passing agonizingly slowly. Her mouth was so dry she had to work to swallow, and her stomach was tied in knots.

Behind her, Brucius Marino adjusted his weight against his desk, sometimes reading, sometimes staring off in thought, but mostly watching Sara out of the corner of his eye.

She was a truly beautiful woman. He admired her in so many ways.

She turned and looked at him. He seemed completely relaxed.

"They've been deliberating for almost six hours," she said.

He nodded to her. "A little more than that."

Sara thought of Justice Jefferson, his pride and exaggerated sense of worth. Were the other justices like him? She didn't know. Did they have the courage to do the right thing? Did they even have the wisdom to know what the right thing *was* to do? Again, she didn't know.

By now, the men inside Raven Rock would know that Justice Jefferson had left their compound. By now, they would have realized that Marino had gathered the two remaining Supreme Court justices and brought them out to Offutt. By now, they would surely understand that the three justices were meeting and that they would soon decide which path the nation ought to take. She knew their future was hanging in the balance, depending on what the three surviving members of the Supreme Court finally said.

Marino watched her, his thoughts much the same as hers.

If the justices found against him, he didn't know what he

would do. He wouldn't have many options. But whatever action he took, he would remain within the law.

If, on the other hand, the justices found against the men in Raven Rock, Marino knew that those men would fight him hand and tooth and nail. No way would they give up power without a fight. They would destroy the country if they had to. For them, so much the better if they did. They would do anything to stop him, no matter what the Supreme Court said.

Which was why he was preparing for open war.

Sara hugged her arms around herself as she stared absently out the window. There were a few security lights around the base entry points and a couple of lighted windows in the headquarters complex, but beyond the perimeter fence that lined the base it was utterly dark, the stars and moon hidden by a layer of clinging clouds.

"Are you nervous?" she asked Brucius as she turned around.

He looked at her and nodded. "I've had a knot of fear inside my stomach since before the nuclear explosion in D.C. It's pretty much been the only thing I've felt for many weeks."

"Funny, you don't seem nervous."

He hunched his shoulders. "All the fears have been squeezed out of me, I guess."

Sara interlaced her fingers nervously. "I wonder how things are going with . . . you know, Sam and the others."

"Sara, if I'd heard anything I would have told you. I'm not keeping any secrets. Last we heard from them, they were on the chopper making their way toward the village where the boy was supposed to meet us. Truly, if I had any information, especially any bad information, I would have told you."

"I know you would."

They fell into silence. Brucius moved behind the desk and started looking through the drawers. Finding a small key, he stood and walked to a locked cabinet, opened the etched glass doors, and pulled down a half-empty bottle of Jack Daniel's whiskey. "You want something to drink?" he asked her.

She shook her head.

He looked embarrassed. "Of course not. My mistake." He started to open the liquor, then changed his mind, screwed the lid back on, and put the bottle back. Locking the door, he moved silently back to the desk.

The door to the office was open and there was constant traffic up and down the hall. Someone appeared in the doorway and both of them turned instantly, their eyes expectant. "Have they made a decision?" Sara blurted out before Brucius could even say anything. The young lieutenant looked at her, uncertain what she was even talking about. Information regarding the three Supreme Court justices had been very tightly controlled.

Sara shot a quick, embarrassed look to Brucius. "Sorry," she almost said before he cut her off.

"Yes?" he asked the lieutenant.

"Sir, would you like me to bring you up some sandwiches?"

Brucius motioned toward Sara. "You must be hungry. Why don't you let them get you something?"

She shook her head. She was far too nervous to eat.

Brucius waited, giving her a chance to change her mind, then turned to the young lieutenant. "You got any tuna fish?"

"I'm sure we could find some, sir."

"That'd be nice. With horseradish sauce and mayonnaise. And lots of Tabasco."

Sara smiled. His order reminded her of her husband and sons. In her mind, she could hear them in the kitchen of the old house in Virginia, knocking down plates of chips and salsa sprinkled with the various hot sauces Neil had collected from around the world, some of them deadly to a normal person with any taste buds left.

Brucius studied her. "What are you smiling about?" he asked.

She shrugged. "Just thinking."

They fell silent once again. Marino bent down and placed the key back inside the desk drawer. Sara walked to the door and poked her head out, looking down the hallway that ended at a set of double doors. Two guards were posted there, mini-machine guns (more effective, if less imposing, than the full-size models) held at the ready in their hands. She watched them, knowing the justices were working behind the heavy wooden doors. Staring down the hallway, thinking of the Court and the direction they would take the country, thinking of the men who had conspired to steal their freedoms, she found her husband's whispered words coming again into her mind, the sudden warning he had told her in the darkness of the night.

"*There are men around the president who want to destroy our country,*" he had said.

She had stared at him, unbelieving.

"*He has put them in position within the government but he doesn't know who they really are or what they're willing to do. They will kill him if they have to. Our government's survival isn't assured.*"

Looking back, she realized that even her husband hadn't understood how dangerous the conspirators really were.

Pulling her head back into the room, she glanced down at her watch again.

Sighing, she took a breath.

Why was time passing so *slowly?!*

chapter forty

Omar turned to the village leader. The *abbu Rehnuma* was a tall man, thin, his arms nimble but strong. He'd had a hard life—life on the mountain was hard—but his trials hadn't hurt him; quite the opposite, they'd made him softer, more patient, more willing to suffer, more inclined to do good. His faith was strong, his gratitude for every day of life full and genuine. He had children of his own now and he loved them as much as any man.

Which was the only hope that Omar had: that this man's faith in his God and his love for His creations, especially those who were small and vulnerable, would sway his decision.

But it could go either way. The leader's love for his children could lead to compassion or it could lead to fear. If compassion proved the greatest, he would allow sanctuary for the child. If fear for his family prevailed, he would send them both away.

Omar held his breath and waited.

The sun was barely breaking over the sheer mountain peaks behind him. The ground was squishy and soft beneath his feet from three days of constant rain. The air was cool and

258

clear as only the mountain air could be, cloudless and clean, with visibility of a hundred miles or more. Looking around him, Omar felt suddenly exposed. For the past week, he'd been traveling under cover of night or fog, but he was standing in the open now, looking down on the village. He knew that it was foolish and he glanced toward the hut, wishing they were inside.

The villager leader remained silent. Omar couldn't wait any longer. "Sanctuary," he pleaded.

The leader shook his head. "I have a family. They would be in danger. It wouldn't be right to jeopardize their safety. I'm sorry, my good friend, but the answer is no."

Omar stared at him, his mouth open. He wanted to take the village leader by the clothes and shake him. He wanted to smash him in the face. He wanted to scream and curse him. He wanted him to see! *This child is our future, the future of our world. Everything you hold dear and holy is hanging in the wind. He is the only hope of a future kingdom in Arabia not based on insanity and rage. The Americans won't let Abdullah survive inside his kingdom. They will come for him. Yes, he has wounded them, but the Americans are still alive. They'll retaliate. They'll surely kill us. This child is our only hope!*

Fighting the rage inside him, Omar didn't say anything. Staring at the village leader, he thought for several moments, his heart beating in his chest. But as he stared at him, seeing the fearful look on his face, he realized the leader wasn't going to change his mind.

Omar glanced down at the boy standing at his side, then put his hand on his shoulder and guided him away. Turning, they started walking up the winding trail that led back into the mountains. Forty steps ahead of them, the trees grew thick. Beyond the first grove of evergreens, the trail dropped twenty meters toward a mountain stream. On the other side of the gushing water, the trail climbed out of the streambed and quickly disappeared in a thick forest of pine and mountain oak.

Looking behind him, Omar felt a sudden sense of hurry. Too long in the open. Too long to be seen. He felt a web of fear running through him and he fought the urge to run.

The village leader stood beside his hut and watched them go, his eyes sad, his lips pulled into a frown.

Omar caught his eye in a final farewell, then took the child's hand and pulled him closer. "We must hurry!" he declared.

*　　*　　*

Above them, hidden in the rocks and low shrubs, the king's sniper spoke into the radio transmitter snapped to his lapel. "Target is exiting the area," he announced urgently.

The radio buzzed in his ear. "Confirm the target is leaving the immediate location?"

"Affirmative. Target is moving back up toward the mountains."

He heard a vicious curse, as angry and foul as anything his language had to offer. "You *must not* let them reach the mountains," his commander ordered. "We've been looking for them for weeks now. If they make it to the mountains, we'll never find them in time. *We can't operate up there!*"

The sniper simply waited. There was nothing more for him to say.

"Is the escort staying with the target?" the voice in his radio demanded.

"Yes, the fat one is with the boy."

"Do whatever it takes to stop them. We're seven minutes yet away."

"I can't stop them without killing him."

"Do whatever you must to stop the fat one, but leave the

boy alive. You know our instructions. We *must* save him for the king!"

*　　*　　*

Looking ahead, Omar saw the trail descend suddenly, winding through a series of short switchbacks toward the rushing stream. He was close enough now that he could feel the moist air kicked up from the water gushing over the boulders in the stream. In fifteen meters they would start descending, dropping out of sight.

He felt the urge to run again. Something was screaming inside his head, the words almost forming in his mind.

*　　*　　*

"Go!" Neil Brighton told him, whispering urgently into the mortal's ears. "Go, Omar. Run now! Your life's in danger. There is danger for the child!"

Teancum stood beside him, not saying anything.

Neil turned toward his friend. "Will you not help me?" he cried.

Teancum reached out and rested his hand on Neil's shoulder. His face was calm and peaceful. "Neil," he offered simply, "this is not why we are here. Father has another plan for this one. It might be his time has come."

*　　*　　*

The village leader watched Omar and the boy walking up the trail. Inside, his heart was breaking. He honestly didn't know what to do! Should he save the boy or save his family? If the foreign military forces came looking for the child—and the village leader knew that eventually they would—they would find him. The village was too small to hide a trinket, let alone a living child. And if the king's forces discovered he had concealed the child, their punishment would be swift and thorough. Best case, they would only kill him. Worst case, they'd make him shoot his wife and children before turning the gun on himself.

So he didn't move as he watched them walk away, his mind reeling.

It wasn't too late. He could still stop them. He could offer sanctuary and protection to the child . . .

As he stood there, a verse from the blessed Koran filtered into his mind: *"There is no God but him, in him I have put my trust."*

His thoughts quickened as he considered. Then his heart seemed to settle and he felt a cooling breeze.

That was his answer. He would put his trust in Allah. He would offer sanctuary to the child.

Calling out, he started running after Omar and the boy.

*   *   *

On the other side of the stream, across a split log used for a bridge, there was a thicket of brush and young trees. There the trail ascended steeply before reaching the forest again. Once in the protection of the forest, Omar knew they would be all right. Their packs were hidden up on the mountain: food, protection, warm clothes. They could disappear and survive up there for days, which would be long enough for him to decide what next to do.

Reaching down again, he pulled the prince along. Once they had reached the protection of the mountain, Allah would lead and guide them.

It was the last thought to filter through Omar's mortal mind.

The fine-grain bullet entered the right side of his head,

metal and pieces of fractured skull exploding into his brain and blowing out the other side.

Omar made a sound as he fell over. Before he hit the ground, he was dead.

The dull *thump* of the bullet crashing into bone was the second sound the young boy heard. Before that, he sensed a slight buzzing, like a surge of electricity, as the bullet passed over his shoulder before exploding into Omar's head.

Looking around him, the young prince stopped and waited for the next bullet to come slashing into him.

*　　*　　*

The village leader didn't hear the gunfire or sense the bullet passing. All he saw was a red explosion out the left side of Omar's head. Then he saw him crumple. Then he saw the child stop.

Then he too, like the young prince, stood and waited for the next shot to be fired.

Inside his mind, the village leader counted, his heart beating like a butterfly, his eyes darting left and right. Were they going to kill the boy? Was there any chance they would let him live? He held his breath and waited, expecting the child to crumple like his friend.

One . . . two . . . three . . .

Five, then ten seconds.

The air gushed out of him like an explosion from his chest. Without thinking any longer, he rushed toward the child.

Sweeping him up in his arms, he held the boy against his chest as he dove over the hill and rolled toward the gushing stream.

chapter forty-one

ALONG THE PAKISTAN/AFGHANISTAN BORDER
EIGHTY-FIVE KILOMETERS EAST OF KANDAHAR,
AFGHANISTAN

A re you sure it's him?"

Bono stared through his field glasses while bracing his elbows on the ground to form a bipod, allowing a more stable view. "His face is partially covered by part of his turban," he answered absently, concentrating more on his viewing than on responding to Sam's question. He moved the binoculars just a fraction of an inch, then dropped them. "Show me his photograph again."

Sam held up his iPod. Small, easy to conceal, password protected, long battery life, capable of holding huge amounts of information, it was a perfect—if completely unauthorized—military accessory. A close-up of Omar's face filled the small screen. Bono looked at it, then swore. Handing Sam the field glasses, he answered, "I'm pretty sure that's him."

Sam looked, taking his time to be certain, then lowered the binoculars. "They got him," he agreed in frustration.

"If they got him, they got the boy."

Sam turned around carefully, positioning his back against the ridge. The rocks behind him were sharp slabs of slate, and he had to be careful as he leaned against the broken fissures.

"They got him," Bono repeated. "We came out here for nothing. The prince is dead. We're all too late."

Sam took a weary breath. For a long moment neither of them spoke; then their radios suddenly crackled in their ears. Sam listened to the report from their reconnaissance leader. "We've identified all of the special units around and in the village," Dallas Houston said. "We've got members of the Sword Knights from the First Saudi Special Forces Brigade and a couple of regular SpecFor units from the 21st."

Sam touched the transmitter on his radio. "So we're covered, then. We've got the right uniforms and the other special equipment that we need."

"Rog that, boss. We were way lucky, if you ask me, but yeah, we got it right."

"So we can go in if we have to?"

"True that. The only problem, far as I see it, is that the prince is probably dead."

Bono looked at Sam with an "I-told-you-so" expression.

Sam ignored it. "Stand by," he told the NCO.

"What's going to happen now, Sammy boy?" Bono asked. "What's the world going to come to? When we go back without either the prince or King Abdullah, there's going to be a terrible price to pay."

"I don't think they got the prince."

Bono didn't move. He was trying to believe that Sam might be right, but the evidence was there before him. He saw the dead man, the young prince's protector, lying on the pathway. The boy must be down there somewhere as well, probably lying facedown. He sighed, weary to the bone already. "Let's gather up the team," he said.

"They don't have the prince yet," Sam repeated.

Bono looked at him in disbelief. "Come on, Sam, it's time to go."

Sam rolled over to face the village four hundred meters to the west. "Check out the dead one," he offered, holding up the field glasses. "Look at the size of the exit wound on the left side of his head. That's a fine-grain bullet, I'm guessing an M118. We know all Saudi Special Forces units use U.S. weapons, too. Take a closer look at that, Bono. How many shells have the velocity to do that kind of damage? The sniper was out here somewhere. He had good position and opportunity, yet Omar was the only one he killed."

"You don't know that," Bono answered after looking through the glasses. "For all we know, he killed the prince first."

Sam gestured toward the path below them. "Do you see any other bodies? Any spots of blood anywhere along the trail? Any evidence that indicates there was another shooting?"

Bono stared through the glasses, then shook his head. "You think he's in the village, then?" he asked.

"I'd bet my life he is."

"But where? And how did he get away?" Bono put the binoculars down and shook his head again. "Where's the sniper, Sam?" He moved his eyes around the terraced hills looking over the tiny village.

Sam pointed with his finger toward the mud and stone hut on the corner of the lowest terrace. The pathway toward the river where Omar's body lay was only forty meters from the hut. "That's the *abbu Rehnuma's* home. Omar brought the boy to him, seeking sanctuary, I would guess. Then Omar left, heading back up the mountain, maybe with the boy, maybe alone. Either way, while he was moving away from the hut, he was taken out by a long-range sniper. But all of the evidence we have suggests the boy was unharmed. We've been here long enough, and we were close enough before that, to have heard any helicopters in the area . . ."

266

Bono started nodding.

"The boy is here." Sam was certain, and he motioned to the village. "Somewhere down there. Maybe hiding by himself, but maybe hidden. Either way, he's still down there."

Bono lifted the powerful set of binoculars and turned them toward the village, studying the rows of huts, outhouses, barns, fences, and pens, all of the things he hadn't taken the chance to look at before. Moving his field of vision, he studied the central market with its arched entryway and pock-marked walls.

There, moving through the market, he saw him. The Saudi soldier made no effort to hide his presence, choosing to move out in the open. He wore a camouflage uniform and flak vest but his head was covered with a black helmet now. His gun was ready and he moved quickly.

Adjusting the glasses, Bono looked farther east. Then he saw it. The military vehicle had been hidden behind a brick wall on the far side of the village, but now it had been driven into the open. A group of Saudi soldiers were moving around the truck. They huddled on their leader, then split up and fanned out, taking up positions among the huts and dirty roads that led toward the market square.

Farther to the east, other military trucks were moving down the road.

chapter forty-two

The sniper moved quickly through the village, his eyes narrowed to a tight squint, his head always moving, his shoulders hunched, his weapon ready. The villagers had a lot of weapons, he knew that—between the local warlords, poppy farmers, and Taliban, Afghani, and Pakistani forces, this area was in a nearly constant state of war. But he wasn't afraid. The villagers might be backward and uneducated, but they weren't stupid. Just the opposite, especially when it came to rules of war. He represented something far more powerful than they were. They wouldn't challenge him, not with their weapons, though there might still be a short battle of wills.

Which meant it was important for the soldiers to establish their credibility from the start.

Listening through his radio earpiece, he heard his brother soldiers take their orders, then begin moving through the village, searching for the prince. Listening to the orders being given, he couldn't miss the fear in his commander's voice.

Their king was on his way, his chopper little more than fifteen minutes away. They had to have the boy by then or all of

268

them would die. The villagers. The soldiers. None of them would survive the morning if they didn't find the child.

Fifteen minutes to find the young prince and turn him over to the king.

Fifteen minutes to kill every man, woman, and child within the village if they tried to hide him.

Fifteen minutes for the soldiers to do whatever they had to in order to save themselves.

The sniper walked quickly, his steps angry and determined. He had seen it all, the *abbu Rehnuma* standing in silent shock at the death of the other man, his hesitation, then quick decision. He'd watched as the *abbu Rehnuma* had burst into action, sprinting up the narrow pathway and scooping up the child before diving over the embankment that held the rushing stream. From his position in the foothills, the sniper had lost sight of them for a few moments but, knowing they would have to emerge eventually, he had waited, sometimes using his binoculars, sometimes scanning the area with his eyes. Minutes later, the *abbu Rehnuma* had emerged, running through the trees to the south, where the mountain stream met the larger river. The water was strong and fierce there, more a series of waterfalls than just a rocky stream, and a light mist formed around the banks of the river, making it difficult for the shooter to see. Squinting, he'd watched as the *abbu Rehnuma*, child still clutched in his arms, had run up the narrow pathway and passed into the village, where the sniper had lost sight of them again.

But they were here, inside the village.

And he would kill everyone inside the rock walls if that was what it took to find the child.

He glanced down at his watch.

Twelve minutes until the king got there.

* * *

In the center of the village square there was a mosque: dusty, open windows, ancient white stone, and a checkered dome that was damaged on one side. Most of the holy structure was taken up by the *musalla,* or prayer hall, but off to the right there was a small wing with a doomed roof and arching windows. The soldier approached the side entrance to the building, a thick, wood door tucked in a narrow archway, and stopped to listen. Lifting his weapon, he used the butt to knock.

While he waited, he listened to the sound of the other soldiers searching through the narrow streets.

"Pile Driver is airborne," his commander announced over the radio in a terrified voice. The king of the House of Saud was coming, the most powerful man on earth.

"Time of arrival, ten minutes. Find the boy now, you pigs, or I will shoot you all myself!"

The sniper listened, then banged again, almost breaking down the door.

The village leader pulled it open, his eyes wide in fear, a tiny wad of spit on the corner of his dry lips. The sniper pointed his weapon, recognizing the leader's face and long beard. "Where is he!" he demanded.

The *abbu Rehnuma* held his ground. "He is safe in the mosque of Allah. He is protected here. He has implored for sanctuary—"

The sniper lifted his weapon and jammed the barrel into the young man's cheek, pushing him back. "Give the boy to me and you will live. Speak another word in his defense, and you will die. It is that simple. Now, where have you hidden the child?"

The young man's mind shut down, thoughts of love and family freezing his brain into a paralyzed state. *My children!*

How I love them. All I wanted was to keep them safe. All I wanted was to be their father . . .

"WHERE IS THE BOY?!" the sniper screamed after watching the young man bow his head to pray.

The *abbu Rehnuma* swallowed and looked up, his heart racing in his chest. Drops of sweat rolled down his temples. His hands trembled. His knees buckled. He almost collapsed in fear.

"Sanctuary," was all he muttered, his voice nothing but the whisper of a man who knew that he was dead. "I have granted sanctuary to the young one—"

The sniper shot the village leader in the head.

Wiping spattered flecks of blood from his eyes, the soldier burst into the hallway. Turning left, he ran into the dark, green-tiled prayer hall. It took him only seconds to find the child hiding there.

Grabbing him by the hair, he pulled him out onto the street.

*   *   *

Far above, half a kilometer to the west, Sam and Bono watched through their field glasses as the soldier emerged from the mosque, pulling the prince behind him.

Sam turned to Bono. "We've got to go!" he cried.

Bono was already on his radio. "We don't have much time, guys," he told his team.

Hidden in the foothills around the village, the U.S. soldiers sprang into action. Most of the groundwork had already been put in place. All they needed now was to implement the plan.

Sam looked intently at Azadeh. "Are you ready?" he asked.

She nodded hesitantly.

"I'll never be far away from you."

271

She nodded again, her eyes flickering with uncertainty.

He took a step toward her and placed his hand on her arm. "Remember back in Chicago?"

She nodded at him, her fear melting.

"It's just like that," he said.

chapter forty-three

The Saudi king's helicopter, a huge white-and-blue Sikorsky, the largest and most expensive chopper in the world, approached low from the southeast. Flying up the valley, it followed the rutted dirt road that came to an end at the stone wall around the village. A thousand feet from the outskirts of the village, the helicopter's nose rose abruptly into the sky, then leveled just as quickly as the chopper settled onto a patch of open grass. The ground around the village was wet and muddy, and there was no blowing dust as the enormous helicopter landed.

The cabin doors instantly pulled back and the twelve-man Royal Security Forces (RSF) team ran down the short steps and spread out. Carefully selected, highly trained, indoctrinated to the point of being brainwashed, the members of the RSF were as brutal and efficient as any security forces in the world. Each of them would happily sacrifice his life for the kingdom. Each of them would kill or torture his own children for the king. None of them had a hint of conscience any longer, for their entire existence was dedicated to only one cause: protecting the king of the House of Saud. Were they

273

ever to fail in this mission, every member of the RSF would die, for they were bound by a sacred oath of suicide. Were they to fail in taking their own lives, they would be hunted down, tortured, and killed, along with every member of their extended families and a viciously large number of their friends.

To say they were dedicated to their mission was an understatement that bordered on the absurd.

The foothills and perimeter of the village had already been secured with other military teams. The roads, buildings, market, and mosque had been secured as well.

Altogether there were eighty-seven Saudi soldiers in the area now, all of them dedicated to protecting the king.

The helicopter pilot kept the engines running but disengaged the rotors, allowing the blades to slow to a stop. King Abdullah watched from the bulletproof cockpit window as the RSF team fanned out around the helicopter. When given the all clear, he moved to the steps and loped down quickly, anxious to get his target and get out of here.

Standing at the foot of the short stairs, he paused and looked around. Two of his guards were hunched down near the gate in the wall around the village, a small cut in the rock barely wide enough for a horse to pass through. Beyond the three-foot wall, he saw a couple of bodies lying in the streets, the water-filled ruts turning red beneath their bodies. On the other side of the village, a fire was burning, smoke lifting quickly into the calm skies, the blackness driven upward by the energy of the growing flames beneath. The village streets had been cleared, the terrified inhabitants told to remain inside their muddy shacks, and none of the villagers besides the dead ones could be seen. The chief of the RSF was standing near the front of the chopper, talking into a radio as the king glanced left and right.

Twenty meters beyond the tip of helicopter's rotors, the

sniper held the boy. The child was small and submissive, but the sniper constrained him as if he were a dangerous animal. The king took out an American cigarette, lit it, pulled a deep drag, the smoke escaping from his nose, pulled again, then dropped the cigarette in the mud and started walking. Approaching the child, he bored his eyes into him. This was his nephew, son of his oldest brother, and he knew the child well.

The boy-prince fought against the guard's steely grip, then fell still and glared into his uncle's eyes. There was no pretense between them now. The child knew why the king was here. His father and mother, all of his brothers and sisters, everyone he had ever cared about was dead. The young father back in Iran, Omar, the village leader, everyone who had taken a risk to help him had been killed as well.

He was utterly alone now.

His uncle had come to kill him.

He bowed his head and waited.

King Abdullah came to a stop in front of the prince and looked down. So much of his time and thought and energy had been extended toward this goal. He had come so far to do this, and it would bring him enormous pleasure to kill the child. But it would be more than just a pleasure; it would also bring him release. This was the last threat to his kingdom, the last human who could ever claim his crown. For this reason, yes, he wanted the boy to die, but there was more to this than that. He wanted to see it, to feel it, to be the direct cause of his death. He wanted to smell the tinge of blood. He wanted to feel the recoil of the gun and see the spattered flesh. He wanted to know and then remember how it felt to kill the child.

He smiled at the prince and licked his lips.

There was a certain honor in the killing. It was a thing that he *should* do. He could easily have ordered it taken care of, just like with most of the others. But he *wanted* to be the one who pulled the trigger. He *wanted* to kill the child.

A sudden chill seeped through him, penetrating to his soul and bone.

How was he going to do it? He didn't know. He hadn't thought that far ahead. He might just shoot him. Simple, if not elegant. Or he might kill him with his bare hands. If he were alone, that would be how he would do it, but with his soldiers all around him it might be awkward.

He stared into the boy's eyes.

The prince stared back defiantly at him.

"You're going to see your father," Abdullah whispered to him.

"You're going to hell," the young prince sneered.

"I'm already in hell, my little princeling. Once we sign up with the Master, once he holds our souls in his hands, then hell is all around us. Hell is our entire world. There is no light or joy left inside us. There is no—"

Abdullah stopped suddenly, catching the last words in his throat. The words had slipped out of him without thought, and he was frightened at his sudden honesty.

How could it matter what he told the prince? In a few moments he would be dead.

But did it matter to Abdullah?

He didn't want to know.

Turning, he thought back bitterly to one of the most powerful memories of his life. Back at his palace. They were talking after the EMP attack. The old man had spoken to him just as the brilliant morning sunlight had broken across the concrete-flat horizon. *"The truth is, my King Abdullah,"* the old man had sneered, his voice wicked and sarcastic, *"I was lying to you then. I promised you everything, but none of it is real.*

276

None of it will last forever. It will all come crashing down. We can fight and scratch and murder, we can lie and cheat and kill. We can plot and plan and muster, but we are never going to win. The sun will still rise in the morning. Light will always chase the dark. We cannot win. We never could.

"And that, my friend, is the only truth that really matters. You have sold your soul for nothing. Now, welcome to my world."

King Abdullah thought, a dark desperation all around him, then turned back to the prince. "I'm going to kill you now."

The young boy didn't answer.

"You understand this?" Abdullah wondered.

The young prince shook his head, tears of fear and sadness rolling down his cheeks. Then, ashamed at his display of weakness and emotion, he gritted his teeth and held his breath.

chapter forty-four

OFFUTT AIR FORCE BASE
HEADQUARTERS, U.S. STRATEGIC COMMAND
EIGHT MILES SOUTH OF OMAHA, NEBRASKA

Almost four hours had passed since the tuna sandwiches, chips, and bottled water had been sent up. Brucius was slumped in his chair, his head back. His eyes were open but his heart rate and blood pressure had slipped into something very close to sleep. Sara was stretched out on the leather couch, the deep burgundy blending with the color of her skirt, her shoes off, her blonde hair falling to one side of her face. Brucius knew that she was sleeping from the slow rate of her breathing and the sudden movements of her feet.

If she was dreaming, and she seemed to be, then she wasn't having pleasant dreams.

A shadow fell across the room from the bright lights in the hallway. Brucius looked up to see his civilian attaché standing there.

He immediately stood up.

"They've decided," the man said.

chapter forty-five

The swearing-in ceremony was broadcast over television and radio stations across the entire United States. Not many people would actually see or hear it, but the word would quickly spread.

Brucius Marino, for twelve minutes now the legally sworn-in president of the United States of America, stood before his staff. The atmosphere inside the conference room was electric with emotion and energy. Everything was clear now, no more uncertainty in the air. All of the participants had known that they were doing the right thing; all of them had been completely committed to helping Brucius Marino retain power. It wasn't any single man or party to which they were committed, it was a cause. But it was a huge relief to have the unanimous Supreme Court decision on their side. Their mission had been clarified. The law had spoken. The Constitution had made them right.

The president looked around the room, and for a brief moment he was so caught up with the emotion that he couldn't speak. He tried. His voice choked inside his throat. He waited, looking down, then raised his head again, but the emotion was still so overpowering that he simply couldn't speak.

Taking a breath, he looked away, then turned back to the people who had risked their lives to help him. Nothing he could say would be sufficient, and any attempt at a speech would only diminish what they'd done. So he didn't even try. Instead, he focused on their mission. There was so much work to do still. "We have to get to Raven Rock," he told them. He nodded to the engineering drawings spread out on the conference table between them. "We've been over all the plans. All of you know what you have to do."

RAVEN ROCK (SITE R), UNDERGROUND MILITARY COMPLEX
SOUTHERN PENNSYLVANIA

Once given the command, the Special Forces units moved in on the compound with great speed, securing every entrance or passageway into the enormous underground national command post. It wasn't an easy thing to do, for there were more than a dozen entries, tunnels, and cargo elevators into the compound. But there was no opposition and it didn't take much time.

Minutes after the soldiers had received their orders, all of the exits to the command post were secure.

President Marino had ordered the military forces not to enter Raven Rock. For one thing, there was no reason. None of the conspirators were going anywhere. And Marino didn't want the risk of bloodshed. He would give the conspirators time to sort it out, to decide what they wanted to do—which was, of course, surrender, utterly trapped in the compound as they were. More, President Marino recognized that most of the military and civilian staff inside the compound weren't the enemy; they were just doing what they'd been told. Very few of them were even aware of the conspiracy, and those who were had already been identified.

While the exits were being secured, other military forces moved to control the compound's communications grid, power sources, air-conveying units, and electrical power cables. Within minutes, everything the occupants of Raven Rock needed to communicate with the outside world was under the control of Marino's troops.

With the Supreme Court having found against them, and with Brucius Marino having been sworn in as the president, the conspirators inside the compound had no choice. Unable to get a message out, cut off from any energy or power sources, including the ability to get fresh air, the residents of Raven Rock had very little option.

Once the leaders inside the compound understood the true hopelessness of their situation, they would surrender.

Security forces were waiting to arrest the conspirators.

They didn't have to wait very long.

chapter forty-six

The morning was calm and quiet, the only noise the muffled sound of the helicopter engines fifty feet behind the king. The pilot had pulled the chopper's engines back to idle, and the helicopter vibrated softly in the mud as he waited for his master.

Abdullah grabbed the boy under the arms and towed him toward the stone wall, the prince's heels dragging through the slimy mud, leaving two light trenches instead of footsteps in his wake.

Throwing him against the wall, the king stared at the boy and sneered. "I hated your father," he hissed as he pulled out a chrome 9mm from the leather holster strapped around his waist. Holding it to the light, he examined the beautiful weapon, the highly polished metal glinting in the sun. "I hated him for as long as I can remember. In fact, my young princeling, one of my earliest memories is of sitting at the evening table wishing he would choke on his wad of meat. Yes, he was my older brother, but I had no respect for him. I wouldn't say that he abused me—quite the opposite, he was patronizing to the core. That was one of the things I hated:

how he treated me so kindly. And I resented from my youth that *he* would be the king. He didn't have to earn it. He didn't have to prove himself. Like a finely wrapped birthday present, it was simply handed to him. Can you really call that *justice?*" He pulled the lever of the Glock, the clicking sound of metal jarring in the morning silence. "I do not call that justice. I do not call that right. I believe you earn what you get and you get only what you earn. That is the world I live in. That is the world as it should be."

He turned and motioned to the pilot, twirling his finger in the air. In seconds it would be over, and he wanted the chopper to be ready.

Even before the king had dropped his hand, the pilot engaged the rotors and the four long black blades started turning though the air.

Abdullah held the gun in both hands, seeming to measure its weight, then focused on the young boy. "And now, my little princeling, I am going to give you a final choice—"

There was a sudden sound behind him. A cry of pain. A cry for mercy. The king quickly turned. A woman was being dragged toward him, frantically fighting the guards who held her arms. She flailed in desperation, her words unrecognizable cries, her legs wobbling underneath her. She was dressed in a black dress, and a dark *hijab* covered her face below her eyes, but the king had enough experience to see that she was young.

"*Sayid, sayid,*" she begged as the two soldiers shoved her between them as if she were a piece of meat. Pulling away from them, she reached out desperately for the young prince. "My son! My son!" she cried.

The king scowled with bitter anger. Who was this woman, and why had the soldiers allowed her to get so close to him? He turned to the guards, members of the Saudi 21st Special Forces. They didn't look at him, afraid of making eye contact, their helmets low on their heads. He would string them up by their intestines for allowing her to get so near.

✷ ✷ ✷

The four American soldiers had positioned themselves strategically around the area. One was shooting from the dome of the tiny school. One of them was much closer, less than fifty feet from the king, hidden in an empty house. Two were shooting from the foothills overlooking the village. Dallas Houston, the team leader, was tasked with calling the targets out.

"Wow, baby," Slapper muttered into his radio. "Look at that. She might have made it—"

"Okay, okay," Sergeant Dallas Houston cut him off as he talked into the microphone near his mouth. "You got the primary target, right, team?"

"Roger that," the second shooter shot back. "The king is in the western style business suit. He is very obvious."

"Okay, okay. Tally on the target. Tally on the woman. Is she in the line of fire?"

"Shooter two is clear."

"Three."

"Four."

All of them called back concisely. The woman wasn't in the way. They all had a clear shot at their targets.

Houston took a breath. Just like they had drawn it up. Still, his face was sweating and he rubbed a sleeve across his brow, wiping the sting out of his eyes.

"Okay, okay," he repeated, his pet phrase when he was under great stress. "All of you call tally on the good guys. We don't want to shoot our own men."

He was talking about Sam and Bono now, who were very close to the king.

"Tally two."

"Tally three."

"Tally four."

All of the good guys were clear.

"Okay, okay. Shooter two and three, you've got the nearest targets. The RSF leader is at the chopper's twelve o'clock position. You take him and the four RSF guards to his right. Shooter three, you've got all of the RSF guards to the left."

One by one, they confirmed the team leader's orders.

Houston moved his assault rifle up to his cheek. "Okay." (Just one okay now. The setup was the hardest part, and he was starting to relax.) "Three, you've got the units from the 21st stationed near the stone wall. I'm the free shooter. Any targets of opportunity are mine."

The team called back, confirming their last instructions.

"After the first barrage, it's every man for himself. But shoot to make your bullets count. And always, *always,* keep an eye on the friendlies down there!"

The U.S. soldiers were silent.

"Okay," Houston muttered for the final time.

He stared through his scope and listened to his heart beating in his ears.

So far, so good.

He took another deep breath.

Everything going according to the plan.

Of course, no one had fired any bullets yet. All plans were good until the shooting started. No plan was worth a wad of spit after that.

*　　*　　*

"That boy is *not* the prince!" the woman cried in terror.

Abdullah turned and looked at her as if for the first time, his mind screaming.

How did she know about the prince?

He glared at her in amazement.

Why did she call the boy her son?

He lifted his hand toward the two guards who had brought her to him, commanding them back. Looking over his shoulder, he shot a glare of warning to the boy who had fallen against the stone wall, his eyes red and teary, his hands trembling in the mud. "STAY!" he commanded, then turned back to the girl. His guards were close around him now and he wanted to push them back. This woman was no threat to him. But what she knew might be.

One of the guards grabbed the woman's arm and brought her forward. Stopping before the king, he bowed so deeply his head was parallel to the ground. "My king, my master, may Allah forgive me for intruding and if it gives you pleasure, please take my life. But this woman says this boy is—"

"He's not the prince," the woman cut in, her voice shrill and frantic. "The one you seek is still hiding in the village. They have tricked you. They have taken him. But I know where he is."

The king looked at her as if she had lost her mind, which she clearly had. The boy before him was his nephew, he was certain of that.

But she knew about the prince. And he had to find out how she knew.

She bowed her head before him. "My son!" she cried again.

King Abdullah reached out to her.

Azadeh lifted her eyes and looked at him, then bowed her head in submission and fell upon her knees.

This was the signal they would be waiting for.

She braced herself for the attack.

*   *   *

With a jerk, Azadeh fell back, a spot of red oozing at her chest. The sound of the gunshot rang out from somewhere in the village, the *crack* echoing against the terraced hills. Then came another shot. Then too many shots to count. The gun blasts echoed off the terraces and sounded across the valley. The king's guards started falling in their tracks, bloody spots in their heads, their chests compressing into gory holes.

The guards were being taken down by an expert marksman.

No, by an entire team of marksmen.

Dallas Houston watched the king's men fall. Hissing into his radio headpiece, he called out to shooter three. "Lay it down! Give it to me NOW!"

Instantly he heard the *thuuuump* from the C4 charges the team had hidden against the stone wall. The explosions were spaced out at all four corners of the village. Even from the distance, he felt the percussion from the explosions and his ears rang from the overpressure. It looked like the entire village was under attack now, smoke rising in the sky, balls of fire inside the rolling smoke, pieces of shattered rock falling through the air. Four seconds later, he heard the chest-crushing *whomp* of the third-generation antipersonnel guided missile. Radar guided, the missile needed no further guidance during flight once the target had been identified. It honed in on the main body of enemy troops, leaving a trail of white smoke to mark its flight. The warhead exploded into the village wall, sending stone and metal fragments in all directions.

Looking on the carnage, Houston almost smiled. Then he remembered his hesitation about the plan and felt a sudden pang of nerves.

In seconds, a dozen guards went down. The king watched in horror, then fell to his knees. In a moment of sheer terror, he didn't know what to do. His mind froze. His heart stopped. His throat was far too tight to breathe. His face was blank and expressionless.

He was certain he was dead.

Did his entire life race before him? Did he think about mortality or the world that was to come? Did he regret his many murders?

No, not for an instant. True to his core, the only question that ran through his mind was, "Will I have time to kill these guards for their failure to protect me before the assassins kill me?"

The king's eyes darted back and forth. Chaos, blood, and smoke swirled all around him. Bodies falling into the mud. The roar of the helicopter's engines. The massive chopper blades turning through the smoky air. Return shots rang over his head now as his elite guards started to shoot back. Gunfire spouting in every direction. His guards didn't even know what they were shooting at! A trail of bullets passed; he could feel their pressure. He could almost feel their heat. Three more members of his RSF team went down, leaving him alone. He rolled into the mud, pretending he'd been shot.

That was when it occurred to him.

Most of his guards were dead around him.

But they hadn't shot him yet.

Which meant they didn't want to kill him.

He shook his head violently.

The two soldiers who had brought the woman to him moved suddenly to his side and pulled him up, ready to sacrifice their lives to protect him. One on each side of him, they crowded close, never allowing the shooters to get a clean shot. Everything around him seemed to slow. He saw the woman dead upon the ground, shot in the chest. He looked at the guards beside him. One of them had light-colored eyes!

A flutter of new fear ran through him.

Why were the guards so close?

Were they protecting him or keeping him from running?

He looked down at the weapons the soldiers had produced from their shoulder harnesses. U.S. made MK-46s.

The fear rose higher in his chest.

"*Sayid,*" the nearest guard called above the chaotic noise.

Abdullah turned to him.

"*Sayid! Sayid!*" the guard motioned frantically. "We've got to get you to the helicopter!" He grabbed his arm and started pulling. "To the helicopter, *Sayid!*"

The guard pulled frantically on his arm.

The king started leaning back.

It didn't make any sense!

His men dead around him?

The explosions from the brick wall, expertly placed. The attack had been a work of brilliance. Snipers from the foothills. Snipers from the village. Some of them were very close. But none of them had killed him.

Yes, they wanted him alive.

The guard pulled him again toward the chopper. Through the tinted glass, Abdullah could see the waiting pilots. The rotors were at full speed now, the chopper light upon its wheels. The instant he was on board, it would spring into the air. He stared at the waiting helicopter. The largest target in the valley. Critical to his escape.

Why hadn't they destroyed it?

His heart jumped up into his throat.

The guard kept dragging him toward the waiting chopper. Abdullah jerked his arm away. Turning to the guard, he spoke in Sahrawi Arabic, his tribe's ancient dialect.

The guard stared back at him but didn't answer.

He spoke again in Sahrawi.

The guard didn't understand.

All his guards spoke Sahrawi.

This man wasn't one of his guards.

Abdullah reached up and jerked off the soldier's helmet, looking into his eyes.

Lieutenant Samuel Brighton stared back at him.

Dallas Houston had been right. The plan was about to fall apart.

chapter forty-seven

The plan Sergeant Houston had been so skeptical about was audacious to the point of lunacy, brave to the point of prideful, simple to the point of childish, and only a few seconds from actually working.

Azadeh would be dressed in local garb. Bono and Sam were dressed as Saudi guards. They were to stay beside her as they dragged her to the king. (What she was to say to him, they had never told her, and Sam couldn't have been more proud when she had come up with her story about the prince.)

The entire operation had only one goal in mind: to confuse the king long enough for them to get close to him without getting shot. Once they were beside him, the hidden U.S. soldiers would attack. Confusion, death, and fear would follow. The king would, of course, be evacuated to his waiting helicopter. The three of them would go with him. Once inside the chopper . . . well, they didn't know. One problem at a time, Bono had told them after explaining the unfinished plan.

*　　*　　*

King Abdullah stepped away from Sam and lifted his handgun, pointing the shiny muzzle right at his forehead. Sam backed up, lifting his hands in surrender while bowing in subjection, still in role. Abdullah kept the gun on him. The bullets continued flying all around him, explosions on every side.

"Who are you?" Abdullah demanded in a deadly voice. "I want to know before you die!"

A burst of Saudi machine-gun fire erupted from the wall. The American soldier's position in the village home had finally been identified. A hail of bullets crashed into the house from no fewer than twenty-five positions, destroying the home in a burst of dust and metal. The king hesitated while the rain of bullets blew the home to pieces. Seeing the destruction out of the corner of his eye, Sam felt sick, knowing the first member of his team had been killed. "No, Slapper!" he almost cried, the young soldier's face bursting into his mind. The king followed his eyes, reading the pain on his face.

In that moment's hesitation, Sam reached out for the king's gun. Grabbing Abdullah's wrist, he snapped it. The bone almost cracked in two. Screaming, Abdullah dropped to his knees in pain and shock, his hand flopping worthlessly beside him. Sam grabbed the handgun and twisted it from his fingers.

Turning, he screamed to Bono, "LET'S GO!"

*　　*　　*

Bono ran toward the prince. Falling into the mud beside him, he commanded, "Come with me!"

The prince looked at him, his eyes wild, his hands still trembling in the mud.

"Come with me!" Bono repeated.

The prince didn't understand. Why didn't the guard speak

in Arabic? What was he saying? Was he threatening to kill him? What was he to do?

"Come with me!" Bono repeated, wishing frantically he could think of the right words to speak in Arabic. "We've only got a few seconds. A few seconds! Come! Come with me!"

The prince pushed against the wall and hid his face.

"Tamanina," Bono shouted. No, no, that was wrong. That meant "don't move."

He tried again. It didn't matter. Unlike Sam, he'd never picked up Arabic. He started gesturing with his hands.

The prince watched and listened. He realized the soldier was speaking English but he didn't know what he meant. From his gestures, he understood the soldier wanted him to go with him into Abdullah's helicopter, which seemed like a stupid thing to do!

Pushing himself to his feet, he threw a fistful of mud into Bono's face and turned and ran.

*   *   *

The king was shouting to his guards now. "Help me! This guard is an American! KILL HIM NOW, YOU FOOLS!" Most of his words were lost in the roar of the helicopter's engines and the constant snap of machine-gun fire. Another missile explosion rocked the village from the American positions in the hills. The king flinched from the exploding rocks around him.

Sam grabbed the king by the arm and started pulling, feeling the broken wrist giving way in his grip. Reaching for his other hand, he dragged the king again.

Abdullah fought and kicked, screaming all the time. Sam tucked the king's handgun in his pants. They were almost to the chopper. Abdullah cried in fear and rage again.

The last surviving member of the RSF heard his master's

cries. He turned from the battle to see a fellow soldier dragging the king toward the chopper. It was the obvious thing to do. Get the king to safety and get the chopper in the air. He watched a second, then turned back to the fight.

The king struggled to escape from Sam, using his weight to pull away from him. "KILL HIM! HE'S AN AMERICAN!" he cried again.

Having lost his primary weapon, Abdullah reached for his ankle gun.

Sam saw him moving for the hidden weapon. He saw the glint of metal in Abdullah's hand. Slamming his fist into the king's face, he felt Abdullah's cheek and eye socket crunch under the raw force of the blow. Abdullah's breath huffed out of him and he rolled over. His eyes rolled back. His tongue extended. His body went completely limp.

The RSF commander had heard the second cry faintly and turned in time to see the soldier slam his fist into his master's face. For a moment, he didn't move, too stunned to react. One of his soldiers had hit the king! It was impossible! *The king!* Men had been killed for looking at him wrong, for whispering in his presence, for stammering as they talked.

And this soldier had just hit him!

It was unthinkable!

It was impossible!

No Saudi would ever, under any circumstances, even think of touching the king!

Which meant the soldier wasn't Saudi.

The soldier turned his gun on Sam.

*   *   *

Bono raced after the prince, sweeping him up in his arms. The child beat upon him, slamming his fists into Bono's face and neck with every ounce of his strength he had. Bono ducked his head and started running toward the waiting helicopter.

"*Áwqafa! Áwqafa!*" the young boy screamed, but Bono didn't understand.

They were almost to the chopper. Azadeh was sprawled out on the ground. "You're clear!" he screamed to her as he rushed by. "GET IN THE HELICOPTER!"

Azadeh opened her eyes and looked around. After giving the signal, she had jerked back and screamed while throwing her hands to her chest, bursting the red paint capsule sewn into her robe. After falling, with the gunfire all around her, she'd done exactly what they had told her to: pretended that she was dead.

Hearing Bono calling to her, she lifted her head to see him rush toward the waiting chopper, the young prince in his arms.

Dead men, smoke, and blood were all around her. Bullets were smashing into the mud. Howls of pain filled the air like crying demons.

Crawling on her knees, she looked for Sam.

*　　*　　*

On the other side of the enormous chopper, Sam watched the Saudi RSF guard turn and point his machine gun at him. Sam also turned his weapon, matching the Saudi's movements almost exactly. In that instant, time stood still. Their weapons pointed at each other, the two men stared. The Saudi fired first, holding on the trigger, the weapon in automatic mode, sending a hail of piercing lead. Sam could actually *feel* the bullets coming at him. He fired his own weapon, sensing his gun recoil from the discharge of the empty shell, then pulled again, a two-shot burst. The Saudi bullets tore into his body, cutting through muscle and bone. The Saudi's neck snapped back and he fell over, shot twice in the head. Another RSF soldier appeared beside the first one. Sam moved his gun and fired again, blowing the guard's chest apart. His eyes darted left and right in horror—no more guards were close enough to shoot—then he dropped to his knees beside the unconscious king, feeling a spring of blood flowing down his chest. For a moment he felt nothing but the flowing blood; then a burning pain spread across his back and neck. His right leg was on fire, the second bullet having passed very near the bone. He tried to breathe, but couldn't. He had no more strength to stand. He rolled on the ground to his good shoulder and looked up at the sky. The day grew dark around him and he slowly closed his eyes.

*　　*　　*

Neil Brighton dropped into the mud beside his son and took him in his arms. He held his head in his lap and brushed his hair back, wiping the mud out of his eyes. In desperation, he turned to Teancum. "What am I supposed to do?" he cried.

Teancum put his hand out and took the father's hand. "It's going to be all right," he said. Reaching out, he touched the mortal lightly, putting his hands across the unconscious soldier's brow, then looked up at his father. "Keep your faith. He needs that more than anything."

Neil Brighton started crying. Cradling his son, he held his head against his chest. "Not now, Sam. Not yet. It's not your time. You have to take care of your mother. She needs you more than I do. You have to be there for your brothers. You've got to fight to stay here, son. You've got to fight to stay here in this mortal world . . ."

Neil felt another man standing there beside him. Lifting his head, he looked up at Sam.

His son knelt down beside him. "It's okay, Dad," he said.

*   *   *

Gunshots splattered around the helicopter. The young prince kept beating on Bono's face and chest, crying to be let go.

Bono was almost to the chopper when he stopped in his tracks. It was as if someone had grabbed him by the throat and screamed, "*STOP AND TURN AROUND!*"

He turned in time to see Sam roll over onto the mud, the king beside him.

Bono almost dropped the child. He stood there unmoving, frozen with indecision. The prince still screaming in his arms, he took two steps toward Sam, then stopped again. To help Sam, he had to let the prince down. But if he put him down, the prince would run—and if he ran, he would be killed. The prince's only chance of survival depended on staying next to Bono.

The little boy didn't understand that Bono was there to help him. Bono *had* to find a way to communicate with him. If he could just speak to him, the boy would know.

But he couldn't speak Arabic.

How could he communicate with the child?

*   *   *

Teancum moved toward Bono, his face peaceful and full of light. In an instant, he was beside the soldier. "You have the Spirit," he whispered in Bono's ear. "You have the gift of attending angels. You have the gift of tongues. Have faith and let me help you."

*   *   *

Without any further thought, Bono started speaking to the child. "*American jundi,*" he told him in perfect Arabic. "*I'm*

297

an American soldier sent to save you. You have to trust me! I'm here to help you. Now run and get inside the chopper. It is safe there. I will follow. Listen to me, or both of us will die here. Do you understand?"

The princeling looked at him in amazement.

"I'm an American soldier! I'm here to help you. Do you understand?"

The prince nodded with hesitation. "I understand," he said in Arabic.

"Go. Get in the chopper!"

The prince nodded once again.

Bono put the boy down and he ran toward the helicopter's steps. Azadeh was in the chopper now and she reached out for the prince. Grabbing his hand, she pulled him up the steps, the blades spinning furiously over their heads.

Bono ran to Sam and dropped beside him. The muddy field beneath him was soaked in blood. To his left, the king lay completely motionless, though he sometimes moaned in pain.

Bono looked around in a panic. They were running out of time! No fewer than forty soldiers were gathering around him. Once they saw him, they would know. He couldn't hide his intentions any longer. He had to get Sam inside the chopper. He had to get Abdullah in, too.

But there was no time.

The plan was crumbling.

chapter forty-eight

Neil Brighton stood and stared at his son. Sam reached out to touch him, but Neil pulled quickly back.

"Dad . . . ?" Sam questioned.

Neil smiled at him. "Do you want to stay?" he asked.

Sam thought awhile, then nodded. "I don't think I'm finished yet."

Neil smiled at him proudly. "No, I don't think that you are."

Sam looked at the blood and carnage all around him. Smoke and spouts of mud, even passing bullets, hung suspended in the air. Time was no more to them. Sam looked down at Bono, who was crying over him.

His dad followed his eyes. "He's a good friend," he said.

"He is, Dad."

"If you have but a few good friends in this life, then you are lucky."

Sam reached down as if to touch Bono's head, then looked up at his dad. "All of us are lucky. We have each other. We have the gospel. I figure that's all we could ever ask."

The two were quiet for a moment until Neil Brighton said, "Will you tell Sara that I love her? And tell Luke and Ammon, *too. They've got so much to look forward to. Their lives are just beginning. So many reasons to be happy. So many reasons to feel joy. And if they do it right, life gets better. Will you tell them that for me?"*

Sam closed his eyes and seemed to lift his head toward the sun. "It feels so good to be here with you, Dad. There's so much I want to ask you. So much I want to talk about. You were taken from us too early. We didn't have enough time."

Neil Brighton nodded slowly. "There'll be more of that," he said. "I promise you, son, there's plenty of time ahead."

Sam looked down and watched Bono place his hands upon his head.

"I'll see you soon," his father told him.

"I love you, Dad," Sam replied.

✳   ✳   ✳

Bono didn't think about what he was doing or what he was going to say. Acting purely by the prompting of the Spirit, he placed his hands on Sam's head. *"By the power of the Melchizedek Priesthood, and in the name of Jesus Christ, I bless you that you might live."*

Sam's body seemed to jerk and he took a sudden breath. Bono didn't notice. Too many guards were closing on him now. No way could the U.S. soldiers hidden around the village keep them all at bay. He had only a few seconds before the entire mission was going to fail.

Pulling his hands away from his best friend's head, Bono turned to King Abdullah. Standing, he lifted the king and threw him over his shoulders like he was nothing but a doll. Where he got such power to lift him, he didn't know, but the king felt light as straw as he hoisted him upon his back.

There were shouts and cries all around him. The Saudi

soldiers were pointing at him now. They knew. And they would kill to stop him.

The king's unconscious body draped across his shoulders, he bent down and put his arm under Sam. With impossible strength, he lifted him, then turned and ran toward the helicopter. Jumping to the third step, he threw the king onto the helicopter's floor.

Watching through the windows at the front of the helicopter, the pilots couldn't see most of the battle or keep track of the king. All they knew was that their master had given them the start-up signal, then the world had exploded in gunfire, smoke, and flames, bodies all around them, explosions along the village wall, bullets and shattered rock flying on every side. In utter terror, they had waited, the pilot's hands on the collective, ready to take off the very instant the king was on board. Once they had their master, they wouldn't wait another second. The king aboard, they would go, leaving the soldiers to sort the battle out.

Looking back through the cockpit door, the pilot saw a soldier throw the king on the chopper floor, his body slumped, his face a bloody mess. "GO!" the soldier screamed from the cabin steps.

The pilot felt his heart race, seeing the blood across his master's face. He almost groaned in panic. *The king has been killed or wounded. There will be no forgiveness for any of us! All of us will be killed.*

Turning in his seat, he hit an electric switch to close the cockpit door behind him, then pulled up on the collective. The heavy chopper started lifting, the massive rotors dropping from the sudden strain. The side door was still open, the stairs hanging in the air.

Balancing on the narrow steps, Sam still under his arm, Bono almost fell back as the massive chopper sprinted into the

301

air. His friend felt dead and heavy, his weight pulling Bono off balance. Grabbing the handrail, Bono caught himself and, with a powerful heave, threw Sam's body through the open door and fell back. Azadeh reached out and grabbed him, pulling Sam inside.

Sam seemed to mumble as she moved him, his eyelids fluttering in pain. "Bono," he called out to the open doorway.

Azadeh turned and reached for Bono, stretching for his hand.

Bono reached out for the handrail. Only two more steps to go. A hail of bullets passed by him, slamming into the helicopter's side and piercing through. Looking down, he saw a Saudi soldier firing at them from the village mosque. Reaching for the handgun holstered underneath his left arm, he pulled out the pearl-handled pistol and fired three times, sending the Saudi soldier falling over the minaret's splintered window and onto the muddy street. Two soldiers stood right below the chopper, both of them firing straight up. Bono aimed and pulled the trigger, hitting one and sending the other scurrying behind the nearest wall. He fired again. The weapon clicked. All six shells were gone. Dropping the handgun, he turned back to the chopper door.

The helicopter was high in the air now and the pilot nosed it over, quickly gaining speed. Bono felt the powerful wind begin to build around him, and the angle of the helicopter almost threw him back again. He wasn't inside the chopper yet. He had one more step to go. He reached out for the doorway. Azadeh stretched for his hand.

The bullet was shot from below and behind him, entering at his shoulder blade and exiting between his two top ribs. Exploding from the front of his body, the bullet continued forward and hit his right hand, the flattened piece of metal as big as a quarter now. The explosion blew his hand apart, sending pieces of bone and flesh flying through the air.

Bono felt his world explode in pain around him.

He couldn't breathe.

He couldn't think.

He couldn't hold on anymore.

The chopper accelerated, the wind growing more powerful. He reached out for the handrail, but his shattered hand didn't move. He looked at the piece of bloody meat that used to be his right hand and realized that he was going to fall.

Azadeh screamed and reached out for him. "Take my hand!" she cried. She leaned out of the doorway. He started slumping, his arm hanging uselessly at his side.

Azadeh screamed again and frantically grabbed at him.

Squinting in pain, Bono reached out through the dimming light. Sweating and bloody, his hand slipped down her wrist and through her fingers.

He was plunging into the darkness.

The blackness was full and warm around him.

Slipping from the helicopter's steps, he fell.

chapter forty-nine

Azadeh stared in terror, watching Bono's body fall. He hit the ground like a broken doll, one leg kinked beneath his body, his arms sprawled out at his side. Seeing his body hit, she cried in horror.

Sam was conscious now and he pulled himself to the open door, leaving a trail of blood behind him, a thick line of red across the carpeted floor. Looking down, he started crying, his face white, his eyes so bleary he could hardly see.

Bono was instantly surrounded by the Saudi forces. Some of them beat upon him while others fixed their attention on the fleeing chopper, sending a hail of gunfire into the sky.

The helicopter shuddered and started jinking left and right as Sam felt the violent force of bullets smashing into the heavy armor underneath the metal floor. Looking out, he saw that Bono didn't move. He was certain he was dead.

The chopper banked onto its right side to almost 90 degrees, sending Sam sliding away from the open door, and then rolled level. By the time he had scrambled back to the doorway, the village was fading in the distance behind him.

Azadeh knelt at the open doorway, completely overwhelmed,

her body heavy with exhaustion, her heart feeling like it was going to break in two. She hardly breathed. She couldn't think. The air was cold and bitter as it roared through the open door.

Looking down, she flinched and pulled back. One of Bono's fingers had been blown off and was lying on the bloody floor. Without thinking, she picked it up and placed it tenderly in the pocket of her dress.

Her thoughts went to Bono's wife and daughter and she started crying uncontrollably, her shoulders shaking, her chin quivering in pain.

She felt a weak hand on her shoulder and quickly turned around. Sam was kneeling there beside her, his face so pale he looked like he was dead. "Shut the door," he shouted to her.

She only stared at him.

"Shut the door," he repeated.

She looked down and saw the green CLOSE switch on the cabin wall beside her shoulder. She pushed it with her palm.

The door beside them closed on its hydraulic pistons and the unbearable noise from the rotors, jet engines, and powerful wind fell away. Sam still had Abdullah's 9mm in his hand but he held it loosely, as if holding it took all the strength he had.

"Listen to me," he said. "I don't know if I'll stay conscious. I don't know how long I have . . ."

Azadeh stared at him, trying very hard to concentrate.

"We've got to secure the king," he told her, handing her a set of plastic handcuffs. She looked down to take them, noting his bloody, shaking hands. "Help me tie his hands and feet . . ."

Sam crawled painfully across the floor, dragging his useless leg behind him. Azadeh moved around him and knelt down before the king. Working together, they cuffed his hands behind him, then his feet, then bound his hands to one of the seat braces on the floor.

It took only a couple of seconds. Sam was almost out of strength. He glanced at the young prince, who was hiding in the corner. "Come," he beckoned to him. The prince hesitated, then crawled toward him. "Bandages," Sam said in Arabic, his voice weaker.

The prince stared at him.

"There's got to be a medical kit somewhere. Do you understand?"

The young prince nodded.

"Okay," Sam patted him on the shoulder to reassure him. The prince stood and ran to the rear of the cabin and started searching through the cabinets in the narrow galley. Sam watched him. He was a good kid. So much stronger than his years. And he showed so little fear. That was the way it was now. Stolen childhoods everywhere.

Turning back to Azadeh, he said, "You have to—"

"I know what we have to do," she cut him off.

Sam slumped across the floor and closed his eyes. "It really hurts," he said.

She leaned over and pressed her soft lips against his cheek. "How many times have you saved me, Sam Brighton?"

He opened his eyes to look at her.

"How many times have you saved me?"

"A couple of times, I guess."

"This is my opportunity to save you now."

He closed his eyes and smiled.

* * *

Dallas Houston watched Bono's fall from the fleeing helicopter, then the beating from the guards. He bowed his head in horror, then looked up at the sun. "Okay," he told himself.

"Keep it cool, Houston, keep it cool. These men are your responsibility now. Do what you have to do."

He swallowed, hard and painful, then turned back to the village and ordered his men to act. "Two, you out of the village yet?"

"Rog," Shooter Two replied. "I'm heading up the trail beside the waterfall."

Houston stared down at the trail. The Cherokee was moving quickly through the underbrush, almost impossible to see.

"Okay, guys, get to the rally point. See you sometime after dark. We'll call for evac from Rally Bravo. Call if you can't make it there."

*　　*　　*

Azadeh stood quickly and took the silver 9mm Glock out of Sam's hand. The helicopter had been airborne for only minutes but it was high and fast now, climbing over the rocky cliffs.

Moving forward, she studied the bulkhead beside the cockpit door, hit the emergency release switch, and threw the door open. Bursting into the cockpit, she pointed the gun at the pilot. Her hands were firm and steady, her face determined.

The pilot turned to look at her, his eyes wide in shock. He made a move toward her, but he was strapped in by the seatbelt system and couldn't get out of his seat. As he lurched toward her, Azadeh shot a single shell through the cockpit wall and he instantly fell back, his hands raised in surrender, a sudden hiss from the outside air blowing through the one-inch hole. Panicked and unsure, in a final show of force, he screamed and lurched for the gun. She stepped easily out of range, then aimed the gun directly at his head. The copilot on the other side started to weep, certain his life was over. Taking half a step toward them, Azadeh reached out and ripped both of their radio headsets off, throwing them onto the cabin floor.

"Do you want to live?" she asked them.

They both stared back at her.

"Do you want to live?" she repeated, her voice hard. She was young and beautiful but the look on her face didn't lie. She wasn't afraid. She'd been through so much in her life already, faced so many evil men, so many evil places, so many hopeless times: the assassination of her father, watching him burn to death outside her small home in the Agha Jari Deh Valley; being expelled by her own people; life in the Khorramshahr refugee camp, with its hunger, boredom, disease, and thuggish guards; the slave trader who was going to sell her as if she were nothing but a barnyard animal; the possibility of rape and starvation on the streets of East Chicago after the EMP attack.

No, she had lived through much worse than this before.

Azadeh stared directly at the pilot. She would kill him if she had to; there was no doubt in her mind. And the helicopter pilot knew it from the unflinching look in her eye.

"Do you want to live!" she repeated for the final time.

Her voice was so cold and hard, the pilot almost shivered. His head was swimming. The entire morning had been overwhelming—explosions and bullets all around them, their master going down, smoke and fire and exploding pieces of rock wall, the master pushed into the helicopter, thinking their king was safe, their own forces firing on them, a stranger now holding a gun to his head. Nothing made sense any longer and he simply couldn't think.

Why in the name of Allah had the king insisted on leaving the safety of his kingdom to come out here? All of his security forces had argued against it. The entire world had gone crazy. He felt his head begin to spin.

He shot a terrified look toward the copilot, then turned back to Azadeh and slowly nodded.

"If you do exactly what I tell you, you'll live to see your children," she said. "If you don't, I'll kill King Abdullah." She moved the gun toward the king, who was tied up, still unconscious, his face bleeding from his broken nose and shattered eye socket. "I'll kill your king, then I'll kill you. Or worse, I'll let you live. They'll hunt you down and hurt you in ways few men could understand. But do what I tell you and everything will be all right. You'll be safe. You'll have asylum." Azadeh was fabricating promises now, but she didn't care. There was only one thing that mattered, and that was getting the pilots to do exactly what she said. "Do what I tell you and the king will live. Divert one inch and I will kill him. We both know what will happen to you then."

The pilot looked at her helplessly, his lips trembling with fear.

She threw a wadded piece of paper onto his lap. "These are the coordinates you're going to fly to." She kept the gun at his head. "You're going to land there. Others will be waiting. Do you understand?"

He picked up the paper and nodded at her.

She kept the gun aimed at his head.

*   *   *

Behind Azadeh, the young prince helped Sam toward a leather couch on the opposite side of the cabin, out of sight of the two pilots. After helping him lie down, he cut away the bloody material from around the soldier's leg, wrapped a thick bandage around the wound, and secured it with white tape. Tenderly lifting his arm, he applied another sheet of disinfected bandage. Sam pressed the wadded cloth to stop the bleeding, then leaned back.

Unsure of what else to do, the prince cradled the soldier's head in his lap and helped him drink some water. Sam drank and coughed, then slowly closed his eyes. The helicopter accelerated, flying west. Time passed and the young prince fell into a stupor, completely overcome. Leaning his head against the bulkhead, he closed his eyes and fell asleep.

Slipping away, he dreamed of his mother singing to him while holding him in her arms.

When the battle is over,
And the evening winds come,
When spear tips glint in the twilight,
And the skirmish is done,
Then I hope that I am standing,
And brother, I hope that you are too,
For on the other side of the war ground,
I will be thinking of you.

"The world is full of darkness. Sin and wickedness is over-whelming the world as the waters cover the great deep. The devil rules over the world in a great measure. The world will war against you; the devil will, earth will, and hell will. But . . . do your duty, and the Lord will stand by you. Earth and hell shall not prevail against you."

—JOSEPH SMITH

chapter fifty

The men huddled in the semidarkness, the room illuminated only by a single battery-powered lantern in
the middle of the conference table. Even that was
growing dim now, the white light having faded to a pale yellow that cast flickering shadows across the wall. Every breath
the group took in had been breathed a couple of times before;
the air inside the sealed compound was growing wet with
human exhaust, the oxygen level falling fast. The power was
out. The air purifiers and circulation systems had been off for
hours. Every telephone, satellite, computer, and communications system was down. There was no heat. There was no
water. The toilets didn't flush. No light but the failing lantern
on the table. Soon there would be no air.

It was ironic, they all realized, how the situations had been
reversed. The chaos from the surface had descended on them
now, all the desperation, thirst and hunger, hopelessness and
fear, falling like a blanket to overwhelm them with despair.

Looking at the group of conspirators, Fuentes realized
they were no less isolated in the compound than they would

be in a prison cell. "What do we do now?" he demanded of his staff.

No one looked at him.

"What are we going to *do!*"

"Shut up, Fuentes!" someone sneered.

Fuentes's face turned sour with hurt and spite. How far he had fallen! No one called him Mr. President anymore. He sat in silence, trying to decide how to react, then, deciding on righteous indignation, stood up from his chair. "I am the president of the United States! I am the—"

The National Security Adviser rose up and faced him. "You are nothing, you ignorant fool! At best, you were a puppet; at worst, a redneck joke. Now shut up, or I'll kill you and save us all the pain of listening to your whiny voice!"

Fuentes stood before the NSA, his breath coming in gasps of rage, his face wild with fear and intimidation. Then, realizing he had no option, he sat down and stared blankly at the wall.

The NSA shot a deadly look in his direction, then turned away and drew a long breath. A couple of days before, he had been on top of the world. Integrated into the bloody trenches of power, he was a player—not the main man, but someone they had to listen to. And his star was only rising. One day, if he played his cards right—and he was very good at this game of cards—he would be the king, or if not the king, then something very close. Brilliant, rich, and completely unfaithful to anything besides himself, he was the epitome of the type of leader the new world was begging for. Power had proven his great aphrodisiac and he was flush with power.

But all of it was gone now. He was a rat trapped in a hole. He was dehydrated. His hair was greasy. He hadn't eaten in two days. His clothes were soiled, his underarms so rank and sweaty he couldn't stand the smell of himself.

Looking into the others' faces, he wanted to throw up on the floor.

All of them were ugly now, their power and beauty gone. They were nothing. They had nothing. They were rotten and hungry and loathsome. He saw their hideous desperation. They had taken their shot and missed.

Staring at the others, the NSA wondered about the old man. Had he slipped through their fingers? Had he been able to escape? "Where is he!" he demanded of the empty faces around the table.

A dark-haired man across the table bowed his head and groaned. "I thought he would stay with us," he muttered. "I thought he was immortal!"

"Shut up, you stupid idiot!" the former president tore into him.

The NSA turned to the old man. "*Mr. President,*" he sneered.

The former president turned and glared.

"You have hated your own country for almost thirty years," the NSA went on. "There was hardly an affair or topic on which you did not pontificate. A dozen books. A thousand speeches. You made millions duping others into believing the United States was to blame. You assured us they would falter. You told us—"

There was a sudden knock at the door.

The room fell into silence.

The knocking came again. Heavy. The butt of a rifle. Determined.

The door started cracking upon its hinges.

The NSA turned and swore.

chapter fifty-one

OFFUTT AIR FORCE BASE
HEADQUARTERS, U.S. STRATEGIC COMMAND
EIGHT MILES SOUTH OF OMAHA, NEBRASKA

Mary Dupree paced the halls, not knowing where she could go but feeling as if she had to move, as if she had to do something, as if she had to act. She was alone now, Sara and her family having left. No one really claimed her, but no one seemed inclined to make her leave, either. They fed her, allowed her to move freely, gave her and Kelly a place to sleep, but otherwise ignored her, unwilling to answer any of her questions, unwilling to tell her what to do or where to go.

After pacing the halls for half an hour, she walked to the cafeteria and ordered a cup of coffee, which grew cold between her fingers as she stared down at the cup.

She knew things were getting better. She could see the trucks outside the base. A little traffic on the highways now. Cargo aircraft flying through the air. A few lights in the distance at night. More, she could see it in the eyes of the men and women all around her. Relief. No more hesitation. A sense of justice in the air.

They had reached and passed the tipping point.

That left her much as she had been when Sara and her

family had first found her: alone with Kelly but not much else. No real sense of purpose or possession. No real sense of hope.

But things *were* different now. She had seen too much, heard too much, experienced too much to ever be the same again. All of it had created a burning question, an intense desire to find the truth.

Forty minutes later she stood, walked down the hallway, exited the headquarters building, and crossed a patch of dry grass. The base chapel was before her. She looked around, then walked inside, not because she was seeking its comfort but because it was empty and the only place where she could be alone.

She sat on the back pew. The chapel was dimly lit. A row of white candles lined the back wall. A stained-glass window was illuminated behind the pulpit, Jesus standing at a large wooden doorway. *I stand at the doorway and knock* was inscribed under the stained glass.

Mary settled on her pew and stared.

Sitting there, alone for the first time in weeks, maybe months—it seemed like years—she thought, her eyes closed, her mind drifting back.

The memories were too powerful to ever be too far away.

A cold morning in Chicago. Her daughter dying in a hospital bed. No hope for the mother or the child.

She shivered as the memory filled her empty soul, recalling the morning she had gone to the hospital to check Kelly out and take her home.

*   *   *

She stepped off the bus, then paused on the sidewalk to glance up at the sky, the autumn sun breaking through the gray band of clouds. She looked left, then turned right and moved down the crowded sidewalk, meshing with the hordes of pedestrians, all of them unaware of anyone around them. Moving slowly, she walked toward the hospital. Though she had steeled herself for this moment, her stomach was rolled in knots, her face a mask of false composure to hide the pain inside.

Her daughter, Kelly Beth, was going to die. Maybe today. Maybe next week. She might even live a month, but she was going to die, there was not a doubt in Mary's heart.

There was nothing more the doctors could do. It was time to take her home.

Mary felt sick at the responsibility and sadness of giving up. But the cancer had won and it was time to concede. It was time to make her daughter comfortable and surround her with love instead of chrome beds and tile floors, with color instead of the grayness of the cracking hospital walls, with friends instead of overworked and hurried staff.

As Mary walked, the skies continued to clear, but each step closer to the hospital made her heart beat faster in her chest. Reaching the enormous building, with its sandstone walls and cement stairs, she slowed almost to a stop. In her mind, she already smelled the disinfectant and highly polished floors. Her stomach rolled inside her and she paused halfway up the stairs.

Once she entered the building, it would be over. She would be committed. She would take her daughter home. And once she took her home, the fight would end.

But if she waited long enough, maybe it wouldn't come. Maybe there'd be a miracle. Maybe her daughter would be healed. Maybe she would wake up from this nightmare. Maybe . . .

Maybe nothing.

Suddenly she felt dizzy and almost fell back on the stairs. Her legs weakened underneath her and she had to grasp the handrail. A passerby paused to help her, but she quickly waved him off. Looking around, she realized she had actually turned around. Facing the street now, she had walked down several stairs.

She took a determined breath, then turned and walked back up the stairs.

*   *   *

Mary shuddered and pulled her sweater close, her eyes focusing on the chapel once again.

Yes, on that day, she had taken Kelly home. But her daughter was alive and healthy now. And Mary wanted to know how it was done.

Looking around, she realized she wasn't alone. A young man was sitting on the pew across from her. She glanced in his direction but he lowered his head as if to pray and she quickly looked away. But something about him seemed to draw her to him, and she looked again. His face was quiet and calm. His eyes remained closed. A gold band glittered from the first finger on his right hand.

When he opened his eyes, she smiled awkwardly and turned back to the altar. Catching her eye, he nodded toward the stained-glass picture that took up most of the front wall. "It's a beautiful picture, don't you think?"

Mary glanced at the stained glass and nodded.

"It's a replica of a window in the Sistine Chapel."

"It's beautiful," Mary said, then stood up as if to leave.

The man caught her eye again. "Do you notice anything unusual about the picture?"

She studied the painted glass a moment. "Not really."

"Look at the door," the stranger told her.

Mary studied the picture, then noticed something she hadn't seen before. "There's no door handle," she said.

The man smiled at her. "He stands at the door and knocks. But the door can only be opened from the inside. We have to take the first step. We have to let Him in."

Mary stared at him, then nodded. "I understand," she said.

*   *   *

Fifteen minutes later, she walked through the front doors of the headquarters building and up to the second floor. The young guard was sitting at his desk. The commanding general's office was down the hall.

Mary hustled toward him. "You're a Mormon, aren't you?" she demanded in an urgent tone.

The sergeant turned and looked at her.

"I saw you talking to Luke and Ammon Brighton. They told me you were a Mormon. There's no sense you denying it, I'll find out anyway."

The black man nodded uncertainly, still unsure of what to say.

Mary took a step toward him. "You've got to teach me and my daughter. You've got to teach us everything you know. I want to understand what this feeling is. I want to understand it all."

chapter fifty-two

President Brucius Marino stood on the crest of the hill, the highest bluff in the area, and looked over the devastated city. A wind was blowing from the southwest, but it was warm and clean, having blown up from the mountains of southwestern Virginia. There was no more smoke in the air. In fact, it smelled clean. The haze of dust and ash was gone now and the sun was warm. His chief of staff stood beside him; behind him, his security detail. All the men were quiet as he looked out.

The Capitol's dome stuck out against the horizon. How had it survived? Half of the Washington Monument protruded even higher, a stubborn, blackened needle jutting into the sky. Looking at it, he felt a sudden sense of pride.

Turning southeast, he squinted against the sun. The city was in ruins still, but there were signs of life around. The Chesapeake Bay was full of ships, military and civilian, enormous freighters and cargo vessels, most of them from overseas. Convoys of trucks were lined up at the ports now, some of them stretching as far as he could see. He knew the same was

321

true at other cities all along the eastern and western coasts. Aid from overseas. Aid from their allies.

Looking across the city toward Andrews Air Force Base, he knew the military transport with fighter escorts would be touching down within the hour. King Abdullah was on board the transport aircraft. They were prepared to prosecute him. Justice would be done.

The worst of it was over now.

It was time to get to work.

The chief of staff waited in the background, giving the president time to think. After a few minutes of silence, he stepped forward. "What are we going to do?" he asked.

The president took a deep breath. "We're going to rebuild," he said.

"Everything, Mr. President?" The COS looked at the scarred horizon.

"Of course," Marino answered. Lifting his foot, he stomped the ground below him, marking the hallowed place. "We're going to rebuild it all. And we're going to start right here."

*　　*　　*

Sara Brighton stood behind the president, looking out on the same scene. But she didn't see any of it. Her mind was somewhere else.

She had lost so much. Her husband. Their home. Their lives together. Everything they owned. They had paid the price for years now, giving up their time as a family, driven by the military to foreign lands, moving every year or two, any sense of hometown or stability for their children long gone. Sara had done her best to raise them, but she had done it more or less on her own. Her oldest son lay in the hospital now, critically wounded. Her other sons? Where were they? She simply didn't know.

But as she stood there, she thought of none of this. She didn't mourn the loss of her husband or her home. She didn't mourn for her children or the world they had faced. She didn't wallow in the bitterness that she could so easily have reached out and embraced.

The only thing she thought about were some of the soldiers she had known.

The young son of a good friend who had died from his combat wounds after being attacked by a roadside IED. One man had been killed instantly by the bomb. Four other soldiers in the HUMVEE had been terribly burned—no more skin, no more hair. For months, each of them had fought an agonizing battle to survive but, one by one, they had succumbed to their burns, the last one, her friend's son, passing away almost nine months after the attack.

Why were they willing to do it? She didn't know. She had asked a young soldier once. "We're just trying to help," he said.

She thought back on an incident Sam had told her about. One of his fellow units had been sweeping through one of the most dangerous neighborhoods in Baghdad when they came upon a car in the afternoon sun, a little boy inside. The windows were rolled up, the doors locked. Inside the car, the heat was deadly. But they couldn't get the boy out.

The soldiers started searching, going from house to house, looking for the parents, anyone who knew about the child. No one claimed any knowledge. Realizing they had to do something or the little boy was gong to die, and despite some desperate warnings, one of the solders had decided it was time to get him out.

Breaking the front window, he unlocked the door. The car

bomb went off, having been rigged to explode when the doors were opened.

Again, she thought of what the young soldier had told her. "We're just trying to help."

* * *

President Brucius Marino turned around and walked toward Sara. Seeing the look on her face, he stepped a little closer. "Are you all right?" he asked, reaching for her hand.

She tried to smile, but didn't answer.

The president waited for a moment. "What is it?" he pressed.

Sara shook her head and looked away.

Brucius waited patiently.

"I want you to know that I'm proud of my country," she finally said.

chapter fifty-three

Luke and Ammon Brighton stood among the small crowd. Only a couple of dozen Saints, maybe a few more, had gathered in the open field. The Church had made no grand announcement of the ceremony—there simply was no time, and they didn't want to stir up opposition, of which there was plenty around. Besides, like most Americans, the members of the Church were consumed with simply surviving, and even if the groundbreaking ceremony had been widely announced, few could have made it there anyway.

It was nothing but a stroke of happenstance that Ammon and Luke were there. That, and the fact that they had followed the Spirit and walked to Jackson County, struggling through three weeks of exhaustion, hunger, and thirst.

The thing that was about to happen was one of the great events of the last dispensation, an incredible fulfillment of prophecy that went back seven thousand years, and there was a sense of disbelief in the moment that went beyond any words.

It's here. It's really happening.

Ammon could hardly think.

As the group of Church leaders assembled in their proper

325

places, Ammon bent down and lifted a single blade of green grass, a stubborn holdout against the coming winter, then pressed his palm into the dirt, letting the rich soil press between his fingers. *This is sacred ground,* he thought as he examined the soft earth. Father Adam. Mother Eve. They and their children walked here! Adam prophesied from this location. A warm shiver ran down his spine.

Looking up, he watched the prophet position himself among the group of priesthood leaders. The spirit of the day was solemn and a reverent feeling permeated the air.

So much work to do here.

So much more to come.

The leaders gathered in the open field, the other members of the Church in a semicircle across from them. The trees behind the group of men were filled with singing birds. The sun was bright, but the air was cool. Luke kept his eyes on the prophet. He was dressed in a dark suit, black overcoat, and red tie, and though he looked as if the burden of the world was on his shoulders, his face was radiant with a spirit of great light.

A temple in Jackson County!

Ammon shook his head again.

How many dispensations had waited for this day? How many prophets? How many people? How many Saints had prayed for this to come, knowing that it would happen but never believing they would see it in their time? There were no words to describe it and he was speechless at the privilege of being there.

There was a short moment of silence as the prophet huddled with his counselors. While they waited, Ammon looked around, then closed his eyes.

Luke leaned toward him. "How long will it take to build the temple?" he whispered quietly.

Ammon shook his head. "I don't know, brother."

"It took them forty years to build the Salt Lake Temple."

"Yes, it did."

"Think this one will take us that long?"

Ammon opened his eyes and looked up at the brown trees and the stark, blue winter sky. "I don't think so," he finally answered. "I don't think we have that much time."

Luke watched him, thought, then nodded. The two young men were quiet for a moment until Ammon leaned toward his younger brother once again. "Mom is going to be proud of us."

Luke turned to him and smiled. "So is Dad."

chapter fifty-four

T he entire facility had been designed to hold enemy combatants from various locations around the world, the final stop for terrorists who wanted to destroy the United States. Capable of holding 400 terrorists in individual holding cells, the camp was empty now. He was the only prisoner there.

One prisoner. A couple of hundred guards. Cement and steel all around him. Security cameras inside his cell. Quadruple strands of electrified wire outside the wall. A classified location.

No way was he getting out of there.

His cell was sterile, with no protrusions of any kind from which he could fashion a hook or weapon. A simple sink with a recessed faucet was fastened to the back wall. There were no windows. He had no desk. A simple bowl on the floor was his toilet, and it flushed automatically. There were no sheets on his bed, and strands of wire had been sewn into the padded mattress to keep him from ripping any of the material into shreds. His prison clothes were made of paper, leaving not a single piece of cloth inside the cell from which he could fashion a rope to hang himself.

How long King Abdullah had been inside the prison, he didn't know. All he knew was that he was going to die here. If they were merciful, they would kill him. If they were not, they'd let him live, leaving him to rot until he died from old age.

The king thought of his friend, the old man, and shivered in a despair so deep he thought his chest would rip apart. The old man had been ancient, more than a hundred years old, he was sure. One of the benefits of their oaths and combinations was the gift of living long.

A good idea when they were young and powerful.

But it seemed like a torture now.

King Abdullah looked around his cell, shook his head, and started crying like a child. He would be completely insane before he grew so old.

"Oh, beautiful for heroes proved
In liberating strife,
Who more than self their country loved,
And mercy more than life!"
—KATHERINE LEE BATES

chapter fifty-five

Caelyn's mother kept a watchful eye on Caelyn. They'd made it through the winter. They had made it through the spring. Time had passed. Everything had gotten better.

Everything except her child.

Though six months had passed, there was no more life inside of Caelyn than there had been on the first day she had come back home. Her face was blank, her eyes vacant, her words soft and unemotional. Sometimes Caelyn would smile at Ellie, but even these brief moments of happiness were forced and fleeting. It was as if she had died along with her husband, as if her life was over, as if she was just waiting now, going through the motions, waiting for her time to go.

It was a tragedy, the way she'd given up. No, it was worse than that. What Greta was witnessing was much worse than a simple death. This was a tortured dying, an unending final chapter to a story that had no end. It was *so* unlike Caelyn to just give up like this. She was young. So much of life was still before her. She still had Ellie, a beautiful and loving child. She had a responsibility to be strong for her, and it made Greta

333

angry to see her giving up like this. "Caelyn, please," she had pleaded time and time again. "I know it's hard, honey, but you can't give up this way. You will heal. It will get better. I know what you're feeling, but it will pass."

*　　*　　*

Late in the afternoon, Greta opened Caelyn's bedroom door. "Someone's here to see you," she announced.

Caelyn looked up to see Sara Brighton standing there. Sara moved toward her and pulled her into her arms, and the two of them held each other as if they would die if they let go. "How is Sam?" Caelyn finally asked after they had moved apart.

"He's good, Caelyn. In fact, I'd say he's completely better. He's on duty now and very happy to be back at work. Those two months in the hospital were, I think, the very longest of his life."

Caelyn smiled at the good news. "Do you still see Azadeh?"

"Almost every day."

"I like her so much. She's one of the nicest people I've ever known."

"We feel the same way, Caelyn. But the fact is, I feel the same way about you. Both of you have lost so much."

Caelyn cleared her throat and looked at the open window. "We all have, haven't we, Sara?"

Sara watched her carefully. "Yes, I suppose that's true."

Caelyn took a step toward the window. Ellie was walking hand in hand with Sam across the yard. Sara moved and stood beside her, both of them looking down on their children, the things they loved more than anything else in the world.

"She looks happy," Sara said of Ellie. "Such a pretty little girl. I can see so much of you in her face, but her spirit is so much like her father's."

Caelyn nodded as she tugged at the lacy curtains.

Sara put her arm around her. "It's been six months," she said.

Caelyn shook her head violently.

"I think it's time for you to do this, Caelyn. You need to do it for Ellie. You need to do it for yourself."

"They said I had as long as a year before they had to officially change his status."

"I know that, honey, but the situation is much more clear than with many missing soldiers. He isn't missing, Caelyn. We have eyewitnesses. We know what happened to him." She hesitated, then continued, her voice a bit softer now. "Caelyn, I'm not sure it's fair to Ellie."

Caelyn shook her head again, her eyes filling with sudden tears. "What am I going to do?" she pleaded. "What am I going to bury? The only thing they recovered was his finger! Am I supposed to bury that?"

Sara reached out and held her close again. "What other choice do you have, honey? What other choice do you have?"

"And now, he imparteth his word by angels unto men, yea, not only men but women also. Now this is not all; little children do have words given unto them many times."

—ALMA 32:23

chapter fifty-six

It had rained all night, thunderclouds rolling in from the Blue Ridge Mountains, boiling with power as they met the moisture from the sea. Lightning and heavy rain pounded the night, then suddenly stopped as daylight drew near. The first line of storms moved off to the Chesapeake Bay and lingered over the sea, caught between the rising sun and the musky coastline behind. The rain wasn't over. What was already the wettest spring in a century had much more to give.

The day dawned cold and dreary. Another band of dark clouds gathered in the morning light, moving in from the west, blowing over the hill that lifted on the horizon. Heavy mist hung in the air until the morning breeze finally carried it away.

The grass around the freshly dug grave was wet and long, with tiny drops of moisture glistening from the tip of each blade. The pile of dirt next to the grave was dark and rich, loamy with many years of rotting vegetation, and now rain-soaked and wet. A green patch of plastic Astroturf had been placed over the pile of dirt and pinned down at the corners to

339

keep it from flapping in the wind. A sad arrangement of plastic roses and baby's breath sat atop the fake grass.

The six-man color guard waited by the grave. Their uniforms were so crisp, they almost cracked as they moved, their boots so highly polished they reflected the gray light from the sky. Tiny blades of wet grass clung to the sides of their boots and the cuffs of their pants. The sergeant in charge stood in front of his men, giving them one final inspection, straightening a shoulder board and tightening a shirt here and there.

The soft clop of hooves sounded from the narrow strip of asphalt that wound through the national cemetery. Glancing to his right, the sergeant saw the single mare, old and slow but still proud, her dark mane perfectly curried and braided to the right. She emerged from around a tight bend in the road, drawing a small carriage behind her. Black and shiny, with huge wooden wheels and a leather harness, the carriage carried a single bronze casket on its sideless bed. Seeing the casket, the sergeant took a deep breath and straightened himself. *"Ten-HUT!"* he whispered from deep in his chest, the order nearly silent yet crisp and powerful. His soldiers drew themselves straight, their shoulders square, their chins tight, their hands forming fists at their sides, their elbows slightly bent into powerful bows.

As the funeral procession approached, the team leader placed his right foot exactly behind his left, his toe pointing down, barely touching his heel, then turned with precision so perfect it looked almost mechanical. The wagon drew close and the sergeant felt his heart quicken. This one was special and he wanted it right.

As the wagon passed under a huge oak tree, he caught a better glimpse of the casket, a dark bronze box draped in an American flag. Beside the flag, a ring of flowers, fresh cut and beautifully arranged.

Twenty-four roses. Twelve red and twelve white.

White roses for virtue. Red roses for blood.

Seeing the flowers, the soldier had to swallow against the catch in his throat. *That others might live,* he repeated to himself.

Next to the roses, glistening in the cold, humid air, a copper medallion and white ribbon had been carefully draped over the stars on the flag. For the first time in his life, the soldier saw the Medal of Honor, the most sacred tribute his nation could bestow upon a man.

His squad stood stone-cold still as the funeral procession approached. And though the sergeant avoided eye contact with the mourners who followed the carriage, he couldn't help but see her out of the corner of his eye.

Young and blonde, the little girl glanced around anxiously, a bewildered look on her face. Her mother walked beside her, a perfect reflection of the child: long blonde hair, dark features, and wounded eyes. Tall and slender, the mother wore a simple white dress. No black clothes. No dark veil or mournful hat. The woman was young, perhaps only a year or two older than he was, but there was something about her, something strong and wonderful.

Even in their sadness, the mother and daughter were beautiful. They walked hand in hand, the mother matching the small steps of the girl, both of them misty-eyed but determined. The child approached the grave like it was a monster.

Thunder broke behind the soldier and rolled through the trees, deep, sad, and somber, the sound echoing across the wet ground as another clap rolled and slowly faded. A cold breeze blew at his neck, raising the hair on his arms. "Please, Lord," he prayed. "Hold up your hand. Give this family twenty minutes before you let your rains fall." Another clap of thunder

341

tumbled across the green, rolling hills. Another flash of lightning. But the rains didn't fall.

The soldier looked again at the roses on the casket.

White roses for virtue. Red roses for blood.

*　　*　　*

The army chaplain directed Caelyn and Ellie to a pair of wicker chairs. Ellie held onto her mother's hand as they sat down, then leaned into her shoulder. The child's white dress fell to her ankles and she reached down to press the wrinkles from her lap. A tiny crown of white flowers had been braided through her hair and she tugged at them gently to keep them in place.

Caelyn didn't look at Ellie as the horse-drawn wagon came to a stop. The funeral procession moved forward and formed a half circle on one side of the grave. Ammon and Luke took up a position on the other side of the grave, Sara between them. Bono's parents stood beside her, his father fighting to hold himself together, his mother more at peace. Someone behind Caelyn reached down and touched her face, and she leaned into the unseen hand.

Outside the small ring of family members, three young officers stood in dress uniforms, ribbons and badges upon their chests: comrades of the fallen, fellow Cherokees.

Sam moved stiffly with his brothers, his injuries flaming up from the dampness in the air. Looking down, he smiled at the young prince. The boy glanced across the grave at Ellie, then looked down at the dirt, his face clouded with shame.

His uncle had done this to them. His uncle had caused this pain.

Sam looked down and read his thoughts from the pained look in his eyes. Kneeling, he whispered to the young prince, then stood up again.

The chaplain nodded to the color guard leader and the sergeant commanded under his breath. *"Element, post!"* The six men moved forward in perfect step toward the carriage, taking up a position with three of them on each side of the casket. Without any verbal commands, they reached out and took the casket by the metal handles and lifted together. Nearly empty, the casket was light in their hands.

The color guard turned crisply, carried the flag-draped casket forward, and placed it over the nylon straps that had been stretched across the grave. After they had stepped back, the chaplain walked to the casket and paused, then turned to Caelyn and her daughter. Leaning over, he offered a few words of instruction, then straightened up again.

"One of Lieutenant Calton's brothers in arms has been asked to dedicate the grave," he said.

Sam stepped forward. The prayer was simple and pleading, and tears flowed as he spoke. At the conclusion of his prayer, Sam turned to the casket, took a short step toward it, and placed his hand on the flag. He wanted to turn away but couldn't move. Bowing to one knee, he touched the flag again. "You were always my hero," he whispered through his tears. "I will love you forever. And I will never forget." He knelt there a moment, then forced himself to stand. The chaplain moved to his side and Sam stepped back to his place.

The chaplain straightened his uniform quickly and began to speak. Less formal than most, he spoke of simple things. Duty and honor. Bravery and truth. The obligations that came with freedom and the price that had been paid to keep a people free. Then he nodded to Caelyn and lowered his voice. "I cannot help you," he said. "In a moment such as this, there is little comfort I can give. Indeed, were I to say too much, my words might only diminish your loss. Only time and the Lord can ease you of this pain. But though I don't have the answers, this much I believe.

"All men will die. All men will be called upon to pass through the veil. But only a few, only a few special men, only those who have been worthy to answer a calling from God, are given the honor to die for a cause.

"And in this life, in these times, all of us will be called on to make a sacrifice. When or in what manner that sacrifice may be required, only God knows. All we can do is wait and prepare and pray that when our time comes, we will be ready to complete the task that He gives, so that when it is over, when we have done all we could, we might look to the Lord and say:

> *I have fought my way through,*
> *I have finished the work Thou didst give me to do.*

"If we can reach that point, if we can say these words to the Lord, then our sacrifice will be over and He will bring us home."

The chaplain paused as he clasped his hands and looked again at Caelyn. "I am so proud of your husband," he said in a low voice. "I am so grateful there are still men like him in this world. He fought for the freedom of others. That's the way we do it here in America.

"And so, Mrs. Calton, I speak for a thankful nation when I tell you that we are not only grateful to your husband, we are also grateful to you. We are grateful for your sacrifice and the price you have paid. Your sacrifice is sufficient. Lieutenant Calton is home. And I pray the Lord will bless you until you are together again."

The chaplain stopped, took a step back, and nodded to the color guard. Two of the soldiers stepped to the casket and lifted the American flag. Another sergeant marched to the side of a huge tree, a dark oak on the hillside that would watch over

the grave. The sergeant lifted a silver bugle and started playing "Taps."

> *Day is done*
> *Gone the sun*
> *From the hill, from the dell, from the sea . . .*

The sound was low and mournful and it trailed through
the trees and across the wet grass, melting over the graves of
the American dead. As the bugler played, the two solders rev-
erently folded the American flag into a perfect triangle. The
junior NCO clutched it with crossed arms across his chest. The
team leader took two steps back and stood at rigid attention,
then quickly drew his fist from his thigh and up across his
chest, extending his fingers as his hand crossed his heart, then
upward until his finger touched the tip of his brow. He held
the salute, the last salute, for a very long time, then slowly,
respectfully, almost unwillingly, lowered his hand. Stepping
forward, he took the flag, turned crisply, and handed it to
Caelyn. "On behalf of a grateful nation," he said.

Caelyn took it and placed it on her lap. The soldier then
passed her the Medal of Honor, and she clutched it in her
hand. The two soldiers turned together and moved to the side.
The bugle faded away and the silence returned.

And with that it was over. The service was done. At least
it should have been over. But none seemed willing to move,
for it was almost as if there was something yet left unsaid.
Every eye turned to Caelyn and Ellie. Caelyn glanced down at
her daughter. Ellie looked up. Caelyn smiled encouragingly,
and the little girl stood up. She moved to the casket, which
gleamed even in the dim light, then turned hesitantly to her
mother, who nodded again. The crowd waited in silence. It
seemed even the earth held its breath.

Ellie stood for a moment, and the clouds seemed to part.

345

The wind fell calm and the thunderclouds paused in silence overhead. Ellie took a deep breath, placed her hand on the casket, and lifted her head. "Daddy, I want to tell you something," she said in a quivering voice. "You are my hero. I want to be just like you. But I don't know if I'm strong enough, I don't know if I can. But I will take care of Mommy, just like you asked me to. I will make her cakes for her birthdays, just like I promised I would. I will be her best friend. I will not leave her alone. And I will try to be strong. But I'm a little bit scared." Her voice trailed off and she looked quickly away. "I love you, Dad. I miss you," she said again to the skies. "I need you here, Daddy, and I don't understand. I wish that I could. I want to believe what you said . . ."

She lowered her head in frustration and clasped her arms at her chest, holding herself as if in an embrace. No one spoke. No one moved. Time seemed to stand still, for there was a reverence in the moment that no one was willing to break. How much time passed, it was impossible to say, but the little girl, sweet and peaceful, eventually lifted her head. When she opened her eyes, her face seemed to shine.

If she had seen a vision, it was not shared with anyone.

But the heavens *had* been opened.

And she *did* understand.

❋   ❋   ❋

That night Caelyn slipped beside Ellie in her bed. Brushing her hair away from her eyes, she held Ellie close. "It was a good day, don't you think, baby? It was a beautiful service. I think Daddy was very proud." Her voice was soft and accepting. No more hidden anger. She was going to be all right.

Ellie turned to look at her, her eyes glinting in the dim light.

Caelyn looked across the pillow at her. "God still has a

plan for us, baby. I trust Him. I know He loves us. Things are going to be okay."

Ellie put her arms around her mother's neck.

"I miss him so much," Caelyn muttered.

Ellie smiled at her. "Daddy is alive," she said.

Caelyn pulled back. "I know he is, baby. He's with Heavenly Father now."

Ellie didn't answer. She was already asleep.

chapter fifty-seven

The photo-reconnaissance technician stared at the imagery from the satellite. Having been in urgent contact with the National Reconnaissance Office for most of the last two days, he knew his time was short.

Now he stared at the results, his head swimming, his heart racing in his chest. Hundreds of e-mails had passed between a dozen offices, and almost as many phone calls, some of them going as high as to the chairman of the Joint Chiefs of Staff. Few of the other Intel officers had agreed with him. But now he had his proof.

He was right. It was a signal. And it had been there for months!

He gathered the series of photographs taken of the mountains along the Afghani border and placed them in order, beginning with the first photograph, which had been taken six months before. There were fourteen photographs in all. Taken individually, they meant nothing. But lay them atop one another and the signal was very clear.

ing he leaned back in his chair and took a long breath, wishing he had a stick of gum—his mouth was so dry he could

348

hardly swallow. Then he sat forward, lifted the photographs, made sure they were in order, and picked up his telephone.

He had only a few seconds to wait until the secretary picked it up. "I have to see the boss," he said.

*　　*　　*

Twenty minutes later, the technician was at the four-star's desk. The white-hair commander of Special Operations was lean and grizzled and as serious as a hand grenade without a pin, his caffeine-charged personality never far from boiling over, his temper always ready to explode. He studied the photographs for the final time. He had seen them all before.

"Okay, go through it one more time," he demanded quickly. He felt a growing sense of dread, the same nervous urgency that had driven him since he was an ADHD kid.

If the captain was right, they had left one of their guys behind. Not only that, but he was alive and had been trying to signal them. The situation was intolerable.

If they had failed him, they would correct it very quickly. If that meant the general had to commandeer the assets and fly the mission himself, he would do it. He would stick a pair of scissors into his temple before he'd leave one of his men over there.

The captain moved forward. The general's aides and senior officers were already standing around his desk. The captain laid the photos out and pointed as he started talking. "This is the *al Kifha* detention center, a prison run by Al-Qaeda—a torture center, really—where they detain heretics, anti-Muslim fanatics, traitors, Christian government leaders, and so on. You know the drill, sir." The general did. He knew *al Kifha* very well. "We've shut it down a time or two," the captain went on, "but all they do is move to another village, take over the local

349

jail, and set up operations again. Interestingly, they always give it the same name. Once you've built a brand name for torture, I guess it's worth holding on to." The captain was tart and sarcastic. The general liked that. He wished all of his warriors were as hard.

"Okay," the captain spoke quickly now, partly out of excitement, partly from knowing the general's time was extremely precious, partly out of the building sense of urgency he felt himself. "We get shots of the prison every couple of days. Nothing much to see there. They never let their prisoners into the yard in the daytime, of course." The captain tapped the photograph showing the wire, mud, and snow that surrounded the prison building. "The poor saps inside *al Kifha* will go years without seeing any daylight, assuming they live that long, which, of course, they don't. The average life expectancy inside the prison is something like two months or so. Still," the captain pointed at the next photo now, "you see this, sir, this thin line in the snow."

The general leaned toward the grainy black-and-white photograph. As far as he could see, there was nothing there. The prison. The brick walls. Wire and four machine-gun towers. A no-man's-land between the prison and the outer walls. Mud. Barren ground. A couple of trails in the dirty snow.

The captain leaned across the desk and pointed. "This line here, sir."

The general looked and nodded at the single line in the snow.

"It's one foot wide and six feet long."

"Okay," the general said.

The captain pointed to the next photograph. "This

photograph was taken four days later. Do you see another line there?" he asked.

The general shook his head. He was getting impatient.

The captain traced the outline with his finger. A half circle in the snow.

"Keep going," the general spouted.

The captain pointed to the next photograph. "Three days later, one of our unmanned reconnaissance drones happened to be flying over the area and snapped a couple of photos just for fun." The captain tapped the next photograph. The general looked. "I don't see anything."

"That's because there's nothing there, sir. But look at this. The next day. Four days after the second photograph." He tapped the second photograph with his left hand while touching the fourth one with his right, indicating another gentle curve in the snow. "The right half of a circle." The captain looked up and smiled. "He knows the schedule of our reconnaissance satellite in the area," he said. "Four days on, three days off, four days on. He's leaving his markings in the prison yard to coincide with satellite passage."

The general sat back and frowned.

The captain saw the look on his face and knew he had only a few minutes to complete his case. Pushing the photographs aside, he threw a computer-generated image on the desk before the general. "Over a period of several months, he left a series of markings in the snow. Taken by themselves, they meant nothing. But if you take them all together and overlay them on each other, the signal is very clear."

The general looked down at the computer image.

BONO was all he read.

The general looked up, his face expectant. "Is that one of the classified identifying words?" he demanded.

"Yes, sir, it is. Lieutenant Joseph Calton. The kid who got the king."

The general pushed his chair back and swore. Standing, he jabbed a finger at his exec. "Get me the president," he demanded. "And tell those lazy air force guys to fire up their jets."

chapter fifty-eight

Bono sat in the corner of the rock and brick cell, too exhausted to stand, too exhausted to even think. They hadn't fed him in almost a week now, three days since he'd had water, and he knew, somewhere in the still-functioning part of his mind, that he was standing on the edge of life.

The end was coming fast. He was quickly sliding down the hill. His mind was a constant cloud of thoughts and memories and it was getting harder and harder to know what was going on in the present and what had gone on in the past, what was a memory or imagination, what was fake and what was real. The only thing that he was certain about was the constant thirst and hunger. And the fact that he was going to die here. And it wouldn't take much more time.

He didn't know what day it was, what week or what month. His cell was in constant and utter darkness. No windows. No vents. The tiny door hadn't opened in many weeks now; all they did was push occasional scraps of food and small cups of dirty water under the two-inch crack above the floor. Though he'd lost all track of time, he knew that it was summer from the unbearable heat that had settled on the prison, the cell walls baking until they were almost too hot to touch.

Resting his head against the wall, he figured it was nighttime, for the wall was a few degrees cooler than it was during the day.

He thought back on his capture—it must have been years before—the cutting pain through his chest and ribs, his hand exploding, his grip on the handrail slipping away, the beautiful girl—what was her name, he couldn't remember—reaching down for his hand, tumbling through the air, falling into unconsciousness, hitting the ground, the pain exploding, his breath gushing from him, then his mind going blank again. He thought of waking sometime later, surrounded by the local Taliban. The king's men were gone now, leaving the American in their charge. With their master captured and on his way to the United States, the Saudi soldiers wanted nothing to do with the wounded American now.

The Taliban, on the other hand, was more than willing to kill him, given the chance.

They had debated for a couple of days before deciding to move him to *al Kifha*. With the United States still in turmoil, they knew they had some time to make him suffer. And that was their entire purpose, to make him suffer before he died.

He thought back on the winter. Knowing it would be impossible to keep him from U.S. prying eyes—and they knew the eyes were everywhere—his guards had let him out only at night, giving him a few minutes to walk around the prison yard. Barefoot, he'd stumbled through the snow, anxious to be moving while savoring every breath of fresh air.

Back then, he was always thinking. There *had* to be a way to escape!

Two months into his capture, he realized his only hope.

Pacing his steps carefully, working from a master plan inside his mind, he walked a slightly different path every fourth night, pounding the new snow into a signal.

If only they saw it. If they could put it all together. If they believed that it was real . . .

Sometime late in the winter, they quit letting him out into the yard. About the same time, they cut his rations back. It was clear that someone up the chain of command had decided it was time for him to die. Tired of playing with him, they wanted him to go.

Another couple of months passed as they slowly starved him to death. For the past few weeks, he had hardly moved. He simply didn't have the strength. Along with his body, his mind was going. He heard things. Sometimes he saw things. Things that weren't real. Plates of food. Jugs of fresh water. New clothes. A soft bed.

But mostly he saw Caelyn. When he closed his eyes, he felt her touch. In the mornings he could smell her hair. He heard her voice as he imagined the feel of her slender fingers inter-laced with his. He pictured Ellie looking at him, all of it so real. He talked to them, begging their forgiveness. Lately, they had started talking back.

Leaning against the wall, he closed his eyes and used his energy just to breathe.

Opening his eyes again, he saw her. What was Caelyn doing here?

And because his mind was tortured with such visions, he didn't pay much attention to the sound of the helicopters that had come to set him free.

chapter fifty-nine

T hey stood outside the same VIP reception building where every POW had been welcomed home since the Vietnam War. The day was hot and dry, but scattered clouds filled the sky and a cooling wind blew. A military band stood at the ready, with the press and a reception delegation sitting under a covered stand just to the right of the red carpet that extended to the exact location where the military transport was going to come to a stop. The president of the United States was among the waiting VIPs, but he was smart enough to know that this first moment was for the family, and he stayed out of their way. "Keep everyone back," he had instructed the security teams. "I don't want any intruders or hangers-on and certainly no press. I don't want anyone badgering these people or getting in the way. I want to give them a few minutes of privacy. You understand?"

His security detail and advance team nodded. It made good sense to them.

Ellie was so excited she could hardly stand still. She skipped up and down the tarmac, then turned back and raced toward her mom, grabbing her by the hand. Sara stood beside

Caelyn, always at her side. Over the past few months they had become the best of friends, having shared so much together, the same loss, the same fears. Sam and Azadeh waited with the others on the tarmac, but they hung back, watching Ellie run and skip and laugh.

Azadeh leaned toward Sam and whispered something in his ear, but at that moment the aircraft came into view and the crowd exploded in a joyful roar of applause.

"What did you say?" Sam asked, leaning into her.

She shook her head and looked away. Sam nudged her. She pointed to the aircraft and started clapping with the others.

Sam watched her for a moment. It was so good just to look at her. So good to see her smile. But something told him that what she had said was important, and he leaned toward her again. "What was it?" he repeated.

Her face flushed with embarrassment, but her eyes were clear and bright. She started to speak, fell silent, then looked at him again. "I hope our children will be as beautiful as she is," she said into his ear.

She turned back to watch the aircraft landing.

He stood there without moving, unable to take his eyes off of her face.

The gray C-17 dropped below a bank of clouds and lined up for the runway. The crowd stood still, a reverent hush falling over them. No one seemed to move or even breathe as the aircraft touched down, puffs of white smoke spouting from its tires. It slowed at the end of the runway, turned, and taxied quickly toward the waiting crowd.

Sara kept her eyes on Caelyn, sharing every moment of her joy. Caelyn shuddered with pure happiness and incalculable relief. Ellie stood beside her, grasping her mother's hand so tightly her little fingers turned white. Caelyn didn't speak. She couldn't. She knew if she tried to talk, if she showed even a hint of her emotions, she would crumble into a pool of uncontrollable tears.

God had given her her husband back.

He was dead, but had returned.

Inside her chest, her heart was racing, thumping loudly in her ears.

"He's home. He's home!" It was the only thing that she could think.

It was a miracle. No, it was more than that. It was something she would never understand.

The aircraft came to a stop and immediately shut down its four engines, falling silent in front of the crowd. Nothing happened for a moment; then the crew door opened and a set of short steps extended. Ten seconds more passed in silence. Then Bono stepped into the sunlight and looked out on the crowd.

Caelyn screamed and started running to him.

Ellie beat her mother to her dad.

epilogue

S tanding to the side, the former son of the morning watched the scene in solemn fury, his eyes dead, his shoulders bent, his face hollow, his soul as empty as a rotting shell. His hordes of followers stood behind him, watching their master suffer and sharing his every pain. The old man was among those followers, having killed himself just a few days before.

Lucifer watched the mother run toward her husband and almost groaned. It was terrible to have to watch their happiness. These Great Ones were so powerful!

Turning away from them, he looked out on the world. So much truth and hope around him! Even after all that he had done! So many had proven faithful. So many had proven strong. Looking farther out, he took in the efforts of the Americans to rebuild their nation. Determined. Still undaunted. Much stronger than he'd expected. It made him sick inside.

Feeling a shudder moving through him, the father of all lies let out a long breath of despair.

Turning from his followers, he lowered his head and stared down at the ground. The sweet earth was still his kingdom, but that would not be true for very long.

Chris Stewart

He *was coming. The day was closer.*
Lucifer's shoulders heaved.
Letting out a moan of hopeless fury, he started weeping.
It was the devil's turn to cry.